THE

"This is a must-read Christian action novel that takes faith seriously and inspires your soul. Terry Paulson is an extraordinary leader, speaker, and encourager."

Nido R. Qubein, President, High Point University

"I couldn't put it down. The action is non-stop, and finally, a novel where faith makes a difference. *The Summit* is a must read that comes off the headlines of today's threats to world peace."

Patty Wu, Taiwan Immigrant and US Citizen

"This new novel by Dr. Terry Paulson is a wonderful mix of faith and fantasy combined with fiction and political intrigue. I'm sure you'll love it as much as I did."

Stephen Tweed, CEO of Leading Home Care, Louisville, KY

"I loved the Christian backdrop weaved into this book. I didn't want to put it down. The authors ability to weave a cornucopia of suspense, intrigue, and joyful expectations make this a must read that will surely be made into a movie."

Patrick O'Dooley, Professional Pilot and Internationally Known Professional Speaker

"Read *The Summit* and let your imagination soar! Terrorism, politics, volatility, fear, danger, and uncertainty! This story reads just like the world today with its non-stop action and fast heartbeat engagement! In this compelling, electrifying read, Paulson sparks us to relate to our own situation, both in the world and personally. Don't miss this exciting story that is un-put-downable!"

Elizabeth Jeffries, RN and Author of "What Exceptional Executives Need to Know"

"A timely, emotion packed drama that puts nations and leaders to the test. It's a story for our times and one that you MUST read. And probably re-read. Bravo, Dr. Paulson!"

Eileen McDargh, Award-winning Author and CEO of The Resiliency Group

"Amazing......finally a great, page-turning CHRISTIAN ACTION NOVEL!! Dr. Paulson, a student of our present world situation, brings to life characters caught in crisis who understand the strength faith can provide. Buy more than one copy, to save yourself from re-ordering."

Naomi Rhode, Award-Winning Professional Speaker and Co-Founder of Smart Practice

"Terry Paulson, a gifted storyteller as a professional speaker and a successful nonfiction author, now gives us a stirring novel of political intrigue. With his vast knowledge of world affairs and his ability to keep his audiences enthralled, this is a page turner!"

Jeff Davidson, Noted Author and Op-ed Columnist

THE SUMMIT

"In the realm of political thrillers, Dr. Terry Paulson's masterpiece, *The Summit*, emerges as a beacon of innovation and timely narrative. This is not just a book; it's a journey into the heart of global diplomacy, political intrigue, and the profound implications of faith in action. *The Summit* is a must-read for anyone seeking a story that marries the intensity of geopolitical tensions with the depth of Christian values. Finally, a Christian action novel that doesn't shy away from the complexities of the modern world, while still offering a message of hope and resilience. *The Summit* is poised to be a hit. You won't want to put it down."

Patricia Fripp, Author Deliver Unforgettable Presentations and Past President National Speakers Association

"It is rare and rewarding to find a great story combined with informed and thoughtful consideration of contemporary realities and infused with a real sense of the role of faith in modern life. This is a must read for thinking and faithful people who are looking for a thrilling literary journey."

Dr. Johnnie Driessner, University Professor and Administrator

"*The Summit* is an electrifying political thriller that will keep you on the edge of your seat from start to finish. Dr. Terry Paulson's masterful storytelling seamlessly weaves psychological insights into a heart-stopping plot, creating a must-read that not only mirrors today's threats to world peace but also explores the depths of human courage, cooperation, and sacrifice. A gripping rollercoaster of emotions, this compelling novel challenges preconceptions and underscores the power of unity in the face of a global crisis. You won't be able to put it down!"

Carlos Conejo, Lean Six Sigma Master Black Belt and
CEO of Lean Six Sigma Specialists

"Put this on your 'Must Read' list! Terry Paulson is one of the world's great storytellers. He's also a man of deep faith convictions with a background in psychology. This makes for a compelling read. You will be moved, inspired, and touched by this timely story."

Jim Cathcart, Founder of The Going Pro® Experts Academy
and Bestselling Author 26 Books

"President Connie Freeman's desperate fight for political survival amidst global upheaval is masterfully depicted in this enthralling political thriller. Terry Paulson's masterpiece captures the essence of today's geopolitical tension, weaving a complex narrative of terrorism, international diplomacy, and a desperate quest for peace that leaves readers on the edge of their seats."

Robert B. Tucker, Futurist and Author of Navigating the Future

"As someone who savors spy, espionage, and political thrillers, *The Summit* rocked me with the depth and complexity of both the characters and story line. I follow the political landscape of many countries. To read this, at a time such as this, is both riveting and compelling. It also gives hope to the possibility of our real world and reluctant enemies working together for the greater good. I loved the incorporation of faith, prayer and Biblical wisdom in the characters. As we know, evil exists, this story actually feels as though it could happen this year.

Paulson is a master storyteller and gifted writer. The treat will be yours to get your hands on this thriller."

Kate Larson, Author of Progress Not Perfection and Developer of Influence-IQ

"*The Summit* is a page-turner and a Christian action novel that takes faith seriously. It's a 'really could happen' story given today's international political tensions. I can't wait for the movie!"

David L. Meinz, RDN and Author of "WEALTHY, HEALTHY & WISE: How to Make Sure Your Health Lasts As Long As Your Money Does"

"A gripping political thriller that masterfully blends high-stakes diplomacy, suspense, and a stark glimpse into the potential for global chaos. President Connie Freeman's battle for survival amidst escalating tensions with China and a world on the brink of disaster is both thrilling and terrifyingly plausible. This book is a fast-paced, thought-provoking journey through the complexities of international politics and human resilience. A must-read for thriller enthusiasts and those intrigued by the delicate dance of global diplomacy."

Joel G. Block, Bullseye Capital Hedge Fund Manager and Venture Capitalist

"Somehow, 'ripped from the headlines' is a phrase that comes to mind reading Dr. Terry Paulson's wonderful new thriller. AND, he masterfully weaves a powerful Christian message throughout at a time when many people need to hear it. I have known and admired Terry for more than 30 years, and I have always been captivated by his story-telling skills. You will as well...promise!"

Lou Heckler, Humorous Business Speaker and Speaker Coach

"Dr. Paulson has written an incredible story that is truly a 'page turner' because I couldn't wait to see what was going to happen next. The characters came so vividly to life as I was drawn into this timely and compelling story. As life does, occasionally, life intruded, and I had to put it down. But I was soon finding my way back to *The Summit*. This could easily be a very successful Netflix series. Thank you for writing a novel that allows faith to play a key role."

Al Walker, Motivational Humorist and Author

THE
SUMMIT

THE SUMMIT

by

TERRY PAULSON, PHD

Most Parrhesia Books products are available at special quantity discounts for bulk purchases for sales promotions, premiums, fund-raising and educational needs. For details visit our website at www.ParrhesiaPublishing.com

The Summit by Terry Paulson
Published by Parrhesia Publishing, an imprint of Leadership Books, Inc.
Las Vegas, Nevada & New York, NY

This book or parts thereof may not be reproduced in any form, stored in a retrieval system, or transmitted in any form by any means – electronic, mechanical, photocopy, recording, or otherwise- without prior written permission of the publisher, except as provided by United States of America copyright law. Permission may be granted upon request.

Copyright 2024 by **Terry Paulson, The Summit**
All rights reserved.

International Standard Book Number:
978-1-951648-10-7 (Hardcover)
978-1-951648-89-3 (Paperback)
978-1-951648-90-9 (eBook)

While the author has made every effort to provide accurate internet addresses at the time of publication, neither the publisher nor the author assumes any responsibility for errors or for changes that occur after publication. Further, the publisher does not have any control over and does not assume any responsibility for the author or third-party website or their content.

This is a work of fiction. Unless otherwise indicated, all the names, characters, businesses, places, events, and incidents in this book are either the product of the Author's imagination or used in a fictitious manner. Any resemblance to actual persons, living or dead, or actual events is purely coincidental.

Printed in the United States of America

ACKNOWLEDGMENT

A special thanks to Rod Peterson, a producer and writer for *The Waltons* and *Falcon Crest*, for his help and encouragement in turning this story into a compelling novel. I also want to express my appreciation to Patty Wu for her knowledge and help in ensuring that the names for my Chinese characters were appropriate. Let me thank my wife Lorie for her help, support, and time invested in editing this work. Finally, without the confidence and support of Mike Stickler with Parrhesia Publishing and Leadership Books, *The Summit* would have never seen the light of day. Thank you all from the bottom of my heart.

Terry Paulson, PhD

THE SUMMIT FOREWORD

My read of *The Summit* brought back memories of my captivity. As a hot shot "Top Gun" fighter pilot, in total control of my jet fighter and my destiny, I was shot down and held prisoner in Vietnam for 2,103 days. I was shocked when the North Vietnamese really did have a gun big enough to shoot down Charlie Plumb. In the mind-numbing tumult of a 90-second parachute ride, I made the transition from king of the skies to scum of the earth!

And just as the superpower leaders in this book who were accustomed to great power felt powerless, I, too, felt I had lost control and was traumatized. I was soon flirting with deep feelings of hopelessness.

What would President Freeman hold onto for solid ground when everything was crumbling beneath her? When everything she ever used to validate her own prominence was in question, she would reach for a foundation, a rock, an anchor to steady her ship-of-self. And just as with the POWs, she found it in her faith, faith in her God, faith in her country, and faith in herself. The things she once thought were surreal suddenly became critically real, seriously REAL!

And just as the principal characters of this novel, we prisoners of war relied on the vital gift of communication. Both President Connie Freeman and General Secretary Wang Da developed a totally different level of conversation from that which was planned for the Geneva Summit. You'll be pulled in by the honesty and the hope for a future which the two world leaders developed in their dialogue. It's a hope that even now is hard but important to imagine.

Will this shared crisis sow the seeds for a change in their trust in each other, a trust capable of sustaining world peace? And how relevant in today's world is Dr. Paulson picture of troubled times and the hope for a more peaceful world? Read this novel and then take time to lift a prayer for the possibility of a peace we can now only dream of.

–Retired U.S. Navy Captain Charlie Plumb, Hanoi Hilton
"Chaplain" and Professional Speaker

CHAPTER ONE

THE DEVILS WILL DO WHAT WE SAY

Dasht-e Lut Desert, Iran

*"And all the people answered and said,
His blood be on us, and on our children."
Matthew 27:25 (New King James Version)*

The isolated asphalt runway brought a stark symmetry to the endless nothingness of the burning desert of sand and rocks. The fading black surface and ram shackled structures stood bravely against the ravages of one of nature's natural ovens, the Dasht-e Lut desert in South Central Iran. The beating sun, along with the heat the asphalt absorbed, gave the air a heavy movement, a pulse of its own. It had been long abandoned as if haunted by specters of the past and fueled by the blood of Iran's turbulent history. If the fertile crescent had been the womb of the earth, this desert had been one of its stillborn offspring.

Two heavily armed men walked slowly towards a waiting jeep. The blazing sun tore into the shirts on their backs casting unfamiliar shadows onto the virgin sand as they moved. They were brazen intruders in an arid land oblivious to the oppressive land around them. The sweat covering their jet-black hair and sun-bronzed faces was the only evidence of the price they paid.

The older man took his place in the jeep, an American marvel left and secured from the Taliban when the Americans left Afghanistan. Turning to face his younger colleague, his words broke the silence of the desert.

"It will work, Abdul," said Youssef, his anthracite eyes fired by years of hatred. "The venom is in place. They will pay for the atrocities done to my father and to our people. Many of our men will die, but Allah will be served! It is a holy war, and we are soldiers of God. For it is written, an eye for an eye and...."

"It will not be easy. There will be many at the Summit to guard them," Abdul cautioned. Youssef stared into Abdul's eyes, not a hint of doubt evident.

"I have heard it said, 'When there are too many dogs to guard the chickens, the crafty fox can have his day.'" Youssef said. "We have more than a crafty fox, we have Ghazi. His men have vowed revenge, and they will show no mercy. They're prepared and are at home with death. With the strength of Allah, we will prevail."

"Finally, we will humble the mighty and the Zionists will die with them," Abdul hissed, his voice low and shaking with emotion.

Youssef continued with a wracked ghost of a chuckle, "And soon, the Americans and the Chinese will have to help us before they, too, pay!"

"The devils will do what we say, or they will die!"

"They will do what we say, but we must be ready when the bombs are delivered."

"We will be ready!" Abdul asserted.

"Praise to Allah!" Youssef shouted. His eyes flared. An expression of cold contempt on his face thinly masked the rage Abdul must now put to use.

"Praise to Allah! May it always be so!" Abdul said fiercely, raising his rifle in support.

Youssef started the jeep. The engine struggled, as if resisting coming back to life in this alien land of death. He turned facing his young friend one last time.

"Soon, Abdul," Youssef said in a soft conspiratorial tone. "We will begin to introduce the world to our fury. Our teams are in place in China and in Bethlehem. Both are ready. They've picked their targets. They have the Chinese missile and the explosives needed. Before the Summit, we will serve up death as an appetizer to the main course. By the time the devils arrive at the Geneva Summit, they'll know who we are and what we can do. Soon enough, they will come to understand the price Allah demands."

CHAPTER TWO

PRESIDENTS ARE NEVER ALONE

The Oval Office
The White House
August 23, 2028

*"God is our refuge and strength,
an ever-present help in trouble."
Psalm 46:1 (New International Version)*

President Connie Freeman closed her mother's Bible but left her hand on its cover. Somehow touching her mom's Bible and reading her notes in the margin brought her back. It reminded her of the peace and comfort they both found reading from the Word of God. As she contemplated the coming Geneva Summit, she needed that comfort.

"You are never alone." That was the first thing President Bush had told her about what it was like to be President. Then she was just an intern spending her summer break on leave from her studies at Stanford. She had never forgotten those words. He wasn't talking about God. He was talking about the never-ending stream of briefings and meetings. As President, it was hard to escape the voices that filled her every waking minute. As she was preparing for the upcoming Summit, she hadn't even opened her Bible. She wanted to spend more time there, but when.

But today, she stared transfixed at the white walls of the Oval Office. Her mind wouldn't let her rest for long. She and her staff had put in hours of preparation for the Geneva Summit—attending endless briefings, reading piles of position papers, and participating in grueling simulation sessions. It had been a difficult three months. In addition to her normal responsibilities, she had endured a steady diet of Chinese political history and their unique cultural quirks, video clips of recent speeches by the new Chinese President, and conversations with every Beijing-watcher she could get a hold of. Now the Summit was only days away.

Connie wondered whether President Reagan felt the anxiety she felt as he prepared to meet in Geneva with Russian General Secretary Mikhail Gorbachev. Even though she and her team were prepared, she knew everyone had too much nervous energy to rest. So, they put their energy to work reviewing material they had covered hundreds of times before.

Connie Freeman had dreamed of being President, but she had always kept her deepest dreams to herself. She had prayed for God's will to be done. She had gotten the answer to her prayers. She was elected. She thought she could make a difference, but had she really? All the spinning rhetoric aside, would this Summit make a difference? Was it just another presidential "testosterone" game where she had to play that game her own way? Some players were old guard and others were new, but all the moves in this game were still potentially consequential. She did not want to make the wrong move.

Before Connie could complete her train of thought, the harsh, raspy voice of her Chief of Staff, Jim Naisbitt, cut through her private reverie, as he burst into the room joined by Neil Thomas, her press secretary.

"It's the same old crap!" Jim exploded, his weathered face and fiery eyes creating an intimidating countenance. For Connie, Jim was the chief catalyst; he kept the juices flowing. He knew how to build and burn the right bridges to get things accomplished in Washington. He wasn't beyond doing the same thing in her security briefings. Jim's tirade continued, "They've been pleading for months for you to have a Summit. When you do, they still find a way to crucify you!"

Turning his disturbed gaze onto the now attentive President, Jim said crisply, "Madam President! Listen to this! The *TIMES*, and I quote, 'We cannot help but wonder at the timing of President Freeman's Geneva Summit. With American foreign policy in shambles, open conflict with Iran and a deteriorating relationship with China over Taiwan on the front page, Congress and the public are clamoring for results. The President had no choice but to find a way to get to Geneva. This is not a major step towards peace as the President would have us believe. This is but a veiled and desperate attempt to silence her critics months away from the November election."

Connie watched as Jim slammed the press reports on the table and turned his stare onto Neil Thomas. His young but expressive face returned the look.

"You've read these, Neil. You're the press spokesman. What is this? Can't we get any positive press anymore?!"

Connie watched Neil's eyes; they showed the resolve of a man beyond his years, a man not afraid of any confrontation. Connie didn't worry about him handling Jim. Neil faced deadlier fire daily every time he faced the press. Even Jim had given him the title "Resident

Zookeeper." Every press conference was a "zoo." The press were the "animals," and Neil the "zookeeper."

Neil's words were controlled but direct, "We don't own the media Jim, as much as you might like to. I doubt whether we ever will. We don't seem to feed them what they want to hear. If you...."

"Damn it, Neil, we don't need...." Before Jim could escalate the argument, Connie leaned forward in her chair.

"Enough! Let the press take care of themselves! It's done; they've said it. I never expected to win any popularity contests in this job. Let's not forget. The media wanted a woman president, but they just never planned on her being a Republican!" Connie said with a smile, pausing and focusing on Jim. Connie knew how to use both conflict and humor to get the best out of her people, but conflict needed to be managed. She kept her emotions in check. "Come on, Jim! After all, they're half right. You've been on my back for months to have this Summit for the very reasons they reported. We *do* need this meeting. That's why we picked Geneva to tie into the parallel to the Reagan-Gorbachev Summit. We need some good news!"

Jim rebutted, "We need a diplomatic victory, but don't forget that China needs this Summit, too."

"Of course, but let them take care of China," Connie countered. "We've been hurt, and the polls are showing it. The Democrats have dug my grave. Unfortunately for them, I think they are dancing on my coffin a little prematurely. They'll have a fight on their hands. Let's not waste our energy on each other before we get into the ring with our real enemy and their new leader. This Summit is coming, and it is just days away."

CHAPTER THREE

CHANGE COMES SLOWLY FOR CHINA

> Cabinet Room
> Great Hall of the People
> Beijing, China

"For the wisdom of this world is folly with God. For it is written, 'He catches the wise in their craftiness.'"
1 Corinthians 3:19 (English Standard Version)

While his hands sorted through unending files as if piloted with a mind of their own, the Chinese leader looked at the empty room and then out the window at the expanse of Tiananmen Square. He had taken every spare moment to prepare for the Geneva Summit and the negotiations that were to come. Winning can never be taken for granted.

After all, his road to leadership had not been an easy one. With the sudden death of General Secretary Xi Jinping, the struggle for supremacy in the Chinese Communist Party left many adversaries destroyed. Most had just become irrelevant. Some of the most resistant no longer were even to be found.

But Wang Da had always been confident that his time would come. He could scarcely remember a time when he seriously doubted that he would not be chosen. He had been trained to take power. He had forged the necessary alliances and nurtured critical family connections and now he had the position and the power.

He had always enjoyed Beijing. In his earlier years, he had loved to walk Tiananmen Square. To his grandmother, it was the gate of heavenly peace separating the masses from the Forbidden City. To many, it was the site of protests, military crackdowns and even massacres. To him it was the place of dreams, dreams of power. As an adult, he often strolled into the square and, as he fondly put it, to restore himself. There against the echoing vastness of the square and the walls of power, he would stand off to one side and watch the never-ending stream of mostly smallish men and women flow in and out of the square. He wondered how many dreamed of taking the position that now, he alone had attained. Probably few; most were willing to be led.

Now he was on the inside looking out, surrendering himself for a moment to the past and to the awesome honor of the position which he and his predecessors in their time possessed. But the glare of the sun and the heat of the day brought his mind back to the Summit. It will be nice to get away from Beijing for a few days, but Wang Da was sure Geneva would be no vacation. He was aware of the many pitfalls, but the many opportunities as well.

He turned his gaze from the window to Lin Feng, as he entered the room carrying the briefing on last Wednesday's Communist Party meeting. Lin Feng, a man of paradox, possessed an intensity and proficiency that had accelerated his rise within the party to his present position as head of the Central Security Bureau. The CSB was charged with protecting their leaders and their families. His motivation was not unusual. Many in power had intensity and drive, but Lin Feng also had somehow remained a person, a person with feelings and personal loyalty. The corridors of power in Communist China were often cold and formal. One seldom found people one could really trust. Wang Da trusted Lin Feng, and a smile came to his face as he welcomed his long-time friend. Lin Feng had remained a true friend, one of the few he could afford.

Lin Feng laid the briefings on Wang Da's desk, "Changes come slowly, my friend." Wang Da didn't need the briefing to tell him that was true. He had lived that reality since he moved into the halls of power in Beijing.

"We are making inroads as fast as we can. But despite good economic reports and improved national productivity, glaring domestic problems still remain. Some of our people are very successful, but far too many are tired of waiting for our promises to reach them. They want more now. They expect me to give them more," Wang Da sighed. He looked straight at Lin Feng with eyes that reflected the depth of his concern and exasperation. He hesitated a moment and then said, "We are strong enough, but the aging gray tigers that still stalk the corridors of the Communist Party are waiting for me to fail."

He continued, "I sometimes feel like a slow-moving creek trying to move a rock. Over time it'll give way. But it takes so much time that I wonder if the rock will win."

"The stone wears down quicker than you think, Wang Da. You have consolidated your power quicker than Xi Jinping ever dreamed possible. Soon the stone will begin to roll," Lin Feng said fervently.

Wang Da smiled, wishing that it could be as easy as his friend wished. But what are friends for but to lie when you need one. He hesitated a moment and then said, "In the Party, they offer words of support, but in practice the Party has done very little changing. Never underestimate the power of the old guard. They have a quiet strength that has up to now given permission for what little movement I've made. Officially, Xi Jinping died of a heart attack; I am not convinced. It was all too convenient. Too much, too fast and I fear I would hear their roar and feel their teeth. I do not plan on giving them a reason for hope of my demise."

"They are concerned about concessions you might make in Geneva. General Jin has already been fermenting rumors in the Army about your soft position on new arms. Even Min Jian has been vocal in the Party meetings," Lin Feng said with a complete, flat honesty that forced Wang Da to agree. Such reports were no surprise.

"Yes, Min Jian would be vocal," he said with a scornful, shaky laugh. "The Gray Fox seeks every issue to consolidate power for my demise. I don't worry about General Jin. He means well, but he's always calling for more military spending. He thinks America is still strong and has the will for war. He can't let it happen, but I fear he is blind to our strength. There is no one for us to fear. It is the world that now fears our power. For us to be fearful with the weapons we have now is ridiculous. It scares me, Lin Feng. More weapons just create their own pressure to use them."

Not wanting to sink deeper into that pressure he so often now felt, Wang Da sought to inject a lighter tone, and inquired, amused, "Have you heard the story about Min Jian that is circulating Party halls? The soldier that got five years of hard labor for calling Min Jian an idiot. Six months for insulting a Communist Party official and the rest for revealing a state secret." They both laughed naturally, an experience Wang Da shared with few. But he knew the laughter did nothing to allay the threat that he knew was still very real.

The Summit

"The Party has given you only the authority to attend the Summit," Lin Feng said gently, but with a trace of growing concern. "They have given you little latitude."

"I don't plan on making concessions," Wang Da said with a calm confidence. "To play into their fears of my betrayal would only give them the power they seek. I will make no concessions in armaments to the Americans. I do not need to give concessions to Freeman. You must understand the American press. Our presence at the Geneva Summit keeps them on our side. Freeman is dancing her dance for November. She needs the Summit, whether she gets substantive concessions or not. I don't think she realizes it yet, but she will get reelected with or without the Summit. But her fear of losing has given us, what do they call it, the trump card, Lin Feng."

"What about pressure from her Western allies?" Lin Feng asked.

"Her NATO Allies have their own problems dealing with Russia after the Ukraine fiasco," Wang Da said with a sarcastic laugh. "They're fatalists who have grown used to appeasement and doing nothing. They settle for depending on America, and America has no stomach for another war. They will not be of any help to Freeman. Besides, we will give nothing because the Party has given me nothing to give. But we will leave with trade concessions and newsreels proclaiming People's Republic of China's continuing crusade for peace. I will also have the opportunity to meet Freeman face to face. I have heard much of this woman, and now I shall see for myself."

"You may be underestimating Freeman," Lin Feng observed with a comfortable smile.

"I do not underestimate her. Any woman who has been able to rise to President of the United States has to be respected," he said seriously. "Freeman has strength. She sees herself out of the mold of Reagan.

Before Reagan, we had great faith in the regression of all elected liberals and conservatives to that mealy-mouthed middle ground, that gutless center that floated with whatever the press wanted. Reagan was a unique President; he had the inner strength and confidence to make a difference. I have read much about him."

After pausing thoughtfully, Wang Da mused, his voice shaded with many meanings, "An individual made a difference. Freeman is the same breed, but she's not as paranoid as Reagan was. She's a realist. Reagan kept riding into the sunset with six-shooters drawn chasing after communists behind every shadow. He was a calculated, hard-fisted warrior. But he was also naive, a "B" grade Hollywood actor at the core. Freeman is strong and smart, but, very soon, we shall see how she really performs under pressure."

"It will not be easy," Lin Feng observed.

"Nothing has been easy lately. Taiwan still remains our Achilles heel, but no one wants to face finding a way out of the stalemate. Iran, our delinquent ally, remains an annoying distraction as they keep rattling their toy sabers. In spite of our constant pressure to show restraint, they remain a loose cannon." Sighing, he again looked out the window. He paused and turned to Lin Feng, his face suddenly beaming with a hint of adventure.

"Let's forget Geneva, my good friend. The Mediterranean is calling. I can feel the sand beneath my feet and the sun on my back now."

"You tempt me," Lin Feng said smiling. "Now, get back to your preparation. We are only days away from Geneva."

CHAPTER FOUR

SOME SYMPOSIUMS ARE BETTER THAN OTHERS

Johns Hopkins University
Baltimore, Maryland

"It is not the healthy who need a doctor, but the sick."
Matthew 9:12 (NIV)

It was a slow Saturday morning, the kind Brian loved. He walked slowly across the freshly watered grass towards his university office. The broad, level lawn was dotted with mature trees, a single Scotch pine and several chestnuts. The sun was still low, casting dark, cool shadows, the only respite from the record scorching heat wave that had hit and settled over the East coast like a pall. There was not even a whisper of wind to cool the sweat that already covered his body. How he hated the summers. In the winters he could manage, creating his own protective womb of warmth. But in the summer, the ever-present heat that clung to his body left him no relief.

He would always remember his college years in Southern California, the beautiful nights on the beach. He could hear the screech of the gulls and the pound of the surf. The air was soft and warm, the ocean breezes cooling. He missed it all, but he'd traded it for the prestige of being part of one of the top medical schools in the world. He had made the choice, taking his first professorship at Johns Hopkins University. He had more than found his place; he had contributed to the reputation of the school.

At the podium of a recent New England Conference sponsored by the American Society for Laser Medicine and Surgery, he heard his name echo through the auditorium loudspeakers, "We are proud to have with us today, Dr. Brian Winters, from Johns Hopkins University. He is a former graduate of the UCLA Medical School. As most of you already know, Dr. Winters has already established himself as one of the most prolific researchers and competent trauma surgeons in the field. His recent research into innovative applications of laser surgery has...." It sounded so nice to hear it said. The humid heat be damned; it was all worth it!

Three massive poplars momentarily blocked the sun, turning his world cooler and a bit darker. He thought he heard his name. As he turned, he paused and then smiled.

"My dear Doctor Winters," Terry Solomon began, with his slow-as-molasses southern drawl oozing from his broadly grinning lips. "You aren't leaving without saying goodbye, are you now?" He wrapped one arm strongly around Brian's shoulder as they marched side by side up the steps towards the hospital's main entrance.

"Unhand me before you give anyone any ideas," Brian pleaded, feigning concern.

"Now, that's no way to treat southern hospitality!" Terry replied, exhibiting all the false hurt he could muster. Brian stopped and opened his briefcase, pulling out the final exam he had labored all night to prepare.

"Now, Terry, remember," Brian said, pausing for emphasis. "Don't let my interns talk you into delaying the final next Wednesday. They should be prepared...."

"Don't worry. I, too, love inflicting pain on my students. I shall not grant them any last-minute reprieve. I promise."

"Pain indeed!" Brian said laughing. "You're the pain around here." They both fought hard to keep life fun. They refused to grow older gracefully.

"Don't make any waves either," Brian said. "I hate leaving now, when I'm up for tenure this year."

"If you're so worried about your classes, why are you going?" Terry countered. "You aren't even presenting any new research. I still can't believe they're letting you go."

"I bribed them," he whispered with an air of conspiracy. "Let me go to the Geneva Surgical Congress, and I'll do a spring semester symposium on recent international trends in trauma surgery."

"You hate doing symposiums!" Terry observed, cocking his head to one side. "Have you got tenure fever?"

"Even better. I'll use the symposium to develop a seminar on the same subject. If I play my cards right, I won't have to be tenured," Brian said quickly. "I'll retire in luxury from the money I make as an author and traveling consultant. How's that for being grandiose?"

"Atlantic City won't even lay odds on that one, my man."

"I'm serious. I want to find an established international colleague to work with me. If I can find the right person, I think I can sell our consulting services here and in Europe. Besides, I want to check up on the new Laser equipment they installed at Cornavin Hospital. Since I helped design the installation, I want to see it in operation."

"Besides, I want to be in Geneva with my President," he added with a smile, but with the dry tone that Terry had come to love. "I want to do my part for world peace."

Some Symposiums Are Better than Others

"I think you'll have more luck than Freeman," Terry confided with a sarcastic tone he saved only for political figures. "What a joke this Summit is!"

"Can you imagine a history class in the next century studying American Presidents?" Brian observed, sharing his contempt. "Freeman was our first woman President, and she kept creating good newsreel footage all the way through her Presidency—Connie the Great takes on the 'New Evil Empire—China!'" Both paused for a laugh. Brian continued, "The woman is self-destructing in front of our very eyes. Maybe it is time we have a surgical professor for President. With all their scheduled surgeries and classes, they wouldn't have any time to do any damage as President!"

"Heaven help us all!" Terry cried, enjoying their excursion into the absurd. "Can you imagine? We would all have to take notes and have a mid-term exam. And no doubt he'd expect to be tenured after two terms!"

"Uh oh! I better get moving," Brian said, taking a casual glance at his watch. "I've got some things I have to get done before I leave, and I still have to finish packing." Facing Terry, Brian continued, "Hey. thanks for covering for me."

"No problem. Just make me Vice President when you get to be President."

"Get out of here! See you when I get back," Brian said, looking upwards as if for support from on high. "Heaven help my class!"

He waved and then turned, running up the steps to his office. Brian deserved a break. No, he needed a break. He was glad he wasn't presenting. After all, Geneva was such a peaceful place for a little "professional" vacation.

CHAPTER FIVE

MOTHER WANTS TO KNOW I WILL BE BACK

> Hutong Alley Cottage
> Beijing, China

"Do not forsake your mother's teaching. They are a garland to grace your head and a chain to adorn your neck."
Proverbs 1:8-9 (NIV)

Outside the drabness that was Beijing lies a landscape covered with high-rise apartments for miles on end. The powerful found homes, often small but the best China had to offer. Those less fortunate settled for an apartment, a place simply to exist. They settled for work that ensured only that they could survive and hopefully remain safe.

Dr. Chen Li's mother was fortunate. She had a small cottage. Most Chinese were hopelessly dependent on the government. Those citizens with homes were rare and blessed.

As a child, Chen Li's family situation was far from the worst. Chen Li had fond memories of her life in her family's courtyard house, where her father built a swing from the roof beam. She smiled thinking of how she used to eat on the swing next to an old locust tree. When it blossomed, she would climb up and grab flowers to eat.

When forced to move after her father's death, Chen Li had used her influence to help her mother secure a smaller cottage in a protected traditional hutong block within Beijing, 27 square meters with two rooms. Her mother loved her cottage and her garden she tended for hours.

It had been months since Chen Li had seen her mom. Her life in Beijing left no time for a busy physician to visit her mother, no matter how much she missed her. After all, her position was far from secure. For years, Chen Li had been told by teachers and authorities to remember her place in society, but she had refused to settle. She had skillfully discovered a labyrinth of opportunity few would ever allow themselves to even hope existed, much less have the courage to explore.

Chen Li had found her way alone, and she had succeeded. She had joined the Communist Youth League at an early age, and she quickly rose in the ranks as a young pioneer. Her active participation and academic achievements earned her the right to attend and graduate from Shanghai Jiao Tong University, the top-rated medical program in China.

As one of the most respected surgeons at Peking Union Medical College Hospital, Chen Li had helped the hospital earn China's top rating for the last eleven consecutive years. As a result, she now had become a valued member of China's Ministry of Health and conducted surgery on some of the Communist Party's ruling elites. She had been told that excellence and creativity were to be the cornerstone of China's education. She had taken them at their word, and she had won. And now, she had secured the rarest and most coveted privilege of all—she was traveling to the West to attend the Geneva Surgical Congress as a representative of the Chinese Academy of Medicine.

Chen Li had a small, innocent child's face, and sparkling brown eyes. Her voice was high and strong, like her personality. She had a spring in her walk that smacked of energy on the move. Dr. Chen. was on her way from a Ministry of Health meeting, her gray pinstriped, fitted jacket and professional manor were natural to her now. The only flaw, her drooping black hair, the result of her long trip to her mom's cottage on the outskirts of Beijing.

She walked past her mother's neighbors. She was the focus of their stares. Yes, they belonged there. They had settled for safety and security. Chen Li picked up her pace as she walked. As she reached her mother's cottage, she stopped and stared. Reluctantly, she placed her foot on the worn steps, remembering past days. The weathered paint and the burned-out light above caused her to pause. If she had been a more faithful daughter, she would have taken care of such things. She knocked on the door, looking at the house and surrounding garden as she waited. The garden was beautiful, but the cottage needed repair.

The door opened. The sight of her mother unleashed a torrent of tears and emotions Chen Li had forced to be dormant for months.

"Mama!" Chen Li shouted, unafraid of who would hear. They hugged, neither wanting to be the first to let go. Chen Li looked into her mother's smiling face. Yan Fang-Yi possessed a completely irresistible smile. It was wide, taking in her whole face, but most especially, it was warm. She looked older than she expected. A few more lines now scored her face, but then her smile still shined through warming Chen Li to the heart. She was home! As much as she tried to escape her past, just seeing her mom brought it all back.

"Li! Oh, Li!" said Yan Fang-Yi. Unable to find other words, Chen Li hugged her mother again. Their tears flowed in one stream, and the words that neither needed to say came slowly. "How are you, my child?" Yan Fang-Yi said, as only a mother could.

"Crazy, as usual, Mama," Chen Li said with a slip of a smile. She refused to let go of her, as if her mother's touch was somehow recharging the batteries she had let drain to dangerous levels. Now Chen Li stared at her and said the message she knew she must say, "Mother, I wanted to see you before I left for Geneva."

Yan Fang-Yi's smile disappeared like clouds racing from a scorching sun. She had a peculiar look in her eyes. When she spoke, her voice was soft as silk, "You are coming back, Li. Aren't you?"

"Of course, I'm coming back, Mama!" Chen Li squeezed her hand, giving her the assurance Chen Li knew she needed. "That's a silly question."

"Wenlan said she had heard of many doctors who never returned from presenting in the West. I have been worried." In her eyes, Chen Li tried hiding some of her own doubts. Many doctors she knew well had not returned. She remembered the interview ordeal she had been through to even make the trip possible.

Like a restless soul, she had wanted to see the West, but she had paid the price to make it possible. The hours of interrogation about her relatives, her friends, her education, her jobs, the never-ending stream of paperwork—her birth certificate, medical report, itinerary, character references, twelve photos. The necessary Communist Party approvals took the most time. The House of Surgeons and the Chinese Academy of Medicine had all approved her attending. They wanted the prestige her presenting would provide. They also wanted the wealth of information from the West that she could bring back to China. But it was her perseverance that had paid off. She was now going to Geneva.

As if convincing herself as much as her mother, she said in a strong but respectful voice, "Mama. I will not be staying. I love my country. I love you. I will come back, no matter what Wenlan says. I'm just going to present a paper on my research on the 'trauma' team concept for rural clinic emergency treatment."

Pausing, Chen Li gripped her mother's shoulders and said confidently, "I WILL be back."

"How long will you be gone, Li?"

"I leave next week. I will be gone one week, Mama. Just one week! I have clearance," she said enthusiastically, showing her the papers she had worked so hard to obtain. Yan Fang-Yi held them carefully as if something sacred might be defiled by her touch.

Seeking to inject a lighter tone, Chen Li remarked, "Enough of this talk. I have only two hours before I must go. I do not want to leave without having some of my mother's cooking."

They both eyed each other, close to laughter, and then they both gave way to it. Yan Fang-Yi shrugged her meaty shoulders and said with humorous indignation, "You lie so well, my daughter! Let us enjoy our time, the little we have."

CHAPTER SIX

MORE THAN A RIPPLE IN THE SOUTH CHINA SEA

American Airlines Flight 8936
Guangdong Province, China
North Shore of South China Sea

*"For behold, they have set an ambush for my life;
fierce men launch an attack against me, not for my
transgression nor for my sin, O Lord."
Psalm 59:3 (New American Standard)*

"What are you going to do in Hong Kong?" Captain Strong asked, looking at his co-pilot.

"My wife and my kids always give me a shopping list for Hong Kong. I call it early Christmas shopping gone mad," Steve replied.

"Yea, great deals," the captain replied. "Don't take the first price."

"I never do," Steve said laughing. "About time for our approach."

"Agreed." The captain initiated contact, "Hong Kong Tower. AA8936 Boeing 777, 15 miles North with American inbound for landing."

"Radar contact," replied the Hong Kong approach controller. "Cleared for the ILS runway two four left. Maintain one seven zero knots. Maintain one two thousand."

"Roger, Center." Turning to Steve, "Tell the flight attendants to prepare for landing and for the crew to take their seats."

"Wait a minute. What's that on the radar?" Captain Strong asked. "It's not supposed to be there!"

"I don't know, but it is coming at us," Steve replied. "It's coming fast!"

"Hong Kong Tower, radar indicating…"

The explosion ripped through the plane, and it was no more. Debris and dismembered bodies fell from the sky, leaving but a ripple as all were swallowed up by the South China Sea.

CHAPTER SEVEN

THE PRESIDENT WILL WANT ANSWERS

President's Office
Beijing, China

*"They attack, they lurk. They watch my steps, as they
have waited to take my life."*
Psalm 56:6 (NAS)

"What do you mean, an American commercial airliner was shot down on approach to Hong Kong?" Wang Da demanded.

"We just got word from Hong Kong International," Lin Feng continued. "American Airlines flight 8936 was shot out of the sky by a missile that initiated near the shoreline from Guangdong Province."

"A missile?" Wang Da asked. "Was it one of ours?"

"No," Lin Feng replied. "We have been reassured by the military that it was not one of ours. They do not know who attacked the plane."

"How many were on board?"

"It was a Boeing 777. The plane manifest indicated 328 passengers, mostly American with some of our own citizens."

The Summit

"We must get President Freeman on the line," Wang Da demanded. "They will be thinking the worst. It is best that we call with what information and assurances we can give at this time. Get everyone busy finding out where that missile was launched and who launched it. With this, the Summit could be in jeopardy. Now, get me all the information you have and get Washington on the crisis phone! She will want answers!"

CHAPTER EIGHT

ATTACK QUESTIONS REMAIN

> The White House
> Washington, DC

"'They will fight against you, but they will not overcome you, for I am with you to deliver you,' declares the Lord."
Jeremiah 1:19 (NIV)

The phone rang in her private quarters, startling her. A call in the middle of the night is never good news for a President. She turned on the light as she grabbed for the phone.

"Madam President," Jim Naisbitt, her Chief of Staff said. "I hated to wake you, but there has been an incident off the coast of Hong Kong. An American Airlines Boeing 777 was taken down by a missile strike ten miles outside of the airport. There were 328 passengers on board. As of now, no indications of any survivors."

"Was China involved?"

"No one has taken responsibility. China has emphatically denied that they are the source of the missile," Jim confirmed.

"Get the crisis team to the situation room," the President replied. "I will be there as soon as I can. Get me all the information you have."

"Mrs. President," Naisbitt replied. "We just got word that the President of China, Wang Da, wants to talk to you. His office says that he is on the crisis line now."

The President paused putting her hand over the phone, she turned to her husband. "Martin, an American Airlines plane has been shot down just miles out of Hong Kong with over 300 dead."

"My God! Who was responsible?" Martin asked.

"President Wang wants to talk to me now. I'm going to have to ask you to leave. It should be a private conversation."

As Martin leaves the bedroom, President Freeman pauses for a momentary prayer, a pleading for the right words.

"President Wang, this was not the first conversation I expected to have with you. This is very troubling news. I have just been informed of the downing of one of our commercial planes and the loss of over 300 lives."

"President Freeman, my condolences for the loss of life," Wang Da said in the best English he could muster. "I was just notified moments ago. I wanted to call you immediately to assure you that China was not involved in the missile attack. I have received assurances from my military that our forces were not the source of the missile."

"You can understand the gravity of this news. Early information is often inadequate. What do you know?"

"The plane had been cleared for landing. There were no indications of any problems on the aircraft. The Hong Kong Tower received a final message from the captain asking about something appearing on their radar. The missile was on the airport radar as well. What we now know was a missile launched from the shoreline of our Guangdong Province."

"The missile came from mainland China?" the President asked, pausing.

"Yes, that is the information we have," Wang Da said. "As of yet, no one has taken responsibility for the attack. I wanted to call you to let you know that the attack was not authorized by us. We will work with your people to find out who was responsible and hold them accountable."

"Mr. President," Freeman continued cautiously. "Your rise to power did not occur without enemies. Do you think it possible that some within your country wanted to sabotage our upcoming Summit?"

"I will not deny that such individuals exist. There are those who do not want the Summit to succeed, but I have no evidence at this time that they would even suggest such an unprovoked attack on a commercial aircraft," Wang Da confided, hoping that what he said was true.

"Mr. President, it is too early to accept your assurances, but I appreciate the quick call and the offer to work with us in holding whoever did this responsible," Connie paused. "For now, we both have work to do and fears to quell and manage. This loss of life is more than tragic. This act is evil and must be dealt with in the strongest terms possible. I hope you understand that."

"I do. That is why I called."

"We will talk again soon," she said. "There will be many questions to answer."

"I understand. Thank you for taking my call."

As the President moved to get dressed, she prayed, "Lord, be with the families of the loss. Give me clear thinking, the right words, and the discernment of the best actions to take." She knew her team would be waiting. She had much to share and much to decide.

CHAPTER NINE

WILL THE SUMMIT EVEN OCCUR?

> Situation Room
> White House

*"And ye shall hear of wars and rumors of wars: see that
ye be not troubled: for all these things must come
to pass, but the end is not yet."*
Matthew 24:6-8 (King James Version)

President Freeman finished her final summary of her conversation with President Wang in the crisis situation room, "In summary, Wang Da has indicated that they do not know who launched the attack. He also denies that he or their military authorized or fired the missile used. But the facts remain, a missile launched from the shores of mainland China took down American Airlines Flight 8936 and 328 people are dead. Is there anything new to report from the military analysis of the attack?"

Connie watched as General "Bud" Williamson leaned forward in his chair. Bud's slow, crusty voice pulled the rest of the room's eyes to his aging but still massive frame. "Obviously, the Chinese military has all the resources needed to carry out the attack. But there are reasons to believe that what President Wang said most likely is true. If it were a sanctioned attack, China would have deployed resources to defend against any American retaliation. There was no change in the deployment of their resources." The general handed out a report to those attending.

As the short briefing paper was shared, Connie thought of the first time she had met the Chairman of her Joint Chiefs of Staff. The General had not been impressed with her or her credentials. Connie hadn't served in the military, and although she talked tough on her support for military spending, it had been more talk than action. To the General, Connie Freeman was first and foremost a woman who didn't know a damn thing about Washington, the world, war, or for that matter, anything military. And the General had told her so. Connie liked that kind of directness. She told the General she liked to fight as long as her people knew when the fight was over and they needed to obey orders, and damned if the General hadn't smiled. Everyone on her Summit preparation team also knew that there was still a lot of apprehension in the armed forces over possible defense cuts as a result of any Summit agreements.

"We can confirm that the missile was launched near the shoreline in the Guangdong Province as the Chinese reported. It is also worthy of note that there are no military bases near that area."

"That doesn't mean it was not them." All eyes turned to Curtis Wayte, the new National Security Advisor. He was young but experienced in fighting terrorists. He had spent seven years in the military as a Navy Seal and a decade with the CIA. He did not waste words, and when he said something, it was usually worth hearing. "A small tactical team with a missile could be deployed to that area to make China's denials plausible. But shooting down a commercial aircraft and killing civilians a week before the Geneva Summit seems provocative and downright stupid."

The Summit

"Initiating an attack like this does not fit what we know and expect from President Wang," Secretary of State Tom Grodin offered with reassurance. "He has not fully consolidated his power base. Xi Jinping's sudden death has just muddied the waters. He is still walking a thin line. The battle for power proved his metal, but he's still 'new generation.' In all my years in the State Department, we've never had anything to compare with this time in China's history. The old guard is finally dying off, but the new leaders don't have a firm hold. Many in the Party are waiting for President Wang to make a mistake, and I wouldn't rule out that fact that some rogue enemies within the Chinese Communist Party might have done this. This attack could be the blow to his leadership they wanted."

"I certainly hope not," Connie said.

"Look. I keep coming back to that one note of optimism" Tom continued. "He spent two years studying at Oxford. He knows the West. He's the first General Secretary to have firsthand experience living in a capitalist country. I think he wants and needs this Summit to succeed."

"But don't forget. From what I've experienced, he was no sweetheart, when we faced him in past negotiations in London," Maureen Trudeau countered. She was Connie's Assistant for Policy Development and the team's most respected woman in her inner circle of advisors. Maureen more than carried her own weight. She had the credentials in both international diplomacy and domestic affairs. She also had the intellect and the heart to keep balance in her prepared policy statements. She could be tough, and she could give where it cost little to bend.

"As I'm sure you remember from our briefings, Xi sent him to lead the delegation in London," Tom said in thoughtful tones. "Xi Jinping was not known for giving his negotiators much room for movement. Wang Da had more than most. He had earned trust."

"I remember my impressions of him," Maureen paused as if trying to build a mental picture, making room for texture and feel. "Wang Da was quiet, not particularly charismatic at all. He didn't waste words, at least he didn't then. But you still sensed his presence. I'm sure our President Wang will be a man to reckon with. I think they've already found that out in Beijing. Only the exceptionally strong make it to the top in the Chinese Communist Party."

"You're not telling me anything new. I never have expected to fall in love with the man," Connie added with a chuckle that was shared by others. "If Machiavelli were alive today and living with China's elite, he wouldn't be a professor—Machiavelli would be a student."

"It's not all bad," added Tom. "As I said, his experience in the West is a plus. He's the first Chinese General Secretary to have lived extensively outside of China. I think that will make him more realistic. He's already experimented with bringing capitalism back on a small scale, and the Chinese economy has been responding. They've rebounded from a dismal growth rate of 1.7% to a projected rate of 4%. He's brought more youth with him at all levels of leadership in the Party's power matrix. He wants to continue moving ahead, but the drain on the Chinese economy for their extensive military buildup is still limiting his success. The costs are high, and the public is clamoring for more from their government."

"I agree with Curtis—a small unit with a missile makes the most sense. If it wasn't China, I'd put my bet on a very motivated terrorist group," Gerald Opfer observed. Gerald, the State Department Director from the Office for Combating Terrorism Crisis Management Task Force. "There are increased tensions in the Middle East. Rogue units within Iran and Syria seem to have upped their rhetoric and increased their support for terrorist incursions into Israel. The Prime Minister wants to strike back, but for now, we have convinced him to show restraint. There are a number of new terrorist groups formed in the wake of Biden's botched exit from Afghanistan and Israel's extended war with Hamas in Gaza. With Iran's ties to China, they don't want this Summit to force Iran to curtail their actions. Some of these new terrorist groups, we have little or no information about."

"Any one of them would love to find a way to upstage the Summit," interjected Jim. "But they usually love to take responsibility, but no group has done so. There has been no indication of increased chatter from any of the sources we monitor. It's hard to believe that any of them could get into China to initiate this attack."

"The media is going crazy and talking about possible attacks on the Geneva Summit," Press Secretary Neil Thomas reported. "There is no intelligence that confirms anything, but some of the Swiss leaders are caught up in the hysteria."

"They have a good man in charge," Gerald added. "Guntram Meyer is in charge of security for the Summit. He's a good man, trained with Chuck Healey with Delta Force when they both took part in a SAS Special Forces training rotation in England. He's prepared, but there's a lot of pressure. I'm sure he'll never forget this Summit. The security is tight as a drum and so are the security personnel's nerves. Both the Secret Service and the Chinese have been giving the Swiss a bad time. This attack has just made things worse. I'm sure the Swiss are already eager for us to leave."

A number of the men laughed. To Connie it seemed a tense laugh—the kind of laugh men use when they know not everything is in their control. Connie knew how to laugh, but she wasn't ready to end the meeting.

"Let me make one thing clear," Connie again took control. "We are moving forward with this Summit. I don't care about the media or the polls. Don't get me wrong. I'm not in love with President Wang either, but in foreign policy, he's made it clear that he wants renewed detente."

"Let's hope he means it," Tom said evenly.

"I plan on doing more than hoping. I pray to God he plans on the same." Connie's voice gave a hint of her resolve. These were more than words to her; she had been praying for months about this meeting.

"Remember", added Tom, "Don't try small talk about God, Hollywood, TicTok, jeans, or American music. He hates them all with a passion! He's come down hard on religion and Americanization of Chinese youth. He's a fanatic about it!"

"I know. I've been thinking. With any luck, maybe I can get Wang Da to talk to our youth. I think they could use it," Connie remarked with a smile. A genuine laughter rippled through the room.

"Madam President," Neil said, looking at his phone. "I just got a confirmed media report. A terrorist group has taken responsibility for the attack! It's a group called Al-Haram. That's a new one, Al-Haram. Has anyone heard of them?"

"No, not even on our new list," Gerald Added. "What was their message?

"Short and sweet," Neil continued reading from his phone, "They give their name, Al-Haram. The type missile used, an FN-6, and a warning, 'More will die soon. Allahu Akbar!'"

"A lot of groups can claim an attack," Gerald explained. "But few list the weapon used that we can check. The FN-6 is a Chinese, third generation, passive infrared, man-portable surface to air missile. They could have got an FN-6 out of Sudan, Iran, or any number of countries."

"You've got work to do," Connie said firmly. "Get me what we need to know about this group. I want them stopped before they attack again. I need to get back to Wang Da."

"Neil, do what you can to get control of the media narrative," Connie asserted. "This was not an attack by China. The Geneva Summit is more important than ever to chart a common course. The military is active in planning an effective response to the terrorist attack by Al-Haram. And end with a call for prayers for those lost and their families."

"Got it."

As her team left the situation room, she got her papers together and paused. She thought of a verse in the Apostle Peter's first letter to Christians that had centered her during tough moments in her campaign: "Humble yourselves, therefore, under God's mighty hand, that he may lift you up in due time. Cast all your anxiety on him because he cares for you." Connie liked Peter, his confidence, brashness, an ability to lead the charge. She could see him yelling at the front, "Forward!" But God molded him into a man who knew when to wait on God and trust him alone.

Connie sat and prayed, "Lord, I feel humbled by this moment, and I am anxious about this Summit and further attacks. Give me the wisdom and the words to do your will. Smite this enemy and put a protective shield around our citizens. Open Chairman Wang's heart that this Summit will create a path that serves all our people and gives us peace. God, I need your mighty hand on these next few days. Give me wisdom, courage, and patience when needed. In Jesus name."

CHAPTER TEN

IF THE PRESIDENT IS NOT CONCERNED...

> Johns Hopkins University
> Baltimore, Maryland

*"They have also surrounded me with words of hatred
and fought against me without cause."*
Psalm 109:3 (NKJV)

The whole campus was abuzz with news of the downed plane. Terry Solomon knocked on Brian's office door and came in without him having to reply, "Have you heard about terrorist group accepting responsibility for the flight 8936? Some new group out of the Middle East."

"Yes, I was watching *Fox News*," Brian said. "They are all over it. It will be non-stop terrorist for a week."

"You're still packing?"

"President Freeman and President Wang are still going," Brian said. "If they are not concerned, why should a lowly medical professor worry? I can see the headlines now, 'Terrorist Attack Misses Summit and Destroys Medical Conference!' Noted surgeon Brian Winters' last words were memorable, "Well, some days you're the bug, and some days you're the windshield!"

"Very funny! You know, lately, you've been developing a kinda bug look! Seriously Brian, you are not even presenting!"

"We are doctors, and as Lord Byron would say, 'Always laugh when you can. It is cheap medicine.' See, just having you come in here to make us both laugh. That's good medicine. And after all, something more important is at play here," Brian said, playing along.

"And just what is that?"

"My tickets are non-refundable, and they weren't cheap because of the Summit. And we both know that the university most certainly won't reimburse me unless I go. So, whether I live or die at the hands of terrorists, I or my estate will be reimbursed for my tickets. The Johns Hopkins bureaucracy rules. Yes, bureaucrats are cheap, but they do eventually pay!"

"No, you're the one that's cheap," Terry continued. "Your life is more important than…"

"Terry, I'm going. Wish me safe travels and pray that I eventually die painlessly in my sleep at 90 and not at the hands of evil terrorists in Geneva!"

"You don't believe in prayer!"

"That doesn't stop me from covering my bets when the going gets tough. If I can believe that Dr. Terry Solomon can take care of my class when I am gone, I can believe that God will take care of me when I'm in Geneva. You might add a prayer for President Freeman. I have a feeling she is going to need God's intervention more."

CHAPTER ELEVEN

A COMMON ENEMY TAKES RESPONSIBILITY

Oval Office
White House

"Let there be a treaty between you and me, as between my father and your father."
I Kings 15:19 (NIV)

"**M**r. President, it is good to talk to you directly again," President Freeman said on her crisis line to Beijing. "I have met with my cabinet and military leaders. Although we have no direct information on the Al-Haram group, their taking responsibility for the attack on the plane confirms what you said."

"Thank you, Madam President," President Wang replied. "We have investigated that area where the missile was fired. I can confirm evidence of their presence, but we were unable to find any of those responsible. It was obviously well planned, including their escape."

"I know you have worked more closely with some countries in the Middle East, including Iran. We are concerned that with our continuing sanctions, they may have been involved."

"I have talked directly with Iran's President in Tehran to get his assurances that they were not behind the attack. As you know, with the passing of their Supreme Leader Ali Khamenei and the years of demonstrations in the street demanding change, the mullahs have lost some of their control. But that isn't to say they are happy. There remain many radical factions. I would not rule out a rogue element planning such an attack, but we yet have no direct evidence of that."

"Can you trust the new leader?" President Freeman asked.

"He is doing his best to balance the factions, but none are happy. But I don't think he has consolidated the power, nor do I think he has the will to do such an attack. I did ask for his help in learning more about the Al-Haram group. He said that his people had no knowledge of this group either. I do not know if that is true, but it's clear that he wants nothing to do with taking blame for this attack. He has enough trouble of his own."

"I have asked our military to get as much information as they can find on this group, but I think it best that we cooperate together on that," Freeman said. "Neither side needs any surprises to add to the tension."

"I have talked with General Jin Yuan, and he has confided that he has had constructive conversations with your Chairman of your Joint Chiefs of Staff, General Williamson," President Wang continued. "I would not say that they trust one another, but there is enough respect and past communication to warrant their working together on this... cooperatively."

"That is good to hear," the President responded. "I will instruct General Williamson to contact the general. We can leave it to them to bring together the people from both our countries to find out more

A Common Enemy Takes Responsibility

about this Al-Haram group. More importantly, to execute a plan to neutralize them. The faster the better!"

"Agreed. We are days away from Geneva," President Wang said, pausing. "I believe meeting for the Summit is more important than ever to quell any doubts of our involvement in this attack and to assure the world that we both want to find a way to get past this tragedy."

"I agree, but this was not a tragedy. This was a premeditated evil attack," President Freeman replied. "I trust that we both know that. Now, I have told our advance team to continue with the planning. Yes, the Geneva Summit must occur. The world needs to see us together to avoid any more rumors of pending hostilities over the downing of this plane."

"Yes, an evil attack. One of my generals noted that the word 'Haram' means roughly 'prescribed by Islamic Law.' As the world knows, evil in the name of religion provides a very strong motivation. But I trust that together, we will find them and destroy them for what they have done," President Wang confirmed. "We will talk in person soon. Mei will still be traveling with me."

"Yes, Martin and I both look forward to meeting you and your wife. Safe travels to you both, Mr. General Secretary."

"You as well."

CHAPTER TWELVE

A PRESIDENT QUESTIONS HER WILL TO RUN AGAIN

**White House Oval Office
Washington, DC**

*"Now therefore, please swear to me by the Lord, since
I have dealt kindly with you, that you also will deal
kindly with my father's household, and give
me a pledge of truth."*
Joshua 2:12 (NAS)

"**M**artin, it's confirmed. We're still going to Geneva," President Freeman said to her husband in their private quarters. Now that is a Presidential name—Martin Freeman. He was so important to her, and she could sense his concern for her in making the decision.

To Martin, her troubled eyes were like open windows to her soul. She tried to hide her doubts, but too much had already been revealed for the shutters to be closed. The last five years had taken a toll on both of them, and she was so stubborn. She would always take everything on herself. He knew she needed him, sometimes, just to be held.

He came up behind her. She felt the warmth of his hands rubbing her neck and shoulders. She closed her eyes. The warmth of his hands and his firm caress melted the tense steel cords, draining her tension.

"Well, I know we're going, but what is it, my President?" said her thirty-five-year companion with the amiable candor she always prized and relied upon.

"Nothing a good massage can't take away," she said with a smile, amazed at the flood of relief and calmness that swept over her just at the sound of his voice and the touch of his hands. "Don't you ever leave me; I couldn't afford to pay for the times I need you to give me one of these."

"Connie Freeman, you're stuck with me. I'm not leaving you," he said, kissing her on the cheek. "But I'm worried about you. With the downing of the plane and the tough campaign ahead, it's a lot to juggle," he confided.

"President Wang wants to meet. I want to trust his motives, but I don't want to be blind to where he wants to take China. So many on my team don't want me to trust him," she said in a thoughtful tone, resigning to the need for their inevitable Summit.

"I want you to take care of yourself. You're worried. I can see it in your eyes. You know what the doctors said last week," he said earnestly. He came around and sat down facing her. He touched her arm, mustering all the reassurance he knew she needed.

"I heard no reason to be overly concerned," she said with a calm confidence that she knew to him seemed almost bereft of sense. "Besides, those doctors are paid to make a big thing out of...."

"You're not fooling me!" Martin said sharply, fixing her with a sudden intense gaze. "I was in the room with you when they discussed your heart. Whether you win in November or not, I plan on electing you for as many consecutive terms as my wife as I can get. But you have to be around a few more years to make that happen."

"You're going to make me a hypochondriac," she said, laughing sympathetically, trying to calm the rising storm signals emanating from her husband. "I'm as healthy as a horse. But all right, I'll take care of myself. After all, I've got to please my one sure vote. It is sure, isn't it?"

"Only if you take me seriously for once. I'm not letting this go!"

"I've changed my diet," she pleaded with a look few else would ever see. "I'm even running with my Secret Service team. And you know I hate running! If God had wanted us to keep running, He would never have allowed cars to be invented."

"You can pick your pace if you run with me. You've made a difference here. You don't have to run again in November," he said with a complete, flat honesty that forced her to pause. The four years HAD taken its toll—the campaigns, the never-ending stream of hands and smiling faceless friends, the long hours, the black box, the hounding press attacks, the rarity of moments where there was time to touch. For a very long moment there in the Oval Office, she stared at him without a sound. Then she sighed, a deep and infinitely tired sound.

She shook her head sadly, speaking but hardly recognizing her own voice. "I've decided Martin," she said gently with a trace of growing firmness. "I've already announced my intention to run. Now is not the time to back away from this. I don't want to be the first woman president and let a few health problems chase me out of office. My God, Biden was one step away from the grave and as senile as they come."

He squeezed her arm without speaking. In a sense they had been spoiled. They had always had it easy as a couple. No issue had ever really come home to hit them in the immediate human way that being

President had. Her Presidency was challenging them deeply in a way that neither could escape.

Finally, Connie grabbed his hands and said, "We've got to finish getting ready. We'll be leaving for Geneva later today. I'm just glad my one sure vote will be with me."

CHAPTER THIRTEEN

NO SILENT NIGHT IN BETHLEHEM

> Air Force One
> An Hour from Cointrin Airport in Geneva

"You will not be afraid of the terror by night, or of the arrow that flies by day."
Psalm 91:5 (NAS)

President. Freeman had found some relief in her private quarters on board Air Force One. But she already felt tired. Reviewing the Summit briefing papers that had been updated before they left hadn't helped. There was much they still did not know.

A frantic knock sounded an alarm. The room echoed with it for a second, startling her.

"Come in!"

"I hate to interrupt you," Tom said in exasperation. Tom Grodin's face said more than words could say. "We just got word of a terrorist attack in Bethlehem a couple of hours ago. A bomb detonated destroying a bus carrying a small group of American tourists just outside of the Church of the Nativity."

"My God, how many casualties?" Freeman asked, grasping for a way to hide her frustration.

"There were 13 Americans killed and 7 wounded. The Palestinian bus driver and two shoppers just outside a nearby store also died," Tom replied.

"Has anyone taken responsibility?"

"Not yet, but Israel does not suspect Hezballah, Hamas, the Palestine Islamic Jihad, ISIS or any of the normal groups," Tom explained. "There was no chatter or intelligence information before the attack, and the regulars are wise enough to avoid attacking Americans."

"Get Bud in the conference room. I want to get his read on what we might need to do to our alert status in the area. I'm sure our embassy is aware, but make sure they're increasing security."

Tom turned to leave and then paused, looking back at the President. "Madam President, I'm sorry. You've got enough on your plate without adding Israel to the mix. This is no way to start a Summit."

"You're telling me," the President said with a ghost of a laugh. "Get together with Jim and Neil. We need to prepare a statement. The press will be waiting for us with bells on. Get as much information as you can, but we'll still want the major thrust of anything we say to remain as positive as we can. We're here to find answers, not add to our problems."

For a moment, she sat down on the bed in her quarters. Connie said, no pleaded, in a momentary prayer, "God, be with me in and through this. Give me the presence and the words I need to handle this. Be with those wounded and the medical team there to help. If it be your will, don't let this escalate any further."

Connie wondered what President Wang was feeling when he learned of this. She doubted he would be taking time to pray. She wondered if past presidents prayed alone in times of crisis. She knew that she needed the peace that prayer gave her.

There was another knock at the door.

"Come in," She again replied. Tom again entered along with Martin.

"We just got word that the same Al-Haram group that attacked the plane is now taking responsibility for the bus bomb in Bethlehem," Tom said as Martin moved past him into the room to be with Connie.

"That was my fear," Connie replied as Martin took her hand. "Get my statement ready. It doesn't change a thing. It just makes the need to deal with these terrorists that much more important. I will be in the conference room in a minute."

As Tom left, Martin asked a question both knew was not far under the surface, "Are you sure the Summit is safe?"

CHAPTER FOURTEEN

A SUMMIT IN THE MEETING PLACE FOR THE WORLD

Cointrin Airport
Geneva, Switzerland

*"A gentle answer turns away wrath,
but a harsh word stirs up anger."*
Proverbs 15:1 (NIV)

Geneva was the meeting place for the world, and Connie had participated in her share of those meetings. The United Nations facility was ideally suited with adequate conference rooms, the multilingual interpreters, and their digital expertise. The Swiss also had the discipline and cultural temperament to keep it all running on time. She remembered the motto on the Swiss five-franc coin, "Dominus Providebit"--"The Lord will provide." She hoped that God would do just that; she could use a little divine intervention right now. She knew she would need it.

Connie Freeman knew the press would be there in force. Her controlled arrival at Cointrin Airport, set the stage for her short, prepared statement. She had no intention of giving them room to ask the questions she knew they would want answered.

Her relations with the press had not always been difficult. When she was first elected, political columnists and TV commentators had praised her character, her earnest but honest conservatism, her integrity and business savvy. And, of course, she was the first woman President! How could she do anything wrong? As the *Los Angeles Times* had once written, "Connie Freeman is ideally equipped for the challenges of our time, the perilous age in which she is called to lead our nation."

But now the honeymoon was over; it had long since withered under the heat of hundreds of difficult decisions. She had been unable to stop the almost constant plaintive cry of Americans who wanted desperately to return to the unchecked prosperity of the past. China, in many ways, had surpassed America's economy on many levels. Poorer countries wanted to participate in prosperity themselves, not just see it in Hollywood movies about America.

When people were in pain, they searched for someone to blame. The world had blamed America. Many Americans, in turn, had blamed her. To many, she had lost her luster. The press was ready to feed the public what it seemed to want, and she was to be the main course. The Al-Haram attacks had just added hot sauce to their waiting dinner!

She heard the incessant questions as she approached the microphone. Jim had told her to be confident, to be short, and to end with the focus on the opportunity the Summit can provide.

"As I am sure you know," the President began the press conference. "A second attack by the Al-Haram terrorist group has occurred in Bethlehem. Early reports indicate that there are fifteen dead and many others wounded. Members of our Terrorism Crisis Management Team are on their way to Bethlehem to assist in the investigation and help in any way they can. We will not rest until those responsible are held accountable. It certainly will be one of the topics President Wang and I will both be motivated to explore together. But let me assure you that no terrorist attack will stop us from the important work of this Summit. We are working to redefine the relationship between China and the United States and renew our disarmament talks in Stockholm. Peace calls us to Geneva, and furthering peace and cooperation remain our goals. I ask the world for continued prayers for the families of those who have lost loved ones at the hands of these terrorists, for a full recovery for those wounded, and for a successful Summit. Thank you."

As the President left the microphone, Martin grabbed Connie's arm and both were ushered by Secret Servicemen as they moved quickly through the gauntlet of probing microphones, cameras and bodies.

"What can you tell us about the Al-Haram terrorist group?"

"What is the American response to the terrorist attacks on Israel?"

"Is Iran behind this?

Like jackals, the reporters pushed for answers, all echoing in unison their version of the same question. Connie Freeman's face showed the discomfort she felt, the forced smile bringing tension across her face. Connie stumbled, but somehow stayed up buoyed by the strength of Martin's grip propelling her forward.

Another reporter screamed, "Is there any truth to the report that your negotiating team is ready to negotiate for substantial reductions in your Pershing 2 missiles deployed in Asia?"

Connie's mind was now reeling. THERE'S A LEAK ON THE NEGOTIATING TEAM. SOMEBODY'S TRYING TO SABOTAGE THIS SUMMIT!

The Summit

Neil was now pushing them both past a final throng of disappointed reporters. Neil shouted in exasperation what none of the reporters wanted to hear, "There will be a full press briefing tomorrow morning! There will be no additional statements now!"

"Madam President, there are reports that the terrorist attacks have already derailed the Summit?" Like a bullet from an unseen assassin, the final question had hit its mark. The terrible attacks and the leak had put an end to quiet diplomacy, and Connie knew it. She realized that no amount of formality or hiding would change that fact. She pulled up suddenly and turned to face the reporters. There was a startled gasp from those reporters closest to her.

Neil tried to encourage her to keep going, but he was quickly silenced by the reassuring wave of Connie's hand. For what seemed like a long time, Connie said nothing. She hesitated and then yielded to the demand of the moment, something she almost never did as President, for she had learned to become thoughtful and careful in her choice of words.

"These terrorist attacks will in NO WAY effect the outcome of this Summit," The President said firmly. "We are here for peace, and peace is too important to be put in jeopardy by any terrorist provocation. Since the first attack, our forces have been on alert and will continue to be on alert. The carrier USS America is positioned to act if needed."

"Madam President, does the leak of your negotiating position concern you?" asked a familiar foreign correspondent from NBC.

"Of course! Leaks always concern me!" replied Freeman. "But it's your job to go fishing for whatever tidbits of truth or rumors that will satisfy the desire for information. But do not miss the historical significance of this event and my commitment to make this Summit a success."

A Summit in the Meeting Place for the World

President Freeman, sensing she was now back in control of her emotions, paused and then said fervently, "Whatever the outcome of our talks, we are taking the initiative for peace. It is a moment of opportunity and, also, danger. We're here to search for substantive dialogue in the midst of our many differences. President Wang's first year as leader of the People's Republic of China has given us some reason for hope. I plan to examine closely with him the possibility of a constructive alliance for peace. The actions of Al-Haram impacting both our countries has just increased the likelihood of that cooperation."

"So you expect substantive progress?" It was a question Connie was used to hearing. She knew they were used to her answer.

"I always expect progress, but the recent breakdown of disarmament talks in Stockholm has been frustrating. I am personally committed to a serious, intensive, and prolonged dialogue with Chinese leaders, one aimed at building a more constructive US-China relationship. Our differences will not be wished away. It will take work. With a good faith effort on both sides, we can make a good start for that change at this Summit."

Before other questions could be asked, she turned to Martin and grabbed his arm. Showing a broad smile, she took a seat in her waiting limousine.

CHAPTER FIFTEEN

PRESIDENT FREEMAN IS NO REAGAN!

> Bar Les Nations
> Geneva, Switzerland

"As for you, you meant evil against me, but God meant it for good in order to bring about this present result, to preserve many people alive."
Genesis 50:20 (English Standard Version)

It was late. Most of the people of Geneva had already gone to bed. The few people remaining were mostly seated alone. The two U.S. generals sipped their drinks quietly, blinking bleary-eyed into the walls staring back at them. Only the occasional brittle laughter that came from one couple in the corner gave life to the room. In short, it was like any late-night bar in any quarter of the world.

Rear Admiral Julian Bishop clutched the back of the worn wooden chair next to his, gripping it with a force indicative of the feelings he tried to control. He waited impatiently for the drinks to be served and the waiter to leave. When alone again, he stared intently at General John Westlake, his Army counterpart in the fifty-member negotiating team sent in advance by Freeman to prepare for the Summit. Finally, Julian spoke in a low voice, but his eyes were blazing with anger.

"I don't care what Bud says, Freeman is going to sell us out!"

"You don't know that," John countered, leaning forward grabbing his beer. "She specifically assured the Joint Chiefs of Staff that there would be no substantive changes negotiated at this Summit. My God, what more do you..."

"That's shit, and you know it!" Julian blurted with controlled savagery. "Freeman is no Reagan! I can guarantee you that. Reagan knew the importance of sharpening your teeth before you risked talking about peace with the Russians! The Chinese are bigger, tougher, and far more dangerous. My God, John. You remember Afghanistan. You know what that's like when a President sells you out!"

"You and I both know they were never going to give up," John stated sharply. "They just waited. They knew we had no stomach for extended wars or even keeping our military deployed. She's no Biden, Julian! She knows how dangerous China can be."

"Don't give me that! China has no intention of living up to any agreement. They never have!" he said, unmoved. "What's a paper treaty when the only thing they respect is power? Let me tell you, John. If this Summit goes well, they'll put the rest of the Stealth Bombers on hold, and they'll nix the Strategic Defense Initiative Deployment that has finally proved itself workable. Damn it, John! They don't want peace! They're now propping up that puppet regime in Iran and Syria. They're going to take advantage of any leeway Freeman is forced to give them. I just get sick of the musical chairs we have to go through from one election to the next. It's a joke!"

"Settle down!" John said forcefully, with a sharpness that surprised Julian. "We don't need to make a scene in here. If you keep this up, next thing you know, we'll trigger a spontaneous peace demonstration all by ourselves."

Julian gave a shaky, sarcastic laugh. "I'm sorry. I just get carried away!" he said slowly, staring momentarily into the glass he held in his hand. THAT'S WHAT THEY SAID TO ME WHEN THEY TURNED ME DOWN FOR ADMIRAL--"YOU GET CARRIED AWAY; YOU STATE YOUR OPINIONS LIKE YOU WERE PREACHING A FIERY SERMON FROM THE PULPIT. THERE'S NO ROOM FOR THAT IN WASHINGTON!"

John said nothing, taking a sip from his drink.

"I retire next year, and, frankly, I'm ready to get out. I just don't need this frustration!" Julian said, again pausing. Feeling John's silence as an invitation to continue, he added, "With any luck, I'll land a consulting job with Tyler Defense Systems. I've been assured of a position there after I retire."

The Admiral paused looking for a hint of disapproval from John that he half expected. Not seeing any, he continued with a humorous bravado, "They said I was a 'tough son of a bitch to deal with' and they wanted me pushing from their side. I can't sell weapons directly, but I know the rules, and I can still use my experience and contacts. The old revolving door from the military to the defense industry looks better and better every day."

Pausing for a moment, John interrupted sarcastically, "Julian a consultant! Mr. Loudmouth pigeonholing legislators for defense contract support. And this time, for fun and profit." Julian's forced laughter failed to mask a hint of criticism.

"But if it's back to detente, the soft money melts away. No more stealth bombers, no consulting job; it's that simple, John. Don't get me wrong, I'm as patriotic as the next guy, but detente doesn't work," Julian asserted, his voice heavy with frustration.

"Don't give up the ship, Julian. I know steering a consistent course is all but impossible in Washington. But after seeing her in office for three years, I think Freeman is stronger than you give her credit for. She won't..."

"Good guys...or gals... make bum Presidents! I like some of what she has done. I even voted for her, but she's just out of her league with China. Wang Da is going to eat her alive at the negotiating table. He doesn't need this like she does, and he knows it. I'm worried, that's all." Julian turned to the bar and waved for a second round.

The drinks came, bringing a momentary respite to their conversational stalemate. Julian picked up the gauntlet as soon as they were again alone. "Damn it! This is not a parlor game. The stakes are too high! We can't afford to have her learn from her big mistakes."

There was a long pause. Julian watched as John stared into his drink and then met his eyes in an intense stare.

"You heard the press on her arrival. Did you leak the information to the press, Julian?"

"Whoever did, I'm glad they did it," Julian answered quickly, looking momentarily at the couple laughing in the corner and then back at Westlake.

"You didn't answer my question. Did you leak the information to the press?"

"If I did, would you want me to tell you?"

"Come on, Julian," Westlake warned, leaning forward in his chair continuing in a whisper, "If they found out who did it, you'd be out the door!"

"I didn't say I did it. I don't think there is any point in continuing this conversation. Here's to a...," Julian said, raising his drink and pausing for effect, "successful, yet survivable Summit. Skoal!"

The Summit

Westlake refused to raise his glass to the toast. Julian knew all too well that much was left unsaid, but he was unwilling to say more. He was concerned that he had already said too much.

CHAPTER SIXTEEN

THE STRANGE ECSTASY OF CATACLYSMIC VIOLENCE

The Palace of Nations
Geneva, Switzerland

"When you go to war against your enemies and see horses and chariots and an army greater than yours, do not be afraid of them, because the LORD your God, who brought you up out of Egypt, will be with you."
Deuteronomy 20:1 (NIV)

In the pregnant silence of the night, only the footsteps of the security guards making their rounds gave life to the building. But even in the silence, the well-lit, sprawling Palace of Nations stood as an imposing monument. Built between the two world wars for the ill-fated League of Nations, it had through the decades earned a reputation as a haven for international diplomacy. Its hallowed halls had provided a nurturing womb for man's struggle for cooperation and peace. It was here that Austria's neutrality was negotiated and the Nuclear Non-Proliferation Treaty was signed. Many nuclear disarmament discussions had been conceived and nurtured there, but all had, as yet, died stillborn.

However, the rocky struggle for peace was continuing. The complex contained offices for over 7,000 U.N. employees as well as numerous conference rooms that were constantly in use. But this night, in the silence, the Palace of Nations was at rest, as if saving energy from the calmness for the demands and challenges that tomorrow's Summit address would surely bring.

Security for the Summit had been massive, and, after the Al-Haram attacks, its excesses had bordered on the absurd, if not the ridiculous. Chinese security men had given a stiff refusal to Geneva trash collectors making their weekly rounds at the Chinese Embassy. They had requested the same precautions at the Palace of Nations on the day the General Secretary and the President were to deliver a joint address to the assembled United Nations' delegates. The Swiss had refused but had compromised, requiring a thorough search of each truck.

The next day in preparations, a U.S. Secret Service agent carrying a concealed weapon had talked his way into the Palace of Nations conference center without having to pass through the metal detector or to show his clearance pass. The uproar created by the incident had reached the press, requiring numerous Swiss authorities to spend hours before the microphone quieting growing fears of lax security. In response to the tension all felt, Swiss security at the Palace had been doubled.

Now, the preparations were done and the palace had given way to the night. The light from the full moon ruptured obliquely through the overcast skies adding rare touches of beauty and peace to the scene.

Inside the echoing hallways, a Swiss guard moved on his appointed rounds. He glanced at his watch; he was right on schedule. He, like

The Strange Ecstasy of Cataclysmic Violence

the rest of the Swiss military, took pride in the meticulous nature of their thorough regimen. He could not understand why others were not always the same way; it seemed so logical. He shook his head as he thought of the last few days. The security had been fine before all the turmoil, but with pressure from the Mayor of Geneva and other Swiss officials, the number of guards had been doubled to silence the clamoring Western press.

To the guard, it was all a useless political charade. There had never been a serious security problem in Geneva. But while the powerful slept, he, and men like him, walked the hallways of this modern-day fortress. Night after night, they scared away ghosts that did not exist. It was good money, but he was tired of the overtime hours. His wife was furious. He assured himself that it would soon be over, and then the superpower leaders and their bothersome press would leave. A sudden muffled sound coming from somewhere down the hall broke his train of thought.

The guard stood motionless, listening for the noise he was not even sure he even heard. In that seemingly endless moment, there was total silence. After hearing nothing else to signal alarm, he resumed his walk, smiling to himself. The predictable cadence of his moving feet produced sounds that filled the empty void, masking the all-but-silent movements of the animals that were lurking within the citadel's walls. He continued on his rounds.

At heart, Ghazi Saud and his men were animals. They lived in a world outside of order and reality. Ghazi's only true companions were Allah and his men, finely-trained men, who shared his contemptuous disregard for human life. But now he waited in silence, staring at his brother Gamal. Gamal's careless dropping of his weapon within their sealed shelter had signaled alarm to the passing guard in the hallway beyond the walls. In absolute silence, he and his men waited for the sounds of the guard's movement that would signal their reprieve.

Ghazi was sure that this guard, as others before him, wanted to believe that nothing was unusual. Like all ego-stroked civil servants, they were willing to remain blind. Would they blame the noise on the rats he and his men had killed? Would they doubt their senses? He gave thanks to Allah for shielding their hiding place from the guard.

All his life, Saud Ghazi had studied but one science, the science of destruction. He knew but one objective, the destruction of the vile order of earthly governments that had wronged his people. In his mind, there was but one principle that mattered, the doctrine of liberation through cataclysmic violence. He had already tasted the strange ecstasy in meting out death to the infidels; now he looked forward to doing the same to their leaders.

The guard was gone; another would return in fifteen minutes. He turned his icy stare to Gamal.

"There is no room for error!" Ghazi said quietly, fiercely. His words, like piercing daggers, found their mark. "You're not an amateur!"

" It was dark, and I tripped when...." Gamal said testily, recoiling only slightly from Ghazi's gaze as he reached down to pick up his lightweight Uzi-9 mm submachine gun.

"There can be no excuses!" Ghazi snapped, openly showing his displeasure. There was no response from any of the men. Eyes locked with other eyes, communicated thoughts and fears. Their olive drab fatigues allowed them to momentarily fade into the shadows. Their faces were unreadable, but attentive. He had said enough; to say more would only add salt to an open wound. Ghazi again turned away, leaving his men to their own thoughts. The lines were drawn clearly; they all knew the ramifications of such mistakes.

The Strange Ecstasy of Cataclysmic Violence

Ghazi knew it had been a difficult week. Like men sealed in a tomb, he and his men had survived hours of monotony in close quarters. They were men of action who were forced to wait. They had checked and rechecked their weapons. They had reviewed plans and contingencies. Now, they were all on edge and would be until they were free of this self-imposed prison.

The small, sealed food chamber for the Palace of Nation's bomb shelter had provided an unlikely and uncomfortable home, but it had left them and their weapons undetected. The lead walls had thwarted the security detection equipment and the shelter rations had provided a tasteless, but adequate, food supply. What illumination there was came from one small lantern they had brought with them.

It had taken months of preparation to find a safe location within striking distance of the leaders and to consolidate a workable plan. It had taken a kidnaping and a threat to the life of the Night Security Supervisor's wife to gain entry. In order to save his wife's life, Joseph Brunner had done his job. Brunner had reluctantly cooperated, but, in the truest Swiss tradition, his meticulous efforts to seal the shelter door from the outside and his orders to his men to leave the bomb shelter sealed had made searches unnecessary. All had gone well to this point. If they could survive one last night undetected, there would be no further need for hiding.

Of course, he had been through worse before. Ghazi and his younger brother had never been able to hide as children. They lived daily in the corridors of hell, first in Iran and then in Lebanon. Ghazi had been one of the first to see his father's mutilated body, riddled with bullets from the gun of a Christian Militia assassin. He remembered clinging to him--the cold lifeless feel, the blood caked on his blue-tinted skin, the stench of glue. They had quickly pulled him away, covering his father before taking him away. During the funeral procession through their Beirut Shia Muslim slum, Ghazi remembered hearing a defiant, rhythmic chant that rose from the multitude of mourners.

"Allah is our God," the crowd roared, "and Hezbollah is our army." That war cry had been imprinted in his soul. There had been no room for tears. He had remembered his father's words, "The more they kill us, the more we grow." He and his brother had joined the holy war. Since then, the enemies of the Hezbollah had felt the weight of his iron fist. But the Hezbollah had not gone far enough; they had grown soft, settling for words instead of retribution. He and his men had formed Al-Haram. The world had felt its destructive sting. Now, he was ready to savor their ultimate victory.

"Gamal," Ghazi said evenly, again looking at his brother. THE TIME FOR MEMORIES IS OVER. "The explosives are in place?"

"Yes. Brunner confirmed that he placed the cyclonite explosives inside the gate control mechanism at the Pregny Gate during the changing of the guards weeks ago. Now activated, when the truck breaks through the gate tomorrow, the pressure will automatically detonate the explosives, within seconds blowing up the guard house,"

Gamal said with a dispassionate tone, his rodent like eyes giving fire to his small, wiry frame. "After Youssef rams his truck through the gate, he will have a direct access to the Assembly Hall entrance with no one left alive in position to stop him. When the truck rams into the limestone exterior at full speed, 200 lbs. of explosives will take half of the complex with him."

"With the forces of hell unleashed on the Assembly Hall, security will be occupied chasing ghosts they will never find," Ghazi said evenly. "We will be free to move from within," His eyes were burning bright, as if feasting off his own words. To Ghazi, the truck bombing

The Strange Ecstasy of Cataclysmic Violence

was a brilliant diversion, a professionally executed snare. Once the trap was sprung shut, the animal would flail back and forth trying to rid itself of the pain. In its panic, it would be left open for the death blow.

"And Joseph Brunner?" Gamal asked, his voice full of suppressed excitement.

"Joseph Brunner and his wife will die tonight," Ghazi said with a grim little smile. "Mohammed will kill them both. They are no longer of use to us. They have been good hosts, but the party for them is over."

Gamal's smile was wasted on Ghazi; there was no room for any humor in Ghazi's world. HUMOR IS FOR THE VICTIM; POWER IS FOR THE STRONG. WHEN IN DOUBT, KILL. ALLAH SHOWS NO MERCY ON INFIDELS. NO LONGER WILL THE POWERFUL ENSLAVE THE WEAK. Ghazi had come to make the weak powerful, and now, in this room, he felt power surge through his veins as never before. That same power emanating from him touched every man in the room. He looked at each of his men before he spoke.

"Tomorrow, they will come to us," Ghazi promised. He smiled benignly. "And then, even the mighty will become beggars! It is time to get some sleep. You will need strength and a clear mind."

CHAPTER SEVENTEEN

A MOMENTARY CONNECTION TO REMEMBER

Hotel des Berguese
Geneva, Switzerland

"When the LORD takes pleasure in anyone's way, he causes their enemies to make peace with them."
Proverbs 16:7 (NIV)

His flight from Dulles had been uneventful but long. The same could not be said about his arrival in Geneva. Brian Winters was sitting at the bar of the impeccably appointed Hotel des Bergues. The lights were soft and low, giving a glow to the cream and burgundy decor. The fine antiques and the waiter's tuxedo created an ambiance that was so elegant it almost set his teeth on edge. In short, the interior of the Bar des Bergues was permeated with the Old-World charm one would expect from one of the most elegant hotels on the conservative right bank of Geneva.

Brian was already comfortable. It wasn't the place or the rooms; they were formal. In the land of clocks, chocolates, and peace, it was the people that stood out. They had already shown a gracious hospitality that he hadn't expected. Voltaire had called Geneva "a city where no one ever smiles." The people were supposed to be cold and unfriendly, but he hadn't experienced that. Of course, maybe it was the cost of the rooms. Brian mused about the 350 Swiss francs a night he was paying. THEY OUGHT TO SMILE. But the University could afford it, and he liked being pampered for a change.

Brain's arrival in Geneva had been more than he had bargained for. As his taxi had left the airport and snaked through the streets and quays of Geneva, all his senses were treated to a smorgasbord of international causes created by thousands of demonstrators alongside the roads leading in and out of the city. The Taiwanese and the Jews berated Wang, while the Nicaraguans, Iranians, and Palestinians waved placards condemning Freeman. The Trotskyites, environmentalists, feminists, the Hare Krishnas, and the students from the International School of Geneva all hurled affable insults on both their houses.

Brian heard one young woman chanting with a bull horn, "Freeman! Wang! Le monde n'est pas a vous." He knew enough French to find the men's restroom and to be dangerous in a restaurant. What she had said was simple enough for him to understand, but it made too much sense to be on a placard--"It's not your world!" But it wasn't true; he knew that the superpower Summit had provided the magnet for those with placards, passions, and causes.

Even the displays that graced the store windows along the Rue du Mont Blanc gave testimony to the impact of the Summit. Before Wang and Freeman had so much as shaken hands, their pictures appeared together on souvenir posters, pins, hats and T-shirts. Geneva didn't seem to care about who or what to be for; both the demonstrators and the Summit would put money in their pockets. They would take the commerce. The rest of the world could keep the arguments.

The Summit

By the time Brian's taxi had pulled up to the hotel along the Quai des Bergues, he had been ready to find a peaceful refuge. As soon as he had walked into the hotel's cool marble foyer with the sweeping central staircase, he had experienced an immediate sense of occasion. The welcome accorded by the hospitable staff had been far less imposing, but no less notable. There were no bellboys; the clerk personally escorted him to his room. It gave the Old-World formality of the hotel a personal quality that made Brian feel honored to even stay there.

The hotel had even accommodated the peculiar needs of the frequent American travelers by putting in a television set in the bar. In spite of the fact that little of the programming made sense, there were enough American shows that would forestall any withdrawal symptoms the chronic "TV-holics" might have.

Brian could care less about the programs; he seldom watched television. But tonight, any program was a welcome companion. Brian stared at his slowly disappearing glass of wine as if through a trance, trying to usher himself to feel sleepy. He was tired, but he hadn't been able to sleep. He had already tried but had found it useless.

A smile formed on his lips as he thought of his dad's favorite saying, "If you can't fight it, join it." So, he had decided to come to the bar to drink with any other night owls that might be suffering the same fate. The bar was mostly empty, so he sat alone. As he found himself watching the unintelligible program droning on before his eyes, he realized why people liked television; it was the cheapest way to have company without having to buy anyone a drink. Television was boring, but it was always there. Watching it, however, he felt no closer to sleep. He knew he would sleep, though, probably tomorrow during the first boring presentation he had to endure. Brian smiled to himself and took another long sip of wine.

A Momentary Connection to Remember

"Sir, would you like another glass?"

He looked up, shrugged his shoulders. "Sure, why not. I can't sleep anyway," Brian said, not masking the frustration he felt. He took a final sip from his glass and, mustering what cordiality he could find, he added politely, "That's good wine. What is it?"

"It is a French wine, sir. Pouilly-Fuisse, by Barton and Gvestier. It is a very fine wine," the waiter said with a certain haughtiness, taking the empty glass away and returning quickly with a new one. Brian accepted the half-filled glass. He swirled its contents to look like he actually knew wine.

"I wish I could say the same for your television," Brian added, seeking to inject a lighter tone. The waiter said nothing. Brian added thoughtfully, "Do you have any English language stations?"

"There are American shows. Most Swiss speak English."

"Thank God, or I'd be lost!" Brian replied, hoping he sounded humorous. For the first time, they exchanged tentative, but genuine smiles. PEOPLE IN GENEVA DO SMILE; YOU JUST HAD TO WORK AT IT.

"There's the USIA's global news network, Worldnet, and it's in English. Let me turn to that channel; you're the only one watching," the waiter said, turning quickly to the channel.

"Thank you. That's perfect," Brian said, with an expression that showed genuine appreciation.

Dr. Chen Li slowly entered the Hotel des Bergues' bar, her senses taking in the richness of this world that she had not dreamed existed. The colors, the furniture, the textures, all like feathers playfully tickling a child's body, brought her both intense pleasure and pain. She took a seat at a table by the door.

The waiter slid soundlessly into her world, asking her something in a voice that came from her past. She replied automatically, with words she had learned well in school, "Le vin blanc, s'il vous plait."

"Certainement, Mademoiselle." He nodded and left as quickly as he had come, leaving her again alone. Her eyes followed him and for a second caught the eyes of a man at the bar. Instinctively, she looked away, a habit honed through years of cautious involvement with Westerners. But a strange scarlet flush crept up her neck, masked by the comforting semi-darkness the dim lighting provided. As her eyes returned to the stranger, she noted that he was watching the television.

Dr. Chen was dimly aware of the wine being brought to her table, and, as if in a trance, thanked the waiter. Her mind was still focused on the man at the bar. He was a remarkably handsome man, but not in the unvarying Hollywood way she expected to see from Westerners. He had a rough-hewn quality that gave him character and strength. His oval face was dominated by his dark hooded eyes that gave him a strong, but sleepy look.

She was attracted to him. She felt a sudden ridiculous panic and took a deep breath in an attempt to alleviate it. YOU ARE NO LONGER A CHILD; STOP ACTING LIKE ONE. YOU HAVE NO ROOM FOR A MAN, PARTICULARLY A WESTERN MAN. She reached for her glass and took a slow sip from the fine wine.

Brian sat straining to hear a short news report on the upcoming Summit meeting. He turned quickly to the waiter and asked politely, "Could you turn that up, please? I want to hear what they have to say about the Summit."

"Certainly." He responded with a grudging hospitality Brian was getting used to. Brian took a sip of wine and watched as a commentator analyzed Freeman's statements on arriving in Geneva.

A Momentary Connection to Remember

"The President shared her disappointment at General Secretary Wangs's response to the United Nations' nuclear proliferation control initiative and China's cancelation of arms control talks in Stockholm. She again stressed that the United States is prepared to work for peace and for a negotiated settlement that will strengthen international peace and security. She briefly referred to the new Al-Haram bomb attack in Bethlehem...."

Brian reacted, "Bombing in Bethlehem?"'"

"Yes, there was a tourist bus bombing that killed many Americans and wounded others," The bartender replied.

"Al-Haram?" Brian asked.

"Yes, they have taken responsibility."

"Tell you the truth. I didn't really trust either of them to do anything with this so-called Summit, but these attacks just speak to the futility of even talking about peace in this crazy world," Brian said continuing with the honesty that had often gotten him in trouble. But before the bartender could even respond, Brian raised his glass of wine in a toast. Looking at the television, he added hopefully, "But here's hoping the Summit doesn't make it any worse! Skoal."

In silence, Chen Li watched as the man sipped his wine. His actions were puzzling, and yet, something about him still attracted her. Having finished her drink and leaving money on the table, she quietly got up to leave the room, but the sound of her chair betrayed her retreat. Brian locked eyes with her. For a long moment, they watched each other. She tried a smile, but it missed. He returned to his drink. She studied him for what seemed like a long time, her gaze disbelieving and her thoughts turning inward. WESTERNERS WERE INDEED DIFFERENT.

The Summit

She did not feel comfortable with what she saw. She could not say such things as he just said openly in public; others would hear. WHERE THERE ARE EARS, THERE ARE POTENTIAL ENEMIES. BUT HE SEEMED NOT TO CARE WHO WAS LISTENING! Her mind struggled with all she had heard as she walked alone to her room.

CHAPTER EIGHTEEN

THE STRAINED PROTOCOL DASHES EARLY HOPES

**Palace of Nations
Geneva, Switzerland
10:07 AM**

*"When you draw near to the battle, the priest shall
come forward and speak to the people and shall say to
them, 'Hear, O Israel, today you are drawing near for
battle against your enemies: let not your heart faint.
Do not fear or panic or be in dread of them, for the
Lord your God is he who goes with you to fight for you
against your enemies, to give you the victory.'"
Deuteronomy 20:2-4 (ESV)*

Protocol rules the day, even in times of crisis. Martin and the President, escorted by President Conrad Honeggar and his wife, continued slowly, almost mechanically, through the line of Swiss dignitaries. The new Swiss President had decided to leave no one out. Fortunately, most introductions were brief and not even fleetingly remembered. Connie had grown accustomed to such lines during her tenure in the White House. She had given up on remembering names;

she had instead learned to discern a feel for a people by studying the mosaic of faces that passed before her.

For years she had honed her skills in reading people; those skills were even more valuable in the political arena. As she looked into the man's eyes, she wished she was negotiating with the Swiss instead of the Chinese. She had a feeling the Chinese would not be as ready to buy what she had to sell.

The arrival of their limousine at the Palace of Nations complex perched on the wooded hills above Geneva had immediately started in motion the complex labyrinth of formalities and protocol that would inevitably bring Freeman face to face with her Chinese counterpart, Wang Da. All the preparation and strategy planning meetings were behind them. There was no time for nervousness, little time for thinking. Both would now have to trust their own preparation and instincts.

With the opening address to the United Nations Assembly scheduled for the afternoon, the world would get its fill of formality whether they wanted it or not. But then, Freeman knew that a little pomp and circumstance never hurt anybody when done with skill at the right time. This was the right time, and no one was better at orchestrating such an event than the Swiss. They had the practice, and the city's economy depended on it.

Freeman caught the eye of one of her Secret Service agents busily scanning the mass of guests and press corp gathered for the event. She felt for them. They had protected her well in her years in the White House. She felt safe, but she remembered the chilling words of a terrorist who called the Secret Service after a near miss on the life of the British Prime Minister visiting Washington—"We need only be lucky once; you must be lucky every day."

The Strained Protocol Dashes Early Hopes

The President was not sure how many lucky days she had to endure, but she knew that the Secret Service had done its part thoroughly, as it always did.

The U.N. employees had been given three days off to avoid unnecessary complications in security preparations. The terrorist attacks had just increased their focus. The Palace of Nations had been scoured for bombs by Swiss security for days. Everyone entering had passed through a metal detector and had been thoroughly searched. Outside the gates, the heavily armed Swiss troops surrounded the Palace grounds. All precautions had been taken. But the President knew it was a strange time, and one never really had guarantees. Geneva was supposed to be a city for peace. Today, she hoped that would prove to be true.

Freeman was aware of music playing and people applauding before she saw the cause. She turned to see President Wang and the Chinese delegation approaching. Grabbing Martin by the arm, the President advanced on the red carpet to greet the General Secretary and his wife. The cacophony of clicking cameras and flashing lights coming from the pool of photographers and cameramen, formed a surreal matting for the pictures of smiling faces and firm handshakes that she knew would grace the covers of papers and magazines all over the world.

"Hello, General Secretary Wang," Freeman felt as if her voice and her hand were extending across an enormous gulf. "It is a pleasure to meet you in person."

Hesitant but firm, Wang had taken her hand. His expressive, dark eyes dominated his face. All the protocol training aside, he was never quite sure his manners were appropriate for the occasion. Their conversations over the terrorist attack had changed things. He was not sure yet how.

The Summit

"The pleasure is mine, Madam President," Wang answered in a firm, well-modulated voice. He used nearly flawless English. "I've looked forward to this meeting."

The General Secretary's face looked relaxed; he was slow to release the President's hand. She felt that somehow reassuring.

"General Secretary Wang," Connie said turning ever so slightly towards her husband, standing patiently at her side, "I would like you to meet my husband, Martin."

"It is my pleasure," Wang told Martin. His quick smile and warm grasp seemingly draining off some of Martin's reserve. "I have heard of the value of your counsel to the President."

"Thank you, but I fear those reports are an exaggeration." Martin smiled.

"Please let me introduce my wife, Ma Mei."

"I am pleased to meet you," Martin said, taking her hand. "I have heard your name means 'beautiful.' Your name fits you well."

Mie smiled, bowing slightly. "You are so kind."

Connie watched as Martin took Mei's hand. Few words were said, but both had smiled. She studied Mei. She knew so little about her. Her previous pictures had not done her justice. The sunlight played tricks on her hair, the garnet highlights spinning off colors that gave a deep richness to her appearance. She was a very attractive woman. It was a pity the Chinese still hid their leaders' wives from public view.

Before any further words could be said, they were all again being escorted past the crowd of dignitaries and diplomats. Heads bobbed, teeth flashed, cameras clicked. The rhythm of the ceremony seemed to quicken as they walked. Faces passed so rapidly that the President's smile seemed to lock into position. But as she moved, Connie again felt a growing concern. In the artificial, circus atmosphere that a Sum-

The Strained Protocol Dashes Early Hopes

mit creates, clear intentions are easily masked. The polite words, the transparent smiles, and the meaningless handshakes created more questions than answers.

The President noted that the comments by both she and the General Secretary had been pleasant but predictable. Wang and his wife's choice to speak in English had been significant and somewhat unexpected. Connie knew that they were both proficient after their years of service in London, but the U.S. delegation had come to expect a Chinese greeting which was more typical of their recent negotiations with Foreign Minister Min Jian. Jian spoke fluent English but refused to speak it publicly. President Wang had already shown that he could speak English, but she knew she needed more than a difference in style. She needed substantive changes on the Chinese negotiating positions and a way forward to deal with Al-Haram.

As they took their positions, the familiar sound of the countries' national anthems played in order echoed against the palace walls. But Connie's mind refused to relinquish more than a fleeting moment to their engaging sounds. She knew there would be the traditional agenda haggling, the reporting of wrongs committed by both sides, and the formal papers. Then, if God is with us, the real negotiations would begin.

Freeman hoped that her early scheduled private talks with Wang would shorten the whole process. She wanted to use what little time there would be to push for substantive progress. She said a quick prayer, "Lord, give me the right words. Help me discern the right path."

The President then listened to the predictable words of greeting from the Swiss President, "On behalf of the government and people of Switzerland, we welcome you to Geneva." The rising timbre of President Honegger's voice pulled Freeman back to his address. She stared at the Swiss President, this wealthy, well-dressed towering man, as he brought his opening comments to a strong but formal close.

"The eyes of the world are upon you," Honegger said forcefully, turning to face both leaders. "We applaud your efforts for peace and are pleased to host this historic Summit meeting. Welcome to our country. Welcome to Geneva." The President joined in on the resounding applause that carried the Swiss official away from the podium as General Secretary Wang advanced on the red carpet and took his place before the battery of microphones.

President Wang paused and then began deliberately, as if pulling all to the rapt attention his silence created. His voice was strong and controlled.

"I bring greetings from the Chinese people to you and your people," he said warmly, turning to the Swiss President. "We are here for peace. The Chinese people want lasting peace. We wish only that all the leaders of the world would join us in that quest. Unfortunately, in spite of the pressing need for cooperation, there are those that would renew the arms race in a futile attempt to secure military superiority. In a world in need of peace, there is no need for maintaining a multi-billion-dollar arms program. There is no need for extending weapons systems into space. And there is no place for any country's self-defined sphere of influence infringing on the legitimate sovereignty of any state."

Wang's strong words, like a sudden thunderstorm squelching a newly started fire, tore at the hopes Freeman had dared to nurture. The President remained motionless. Only her rapidly accelerating heartbeat gave evidence to her growing discomfort. She listened intently to the General Secretary's every word.

The Strained Protocol Dashes Early Hopes

"We express our concern regarding the recent loss of life at the hands of terrorists. Such reckless and barbaric attacks speak to the challenge of finding any peace. Our only hope is that President Freeman will heed the similar objections raised by sober-minded politicians and prominent personalities in the United States to her calls for increased military spending. It is in that hope that we are here. It is imperative that our talks here in Geneva prove fruitful. There is no task greater and more important for mankind than the prevention of nuclear war. We must find a way to curb the senseless arms race and to erect obstacles in the way of the aggressive aspirations of imperialism. We have heard many words about 'flexibility' coming from Washington. We are here to see evidence of that flexibility in a true commitment for peace. China, which embodies a true government of the people, seeks only to preserve world peace. In that spirit, we come to this Summit for peace."

President Freeman watched as President Wang waved his hands to the expected applause and waited for the President's response. Wang had not once attempted to catch her eyes. The President stopped her restrained applause. As she passed Wang on her way to the lectern, there were no words spoken between them, but their brief moment of eye contact left her unsettled. Was it strength or was it a subtle pleading that she caught in his eyes?

Freeman took her prepared speech and laid it on the lectern. She gazed at the sea of faces and poised cameras. After nodding politely to the Swiss officials and the Chinese delegation, the President's voice took on a firmness even she had not expected.

"Greetings from the people of the United States of America. We are here to work for peace and negotiated settlements that strengthen international peace and security. We have no desire for war. We stand together against terrorism. We want lasting peace."

"We cannot count on the instinct for survival alone to protect us against war. Peace requires more than deterrence and rhetoric."

Turning to face President Wang, she continued, "Real progress requires constructive negotiations and tangible agreements on arms control, a worldwide effort to contain and then eliminate terrorist activity, and progress in human rights for all nations. The world is well aware of where the obstacles to world peace truly lie."

Freeman paused, her voice softening as she continued, "There is, however, no more time for, nor value in, affixing blame. There is no sane alternative to negotiations, arms control, and super power cooperation. The capacity exists to destroy civilization as we know it. To fail to control such a sobering power would be insane. This is a view that is shared by virtually every country in the world, and, as you have heard from the General Secretary, by China herself."

"Responding to this ever-present potential for catastrophe, leaders from around the world have joined us here in Geneva to work for peace," The President said, breaking momentarily to gather strength for her close. "Here, before this historic Palace of Nations and before this assemblage of world leaders, I challenge ourselves and China to take a giant step on the path to mutual understanding and cooperation. As General Secretary Wang has already stated, there is no more important task that faces the world today than finding peace. I trust that common reality will help bring us together at this Summit."

The formality and the staged words had all been said. The parade of dignitaries and guests circulated for one final pass at cordiality for the benefit of the assembled world press. But as the Chinese and American delegations found their way into the stately Palace of Nations, strange, alien stirrings had already begun from within this ageless womb of peace that would soon shatter the world's best laid plans.

CHAPTER NINETEEN

THE GOOD, THE BAD, AND THE UGLY

> Palace of Nations
> Geneva, Switzerland
> 11:17 AM

"Death and life are in the power of the tongue, and those who love it will eat its fruit."
Proverbs 18:21 (NKJV)

Jim Naisbitt had needed to be alone, to think. Being chief of staff had its perks and its challenges. It was his job to help bring order to chaos. He needed to get away from the hordes of people and press. He paced up and down in front of the big conference room windows looking down on the beautiful grounds. The stark green trees and the ever-present lake formed a backdrop one could never really forget. Only the presence of the Swiss military men on patrol ruined the pristine beauty of the scene. He really didn't mind; he knew there would soon be little time for scenery. He was ready for the preliminary negotiations to begin. He was always restless. This Summit took him to an entirely different level. He couldn't sit; he just kept moving.

The morning and the reception had gone well. The Swiss had outdone themselves, even by Western standards of elegance in decorum:

ferns and wildflowers on snowy white tablecloths, the gleaming elegance of old silver, the soft glow of fine china, the ageless touch of antique chairs and tables, and candlelight and crystal everywhere.

But now, the gala reception, opening comments, and luncheon were concluded. It was time to start the preliminary negotiations. Jim glanced at his watch, his mind mentally reviewing the tight schedule of Summit events. They would start with two hours of opening negotiations before Freeman and Wang were scheduled to address the assembled body of United Nations' delegates and invited world leaders in the Hall of Nations. Jim was afraid it would be just another show for the Western press, an exercise in atmospherics and political posturing that would just waste time. Prior to the terrorist attacks, he wondered why they were even meeting. But the attacks had thrown a wild card into the mix. Since one of the attacks was in China, President and Party General Secretary Wang needed this Summit to prove they were doing everything they could to bring the terrorists to justice. With any luck that cooperation could be contagious, or negotiations would just regress into the Chinese finishing their long list of grievances.

The conference room looked ready for work. Jim surveyed the room. It was a large room, spacious and airy, with few distractions to tempt the senses. The large conference table dominated the room with six chairs on a side, six for the good guys and six for the bad guys. IT STILL CAME DOWN TO THAT--THE GOOD AND THE BAD. He stared down at the hardwood floor. He laughed to himself as he remembered the names he had been called in the European press--"The Cold Warrior," "the intellectually vulgar, naive, hard-fisted American." WELL, SCREW 'EM! SOMEBODY HAD TO GET TOUGH ON THE CHINESE. He hated the press and the fatalistic, complacent, and always bending, European liberals.

The Europeans had perfected the dangerous dance of appeasement. They always hated the heavy-handed, military approach of the Americans. To them, he was, at best, crude. The Europeans valued their sophistication. As far as he was concerned, their sophisticated liberals would placate, adjust, lose gracefully, and then bend again, until they were so damn enfeebled that they'd be bowing at the gates of Beijing.

Unfortunately, from the earlier caucus meetings, Jim sensed the same kind of attitude from Tom Grodin and the rest of his team. He wondered why "nice" people never learned. IF YOU DON'T LIKE GETTING SHIT ON BY THE CHINESE, THEN GET OUT FROM UNDER THEIR LEGS.

The sharp click-clack of heels on the hardwood floors brought Jim's mind back. A grin formed on his face as he thought about shit, and how he didn't plan on eating any today. He watched as Tom Grodin and Foreign Minister Min Jian walked into the conference room a safe distance apart, followed closely by a bevy of obedient but lackluster aides. As if ready to do their part in this charade for peace, Jim watched as the members of both the Chinese and American delegations went quietly to their assigned positions. Tom Grodin left Min Jian to his papers and walked slowly towards Jim's position by the window.

"Looks like one happy family already, Tom!" Jim said in a tone that he knew had a knife-edge to it. He was immediately aware that he had said more than he wanted to say to this man he often disagreed with but still respected.

"You don't need to worry. I doubt whether Min is close even to his own family. He doesn't know how to smile. He is more machine than man," Tom said flatly. Jim watched his eyes, but Tom's experience-honed reserve did not break. Tom abruptly spoke again, "I honestly thought President Wang was going to be a different breed. After hearing his opening statements today, I think I may have been mistaken about him. I hope that tirade was just for the media and the old guard cronies he had to impress. I hope having to work together to figure out what to do with Al-Haram will create some momentum for cooperation. If not, this could be one frustrating week."

"You're telling me," Jim said with a sigh. "The attack in Bethlehem is still the lead story. It's taken the spotlight away from Geneva, but the opening remarks were broadcast. The Democrats are going to love the news coverage tonight. I can see the headlines tomorrow, 'Summit Sets in The East for Freeman's Re-election Bid.'"

"Frankly, I felt she handled it the best she could under the circumstances," Tom replied. "For a minute there, when she left her prepared speech, I thought sure she was going to level both barrels at Wang. I was starting to have visions of Reagan's 'Evil Empire' speech. Thank God, she didn't go that far."

"As far as I'm concerned, she didn't go far enough," Jim said, his eyes staring back intently.

"I know how strongly you feel, Jim, but hold it in check here. I haven't given up on Wang. He probably had to play uproar to appease the hard-liners. Let's hope it's more bluster than substance," Tom said, trying to convince himself.

Jim said nothing, choosing rather to look at his watch. He wanted nothing to do with a useless argument with Tom Grodin, an argument that might only strain their already fragile relationship. He turned instead to look at Min Jian neatly arranging a pile of papers. He whispered to Tom as they headed for their seats, "By the look of the size of

Min's stack of papers, we've got a shit pile to go through before we get out of this room. I hope you brought plenty of toilet paper."

Both men gave faint smiles. Both knew it was true. But it was time for the negotiation dance to begin.

CHAPTER TWENTY

TERRORISTS CATER A DISASTER ON DEMAND

Geneva, Switzerland
12:50 PM

"Violence is a healing medicine for all our people's diseases."
Fatah

"Beloved, never avenge yourselves, but leave it to the wrath of God, for it is written, 'Vengeance is mine, I will repay, says the Lord.'"
Romans 12:9 (ESV)

The road into the Summit had been alive with activity. The Limousines and town cars had been three deep in front of the Palace of Nations. It looked like any of the many catering trucks used to feed the thousands of conferences that keep the economic heartbeat of Geneva pulsing. The detailed lettering on the side of the truck marked its pedigree, Le Beaujolais, one of Geneva's finest restaurants. According to a favorable article in the morning paper, the van was carrying "food fit for the Presidents." Le Beaujolais had been picked to cater the Summit; their trucks had been visible all morning at the Palace of Nations bringing the gourmet foods that would fuel the festivities.

As the van picked up speed along the Rue du Rhone, Youssef Hassan could feel the throbbing engine beneath him like a heart, rushing power through his veins. He cruised close to a high rock retaining wall, and, for an instant, the sharp scent of the van's fuel was sent back to him.

The odor stimulated his heightened senses. It reminded Youssef of his first memories on the streets of Tehran. He remembered the crowd's roar of approval as they burned the last vestiges of the Shah's hated regime. He had experienced the cleansing power of violence early. As a child, Youssef had been pushed forward by the mass of bodies as they careened onward through the streets, unstoppable and majestic in their raw power. He had remembered his father had been there when they tore down the gates and overpowered the American Embassy annex. As if yesterday, he remembered the gleaming eyes, the faces twisted with hatred, and the litany of chants that echoed through the streets--"Death to America! Death to Israel! Death to all who oppose the revolution!"

Youssef had again felt the pride of his people surge through his body as they humbled the paper tiger from the West in Afghanistan. He also had felt the strange ecstasy--a healing and purifying force--in meting out death to the innocents of the vile order. The recent attacks had introduced Al-Haram to the world. Now it was his turn to die. PRAISE TO ALLAH! DEATH WILL BE MY SUPREME REWARD. I WILL DIE, BUT MANY WILL DIE WITH ME. A smile of quiet assurance crossed his face.

Wiping his eyes, he pulled at the gear shift as the van leapt ahead, skidding around a sharp turn. The crisp air whipped by him like spirit sails, driving him closer to his destiny. Soon there would be nothingness and then oneness with Allah.

The Summit

Even as he prepared to die, odd echoes from times past hugged at his consciousness. After the excitement of those early days of the purge, he had wandered the streets of Tehran alone. Full of fear and suppressed anger, Youssef had felt a victim to a new kind of bondage, the bondage of a rage that would not go away. After he had discovered Ghazi and the Al-Haram revolution, his anger had been freed to find many deserving targets. Youssef had found his place in Allah's plan. Ghazi had called him, had needed him. Now, he would not fail Ghazi.

The sun seemed to wink at Youssef through the passing foliage, having an almost hypnotic effect. His body felt at one with the caged power beneath his seat, a half-ton of cyclonite explosives poised for destruction. With his eyes riveted on the street before him and his jaw set, he leaned forward and clinched the steering wheel as he moved closer to his appointment with the Palace of Nations.

There was only silence in the underground hallway. The clock above the bomb shelter sign read one-fifteen. The intricate machinations of Summit negotiation were now ready to move into high gear. The shelter was always still, an unused, unseen, long-forgotten appendage added to this palace because of past fears. Annually, like clockwork, the food and water supplies were checked and changed, an automatic ritual to appease the superstitions of men long since silenced by death. And then the shelter would be sealed.

Inside the bomb shelter, Ghazi cautiously depressed the handle from the inside of the airtight food storage chamber. As a surge of air rushed past the seal, the door began to open. First his hand, then his arm sleeved in olive drab fatigues emerged from the room.

Ghazi moved silently out of the shelter. Standing motionless and erect, he listened for any sounds coming from the hallway. There were none. In the darkened room, the pupils of his eyes were enormously expanded to take in all available light. His ebony irises combined with the dark of his pupils made a seamless whole, giving his eyes a deep, almost alien, appearance. Unconsciously, his lips were drawn back from his teeth, forming a wolflike mask that would have frightened anyone who saw it. No one did; it was not yet time for anyone to see his face. He stared ahead; his hands, wet with sweat, resting on his gun. IT IS TIME FOR VICTORY. FOR ALLAH'S SAKE, WE WILL DESTROY.

Turning back towards the opening, Ghazi motioned for his men. Within moments, the shelter was emptied of life. Moving with a feral stealth like the skilled predators they had become, all eight of his men went silently to their positions. They all knew to be detected now meant certain death and failure. But Ghazi knew they would not have to hide long; soon they would be in control.

In the darkness of the alcove, Ghazi checked his weapons one last time, as he and his men had done day after day to help pass the time in waiting for their fast-approaching moment of truth. This time it was different; soon the weapons would be used.

Each man had a 9 mm Skorpion machine pistol with silencer capable of firing over a thousand rounds per minute. The weapon was small, accurate and had the penetration power befitting of a Holy War. Two of his men worked on their Israeli made Uzi 9-mm submachine guns. The devil made good weapons; his men would enjoy using them for Allah's work.

Ghazi Saud looked with pride at his new AM 180; its unique laser sighting system was capable of concentrating firepower on a single red dot projected by a laser light. Few if any obstacles he would face would be impervious to his assault. He smiled to himself thinking of the American ingenuity that had made such a destructive weapon possible. But Ghazi knew he wanted more. Soon he would have all the power for destruction he needed.

Ghazi turned to face his men. His body commanded their attention, tall, brown and hard-muscled. All eyes focused on him.

"It's nearing the time." His voice had a low menacing tone. "You all know what to do. When you hear the explosion, you will take your positions. You know who we are after; I will take care of them. There are to be no other survivors. The urge to destroy is a creative and holy urge. Allah acknowledges no other action but destruction. Everything you do today is sanctified by the revolution. We must remain committed to the sacred cause of rooting out evil in the world."

Ghazi's hand balled into a raised fist. His men responded in kind, raising their fists in a silent salute to their leader. Their eyes were fever-bright, gleaming like predatory beasts ready to attack out of the darkness. For Ghazi, no other answer was needed. Theirs was a sacred journey for destruction that his men were prepared to take. No one spoke. Ghazi's face was set in an unchanging grin, but underneath the surface was a coldly calculating force, like a caged tiger waiting to attack.

CHAPTER TWENTY-ONE

SUMMIT GLADIATORS POISED FOR MENTAL WAR

Palace of Nations
Geneva, Switzerland
1:32 PM

"Woe to those who call evil good and good evil, who put darkness for light and light for darkness, who put bitter for sweet and sweet for bitter."
Isaiah 5:20 (NIV)

She tried to fight the feeling of being more like a gladiator poised for battle than a head of state prepared for Summit dialogue. Their initial handshake was partly an embrace of a deeply hidden hope, partly a challenge, and partly a test of strength. There was another moment of silence as the two leaders studied each other.

Over the years in office, many negotiations had become a necessary mental war. As the first female President, she had been discounted. She had to earn respect. She had proven her mettle as a negotiator with Congress. She'd learned that the first step in mental combat was always to assess one's opponent, to determine his attitude and intentions. Only then could she proceed. Now, she was ready to see whether the man she faced today was like the one her critics feared or would he be more like the man she came to know handling the Al-Haman crisis. She hoped the later.

The preliminary greetings had passed quickly. The President walked with the General Secretary as they left their aides and turned to enter their private palace conference room. As the door closed behind her, Freeman smiled. She wondered if the private room was to keep the world out or if it was the world's way of locking them in until some sanity emerged. Both leaders took their seats facing each other.

"I appreciate your offer to conduct our private sessions without the use of interpreters," the President said evenly with a smile she hoped would communicate none of her own discomforts.

"I am comfortable with my English. I will enjoy getting the rust off."

"You hide your rust well. In our recent conversations regarding the attack, you were more than proficient. You are fluent."

"Thank you. I think that work will serve us well. Now, we've also endured the obligatory rhetoric to placate our respective media. Here we are alone. As your former President Reagan was so fond of saying, *It is time for some straight talk.*" Freeman leaned forward, staring into Wang's steady eyes.

"I would welcome some straight talk," The President replied evenly. "If I can judge from your opening remarks, this conversation is occurring none too soon. I did not expect...."

"What?" Wang interrupted. "Our need to deal with Al-Haram does not change the realities we both face. We both have hardliners who fear the worst—peace! There is barbed wire on top of the fence around this Summit, Madam President. If either of us go too far, we will pay a heavy price. To deny that is not necessary if we are to do *some true straight talk.*"

"That is true, and what comes out for public consumption must reflect necessary boundaries," Connie said respectfully. "But I would hope that the way we talk in this room could capture some of what we found together in handling the crisis. We earned that."

"Yes, we did," Wang said with a smile. "Now we must earn the reluctant respect of those that hope we fail. We need progress without impossible promises. True peace will take time and trust, trust our people do not have."

As Youssef moved his van down the Rue de la Servette, he talked to himself. *Drive carefully, move softly and silently like a crouched tiger stalking its prey.* He tried to keep his elation in check. The world would soon know the power of his faith. His senses grabbed at the world around him, pulling in the last images of life he would take with him to paradise. It was a luxury only those who know when they will die can ever experience. For Youssef Hassan, death was a victim to be stalked.

As the van turned onto Avenue Giuseppe Motta, Youssef's eyes focused on the rapidly approaching Palace of Nations. He saw death reaching out to him, daring him to taste its unseen treasures but baiting him with momentary flashes of uncontrollable terror. He fought back his doubts. Allah would not lie.

A mist was forming in his brain, making the road in front of him disappear into a red swirl of colors pulling him forward. His lips peeled back from his dry teeth, sensing the death ground he now traveled. In these last fleeting minutes, he did not have to think, merely feel the visceral pull of death as if it were a tide drawing him out to sea and the void beyond.

The Summit

To the Swiss security guard, the Summit had finally come. Hopefully, it soon would be over. He stared transfixed at the long list of authorized vehicles, checking off one of the last straggling limousines as it passed the Pregny Gate entrance to the Palace of Nations. The impressive itinerary of afternoon events had already begun. The seemingly never-ending stream of dignitaries and service trucks had finally slowed to a trickle. It had been a hectic morning, but at least there had been something to do. For all the Swiss guards stationed all over the Parc Ariana grounds, the last two days had been nothing but waiting, security checks, and more waiting.

It was the press, the blasted Western press! They didn't care about peace. Instead, they seemed to relish uproar. It had all meant overtime for he and his colleagues. The press had done its best to ferment rumors of trouble, but as he had expected, nothing had occurred, not even a morning demonstration.

Both the superpowers and the hordes of hovering reporters seemed to enjoy peddling images of fear. They saw intrigue behind every tree. But he had to be thankful for those fears. Without them, he would not have had a job. Suddenly, his eyes were drawn to a rapid movement. He focused on the white Le Beaujolais catering van quickly approaching the checkpoint along the Avenue de la Paix. He looked down, scanning his list for confirmation of entry, but couldn't find one.

Then with a crack like a rifle shot, the reinforced van burst through the checkpoint barrier. The guard looked up and saw the blurred image of a white metal monster lurching toward him. Like some horrific, uninvited guest, the vehicle picked up speed as it turned off the avenue, its wheels screeching as it bore down on the Pregny Gate. The guard knew it had no intention of stopping. A momentary frozen silence filled the guardhouse with an odd kind of chill as the guard's mind tried to negate the image of a ghost he knew couldn't exist.

The guard's face was pale, his mind engulfed in sudden waves of terror. His body instinctively moved into action. As he reached behind his chair for his rifle, he heard the steady stream of automatic rifle fire coming from the other guards stationed outside the guardhouse. But as the guard brought his own rifle to bear, it was apparent that the van was not veering from its course. As he squeezed on the trigger, his eye focused on the face glaring through the van window. It was a demonic face, the face of a man coming to die. He continued to squeeze, sending a stream of leaded tears into the rapidly approaching abyss of death.

Then, in one searing moment of impact, as the van tore through the restraining gate, he was left with a momentary vision of the destruction that was to follow.

Peering through the shattered glass, Youssef tried to guide the van as it careened the last 50 yards toward the entrance to the Palace Assembly Hall. He hunched over the steering wheel, his fists like claws unwilling to release his prey. He could still hear the staccato burst of gunfire and the sound of bullets exploding against the reinforced van housing. Youssef knew it did not matter now; he would be dead in a matter of seconds.

In those final moments before impact, he stared transfixed at the limestone pillars rapidly closing in on him. The sight of reporters and diplomats that had not yet entered the hall scurrying for cover barely registered in his brain.

He had done it! Suddenly, he felt a jolt of pain in his chest, and he knew what it was. Fear–pure, raw fear. He was remembering memories within memories. His mind returned to a city in rubble, to the terrible sounds of mass execution. Then and now, there would be victory for Allah. Youssef had stalked death; it was now time for him to taste paradise.

The frame of the van disintegrated as it ran into the curb, sending the van airborne like a missile now unable to be recalled. A one-half ton of cyclonite explosives in a metal coffin slammed into a startled edifice of peace.

Within seconds there was an eruption, a fireball of orange and crimson flames. An incredible flame engulfed Youssef and all in the area. They were no more. The foundation of the palace hall exploded, rocketing twisted shards of stones, hot metal, and piercing fragments of glass into an unsuspecting world of shattered tranquility. The sharp report from the explosion echoed through the city, followed by more death and columns of dense black smoke.

CHAPTER TWENTY-TWO

A SUMMIT PEACE SHATTERED

> **Palace of Nations**
> **Geneva, Switzerland**
> **1:47 PM**

*"As I have observed, those who plow evil and those
who sow trouble reap it."*
Job 4:8 (NIV)

The Summit's fragile peace was shattered by the midday explosion. All the Swiss military guards stationed near the Pregny Gate had been killed in the initial explosion leveling the Palace of Nations' Assembly Hall. Flying glass, stone, and metal were hurled in every direction. The force of the explosion had pierced flesh and stripped the lush foliage for blocks, even taking out windows in the International Red Cross Headquarters and the Soviet Embassy located Northeast of the Palace grounds.

For the international delegates assembled in the Palace Assembly Hall, there had been no time to think; death had come swiftly for most. For those that had the misfortune of surviving the initial blast, the weight of the limestone and marble debris quickly choked off their fragile grasp on life.

The Summit

"My God! What was that?" Jim Naisbitt said, grabbing the conference table to steady himself from the force of the explosion. It was a question that needed no answer. He watched the anxious glances between the Chinese and American diplomats. Like ice water thrown into slumbering faces, they were suddenly brought together in the reality that faced them.

As the Chinese First Deputy Foreign Minister ran to the window, Jim quickly went to his side. He saw the emotion reflected in the diplomat's eyes before he himself saw the destruction. Jim needed no interpreter; fear looked the same in any language. One by one, they joined the two men, all straining to see evidence of what they hoped would not be found.

"It's gone," Tom Grodin said slowly. "My God, it's gone!"

Through the smoke, everyone could plainly see that the Palace of Nations Assembly Hall was no more, leaving the north and south wings of the palace complex standing alone as severed appendages. The grand hall lay in shambles, a mass of twisted steel and shattered stone.

Jim had felt the venom from the terrorists' sting during his brief diplomatic tour in the Middle East. That time a truck bomb had been stopped short of its target, but still, the damage had been severe. Forty-two had died; many more had been injured. Fortunately, he escaped with only minor injuries. As he looked at the devastation before him, he knew few could have survived.

As Curtis Wayte ran for the conference room door, many turned to watch.

"Don't go, Curtis!" Jim shouted.

"Why not? We should be out there helping!"

"Security would want us here! We'd just be in the way."

"My God! There are people dying out there."

"Precisely! That's why we should stay here."

Curtis reluctantly returned to the window. Jim stared at Tom and then turned his attention outside. He could see security forces scurrying through the ruins pulling frantically at the bloody remains of victims. Most looked more dead than alive. Swiss military vehicles had begun arriving from the South, establishing positions around the courtyard.

With no warning, there had been a thunderous explosion, like a thousand earthquakes unleashing their power in one searing second. The walls seemed to shudder, sending pictures and cabinets onto the floor, shattering windows into a million pieces. Instinctively, Freeman had tried to steady herself in her chair. Fortunately, the movement had stopped as quickly as it had started. Wang had been the first to move; the Chinese leader had run to the now broken conference room window.

The President quickly joined him. In silence, both strained to see something to explain the nightmare. From their vantage point, they could see only the Parc de L'Ariana and Lake Leman beyond. The sound of sirens blaring and the sight of security forces running around the building only added to their frustration. Nothing, however, could mask the sound of the President's own heartbeat booming in her ears. As she felt an involuntary shudder, she was not sure whether it came from a sudden burst of wind or from her own fear.

In a moment, a Secret Service agent appeared, a walkie-talkie in one hand and his service revolver in the other. Connie turned and saw an unsettling alarm in the agent's eyes.

"Madam President, please get away from the window!" Ted Armstrong said anxiously. Tension had creased his worn face.

"What is it, Ted?" Freeman asked, trying to keep the note of alarm from her voice. Both leaders retreated from the window as Ted moved toward them.

"Are you both all right?" Ted asked.

"Yes," the President replied, looking briefly at President Wang for the confirmation she expected before continuing. "A little shaken, but fine. What's happened?"

"A truck bomb, Madam President."

"Oh, my God!" Freeman replied.

"How many are hurt?" Wang interjected.

"We don't know," Ted answered. "It was bad. From what I've been able to pick up, the Assembly Hall has been leveled. Thousands were in there when it happened."

"Where are my men?" President Wang demanded, his face darkening for a moment.

"They're outside, sir," Ted replied evenly, "helping one of our agents cover the hallway. We're short-handed here. Most of the backup Swiss security on the floor left. Many of their men were killed in the initial explosion, and they're trying to move men to secure the perimeter from any follow-up attack. I told them to stay, but they left. We don't have any authority over them, sir."

"Do you anticipate any more attacks?" Freeman asked.

"Madam President, we didn't anticipate the first one, but it happened. We're supposed to think the worst and be ready for it. Right now, if the worst comes, we're in trouble. I don't anticipate that there will be any other problems, but I still don't like it."

"What do you want us to do?" asked Freeman.

"Stay here and stay away from the window. There may be snipers out there. Until the whole area is secure, we'll take up positions in the hallway and try and get some Swiss security back up here."

"Fine, but keep us informed, Ted."

"Yes, Madam President."

"Ted," the President said abruptly, halting the agent's exit. "Was Al-Haram responsible for this?" She was having a hard time trying to hide the growing anger she felt for those lost.

"We don't know. As soon as anyone claims responsibility, we'll let you know," Ted said politely as he turned to leave the room. For a moment, nothing was said.

"We've been bitten by the very wolves in Iran that you help feed!" Freeman said in her frustration, turning to face President Wang. "You can't expect terrorists to–"

His face was suffused with indignation. "We do not even know who is responsible. It is your support for the Zionists that stirs their rage. Is it no wonder the Iranians and Palestinians call you the devil!"

Freeman stopped abruptly, and their eyes locked. Both knew they had said enough.

CHAPTER TWENTY-THREE

EVIL WINS WHEN CHAOS IS ALLOWED TO REIGN

> Palace of Nations Grounds
> 1:55 PM

"From their callous hearts comes iniquity; their evil imaginations have no limits."
Psalms 73:7 (NIV)

"Secure the perimeter!" Guntram shouted through the walkie-talkie. Being in charge of the Summit security had now become a nightmare. "The Pregny Gate is gone! Close down any access! Take up positions along the Avenue de la Paix and the Route de Pregny. I want no room for a second attack to occur while our defenses are down! Now get to it!"

Slamming the walkie-talkie onto his belt, Guntram moved quickly towards his new command position on the high ground just north of where the Pregny Gate had been. There had been little time for thinking after the explosion. Like treating a body suffering the loss of a limb, he had tried to move his security forces to stop the bleeding. All remaining security forces had moved to neutralize the attack and secure the perimeter from additional assaults. For Guntram, the unthinkable had happened; a truck bomb had been able to overcome periphery defenses and attack the Summit directly. He had failed but thank God the President and the General Secretary had not been in the Assembly Hall!

The palace destruction and the death of innocents meant nothing to Ghazi and his men. Their international network of death had killed many more on numerous occasions, but the truck bomb was the appetizer for the feast that was to follow. The so-called experts on international terrorism had not expected and, therefore, had not fully prepared for a direct attack on the superpower leaders. Their rigid concepts and statistics had limited their thinking, leaving them vulnerable to the creative urges of a destructive genius like Ghazi. He had known that none of the security forces would trust the proficiency nor the allegiance of the other guards. Without trust, there would be no order, only isolated units trying to control the chaos but unable to mesh any effective, coordinated defense.

While many Swiss security forces left their assigned positions to chase non-existent attackers, Ghazi's band of highly trained terrorists moved silently and systematically through the now dark halls of the Palace of Nations. Their silent but efficient Skorpion machine pistols neutralized the remaining, surprised, and confused security forces they met on the way.

Long before the palace generators were able to restore power back to the remaining structures, Ghazi and his men had already disabled elevators and placed pinpoint explosives to seal off strategic stairways. With his limited force, Ghazi needed secure perimeters. He knew all too well that once the security forces of the superpowers realized their

The Summit

leaders had been captured, reinforcements would return like an enraged swarm of killer bees trying to rescue their stolen king and queen. He did not plan on giving these forces easy access. He was locking the enemies out and the victims in!

CHAPTER TWENTY-FOUR

LEFT ALONE TO FACE DEATH

> **Palace of Nations**
> **Summit Conference Center**
> **2:07 PM**

"Because of the voice of the enemy, Because of the pressure of the wicked; For they bring down trouble upon me, and in anger they bear a grudge against me."
Psalm 55:3 (NKJV)

"Where the hell are your men?" Ted Armstrong yelled into his walkie-talkie as he knelt down for cover behind the overturned oak cabinet in the hallway outside the room where the leaders were meeting. "I don't care what you've got outside! I want this floor crawling with security! Understand?! We got a President and a General Secretary up here, and we're damn near protecting them naked! Don't you give me any shit! No, there's nothing happening now, but have you ever heard of a diversion? You get some men over here!"

"Damn it!" Ted shouted as he slammed the walkie-talkie onto his belt. Momentarily, he turned his gaze from the hallway to face his long-time partner, Chris Toomey. "I told them this would happen!

The Summit

'*Two operatives are all you get,*' they told us. '*The Swiss will provide backup security.*' Backup, my ass!"

Starting to rise to his feet, Chris said, "They should be here by now. I'm going to get back to the President."

"Leave 'em in there!" Ted said crisply, grabbing hold of his partner's arm. "We aren't moving! We watch the hallway." Chris returned to his former position. Both men stared down the hall. There was only silence and the sounds of their rapid breathing.

"What about our Chinese counterparts, our good old Chen brothers?" Ted asked.

"Nothing to report. There's been no activity from their position either," Chris said evenly.

"Can you believe this? What a fiasco!" Ted said tautly, checking his service revolver one more time. "Years of Secret Service training, and do they listen to us? *Shit!* They break every rule in the book to placate a bunch of politicians! *Damn politics!* Here we sit with two pea-shooters and a couple of rounds of ammunition, depending on two communists to guard our rear! God, when I get back to Washington, they're going to get an earful on this one!"

"Listen, there's nothing we can—" Chris remarked, his words cut short by a sudden movement at the end of the hall. His eyes focused on figures knifing through the doorway. "*Shit!* They're not Swiss..."

He was unable to finish his warning as gunshots erupted. Chris's body arched backward. The first bullets penetrated his skull, ripping most of his brain from his body and propelling him backward--a marksman's eye delivering a marksman's score. There was one final spasm, and then all movement stopped.

Instinctively, Ted ducked behind the cabinet; there was nothing he could do for his partner. The staccato clatter of the terrorists' gunfire ripped through the hallway, bullets exploding into the solid oak cabinet. He tried to return fire with his revolver in hopes of stalling their advance, but he knew he was no match for their firepower. In a matter of seconds, Ted knew he would be dead. He grabbed for his walkie-talkie as a final stream of bullets tore through the cabinet and into his back, severing his spine.

As he felt his lifeblood flow from his riddled body, Ted Armstrong tried to give one last parting gift to the President he had vowed to protect with his life. As his fingers wrapped in a vice-like grip on his transmitter, he used his last ounce of strength to draw it to his face. His lips moved in an all but silent litany of death, *"They are here..."*

Inside the Summit conference room, a volley of machine gun fire ripped through the door from outside. Jim Naisbitt moved behind the conference table as the rest of the Chinese and American diplomats scattered in all directions. Bullets ripped a line across the wood paneling at the end of the room.

Through the corner of his eye, Jim caught two Chinese military attachés, their bodies nearly cut in half by the opening salvo. They were dead even before they saw their attackers. Their blood splattered on the wall, on the conference table, and on the diplomats who were more used to talking about weapons than experiencing their ultimate use. As Jim wiped blood from his forehead, he knew it was not his own but could have been.

The great wooden door to the conference room flew open. Foreign Minister Min Jian was the first to speak as two terrorists charged into the room.

"What is the meaning of–" Min demanded, but the foreign minister's words were cut from his mouth as the piercing metal bullets from the Uzi riddled his face.

"Everyone! Hands behind head! Do not move!" Gamal Saud demanded with sudden harshness. His broken English was not clear, but the now still body of Min Jian made no further explanation necessary.

"Please, what do you want from us?" Tom Grodin pleaded, his slow, calming voice breaking the silence. But his question went unheeded.

"Shut up! I tell you when to talk!" Gamal snapped, his eyes darkening. Gamal stood tall, unshakable, his Uzi machine gun grasped in one hand and pointed directly at the graying Secretary of State. With one quick hand motion, Gamal waved Mohammed Shirawi to the other side of the room.

The smaller man, with a dark complexion and stern countenance, advanced quickly through the room, reloading his weapon as he moved. His eyes darted from face to face. The frozen, frightened expressions of his captives only seemed to heighten his perverse pleasure. Jim stared as if drawn to a demon. Their eyes locked, communicating thoughts and fears. *The man was possessed.*

The methodical click of a new ammunition magazine being inserted in Gamal's Uzi broke the spell. Jim turned, his eyes riveting first on the weapon and then on the terrorist's eyes that communicated a message Naisbitt did not want to face. *They were going to die.* The stunned silence lasted five seconds.

An American aide raced past Jim for the window. The terrorist effortlessly aimed his Uzi. The aide never saw the face of unadulterated hatred that zeroed in for the kill. Jim did.

The air again buzzed with the sound of steel-jacketed bullets that flashed from the terrorist's weapon of death. The aide's body crumpled to the ground, motionless in a pool of blood.

"My God, you didn't have to kill him!" Tom shouted as he moved toward his aide's now lifeless body. His plea was half a cry, half a scream.

"No! Tom, don't–" Jim Naisbitt said sharply, reaching out his hand to restrain Tom. He missed. Jim knew how to react to these animals, something Tom was too civilized to really comprehend. But now Jim was powerless to do anything.

Without a word of warning, both terrorists trained their weapons. There was no time for protest, no pleading, no negotiation. Tom arched backward, the bullets penetrating his chest and puncturing his heart and lungs.

"You bastards!" Jim shouted in one final futile protest. A bullet entered the front of his neck, sending him against the conference table, his fingers clawing the air, his blood-streaked face mercifully obliterated by a second bullet.

Both men died immediately. For the others in the room, death came equally as swift. The will of Allah had been done.

The door to the room bolted open, exposing the leaders to their own worst fears. Standing in the doorway was Ibn Shirawi, his glare riveting Freeman's eyes like an animal of the night drawn to the paralyzing light of a poacher. In the terrorist's hand was a large, black 9 mm Skorpion machine pistol. There was a click; more ammunition was snapped into place, echoing like thunder through the painful silence. A tall, powerful figure made his way past the terrorist, his cold black eyes gleaming in the limited light.

"What is this?" Wang said, trying to meet this alien force head-on.

"Shut up!" Ghazi said.

Not yet prepared to back down, Wang complained, "You can't just–"

The Summit

In one sudden strike, Ghazi hammered the butt of his gun into the midsection of the unsuspecting General Secretary. Where there had been words a moment before, there was now only silence. Wang staggered, his legs all but giving way as he bent over in pain at Ghazi's feet. Ghazi stood over him, Wang immobilized by the pain shooting through his body. He held his stomach gasping for air.

"That's better! You'll learn how to bow to Ghazi!" Ghazi said, kicking Wang in the side. The President moved toward the man to help, but the terrorist's gaze pulled her up short.

"You are both insolent dogs! I will be forced to teach you to cooperate!" Ghazi said, menace cradling each word. "Get up, dog!"

Ibn grabbed the General Secretary to his feet. He held onto the back of a chair to steady himself. Ghazi turned to face Freeman. The President offered no response at all, staring back with steady, stonefaced defiance. A grim little smile formed on Ghazi's face.

"You think you are important people. To us, you are nothing! If you do not cooperate, we will make you. We have the means. We are not equals, you and I. You have no rights, no choices. You will obey, or you will be punished."

While Ghazi spoke, the chords of his neck stood out with strain as he grabbed the President's jaw in a vice-like grip.

"You will speak!" Ghazi growled, letting go of Freeman's jaw as she staggered to gain her balance. The terrorist's rough, flat palm whipped across the American's face, then slashed back, his knuckles hitting her in the mouth. Freeman moaned, almost falling from the blow. She had never been hit. Blood was visible from the side of her mouth. She righted herself, stiffened, and stared at their attacker.

"You think being a woman will protect you. Do as I say, dog! *Speak!*" Ghazi screamed, hitting the President again with the back of his hand.

"You are Al-Haram?" Freeman snapped, recoiling from the blow.

"In time you will know, dog! This is but one lesson you will learn. There will be many more!"

In a moment, Gamal Saud appeared, pushing a Chinese security agent into the room at gunpoint.

"The coward deserves to crawl," Gamal said, with just the right amount of derision. "He had no stomach for dying."

"I told you to kill them all!" Ghazi said, glaring at his brother.

As if realizing he was about to die, the Chinese agent leaped at the unsuspecting terrorist leader. Almost with a second sense, Ghazi moved so that he took the attack with his right side. With great fluidity, he extended his right hand like a sword driving it between the attacker's outstretched fists and slashing into the guard's sternum, collapsing his lungs like a punctured balloon. Ghazi used his body to redirect the momentum of the attack to the side, and the Chinese agent's flailing, wasted body fell to the floor with a shuddering force.

No weapon had been used; none had been needed. As Ghazi turned to face Freeman and Wang, his lips curled in an odd smile. Without warning, his right foot left the floor, and his powerful leg muscles flexed in tension, slamming his heel into the guard's neck, killing the man instantly.

"You are our captives! You will do as I say, or you too will die." Ghazi said, continuing in a dispassionate tone. "Your countries will do as we demand, or you will do worse than die as the world watches. Tie them up!"

CHAPTER TWENTY-FOUR

THE ATTACK ON THE SUMMIT TAKES CENTER STAGE

Hotel des Berguese Conference Center

"But suddenly Babylon, too, has fallen. Weep for her. Give her medicine. Perhaps she can yet be healed." Jeremiah 51:8 (New Living Translation)

Dr. Brian Winters regarded her curiously, his eyes moving inconspicuously as he studied Dr. Chen Li as she was being introduced. There was no need to listen to the words; he had read of her work. As one of the bright young stars in an otherwise bleak tapestry of Chinese medical mediocrity, she had used her position and expertise to help develop mobile trauma units to extend quality care into previously inaccessible rural areas. Although the laser equipment she used was outdated, her innovative use of laser surgery in the trauma field had brought her international medical attention, attention that was well deserved.

A momentary flash of light distracted him, but it was gone as quickly as it had appeared. The entire right side of the symposium conference room was made up of a series of windows through which the city shone in all its beauty. The deep green curtains had been pulled back; the early afternoon sunlight still flooded part of the room. But the beauty of the city provided him only a momentary distraction.

Brian again returned his attention to Dr. Chen. He was acquainted with more than her medical expertise. He realized he had seen her last night in the bar. As she rose and approached the podium, his eyes remained focused on her. She showed an innate delicacy and sense of fitness that he appreciated in a woman. As he studied her small but attractive face, his eyes moved to her piercing dark brown eyes. But then she smiled, a completely irresistible smile, he thought. She spoke in English with an almost poetic cadence. The Chinese accent was there, but her voice was like silk, caressing her words.

"The Chinese Ministry of Health has made great strides in bringing quality health care to all the people. One example of that continuing commitment has been the development of mobile trauma units that provide..." Dr. Chen. said earnestly, her face aglow with mission and passion for her work.

A sudden bleep from Brian's watch alarm brought his other hand instinctively to silence this somehow out-of-place, high-tech intrusion. Brian needed the reminder. He had to call Terry stateside to catch him before he left for class. Obviously agitated by the distraction, a nearby participant turned to face him, eyes glaring and unforgiving.

Trying to be light, Brian pointed to his watch and smiled. It missed. The man-made an arrogant slow turn, unwilling to forget and forgive. Brian chuckled to himself as he supplied his own words to the weathered physician's expression—*another damn American with his obnoxious gadgets.* And he was right; Brian loved his new toys. He hoped he never really grew up. If growing up to be a professional meant looking like you were in pain most of the day, he wanted nothing to do with it.

Brian closed his notepad. After a quick glance at his schedule, he rechecked his watch and got up to leave the room. He tried to leave with a minimum of distraction, but his movement brought Dr. Chen. eyes to his. He smiled disarmingly and lowered his head while raising his eyebrows as if to apologize.

For a moment Dr. Chen. seemed to pause, watching him move down the aisle. He smiled, but she turned away without as much as an acknowledgment, continuing her lecture as she returned to the sea of blank faces that populate most medical conferences.

Brian closed the conference room door quietly. Only the sound of his heels on the hall tiles echoed through the ornate hallway. He took out his cell phone and let his fingers play on the keys to connect to another world now only seconds away. As he listened to the phone ringing, he sat staring at the stately beauty and old-world charm of the lobby—a sight that was everywhere in Geneva. Somehow the new technology didn't fit. Like toilet seat covers in a marble john, it somehow defiled the existing order and peace of a world in touch with its history. The sound of his friend's voice pulled him quickly from his reverie.

"Terry, is that you?" Brian said effusively, his eyes lighting up.

"It was the last time I looked," Terry said with humorous indignation.

"My God, it's great to hear your voice," added Brian. "How are things stateside?"

"I bet we're seeing more of Geneva than you are. That's all the networks are talking about. It's so bad that I'm seeing images of Freeman and Wang in my dreams. I'll be glad when it's over, and we can get back to our run-of-the-mill disaster coverage."

The Attack on the Summit Takes Center Stage

"I haven't had time to keep up with it here. What about my class?" Brian asked thoughtfully.

"You were right; they didn't like your exam. But they'll survive. I just hope I will. They've helped remind me why I never wanted to be a substitute teacher," Terry said with a good-natured chuckle.

"I understand. It's tough when their *favorite* professor leaves."

"Yeah, sure!" Terry countered. They both gave way to genuine laughter.

"How's the conference going?" Terry inquired.

"Good. I just heard, ah, Dr. Chen..." Brian said slowly, pausing to look through his schedule to confirm her name. "Dr. Chen, Dr. Chen Li. She's the doctor from Beijing who's been working with those mobile trauma units. Frankly, I wouldn't mind having my own personal summit with this lady. If I hadn't had to call you, I would still be enjoying the view."

"And you call this work! I slave over your class to let you ravage the women of the world!"

"Eat your heart out!" Brian said effusively, but he continued deadpan. "I fly now but pay later. Remember my spring symposium?"

"That's fine for the hospital, but what about me? I suppose I'll get to read your diary?"

"I'll even leave in..." Brian said in a soft conspiratorial tone, but stopped short, startled by the sight of a man running past him through the hallway heading towards the manager at the front desk.

Oblivious to Brian's presence, the man shouted at the manager in a voice fraught with emotion, *"There's been an attack on the Palace of Nations!"*

Brian felt a quick contraction in his stomach. There was only heightened attention and a swarm of uncomfortable thoughts.

115

"Brian! What's the matter?" Terry asked, breaking the silence.

"There's been an attack on the Summit," Brian said slowly with an odd kind of calmness. His words seemed to hang in the air.

"What?" said Terry incredulously.

"Just a minute. Hold on!" Brian said abruptly. He moved toward the man in the lobby who was about to leave.

"Wait a minute! Pardon, Monsieur!" Brian said, waving his hand, knowing that his own eyes revealed his bewildered concerns.

"There has been an attack on the Palace of Nations," the man said flatly. He seemed to eye Brian suspiciously.

"What happened? Is the President hurt?" Brian asked questions as if sharing his stream of consciousness. Brian's hand dug into the front desk as he talked.

"I do not know. Reports are that there was a truck bomb. The Assembly Hall is in total ruin. Many were killed. I have heard nothing about your President," he said tautly, shrugging resignedly as if he had made a great concession and was unwilling to disclose more.

Brian was struck with the irony of the conversation—*The true hospitality of Geneva was finally showing its true colors.* But the thought died stillborn, strangled by the harsh reality of the horror unfolding in Geneva. He half-heartedly thanked the man and waved at him as he returned quickly to Terry on his phone.

"My God, Terry, are you there?" Brian said anxiously, taking a deep breath and hardly waiting for a response. "There was a truck bomb that went off at the Palace of Nations. Apparently, much of it is in ruins. A lot of people were killed. No one seems to know anything about Freeman or Wang."

"I can't believe it!"

"Neither can I. I suggest we both get to a TV. With all the coverage of the Summit, that'll be the quickest way to find out what's happening. I'll get back to you, buddy. Here's hoping it's only exaggerated reports," Brian said, trying desperately to grab for a ray of sunlight after a hideously destructive storm.

Brian stood very still, mastering his emotions as every surgeon is forced to do each time he faces a life-or-death operation. He let it go, concentrating on what to do next. He moved quickly down the hallway towards the bar and its television, man's ever-present lifeline to world crises. Brian joined the stream of conference delegates moving from the meeting rooms. Their startled faces told the story no words could express. The conference would never be the same. No, it was over.

He took his thought one step further; the world would never be the same.

CHAPTER TWENTY-FIVE

SWISS SECURITY CAUGHT IN THE BLAME GAME

Avenue de la Paix Blockade Entrance

"Therefore do not worry about tomorrow, for tomorrow will worry about itself. Each day has enough trouble of its own."
Matthew 6:34 (NIV)

Like vultures shredding flesh from a corpse, the talons of the press latched on to any official that tried to make their way to the palace grounds. A total of 1,678 reporters were assigned to cover the Summit, the largest press corps assembled since the first Reagan-Gorbachev Summit in the fall of '85. Most reporters were now encamped outside the palace grounds, ready for what they were sure would be the story of their lives.

Although the press blocked every entrance, they were held back by the Swiss gendarmes and other military units that had quickly secured a defensive perimeter around the now embattled and defiled monolith for peace. Dressed in light camouflaged battle uniforms and carrying Swiss-made assault rifles, one thousand infantrymen from the 10th

Regiment had secured all entrances to the Palace of Nations. These peace-loving men from the Swiss cantons of Aargau and Solothurn, now supported by fifteen lightweight tanks, were trying to keep out the elusive ghosts that had left their monument in shambles. The soldiers' orders–*"Shoot anyone who ignores your command to stop--anyone!"*--kept even the press at a distance.

Most of the Swiss gendarmes and soldiers kept their backs to the carnage. The clamoring media, digging for news and reaching for rumors, had been pushed back from the palace preventing the newsmen from obtaining the stories they craved. As much as the Swiss tried distancing the cameras and crews from the ruins, they could not hide the destruction from the world. The tragedy would not magically disappear. Some early video footage of the destruction just played on every station in a disturbing loop.

For years Geneva had basked in the free publicity of the crusade for world peace. The city did not now want the world to see its failure. The protests of the clamoring world press fell on deaf ears. The guards' hardened, expressionless faces revealed nothing of the Calvinistic brutality raking unmercifully at their souls. No one needed to tell them what they already knew. The Swiss had sinned and fallen short of the glory of God. They had failed the world.

An American Embassy car pulled to a stop in front of the first barricade checkpoint on the Avenue de la Paix. Neil Thomas jumped from the car, but before his feet were firmly planted on the ground, he was quickly engulfed by uplifted arms, dangling cameras and microphones. He pushed his way through the stream of eager, probing faces. The reporters' indistinguishable, moving lips were screaming–a deafening noise no one could really understand. There were brittle shouts. Someone tripped, went down, bobbed up again, and kept coming.

The Summit

As Neil tried to move through the crowds of media, it seemed to him there was an urgency and a tension that went beyond any he had ever experienced. This group of experienced media professionals appeared actually frightened, wrapped up in horror beyond even their imagination. But like a stunned animal moving on autopilot, they all kept pushing and shoving to get close to the story.

"Neil, what's the condition of the President?" shouted Ann Hallard, a long-time friend and senior foreign correspondent for the *Washington Post*. Her high-pitched, familiar tone found its mark through the shouts, drawing Neil's eyes to Ann's pleading expression. He could read her frustration. He had been on her side of the story before.

"We don't know at this time!" Neil shouted fervently to Ann. "Please let me through!" Breaking eye contact with her and using his outstretched arm as a wedge, he again tried to force himself forward through the unmoving crowd. Unappeased and encouraged by Neil's brief comments, the mass of reporters launched into a new crescendo of questions.

"Then you're confirming that the President was in the Palace building when the explosion occurred?" one reporter yelled, wanting the truth no one really dared to face.

"Yes, President Freeman and General Secretary Wang were both in private conference away from the main hall..." Neil said crisply in a calm, self-possessed voice that discounted the feelings churning inside. His words were cut off before they could find their mark.

"How many terrorists are involved in the attack?" Ann pleaded. "Is it Al-Haram?"

"We don't know. We'll let you know as soon as we have more information. There will be a press conference when we can assess the situation," Neil confessed, looking firmly into Ann's eyes. She gave him a look of betrayal that sent a sudden chill down his back. She had been his friend. Now, he was just another source. He broke away, turned, and pushed for the final few steps to get past the blockade. Then he was through, out of their grasp. He knew their frustration, and he felt it as well. There was so little he really knew.

As if in a mindless fog, he pulled his identification papers out of his coat and thrust them into the waiting hands of the perturbed but thorough guard who eyed Neil suspiciously. He stared for a moment at Neil and then at his passport picture. He then shrugged resignedly as if he was giving up a great concession by allowing Neil to enter.

As Neil moved, he thought about the grueling session he had just had with the Swiss Chief of Information and Protocol. They had haggled for hours over worthless plans no one would now need to use. For a moment, he hated his job. Nothing was really newsworthy unless someone was hurt or killed. Then like vultures, the news media flock. And now it was Neil's friends who were the victims, and—*my God*—the President.

Neil shuddered at the thought of the shock he had felt when he first heard the news. He would always remember that moment. Yes, like the day the Twin Towers went down, everyone would remember. Like the scorched earth after a fire, the brain of man seems to retain the scars of its collective horrors. He prayed that this moment would not end the same way, taking the life of another great leader, a woman he so respected. She was more than a President; she was a friend.

Neil was moving now, and his eyes were taking in the carnage and the chaos that had once been the beautiful Palace Assembly Hall. It was, in the same instant, absorbing and disquieting. He had never seen a battleground firsthand, just endless hours of cosmetically prepared news war footage. It had done nothing to prepare him for this reality ripping at his senses. He lost his footing for a moment, slipping on what to his horror turned out to be a shred of bloody flesh. He instinctively vomited. The dry heaves wrenched at his stomach, bringing forth more liquid than substance. He had had no time to eat and doubted he would have the time or the stomach for it in the hours ahead.

He heard the voice of Guntram Meyer before he saw him. Neil had met the head of Swiss Security three times previously, and each time he had been taken by Meyer's distinctive, deep voice. It was the kind of voice all television commentators craved. As he walked toward the security head, he cleared his throat trying to wash the disturbing taste from his mouth. He listened intently as Guntram directed one of his men.

"I want the mobile control unit in position south of the Palace. Then get your men into position where they have a clear shot at the window," Guntram shouted to a soldier with an authority Neil knew would be very difficult for anyone to refuse.

"Guntram," Neil called to him as he advanced on the Swiss officer's command position. Meyer had already started to turn, picking up Neil's movement in his peripheral vision.

They shook hands. Looking up squarely into Guntram's eyes, Neil saw no hint of cordiality. Guntram was all business. "Is there any report on Freeman or Wang?"

"Nothing confirmed at this point. Five minutes ago, a soldier saw what he thought was General Secretary looking out the conference room window. That's all we have. The spotting does correspond with our last known location for their meeting. If he was accurate, then at least Wang Da was alive at that point. There has been no sighting of the President."

"That President Wang was alive in the room is good news!" Neil said desperately, looking for any ray of hope.

"That's better than can be said for most of the visiting dignitaries," Guntram said, turning away momentarily from Neil's steady gaze. "It's hard to establish any kind of reliable headcount, but the death toll will be well over a thousand. The explosion was effective. It did a lot of damage and provided a good diversion for the follow-up attack. There's no telling how many American and Chinese officials were killed in the conference area assault. Heavy fighting was reported around the Council Chamber, but we can't get in to get any confirmation. They've sealed off the whole area."

"Who are the terrorists, and how the hell did they get in there?" Neil said testily, both anger and frustration leaping through him.

"We don't know yet," Guntram snapped, refusing to break his reserve. His eyes fixed on Neil cooly as if repelling the blame that he himself was finding hard to escape. "We know there was one in the catering truck that rammed through the guard gate and into the Assembly Hall. Nothing we threw at that truck stopped it. This was an incredibly well-planned and well-financed operation. That truck was designed to get through our security gauntlet, and it did."

"The explosion pulled most of our security men from their assigned positions. They wanted to be the hero. Instead, they ended up being the goat. From what we can piece together, in the confusion, a small group of terrorists attacked and neutralized the remaining internal security forces. They have now effectively sealed off the area with controlled explosive charges. The security in place to protect against such things is now working against us. They have closed-circuit TV cameras and monitors with emergency power capability. It won't be easy to get to them. What's worse, we don't know what they've done to the people they captured. We don't know how many terrorists there are, but we do know they are professionals and are well-armed."

"How did they get in?" Neil pleaded, still confused.

"We don't know! There were no reports of an aerial or ground assault by any hostile forces. They almost had to have been in there for days. All the internal security supervisors have been accounted for except for Joseph Anders. He was responsible for night security. No one has seen him since yesterday, and we haven't been able to reach him. There is a secured bomb shelter in the basement of the southeast wing. Anders had assured us that it had been checked and sealed. It's the only area big enough for a small attack force to hide. It also has all the provisions they would need to stay there."

"I can't believe it wasn't checked!" Neil said with some venom.

"It was checked! Anders checked it!" Guntram said testily, his nostrils flaring.

"I'm sorry. It just all seems so impossible. It's done. We can't do anything about that," Neil said softly, not wanting to polarize this man he knew he would need to work with. "Do you know anything about the condition of the negotiating teams?"

"No, but with the extent of machine gun fire heard from the Council Chamber area, I have a feeling there will be extensive casualties. How many, I don't know. But we can't get in there to help the wounded until they talk to us. We're waiting for them to establish contact. Obviously, in light of the attacks by Al-Haram, we are assuming that they may have been involved. We won't do anything else until we know more. For now, we're content to secure defensive positions around the grounds and to treat the wounded we can locate. We have men covering all the entrances on the second and third floors that the terrorists have sealed."

Both men were distracted by an ambulance that came to stop next to them. A mutilated body, more dead than alive, was being pushed through the open doors. The air was permeated with the smell of death and burning flesh.

"They're prepared to help survivors. Unfortunately, they're finding most dead," Guntram said, his voice low. He drew a deep breath. Many of the dead were his people.

There was silence, and an emerging sadness as the full impact of the human tragedy rushed in. The painful intensity of the scene became too much for Neil. He needed structure to hold onto. There was no time to succumb to feelings. He had work to do. He needed work to do.

Turning again to Guntram, Neil said in a strange faraway tone he hardly recognized as his own voice, "With the President being held and no way to clarify her status, Vice President Wallace has already moved to alert status. Reports are that the Chinese have done the same thing. It looks like for once we were both meant to be victims. Well, I need to call Washington to give Wallace a report. I'll get back to you after I've talked with him."

"I'm sure I don't need to tell you this, but remind Wallace not to make any public statement on your no-concession policy. You remember what happened when the press pushed Nixon into revealing that he would never give in to terrorists. His message was broadcast in the Middle East, and two Americans were immediately killed in Khartoum. We can't afford that here," Guntram said emphatically.

"I understand. You know our position is no concession. I can't imagine that changing, even in this situation."

"I understand," replied Guntram. "The Chinese position is the same and always has been—no concessions. But we need time. Get

Wallace to stall. Tell the media he's staying secluded for security reasons. Just keep him from making any off-the-cuff remarks. The less said the better. These terrorists are no amateurs. You don't pull this kind of operation without wanting something in return. When they talk to us—and they will talk to us—we want to string them out, give them time, and keep the negotiations private. That means speaking with one voice and keeping the media out of the way. This is still our country, and I don't want the media adding logs to the fire when we're trying to salvage what's left of this nightmare. Our primary goal is to save lives here, very important lives, I might add. We need to borrow as much time as we can."

"I'll do my best. A no-concession position doesn't mean no negotiation," said Neil. "You are the host government. We have no choice but to leave room for local control. Your Swiss position has always been clear: negotiate. As for Wallace, I should have no trouble keeping him away from the media. With this crisis, he knows he needs to be in a secure location." Neil spoke with more assurance than he felt. Wallace was not known for his reserve. Controlling the Vice President's comments would be extraordinarily difficult, but the costs were too high not to.

Both men shook hands, and Neil turned to leave. Before he could finish taking two steps, he stopped and turned back to the Swiss officer.

"Guntram, I forgot to mention Gerald Opfer, our State Department Director from the Office for Combating Terrorism Crisis Management Task Force, and Col. Chuck Healey, our European Delta Force commander, are on their way here. They want to coordinate operations with your men."

"Yes, I know Col. Healey well. I like him. He's a good man. I've also met Mr. Opfer," Guntram said with complete, flat honesty. "I will work with them but let me be clear. No heroics. This is an extremely dangerous barricade hostage situation, and I will not condone a siege mentality. This group is not a group of amateur idealists, these are gun-wielding, experienced gunmen, who know how to use explosives with precision. The danger of any rescue operation against a group of trained professionals like this could be signing the death warrant for Freeman and Wang. Your men can be part of the negotiating team task force, but we'll do things our way."

"You *do* understand they have our President. We want her back alive, not in a casket. We'll work with you, but our men will be ready to act if you require."

"Good, we understand each other. You should know, I've had a similar request from the Chinese, a Colonel Tang Wei. I've never met the man, and General Shen Gao, both Chinese special forces. They're flying in from Beijing, but I'm sure Colonel Healey and I will get to know them both quite well. I don't look forward to playing politics, but I'm afraid I'm going to have to," Guntram added.

"I don't blame you. I don't think any of us are looking forward to any part of this nightmare. Colonel Healey told me to tell you that Rip Devins is flying in to work with you. He's also bringing information on blood type, medical history, and secret communication codes that the President might use to get information to us. It should prove helpful. President Freeman was briefed just last month on the codes. Let's hope she remembers and is alive to use them," Neil added thoughtfully.

"That could be helpful," Guntram said. He paused and then, in a voice strained with sadness, "Neil. I'm sorry about this. We had the tightest security we've ever had for any event."

"I know," Neil squeezed his arm, offering genuine support. "We've had Presidents shot in our own streets, and the would-be assassins weren't even professionals. If the crazies want to get you, it's hard to stop them. Who would have thought they would pick the first Summit for peace we've had in years. It's clear that some people don't really want peace. It's a crazy world."

"I think it's getting crazier."

CHAPTER TWENTY-SIX

COMFORT FROM SOMEONE WHO WOULD UNDERSTAND

The Domaine de Châteauvieux

"Be strong and courageous. Do not fear or be in dread of them, for it is the Lord your God who goes with you. He will not leave you or forsake you."
Deuteronomy 31:6 (ESV)

He felt so helpless. Taking a deep breath, Martin Freeman stood staring out his high bedroom windows at the natural tapestry of colors displayed on the chateau grounds. It was a pity, he thought to himself, that Connie and he couldn't just vacation here like they used to. Instead, everything was tempered by political realities, and now, it was the only reality. As much as she hated politics, he hated the press more.

They were swarming around his every move. He couldn't blame them for involving him in one of their prime coverage angles. They were saying that, now, the real summit was being held between him and Ma Mei.

Martin fought off waves of exhaustion. He was not sure he had actually slept at all since they arrived. For a moment, he took in their spacious bedroom. The walls were painted a lustrous midnight blue. They were covered with handwoven tapestries and gold-framed paintings of men that had shared these quarters through the years.

Martin focused on the gold-leafed canopied bed that dominated the room. He wondered if the leaders in the paintings had spent more time outside the walls of their majestic chateaus than in their beds with their wives. As for him, there had been no time for sex with "the President" in weeks. He felt a moment of guilt. *She is here to bring peace to the world and, like men through the ages, he's worried about when he can have sex.* In reality, he missed the time to just be next to her in bed. She called him her *"White House heater."* But she also knew he was *very cold* on her running for four more years. He just wished she felt the same way.

Martin heard the waiting room door open, sigh shut, then Maureen Waters' voice, *"Martin."*

In that moment, sensing an alarm in Maureen's voice, he turned to greet Connie's aid and friend. Instinctively, fighting back a growing sense of apprehension, he went to meet her.

As Maureen entered the master bedroom, she barely managed to keep the note of hysteria out of her voice.

Maureen said with a stark directness she knew Martin demanded, "Martin. There's been a truck bombing and terrorist attack on the Palace of Nations. We don't..."

For an instant, it seemed as if Maureen's words hung like icicles frozen in time. Suddenly, the demons of past nightmares were brought to life. His eyes stared.

"Martin, I'm so sorry," Maureen spoke softly in a trembling voice.

Comfort from Someone Who Would Understand

"Is Connie alright?" Martin's voice was anguished but demanding.

"They don't know," Maureen said carefully. Trying to provide a ray of hope that she herself was clinging to, Maureen quickly continued, "Martin, we do know she wasn't killed in the initial truck bomb attack. She wasn't yet in the Assembly Hall. She was still meeting privately with the General Secretary before addressing the assembly."

"Have they gotten them out?" Martin asked, assuming security would have done their job to protect the President.

"No, they can't get to them. The conference room where Connie was meeting with General Secretary Wang is being held by the terrorists," Maureen continued, quickly filling in the details as she knew them.

Martin's mind tried to follow, but the pallor of the word "terrorists" was like hearing the word "cancer" from your doctor. The mind moves quickly to death. Sure, some hostages survive, but to him, terrorists had always meant death. Now they had brought it to his doorstep.

Martin interrupted, "Is this Al-Haram?"

"No one has taken responsibility. It is chaos with only questions."

"What about Tom and the rest of the negotiating team?" Martin asked.

"We don't know. There was a lot of shooting heard on the phone coming from the conference room. We haven't been able to get in there, either. There are indications that many have been killed. They're waiting to hear from the terrorists," Maureen confessed, staring into Martin's eyes.

"I remember watching Nancy Reagan interviewed about the day Reagan was shot She said that she was never the same after that," Martin stated evenly. "Connie knew it could happen. Al-Haram has been brazen in their attacks! We even talked about it, but you never expected them to attack the Summit, the President!"

In pained silence, with tears in her eyes, Maureen gave Martin a hug. She held a moment longer in support.

"I'm sorry, Martin. But I needed to be the one to tell you as soon as I heard." Maureen said.

"Thank you, Maureen."

"I wish I knew more, more to tell you," Maureen added.

"I want to go there, Maureen. I want to be there."

"You can't," Maureen said softly but forcefully. "It wouldn't be wise, and security has made that clear. No way. They'll have enough of a problem dealing with the terrorists and trying to free Connie without having to protect you as well. The Secret Service has tripled security here at the chateau, in case the terrorists try something here, too. You'll be safe here. Connie would want you to stay."

"Connie would want us to pray. Pray right now," Martin said in earnest. "Will you pray with me, Maureen?"

"Yes, of course."

Martin grabbed her hands as they both bowed their heads, *"Dear Lord, we pray right now for Connie and all those being held. Be near and comfort those who have lost loved ones. Bring healing to those wounded. Lord, be with Connie. Give her comfort and safety. Lord, we pray that it be your will that she will be rescued from this attack. Give wisdom to those dealing with the hostages. Lord, give me patience and comfort. Guide me in what you would have me do. Be with Maureen and the team as they struggle with this attack. God, come save her."* A tear formed in the corner of his eye as he squeezed Maureen's hand.

"Amen," Maureen added. Both paused, trying to find God's peace.

Comfort from Someone Who Would Understand

"Maureen, I know you're right. I will stay here for now. Keep me informed. I will be watching the TV to get caught up," Martin said emphatically.

"We'll make sure you have a number of monitors to follow coverage from the different media sources," Maureen said, glancing quickly at her watch. "Martin, since I'm one of the few Presidential staff members left here in Europe that weren't involved in the attack, I've got to get the satellite conference call set up with the Vice President. We've got a lot of planning to do. I'll come back after the call to check in."

"No, that won't be necessary. You have more important work to do, but please keep me informed," Martin said. He knew the team needed to focus on dealing with the real problem, the terrorists! He watched as Maureen left the room.

Martin turned, scanning the luxury of his suite, once a secure refuge, now a prison of helplessness. He stared at the painting of a Swiss nobleman in uniform. He spoke out loud, "Did you leave your wife here alone to go die for the cause?" Had those wives felt the pain of loss he was feeling? He was sure they did.

Taking a deep breath, Martin struggled to find the peace his Lord and savior had promised. He felt the Spirit bring him to one of his favorite verses from Isaiah, *"They that wait upon the Lord shall renew their strength; they shall mount up with wings of eagles; they shall run and not be weary, they shall walk and not faint."*

The words came to him, splashing onto his pained soul, *"Please God! I don't care if Connie never soars with eagles or if she ever runs again. But God, give her back to me alive! Oh, my God! If it's your will, may it be so. Be with her, Lord. May your Spirit give her strength and keep her safe." After a moment's pause, he resumed, "Wait on the Lord! Oh Lord, give me your strength and a little peace. I hate waiting!"* Suddenly, like a dam weakened by an overpowering flood, tears came falling off his cheeks.

"I don't want to wait!" he yelled out loud. His shout echoed through the room. He wanted to negotiate with God, but he resisted. Without success, he searched for the words of comfort that struggled to come. Perhaps it was because, at that moment, he didn't want to find them. He wanted to do something–anything!

CHAPTER TWENTY-SEVEN

A SURGEON UP TO HIS ASS IN ALLIGATORS!

> Hotel des Berguese Bar
> Geneva, Switzerland

*"Is there no medicine in Gilead? Is there no physician
there? Why is there no healing for the
wounds of my people?"*
Jeremiah 8:22 (NLT)

Brian stared at the screen. It was hard as a doctor to witness so much death. The camera's eye panned the rubble of what was the Palace of Nation's majestic centerpiece. He leaned forward against the bar as he took another sip of coffee, watching attentively as the rescue units moved frantically to find and care for the wounded. Far more were beyond help.

He had seen death many times in his life; it was something physicians learned to live with. But never had he seen it so poignantly visited on the house of the mighty. The powerful had always had it easy, playing diplomatic games with the lives of the young and expendable. Few ever dared bring death to their doorstep in such a primitive way. As Brian reached for his coffee, the drone of the commentators left his mind free to pursue his own thoughts.

"...and over 600 wounded," reported the newscaster in a controlled voice that somehow masked the reality of human suffering. The words pulled Brian back to the screen.

"What did he say? How many were killed?" Brian spoke, asking no one in particular.

"There are over a thousand known dead, roughly six hundred wounded, and hundreds still unaccounted for," Dr. Chen said softly. He had not seen her come in and take a seat nearby.

He turned to face her, not even realizing that she had been there. His eyes searched hers. As he looked at her face intently, he realized that she was more beautiful than he had remembered. They both risked a small smile.

"Dr. Chen, I'm sorry. I didn't even notice that you were here. I'm Dr. Brian Winters from Johns Hopkins University. I saw part of your presentation earlier," Brian said, still studying her face.

"I know who you are, Dr. Winters. I have read much of your work," Chen Li replied with a clear, incisive voice.

"I'm honored," he said, again smiling as he gained confidence. "I guess that's assuming you enjoyed what you read." He laughed awkwardly at himself, a disarming laugh that had always been his trademark.

"I did. Probably more than you enjoyed listening to my program, considering how quickly you left," Dr. Chen said with a grin.

"Let me assure you it wasn't because of what you were presenting," Brian pleaded. He brought his hands together as if praying for forgiveness, and his voice took on a conciliatory tone. "I apologize. I had to make a call back to the States. It had nothing to do with your presentation. I've read about your mobile trauma units, and I..."

Suddenly, she smiled disarmingly. "Let me assure you, Dr. Winters, I did not take it personally." For the first time, they exchanged tentative but genuine smiles.

Again, their eyes were drawn back to the TV screen where the newscaster was announcing that Vice President Harold Wallace was about to make a statement from Washington. The tall, lanky, well-dressed Vice President walked stridently to the podium in front of the crowded press conference. He raised his hand to stop the barrage of questions that had already started. After there was silence, Wallace looked straight into the cameras and began to speak with a controlled but confident voice.

"By now, you have all heard the tragic news from the Geneva Summit. A highly organized terrorist attack on the Palace of Nations has destroyed much of the building and left hundreds dead or wounded. Although not impacted directly in the initial truck bomb attack, we have unsubstantiated reports that President Freeman and General Secretary Wang have been captured and are being held hostage," Wallace said deliberately, to the murmur and raised hands from the press in the room. "There is every indication that both are alive and are being held by a yet unidentified terrorist group. No direct communication with the terrorist group has been established at this time, but we expect some contact soon."

The Vice President stopped for a moment, coughing into his hand and glancing at his prepared text on the podium before him. He continued, "I wish to assure you and the people of the world listening, that whatever the result of today's tragic episode, an orderly and efficient transfer of emergency powers has already occurred. I, along with the Speaker of the House of Representatives and other congressional leaders, have met in consultation with military leaders to ensure that we are ready and able to respond to this crisis."

"Although an attack of this nature warrants an immediate increase in our worldwide military alert status, quick communication between us and our Chinese counterparts in Beijing have helped keep any potential suspicions from escalating. There is every indication that both our countries and the world have fallen victim to an unprovoked terrorist attack."

"Let me stress that there is no need for world alarm. We're working together at this very moment to handle what is a tragedy for both countries. Due to the sensitivity of the situation and security considerations, there will be no further statements," Wallace stressed, continuing to talk over the growing buzz of complaints and questions from the assembled press.

"We will keep you informed when there is more to report. We ask for your prayers for the families of those already dead and for the others whose lives remain in the balance. Thank you."

Abruptly leaving the podium with head bowed in a determined retreat, he silently made his way with Secret Service escorts out the door without responding to the stream of questions following him.

"Wallace, saved by the teleprompter!" Brian said dryly. He had never liked Wallace's mock bravado and stale rhetoric. Although Brian had not voted for Freeman, he at least respected her. She had integrity and strength. Wallace had neither, but he had a lock on the Southern vote. Brian would never vote for Wallace. *God help us,* he thought, *if we're stuck with him.*

"With all the weapons the superpowers have between them, they are suddenly powerless. Their great weapons don't matter. There's nothing they can do," Brian continued, adding his own commentary

A Surgeon Up to His Ass in Alligators!

to the drone of the network reporters. "The terrorists are in control. They win even if they die. They've succeeded in bringing two of the most powerful countries in the world to their knees."

Brian's heartfelt commentary was brought to an abrupt stop by the sudden pressure of Li's hand on his arm. He looked first at her intent expression, and then back at the screen she was watching. A live Chinese news report was being broadcast from Beijing. He could not understand a word the Chinese newscaster was saying, but the warm touch of her hand pressing against his arm communicated something he could understand. A hint of a smile played around Brian's mouth as his eyes went from the screen back to Li.

"What did he say?" Brian asked, surprised by the brevity of the report. Li paused and withdrew her hand, looking away momentarily before speaking.

"He said that there were reports of terrorist activity in Geneva. Many Swiss security guards have been wounded, but they expect the peaceful goals of the Summit will still be realized," Dr. Chen. said with an almost apologetic tone.

"You've got to be kidding!" Brian said incredulously. "My God, the whole world is being held hostage, and they report the Summit is still going fine! They didn't even mention the bomb's destruction or the capture of Wang or Freeman?"

There was a moment of silence between them before Dr. Chen. spoke.

"Our people do not like to hear negative news," Li said, pausing to avoid being defensive. "Our leaders feel they know best what the people need to know. They do not want to upset their people unnecessarily."

"Doesn't that bother you?" Brian asked, but with a softer conciliatory tone, trying to understand how such a strong, intelligent woman could accept such a blatant denial of reality. "What about all that talk about 'transparency,' Wang's new openness?"

"General Secretary Wang has been trying to become more open, but it has not been easy for him. Not every leader or citizen agrees with his changes. Many do not want to know. Many have experienced enough pain in their life; they do not want to experience more. They desire a simple life," the good doctor said with a flat honesty that even Brian could not deny. "I think it would be hard for an American to understand."

"You're right. I guess maybe I don't understand," Brian confessed with deliberate slowness and emphasis. He turned to look briefly at the television screen and then back to Chen Li. "I have a feeling all of us will soon find out more than any of us will want to know."

"Dr. Brian Winters!" The urgent sound of his name echoing through the bar startled him.

"Yes, here!" Brian said, waving his hand toward the bellman.

"There's an urgent message from a Dr. Jean Guye," the bellman said, pausing as if struggling to find a way to delicately express the confusing message he had before him.

Turning first to Dr. Chen, the bellman apologized, "I am sorry, Madame. It is a message Doctor Guye said would be understood." The young man cleared his throat, turning nervously to Brian. "The doctor reports that he is *up to his ass in alligators,*" The bellman again turned to Dr. Chen, apologizing as Brian laughed.

It was his turn to touch Chen Li arm as he reassured them that it was quite all right. The bellman left.

"I called Dr. Guye when I got word of the attack," Brian said with a calm assurance. "I told him to holler if they needed help here. With the casualty report they've been talking about, it sounds like they do."

"What of these alligators?"

"Oh," Brian said, squeezing her arm while laughing. "It's just an expression I use that he likes. We worked here in Geneva together in setting up one of the laser-assisted operating rooms. It means the Swiss have got more problems than they can handle, and they need help."

As both doctors instinctively got up, Brian reached in his pocket to leave money for the coffee. He plopped down more Swiss francs than he needed and then turned to the doctor.

"Dr. Chen, would you care to join me?" Brian asked. He continued with an engaging smile, "It's time the teachers see if they can still perform under fire."

"Do you always make jokes, Dr. Winters?" Dr. Chen asked, returning his smile.

"Only when it hurts," Brian said, "Which is most of the time."

Brian smiled and then lightly grabbed Chen Li's arm as he propelled her toward the door. She turned to him as they rushed for the entrance and an available taxi.

"Dr. Winters," Chen Li said, her voice light but neutral.

"Yes?"

"I don't teach. I work," she said, her smile broadening.

"Now who's joking!" Brian said with a chuckle. Then he added, half seriously, "I have a sad feeling there is going to be more than enough work for both of us."

CHAPTER TWENTY-EIGHT

TERRORISTS HOLD THE WORLD HOSTAGE

**Parc de l'Ariana Command Center
Geneva, Switzerland**

*"Be alert and of sober mind. Your enemy, the devil,
prowls around like a roaring lion looking
for someone to devour."
1 Peter 5:8 (NIV)*

Swiss security was caught in a nightmare. Guntram Meyer moved quickly down the steps leading out of the temporary command trailer that had been strategically positioned in the Parc de l'Ariana, southeast of the Palace of Nations. It was out of sight of the terrorists, but close enough to provide the central nerve network for the computer-monitored security operations. By providing an up-to-the-moment location of security forces, the computer was able to spotlight security gaps and problems as soon as they appeared.

The command post was equipped to receive video transmissions from security cameras placed around the perimeter of the Palace complex. The equipment was already recording and processing movement patterns from the infrequent terrorist sightings that had already occurred.

Terrorists Hold the World Hostage

There had been little to work with until moments earlier, when one of the terrorists had come to the window and asked by bullhorn to talk. Guntram had immediately notified the American and Chinese security departments stationed nearby.

Walking briskly through the cedars and cypress lining the park, Guntram tried to clear his mind. As he moved quickly up the hill, the sound of the express train from Paris arriving at the Gare de Cornavin momentarily distracted him. Thankfully, he thought, some things in Geneva were still operating normally.

Guntram moved stealthily the last twenty yards toward the make-shift bunker erected behind the Armillary Sphere after the terrorists' attack. The often-photographed bronze monument to peace given to the Swiss by the United States in honor of President Woodrow Wilson was now but a shield in a modern-day war. After entering the bunker, Guntram took his position and found Gerald Opfer from the US Crisis Management Task Force, who had already arrived.

"Have they said anything else?" Guntram asked.

"No, he came to the window three minutes ago and said in English that he wanted to talk. We called you, and you saw it on the monitor. He hasn't said a thing since," Gerald. spoke with a hint of frustration. He looked directly at Guntram and then turned to look for the unknown terrorist, who seemed to relish the opportunity of riveting the attention of the world on him.

"Any sign of the hostages?" Guntram said calmly, trying to assess the situation as they waited.

"No. Wherever they are, they haven't been visible. It's been awfully quiet up there," Gerald. added in a matter-of-fact tone. Guntram wondered what kind of thoughts this man must be having. It was

143

his President in there. Guntram turned to face his top aide kneeling beside him.

"Get me the bullhorn. I want to be ready to talk to him when he decides it's time," Guntram said with more confidence than he actually felt.

Guntram's movement was not lost on Ghazi. He knew the time to talk was at hand. As he returned to the window, Ghazi stood erect and pulled his own bullhorn to his mouth, drawing the immediate attention of all the security forces and cameras trained on him.

"We have drawn first blood in the final war against the Zionists and their so-called superpower friends," Ghazi spoke, each word like a sledgehammer. He balled his other hand into a raised fist as he continued. "Al-Haram recognizes no other action but destruction! Everything we do is sanctified by the revolution! We are committed to the sacred cause of rooting out the evil that defiles the present world order. There are no innocents in this struggle. Violence is our purifying force, the healing medicine for all our people's diseases. This Summit of superpowers is but another sacrilege to peace. It is a sham meeting between sham leaders. There can be no such thing as negotiation with evil tyrants. We have captured these so-called leaders, these monsters, who under human guise conceal the cruelty and ferocity of wild beasts. They shall be severed from the common body of humanity as sacrifices to the cause unless their countries cooperate in the final war against Israel."

"He's Iranian," whispered Opfer in a voice touched with tension. Guntram asked, "Where's Lin Feng? He should be here to hear this."

"He was notified, and he's on his way here," Gerald. said, his eyes and ears still focused on the terrorist at the window.

"Our demands are simple," Ghazi continued in a dispassionate tone. "You are to deliver three one-kiloton nuclear bombs intact to a base of our choosing in Iran. The bombs are to be used in the final war against the infidels that defile Arab soil. Unless the bombs are delivered within three days, the hostages will die before your very eyes. We will destroy our enemies and walk over their ashes for all eternity. Al-Haram has given you our demands. The choice is yours."

Ghazi's words--*nuclear bombs*—hit their mark. They now knew what they wanted. An unnatural silence hung over them all as the scope of the primordial struggle took shape. Guntram could feel the tension in his knuckles wrapped tightly around his bullhorn.

"He didn't say anything about any other hostages?" Gerald said incredulously, seeking all the information he could get.

Guntram stood and stepped forward, thrusting the bullhorn to his mouth, "What about the other hostages? When will they be released?"

"The dead are silent," Ghazi's words worse than expected.

Guntram steadied himself, "What of the wounded?"

"There are no innocents in the cleansing revolution. ALL are silent. There are no other hostages," Ghazi said contemptuously, lowering his megaphone. Despite the distance, They were close enough to see Ghazi's sadistic smile.

Guntram's megaphone momentarily dropped to his side. Disgust and anger welled up inside of him. *THEY HAD KILLED THEM ALL!*

"Did I hear you right? All of them are dead. Tom… Jim…" Opfer said in a soft, almost mechanical voice. "All of them dead."

Pulling the megaphone to his mouth, Guntram spoke carefully, "Where are the bombs to be delivered?"

The Summit

"You will be informed at the right time," Ghazi said with a wracked ghost of a chuckle. "You will be with us, because you cannot afford to be against us."

Almost disregarding Ghazi's statement, Guntram pushed for more information, "If the other hostages are all dead, how do we know President Freeman and General Secretary Wang are still alive?"

"The monsters live for now, and we will give you proof," Ghazi replied. "But in three days, they will die unless you join us in this sacred war. Let me warn everyone who contemplates any foolhardy attempt to free the hostages. The fate of your leaders would be much worse than the death you have already experienced. We will show no mercy. There is nothing left to say." Ghazi's ominous frame left the window.

Turning to Opfer, Guntram said, "This is impossible. We know what they want. Their demands are unreasonable, but we also know what they are capable of doing to their captives if they don't get what they demand."

"So does the rest of the world," Gerard said. "Because of that bullhorn, within minutes, Al-Haram's demands will be spread around the world. I'm afraid we're going to have more trouble to deal with than just these terrorists. It's more than Israel's future. The whole world is now being held hostage."

CHAPTER TWENTY-NINE

UNLEASHING THE PURIFYING FORCE OF VIOLENCE

**Palace of Nations Conference Center
Geneva, Switzerland**

*"Then Jesus was led by the Spirit into the wilderness
to be tempted by the devil."*
Matthew 4:1 (NIV)

The captives heard Ghazi's projected demands. Freeman searched for logic to shield her from the implications, her emotions overruling. No one would give that man nuclear weapons, no matter what the price. *But what if they did?* She glanced at Wang. No words were exchanged. She saw the torment in the Chinese leader's eyes. They both felt the same painful reality. The cost of their release was too expensive for the world to pay. The President moved and winced as the ropes around her wrists pinched her senses back to the helpless reality of their captivity.

Like a predator returning to gnaw on the half-eaten carcasses of their fallen prey, Ghazi and Ibn confronted their captives. Ghazi raised his weapon into the air defiantly. His eyes gleamed, and his lips formed a wide, wicked smile.

"We are now allies in Allah's final struggle against the infidels," Ghazi said, his other hand now balling into a fist as his eyes bore into Freeman. She felt the cold, calculating, inhuman, force standing before her. She had already tasted Ghazi's venom, and she wanted no more of him.

"Who are you?" The President asked with far more strength than she felt. Her tone was restrained, cautious.

"I am Ghazi Saud, Leader of Al-Haram. It's a name you and the world will come to be very familiar with. To you, I am your master. For now, that is all you need to know."

"We heard your demands," The President replied, still in a strong voice. "Even if the two of us were to sympathize with your cause, do you really think our countries would give you nuclear weapons to free us? It's not even legal under international law. They can't!"

"That is paper! Paper laws can be changed! You are flesh and blood. The Americans cannot let you die. They will find a way to give us the help we want. Now, come with us!" Ghazi grabbed Freeman's arm, pulling her to her feet, the tight bonds tearing into her wrists. She felt flashes of dizziness as the blood drained from her head as she was pulled forward. She staggered but found her footing.

"Why are we…" Freeman began to speak.

"Was not one rifle butt enough, dog!" Ghazi screamed through clenched teeth, "Come!"

The President watched silently as Ibn pushed the General Secretary past him out of the room. Ghazi's hands lifted her effortlessly and propelled her out the doorway and down the open hallway. She was immediately aware of the immense strength of this man. Momentarily resting in the power of her captor, Freeman tried to center her attention on the palace that was now her prison.

She tried to make mental pictures of every room and corridor. There were no bodies to be seen, but blood stains were clearly visible at many locations. Observing two other armed terrorists she had not seen before, her eyes darted from side to side, trying to observe and remember every detail. She would need all the information she could collect if there was to be any chance of escape.

For a moment, she laughed at herself. *Escape!* It suddenly felt like whistling on the way to the gallows. Who was she kidding? Then she saw a familiar sight, the glaring lights of the palace press room with the out-of-place Summit finery, the cameras, and microphones. This time the press was missing.

"Are you ready with the camera?" Ghazi said abruptly to his brother Gamal, who was busy preparing the equipment. "This will be a short recording."

"Yes, I am ready," Gamal said calmly, his hands moving deftly over the recording controls.

"What are you going to record?" Freeman asked without hesitation, asking more out of habit than expectation of any answer.

"You will talk when told!" Ghazi's hand still locked around the President's arm in a vicelike grip. "They want proof that the two of you are alive. We will give them proof that they can show the world. You will have no makeup, no speechwriters now. You will tell them you are fine and to agree to our demands. They will see you for what you are, obedient dogs!"

Before she could react, she felt her world spinning around as Ghazi forced her into a chair. As Ghazi untied the ropes that bound her, Freeman pulled her arms forward, freeing her hands. She rubbed

The Summit

her wrists, blood returning to her hands, sending tingling sensations throbbing through her fingers. Her fingers had survived. God willing, she would survive.

"Turn on the recording!" Ghazi said with derision. For Freeman, the bright lights and camera activity triggered images of safer days–days she feared she might never see again. The defiant, fierce tone of Ghazi's voice, as he began talking, pulled her back to the horror unfolding before her eyes.

"Al-Haram now gives you the proof you wanted that the monsters live! They have defiled Allah, and they will know his revenge!" Ghazi flared, his face darkening as he raised a portable radio spouting now stale news about the tragedy that was just beginning to unfold. "You can hear the radio playing. You are smart enough to check the programming to establish the time. These monsters are alive, but they will not stay alive unless the nuclear weapons are delivered!"

Ghazi turned with methodical control as he handed the microphone to the President. Freeman stared at Ghazi. He said softly, fiercely, "Speak, dog!"

Freeman, looking momentarily at General Secretary Wang sitting next to her, again feeling a silent bond. She licked her lips and tried to muster what dignity she could find. Her brain searched for the words she had recently reviewed but hoped never to have to use, words that were part of the secret communication code she knew would have meaning to those who would hear them.

"We are both well. We have food. Although our treatment has been harsh, neither of us has been hurt in any way. Martin, I am okay," Connie said, her eyes moistening, tears she had no intention of letting surface. "No matter what the demands of Al-Haram, we do not support the–"

Again, the butt of Ghazi's gun smashed into the President's mid-section. A peculiar sound came from Connie's mouth, and tears again formed in the corner of her eyes. Her arms instinctively drew inward, her body recoiling into a protective ball that folded into the chair.

Ghazi grabbed the microphone, clenching his fist as if strangling the words that had escaped. The cords of his neck stood out with the strain. His eyes stared straight at Freeman and then at the silent Wang. Abruptly he hit the table in front of the leaders and turned his burning eyes toward the camera lens.

"That is enough! These so-called leaders are criminals, murderers of all the underprivileged on earth. This is our holy act of war to wash away the stains of the blood of our brothers and our children. For now, they are alive!" He snorted. "As with all pets, they have been kept well. Join with us in the Holy War of annihilation, or you will watch them be executed. By 20 hundred hours this evening, I will expect to hear on this station, twelve hundred megahertz, of your total acceptance of our demands. Specific instructions will follow for the delivery of the weapons."

Freeman could hear Ghazi approaching. Before she could react, she felt the cold sting of the muzzle of Ghazi's Uzi biting into her neck. Her eyes flew open. She felt her body pulled upward in pain as Ghazi forced her to stand. She was embarrassed to feel urine run down her leg. Ghazi held her steady as he pointed the Uzi to her temple. His eyes noting the puddle on the floor.

"Now that you know our demands, shall we show the world how the mighty Yankee President has relieved herself," Ghazi said with a harsh laugh. "A shameful act for a world leader, a common one for a dog!"

The Summit

She could feel the anger leaping through her body. She impaled Ghazi with a stare, but the Arab just stared back defiantly.

"Dogs wet themselves in the face of death. We do not fear death. We spit on death!" Ghazi said emphatically, his voice taking on a steely edge. "Turn it off!"

The recording was completed, but Ghazi was not through. He turned again to face the President, "Don't ever speak out in defiance of me again!" Ghazi ordered with harshness. "You are to say only what you are told! It may shock you, but you have no power here. You have no allies. Do you understand?"

Provoked by the President's defiant silent stare, Ghazi smashed the heel of his fist into the side of her exposed neck. The President cried out. She staggered for a moment but then quickly returned his stare. She could be hurt, but she refused to cower. More than ever, she vowed to survive this.

"Say you understand, Madam President. Your petty display of courage means nothing against the power we have over you. It is a useless display." Ghazi stated in a disgusted tone.

"She understands. You have hurt her enough," Wang interjected fervently, breaking his silence.

"Who gave you permission to speak?" Ghazi flared, his eyes squinting leaving Freeman, he moved slowly toward the General Secretary. Ghazi's dark eyes were like piercing swords inflicting wounds without marks. Wang remained silent.

"Of course, you understand, don't you?" Ghazi said slowly in cruel derision. "You are wise, Mr. General Secretary."

Freeman watched as Ghazi used his huge hand to grip Wang's jaw with vice-like pressure. She had felt that pain and knew it must be intense, but she saw no reaction from Wang as Ghazi continued.

"Are you wise enough to understand that you are alone?" Ghazi said with a harsh laugh, letting go of his grip and pushing the General Secretary away. The terrorist continued to mock him. "It will do no good for either of your countries to pretend to cooperate or negotiate. I have read your books on handling so-called terrorists. Maintain a passive attitude, do what your captors say, stay calm, and try to talk to us to win us over with kindness."

"You are not our friends!" Ghazi snapped, his voice shaking with cold anger. His body tensed, "You insult us! You cannot win us over with words. They are words used by liars–the devil's liars! You are monsters. Both of you. Let me assure you that your lives are worth more to the world than they are to us." The force of his words hung in the air.

"Do not expect to be rescued. They may try to free you, but they will never get you out of here alive. Allahu Akbar. Allah and my men will see to that," Ghazi said, turning to Ibn and Gamal and motioning them to take the prisoners. "Take them to their new cell and do try to make them comfortable."

Ghazi's mocking laughter remained with the President long after she had been led from the room. She was sure the memory would be with her for as long as she lived. However long that would be, she was not sure.

CHAPTER THIRTY

TRAPPED ON THE WRONG SIDE OF A HOLY WAR

> Parc de l'Ariana Command Center
> Geneva, Switzerland

"Proclaim this among the nations: Prepare for war!
Rouse the warriors! Let all the fighting
men draw near and attack."
Joel 3:9 (NIV)

"That is enough! These leaders are criminals, murderers of all the underprivileged on Earth. This is our holy act of war to wash away the stains of the blood of our brothers and our children. For now, they are alive!" Ghazi all but shouted, his image on the screen as captivating and powerful as if he had been in person. "As with all pets, they have been kept well. Join with us in the Holy War of annihilation, or you will watch them be executed."

Neil watched Gerald Opfer lean against the detailed layout of the Palace of Nations taped to the conference room wall. Gerald's eyes, along with those of others in the room, were riveted to the monitor screen as they watched for a second time their President beaten by a

154

madman. Neil didn't want to look; he had seen enough already. Instead, he stared at the man he knew would carry most of the weight of American involvement in the local negotiating team. Although Gerald Opfer was short in stature, he could control a room. Critics in Washington said that he could strut while seated, but he was clearly a firm and effective negotiator, two essentials needed as a Director of the Office to Combat Terrorism.

"It's a crime!" Glen Lawson exclaimed, pounding the table with his fist as the tape ended. "It should never have happened! There was too much paper pushing at the top! We told the Swiss this could happen, but they sat back, analyzing military intelligence reports that told them what they wanted to hear. If they had put adequate numbers in the parameter and helicopters in the air, the President would be safe. But no, they wouldn't budge. I offered them more than enough Secret Service men, but they felt we were too noisy, too visible. They like to do it quietly. We were limited to two men with guns, and they went early."

Neil could see the veins straining on Lawson's aged but muscled neck. As head of the Secret Service, he and his men were dedicated to protecting the President with their lives. And now he could do nothing.

"I'm not sure it's the fault of Swiss security," Col. Chuck Healey said with a calm confidence befitting the head of the Delta Force Special Forces Group.

"And just whose fault is it then?" Glen countered. "Some of the 'so-called' Swiss terrorist experts are holding onto their collective ass to make sure they know where it's going to be kicked!"

"We're not here to kick anyone's ass!" Gerald Opfer said forcefully, trying to bring back control. "We're here to solve a problem. Blaming people will get us nowhere." He looked directly at Lawson.

As if calling a tense draw to a conflict neither man wanted to escalate, Gerald turned and moved toward Col. Healey, "You were going to say something, Chuck. What was it?"

"You know as well as I that the success of this terrorist attack is nothing magical," Chuck began. "Ghazi Saud's Al-Haram appears to be one of many dedicated Sharia secret societies. We've already seen how destructive they can be. They're smart and prepared. They have a small, highly trained, mobile force. We're beginning to get some information on Ghazi. He knows Europe. He went to school here and in England. They want exposure, and this Summit, with all its media coverage, is perfect for them. Martyrdom, for them, is life's ultimate reward. To drive a truck bomb into the Summit building is not to pass 'go,' not to collect two hundred dollars, but a direct ticket to the promised land. It was only a matter of time before Ghazi Saud's determination, skill, and a little luck provided the opportunity. And unfortunately, that time has come," Chuck concluded with a complete, flat honesty his peers respected. "To them, it's a Holy War against the hated infidels. And I'm afraid that we are on what they consider the wrong side."

A sudden movement at the door as Guntram Meyer entered the conference room pulled all eyes to him. Neil knew Guntram had to be tired, but it didn't show on his face. Instead, his face was ablaze with determination.

"Glad you could join us," Gerald said simply. "Do you know any more about what we have facing us?"

"Yes, we do. We found Joseph Anders and his wife dead. He was in charge of night security. We also found some plans of the Palace's basement bomb shelter at his home," Guntram said evenly, moving to the Palace plans and pointing to the location of the bomb shelter. "What we can assume at this time is that Anders, for whatever reason, helped the terrorists find a way in days before the Summit. From the notes found on Anders' plans, I'm assuming that we are dealing with a group no larger than eight. With the storage area used, we can also assume they have enough ammunition, water, and food supplies to last for weeks. So they don't need to negotiate with us for that. It confirms what we already knew. This was well planned."

"Have you made additional contact with Ghazi?" asked General Bud Williamson.

"Not yet. He does not respond to our efforts to reach him. He clearly wants control of the timing for any negotiations."

"If we can't initiate direct conversations, this whole thing is going to escalate into a media circus!" Glen Lawson again interjected with a warning that seemed to surprise Guntram. "They literally are forcing us to use the media as our link, allowing the world to watch. We can't afford to let that continue!"

"We are doing what we can. We are well aware of the possible ramifications," replied Guntram, not flinching in the face of Glen's glare. "We have until six to contact them directly. The media, so far, has been willing to work with us and cooperate in any way possible, but we all know that could change. If we can secure direct contact, we will."

As Guntram turned from Glen to Neil, Neil saw an odd kind of defiance in his eyes, a look he could not quite decipher. Guntram continued, "I agree with Mr. Lawson. We need to control the press if at all possible."

"I've told you. They aren't going to like any attempts to control access," Neil cautioned. "It's the story of a lifetime. They're going after every lead like vampires going for blood. They're not known for their patience, and they're being pressed from every corner for the latest scoop. They all want to be the source of the next headline."

"I don't expect them to like it, but once we secure direct communication, that's the way it'll have to be."

"Alright. When that happens, I'll do whatever I can, but with the limits you want to impose, I'm not even sure we have that kind of control out there," Neil said in exasperation. "I'm not even sure we shouldn't be giving them some information. Keep in mind, using information as a media 'carrot' may be the only way we have of getting information from the President."

"What do you mean?" Guntram asked sharply.

"Until we have direct contact with the terrorists, the tapes provide the only way for Freeman and Wang to communicate with us. Assuming the President is using the pre-established communication codes we reviewed last month in Washington, the videotape has already told us two things. By using 'well' and 'ok,' we know they're being held captive together and that they are bound. We have no way of knowing if that has changed after the taping, but it does give us some information to work with. If Ghazi hadn't wanted to use the media, we wouldn't have that information," Neil concluded.

"I hope we don't have to make it public to use it, but your point is well taken," said Guntram thoughtfully.

"The media aside, what do you know about the present location of the terrorists and the hostages?" Chuck Healey asked calmly.

"As I reported earlier, we don't know much at this time. We do know where they could be and can make some educated guesses about where they are," Guntram said as he moved to the Palace plans, hesitated a moment, and then pointed. "Here is where the taping was done. The Palace of Nations is the press headquarters for Geneva. It must have been part of the terrorists' plan. They have control of the press room and the recording and communication facilities. From the previous recording, it is apparent that someone knows how to work the equipment. We also know there are three easily fortified rooms under their control that could be used to hold the hostages."

After pointing to the three locations on the plans, Guntram turned to face the members of the task force, "Unfortunately, we do not know which one."

Again pointing to the plans, Guntram continued, "The hallway entrance is barricaded at this point and here on the other side. The hostage demands were announced from this window. The General Secretary was last seen at this window, but, as you know, we have made no additional sightings. This probably suggests they have been bound and moved to one of the more easily defended rooms. Here is the conference room where the diplomats were killed; we don't know if it is sealed off or being used. So far, we've seen four different terrorists, although we assume from Joseph Anders' notes there may be eight. The outside perimeter is secure, but they have plenty of room to roam. We need more inside information that only direct contact will provide. In short, we need to talk to the terrorists."

"Who will be doing the direct negotiating?" Gerald asked.

"That is one of the reasons I am here. We have decided to use Kamal Harazi to head the local negotiating team," Guntram said carefully, subtle waves of apprehension showing on his face.

The Summit

"Of all the ridiculous decisions!" Glen Lawson interrupted, his voice cold, controlled. "For all we know, he may have helped them! He's despicable. I know he has been working with the Chinese, but what makes you think he can be trusted!"

"May I remind you the General Secretary is also a hostage, or have you forgotten?" Guntram objected.

"Just how sure are you that the Chinese want Wang alive?" shot back Glen.

Neil tried to reject the thought, but its impact lingered. *Could it be true? Could they want Wang dead?* Neil was sure he was not the only one struggling with this feeling of doubt and distrust.

"On what grounds do you make that allegation?" Gerald responded.

"Decades of lies! I don't trust their words; I look at what they do. They parade for peace while they destabilize Iran, Africa and Central America!" Glen said, his square face suffused with indignation. He pointed his finger at Guntram, his voice taking on a controlled but steely edge. "After Xi Jinping stopped giving them all they wanted. They said he was sick, but we were never sure. Where is he? Dead—by a convenient heart attack! Wang was never popular with all of the Party, and he's conveniently captured by terrorists. Now, the Chinese play poor victim to the world while they watch a pro-western and unpredictable General Secretary get killed by the crazies they helped arm!"

"You don't know that!" Guntram countered.

"My young man, you do not know the Chinese. Do you?" Glen said, waving his hand at him. He snorted in disdain for a man he did not trust.

"General," Gerald interrupted. "I believe this conversation is going nowhere. We have less than a day to find a solution to a very serious problem. I suggest we set our reservations aside. I suggest we discuss Guntram's selection for chief negotiator," He leaned forward, and taking a conciliatory toned, looking directly at Glen.

Gerald continued, addressing Glen, "You described Kamal Harazi as a despicable character. I found that an interesting comment, because he is *far* from the most despicable character in the Middle East. Harazi has been helpful in past negotiations with Syria and Iran. It's true, he's had Chinese leanings, but he's been a moderating force in behind-the-scenes negotiations." He turned to face Guntram, "I'm certainly not opposed to using Kamal Harazi, but why him?"

"He has successful experience in negotiating with terrorists in the Middle East. He's actually met Ghazi, and he knows men like him and what they want. Kamal is intelligent, approachable, and he volunteered. We can't let all Muslims become the enemy here." Guntram said with a complete, flat honesty that impressed Neil.

Pressing for more information, Gerald asked, "Why did he volunteer?"

"He's not the only Arab who has volunteered. They're embarrassed by this episode. If either leader dies, Ghazi and his men will have set back Arab interests in the Middle East for decades, so they want to help. As much as the Arabs struggle with Israel's presence, they don't want the Middle East left in nuclear ashes. They know Israel's reaction will be swift and deadly. They have over 20 nuclear weapons ready to be deployed. They also have the equipment to deliver them. Add to that the unconfirmed reports that Iran may also have gotten nuclear weapons from North Korea, and we have an Armageddon in the making!"

Neil watched as Glen glared silently at Guntram. Guntram seemed to gain confidence as he continued, "Kamal Harazi can help us gain and maintain contact. He can give us time. As a foreign negotiator

The Summit

with no authority, his involvement in the Local Negotiating Team will help stretch out negotiations. He will need to communicate with all the superpowers to get approval on any offers. We need that time that he can demand."

"Who else do you want on the LNT?" Gerald asked quickly.

"We want to keep it small and to speak with a single voice," Guntram said, looking at Gerald. "I had planned on having you and two other United States representatives. Lin Feng, head of the Central Security Bureau, will be heading the Chinese contingent. His close friendship with Wang may also help us know better how the General Secretary may respond through all of this."

"That sounds fine to me," Gerald concluded. Then he turned to Dick Bonner, head of the FBI Hostage Rescue Unit. "Dick, I'd like you to join me."

Dick nodded his consent.

"General Westlake," Gerald continued, now facing the general. "Colonel Healey will be reporting to you. I want you on the LNT as well."

"Yes Sir."

Guntram again took the offensive, talking directly to Col. Chuck Healey, "While we negotiate, I want you to work with the Swiss Military and Colonel Tang Wei to develop the best possible hostage rescue plan. If their demands don't change, we may have to take matters into our own hands. We have to be ready, so I want your best men. Seventy percent of hostages killed during rescue attempts are killed by the rescuers. We can't afford those kinds of mistakes in this operation."

"I know the men I want," Chuck said calmly. "They'll be the best we have."

The harsh sound of the secure phone disrupted the cadence of the planning. Gerald Opfer reached quickly, identified the caller, and paused briefly before replying evenly into the receiver, "Mr. Vice President. We are in the middle of our task force briefing with key personnel and Swiss security. Can I put you on speakerphone for the whole group? I'm sure they will be interested in what you have to say." Gerald enabled the speakerphone as the voice of Harold Wallace filled the room.

"Gerald, ladies and gentlemen, I've been talking with congressional leaders. I'm calling to confirm what I'm sure you already know. There can be no exchange. It was agreed in 1980 at the Convention on the Physical Protection of Nuclear Material that it's illegal to arrange for the 'transfer of nuclear material which causes or is likely to cause death.' No intimidation or hostage threats will negate that fact. As aware as I am of the possible cost, there is no room for negotiation. There is only one choice. You must find a way to change their demands or, if necessary, rescue them."

With deliberate slowness and emphasis, Gerald replied, "Mr. Vice President, we realize there's no room for negotiation for the transfer of the requested nuclear weapons. The Swiss team is here, and they have been listening. Even though giving nuclear weapons is out of the question, we still need time and information to develop any workable rescue plan. Col. Chuck Healey and select men from the Delta Force team will be working with their Swiss and Chinese counterparts in developing a rescue plan. Dick Bonner, General John Westlake, and I will be working with the Local Negotiating Team in getting the information and trying to buy the time we need. These terrorists are professionals, sir, and we must lead them on about the possibility of an exchange. We know it isn't possible to give them weapons, but we can't let them believe that. We need your help in avoiding any public statements that negate our efforts."

As the silence followed, Neil watched Guntram Meyer. He remained motionless, his face somber, staring down at the phone as if mesmerized. When the Vice President began to speak, everyone in the conference room was again hanging on his words.

"Gerald, I understand the value of that time," Wallace said slowly, his voice sounding strained. "I also understand how much panic is increased worldwide every moment we do not take a public stand assuring Israel and the world, for that matter, that no bombs will be given. The world leaders will not settle for our private assurances. Many are readying their own weapons. The Israeli Prime Minister has promised to shoot down any American or Chinese plane believed involved in transporting nuclear weapons into the Middle East. They have all but implied that they are ready to deploy and even launch their own arsenal of nuclear weapons if the threat escalates."

Wallace paused. Neil felt a small chill race through his body. *Was the world finally unraveling?*

"You'll have my silence until midnight tomorrow," the Vice President said with a slight sigh. His voice was anguished. "After that time, I can't promise that there won't be a public statement." He paused again.

"Gentlemen, you have a challenge of immense proportions. The world is being held hostage in Geneva. Our prayers and the prayers of the world are with you. China is also a victim of this catastrophe. We can't afford for any of our rescue efforts to be misconstrued as an attack on General Secretary Wang. You must work with the Chinese and the Swiss to make your best effort. Keep me posted on your progress. I know your time is valuable, so I won't take any more of it."

"Thank you, sir. We'll keep you informed," Gerald said in a voice that displayed more confidence than anyone in the room felt. They heard the phone click, again leaving each of them with their own doubts and fears.

Looking at his watch, Guntram interrupted, cutting off any retort by Lawson. "I was supposed to be with the Chinese ten minutes ago. In light of the time constraints we are facing, I suggest those of you involved with the negotiating and rescue teams come along. We've got a big job ahead of us all."

"I'll meet you there," Col. Healey said with an even tone, "Major John Kerins is picking up Rip Devins and two of his men at the airport now. They're returning from maneuvers stateside. As soon as they arrive, we'll join you. By the way, for the record, the Delta Force code name for the rescue operation is *Urgent Eagle*… If that's okay, we could use that as the combined team."

"That's as good a name as any," Guntram agreed. "We'll suggest that with the Chinese team. I think a shared name for the operation will be the least of our issues."

"I hope all of us can remember how to work together or learn how quickly!" Neil said, looking directly at Glen Lawson. No response was expected; none was given.

CHAPTER THIRTY-ONE

DOCTORS MOVE FROM CARNAGE TO CARING IN ACTION

Hôpitaux Universitaires de Genève (HUG)
Geneva, Switzerland
4:17 PM

*"He went to him and bound up his wounds, pouring on
oil and wine. Then he set him on his own donkey and
brought him to an inn and took care of him."*
Luke 10:34 (NIV)

The afternoon blue sky at 4:17 p.m. still highlighted the bright colors that surrounded the Hôpitaux Universitaires de Genève, called HUG for short. The repeated shriek of fast-moving ambulances bringing a steady stream of patients from the nearby palace grounds had only now begun to slow. The medical teams were working feverously to save those who could be saved.

Within the hospital, the operating rooms hummed with activity. Surgeons from Lucerne and other Swiss Cantons were arriving to relieve the exhausted local physicians.

Doctors Move from Carnage to Caring in Action

Walking down the long hospital corridor, Brian contemplated how glad he was to get a break from the constant surgery. As he passed OR after OR, he could see clusters of figures bent over what he knew were seriously wounded patients. He had never seen war. Now, after today, he knew he never wanted to again.

A hospital gurney approached them with a scrub nurse and an anesthesiologist attending. Brian could see the anesthesiologist matter-of-factly holding the patient's shrapnel-riddled chin back while the patient retched violently. He could see no emotion on the face of the nurse as she wiped the vomit. They were healthcare workers doing their job. But the image of the tortured face of the patient stayed with Brian. He shuddered. He was not sure he would ever really get used to the feeling of helplessness at the sheer numbers.

As Brian pushed through the swinging doors and walked out of the OR's "clean area" and passed the main OR desk into the doctors' dressing room, he became aware of the rustle of the paper booties over his shoes as he moved towards his locker. He took off his hood and finally lowered his mask. Taking a deep, unencumbered breath, he looked at his watch. Dr. Chen would be off soon.

Brian was amazed by the sudden flood of relief and calmness that swept over him as he thought of her. She evoked something in him he hadn't felt in quite a while. His face cracked a smile. He laughed to himself as he thought of Chen Li unceremoniously changing into her scrub suit in the doctor's dressing room, previously in Swiss history the domain of men only. Before he could warn her, she had entered the room, the surprised male surgeons in skivvies searching for clothing. Oblivious to the excited clatter of male voices emanating from the dressing room, the good doctor had approached a vacant locker, grabbed a pale green shirt and pants, and proceeded to undress.

The Summit

Brian had decided that it was no time to be shy and had enthusiastically joined in the task at hand but found it difficult to concentrate. He had to admit that he had given up long ago on the assumption that doctors could be totally detached when looking at the female body. He hoped he never would be. Seeing Chen Li's nearly naked body was the most sensual sight he had seen in months.

He had broken his stare as he scurried into his green scrub pants. He had seldom felt embarrassment, but the rush of blood to his face and the almost boyish grin that crossed his face must have been something to see as Dr. Chen glanced at this fumbling eminent surgeon. He laughed at himself trying to decipher what she must have been feeling.

Momentarily shaking off his memories, Brian removed and threw away his mask and surgical boot covers on his way to the adjacent lounge. In sharp contrast to the hustle and bustle in the OR, the surgical lounge seemed a luxurious, isolated oasis. Only the unattended blare of the television sought his company. He walked to the sink filled with thirty-odd coffee cups mostly half-filled, a testimonial to the urgent crisis that had demanded caffeine but had allowed no time for cleanup. He washed out two cups and refilled the coffee maker as best he could. He hoped his poor track record making coffee would not add to the surgical team's problems.

The television commentator's sharp voice interrupted Brian's thoughts. He moved to the set and turned up the volume.

"In spite of pressure from Israel, there is as yet no clear statement from Washington on whether the nuclear weapons demanded will or will not be given to Al-Haram," the newscaster said calmly with a detachment that to Brian seemed almost bereft of sense. "A spokesman for Vice President Wallace did say, '*The United States will negotiate for the release of both Presidents in good faith within the constraints established by international law."*

The news anchor continued. "It must be noted that under the provisions of the 1980 Convention on the Physical Protection of Nuclear Material, the transfer of atomic weapons is illegal. However, when questioned, officials refused to comment on whether that specifically ruled out negotiation for the release of the hostages. Highly critical comments were voiced in New York at an emergency session of the UN, when Moshe Peres, the UN ambassador from Israel, demanded an immediate strong response."

Brian watched as the fiery Moshe Peres spoke from New York, "Israel denounces the terrorists' attack on the Geneva Summit and the resulting demands. This is but another in a series of attempts to annihilate the Jewish people of the world. We will not stand still for another Holocaust at our expense. We demand the immediate repudiation of any and all attempts to negotiate with the terrorists, a blackout of media coverage of their demands, and strong international reprisals for countries that provide havens and openly promote terrorist activities. It is time to send a clear message to all such groups that the world will not tolerate their madness."

"Whoa," Brian said quietly to no one, "What a mess."

His words were barely out of his mouth when Dr. Chen entered the lounge. He greeted her with a smile. Staring at her, he knew he must look like some moon-struck adolescent. Then she smiled, a completely irresistible smile, warm and wide, taking in her whole face. However, the unfolding crisis on the television screen took their attention. Chen Li moved next to Brian's chair, lightly leaning against his shoulder as they both listened.

The commentator continued evenly. "Although Washington and Beijing refused to give direct assurances to Israel, moderate Arab leaders meeting in Damascus for OPEC negotiations came close to giving such support. Saudi Arabian Foreign Minister Abdul Safad, at a press conference, called for world calm."

The words from Abdul Safad were reassuring, "I speak for my own country and for the majority of Arabs in the Middle East when I denounce the abhorrent attack on the Geneva Peace Summit by Al-Haram. In the name of Islam and all that is good, we call upon Ghazi Saud and his men to surrender and release the hostages. We do not want war with Israel, nor do we condone any terrorist attack. We do not want nuclear weapons in the Middle East. We will cooperate in any way to contribute to the quick and safe release of the hostages. Our prayers, along with the rest of the world, are with the United States and China along with their leaders in this time of crisis."

"More about the hostage crisis and Chinese reaction when we get back," said the commentator abruptly, giving way to an innocuous stream of commercials that seemed oddly out of place.

Brian looked up to Dr. Chen. "It's good to see you," Brian said. "Would you like some coffee? After the work you've just put in, you probably need some."

"Yes, I would," she said, her smile beginning to fade. He could see in her eyes that it had been a tough afternoon. Brian poured her a cup of the brown brew.

"You may need to add water to dilute this poison. I confess I made it," he said with a smile.

"I'll trust you," she said softly. After tasting it, she made a face, "That is, I'll trust you if you have some, too."

"Don't worry, I already have. I need it just to stay awake," he replied. There was silence as she turned toward the window. He saw the late afternoon sunlight touching her face as if trying to recharge her batteries.

"I now understand the words of the poet Yulia Drurina," Chen Li said thoughtfully as she stared out the window. "She was a nurse. She was wounded in war and wrote from her hospital bed, *'Only once I saw a fistfight—once awake, and a thousand times in dreams. He who says war is not dreadful knows nothing about war.'"*

Brian said nothing, waiting for what he sensed was still to come. As Chen Li turned to look at him, her eyes were moist. She bit her lip, shaking her head. "Those men and women we saw today have been to war, Brian. I hope I will never see such bodies again. I will not have to see more to remember."

Brian reached out, put his arm around her shoulder, and pulled her to him. He said nothing, staring with her out the window across the lawn. She sighed a heavy sound that seemed to come from somewhere infinitely deep inside.

Brian shook his head sadly, speaking but hardly recognizing his own voice, "Nothing can prepare one for this kind of carnage."

Again, the television commentator's words brought them back, "In China today, *China Daily*, the official state newspaper, has again stated that the terrorist attack was carried out by 'imperialist reactionary forces' precipitated by the US and Israeli excesses in the Middle East. *China Daily* also reported that both leaders are being held hostage but gave no mention of the terrorists' demands."

"I can't believe it!" Brian shouted. "It's always our fault—the bloody imperialists! That's ridiculous!"

The Summit

"I'm sorry," Chen Li. said, searching for the right words. This time Brian felt her restraining touch on his hand. "I know it's hard to understand. But in China, we do not expect the whole truth, but many seek and know the truth. The Internet, even though monitored, has made it hard to control information."

"I know, but just this once. After all, it's their General Secretary, too," Brian said still frustrated but placing his hand over hers and trying to smile. "Look, I'm sorry. I know it isn't you saying that. I wish all the Chinese were more like you."

"Many are. We have many wonderful people, and they want change. We have been hopeful that General Secretary Wang would help make that happen," she said with a hope now more fleeting.

"Has General Secretary Wang brought any improvements?"

"Yes, I think he has and is trying to bring more," Chen Li said with pride. "My brother Tian is an example."

"I didn't know you had a brother," Brian said with interest.

"There is a lot you do not know about me. Yes, I have a brother, but I do not see him often. He lives in Shanghai. He is the general director of a manufacturing plant there. He has told me that he is pleased with the support Wang has provided. He can now make his own business plan without submitting it for central planning approval. He can now boost a typical worker's monthly wages by 50% if the person works hard. My brother's plant is also installing robots. They are modernizing the equipment that has been in place for twenty years."

"Is the pay enough, even with incentives," Brian said thoughtfully.

"It is more than enough for most Chinese. The state gives us most basic necessities free, or at least very cheaply. Like most people, I save most of my earnings. But everything most want to buy—the luxuries, such as nice clothes–they often do not have in public stores. But even

Doctors Move from Carnage to Caring in Action

that is changing. There is more quality in the stores today. I think the incentives are working. If you come to China, you will see well-dressed young people, many in very fancy cars. For the men, that attracts many pretty young women. They like that."

"Now, attracting pretty young women. I can understand that incentive. With that motivation, we may make capitalists out of China yet!" Brian said, grinning.

"I can't let you soften me up," she said, leaning towards him, their faces only inches apart. "I'm sure you are part of the dreaded American Imperialist Reactionary Forces we must resist."

"Okay, I am part of a reactionary force. I'm reacting to getting to know you! By the way, did you catch the initials for this hospital—HUG? I think you deserve one." Brian said laughing, pulling her to him in a hug he did not want to break.

CHAPTER THIRTY-TWO

FROM THE PAIN OF CAPTIVITY TO THE POWER OF PRAYER

**Palace of Nations Conference Center
Geneva, Switzerland**

*"Because you have kept my word about patient
endurance, I will keep you from the hour of trial
coming on the whole world to try those who
dwell on the earth."*
Revelations 3:10 (ESV)

The terrorists had looked in again and left. Like clockwork, the hostages were checked and left alone for what seemed to Connie like thirty-minute intervals. By now, she was beginning to distinguish the differences in the approaching footsteps. The quick, energetic steps of Gamul Saud, Ghazi's brother, matched his temperament. He seemed always agitated, almost hyperactive, his eyes darting from side to side. He barely entered the room, except to snarl and unleash an occasional Iranian epitaph, or at least what sounded like one to her.

In contrast, the gate of Abdul Gosaibi was slow and controlled. He was always more thorough and seemed less emotionally charged than Gamul Saud. Each time Abdul visited, he checked the ropes that bound them. He would say little. When he did talk, it would be in broken English. Although his tone was not friendly, he was approachable. On two occasions, he had taken time to feed them ration biscuits by hand to supplement the hostages' minimal meals.

On these occasions, both Wang and Freeman tried to be friendly. Their advances had not been encouraged, but they had not been punished. Unfortunately, Abdul rarely came. The President now listened as he heard Gamal scurrying down the hallway.

As the President tried to shift her weight in her chair, the ropes again tore into her wrists. She grimaced and then again surveyed the room. Unfortunately, there were no windows; any rescue or escape would not be easy. Connie quickly reviewed in her mind the route they had taken to reach the room. As best as she could remember, they were now right next to the Council Chamber. Intuitively, she knew she needed to keep her sense of observation and memory sharp. Since she had time for review, she would make sure she would not be found wanting when her observations would prove useful.

The President looked momentarily at Wang as he patiently tried to loosen the ropes that bound him. The man had a resourcefulness and persistence she had come to respect. Every time they had been left alone, Wang had insisted on ten minutes or more of rehashing and rehashing, elaborating and re-elaborating every conceivable plan and contingency both could remember. They had shared observations about the terrorists they had met and about strategies for dealing with them and their outbursts.

There had been little time wasted. Unfortunately, there were few tangible results for their efforts. They knew approximately where they were, but they didn't know how long they would be there or how to get that information out to any rescue team. As their conversations had become redundant, both gave way to long periods of silence. Even when they had talked, memories of Martin and her children kept intruding her thoughts. She took time to pray for their health and peace, *"God, be with them. Comfort them. Give Martin strength and the right words to reassure them as best he can. God, if it be your will, help us find a way out."*

Now, she saw Wang's shoulders slump with a sigh and his eyes move sullenly to meet hers. The ropes had again proven to be secure.

"They say men faced with death think mostly about people—people that are important to them," Freeman said gently. "Do you have people you're thinking about?"

Wang stirred slightly in his chair. He remained silent for what seemed minutes. Connie wondered what he was thinking. His hooded eyes revealed so little. Then, she observed a slight smile at the corners of Wang's mouth.

"I've been thinking about a lot of people," Connie went first, amazed at the calmness that swept over her as she talked to this man she hardly knew. "I know this must be hard on our families. I know my husband is strong, but this is so frightening. He doesn't know what has happened to us, or even if we are alive."

Giving away again to silence, she shook her head sadly, moisture coming to the corners of her eyes. "He's had to go through so much for me. He doesn't even like me being President. I know he would rather I not run again." She turned her head toward Wang, her voice reflective and strong, "Do you think of death?"

"We are people too, Madam President," General Secretary Wang said, looking at the President. "Death is easy; life is hard. Mei will

From the Pain of Captivity to the Power of Prayer

shed her tears, but she is a strong woman. My wife knew this could happen. She will be fine."

"Yes. Martin is strong, too. I'm not worried about him, but he doesn't have many people to talk to in Washington. I know seeing us with Ghazi will reassure him that I'm alive, but it'll worry my children," Connie said, looking at Wang. There was pain in the General Secretary's face, a certain admission. Connie looked away to give him the personal privacy so many men needed. She continued.

"It's funny, Martin and I planned on being in the mountains this week until the Summit changed all that. Frankly, I'd rather be canoeing on the lake, smelling the clean air, even preparing food on that lousy cabin stove. Yes, this President does cook." They both smiled. Connie let her laugh be heard.

"Do you have a special place you go to when you want to get away?" Connie asked, trying to make a connection.

"You know I do, Madam President," Wang said, smiling.

"You're right. I'm sure we both know more about each other than we even care to know or would care to admit," the President confessed. "Although I know the places you go, I don't know which one is special to you. I'm sure like Presidents, General Secretaries must go many places they don't really enjoy. For me, my mountain retreat is not just a place; it's mountain therapy, a kind of wilderness healing place. Unfortunately, it does give the Secret Service team fits."

"There are many places one has to visit as General Secretary because of their connection to China's revolution. Of course, you must visit Shaoshan, the hometown of Mao Zedong. Of course, any leader must read some of the stone tablets of Mao's poems. Mao's Memorial Garden is beautiful. I like it better than his poems."

"Give me gardens over poems any day," Connie said, smiling.

"You must visit Yan'an. It is considered the holy land of China's Communist Party revolution. It was Mao Zedong's revolutionary base area when the Red Army arrived there in 1935. You can actually see some of the caves hollowed out from the local plateau where men were forced to stay."

"You have your history, and so do we. Are any of them a refuge for you? A place you long to visit again?"

"Yes, Jinggang Mountain. It is located near Ji'an City, in the Jiangxi Province. It is rich in historical sites, including the former residence of Mao Zedong, the first hospital of China's Red Army, a revolution museum, and a battle site. But if you visit them once, you have seen what you can see. It is the area I love. It is a place with towering mountains, graceful waterfalls, lush trees, and always adds a spectacular sea of clouds. My family loves to take time there. We even hike the mountain trails."

"It sounds beautiful," Connie said, relishing her own refuge in the mountains.

"My family almost always comes when we go there. My little granddaughter loves it there, and I love to be with her. It, too, renews my health to be there," Wang said slowly. "Our jobs are demanding, are they not?"

Connie said, "But I don't think even they wanted it to get this demanding."

"I, too, am sure there are some in Beijing who are quietly celebrating my misfortune as well," Wang replied in a more serious tone. Then, with a disarming smile, he asked, "Do you always use humor?"

"Probably will as long as I live," she confessed. "But it's gotten me in my share of trouble over the years. If you ask my press secretary, he could list the occasions my timing and choice of stories were not always on target. I do mean well, but the press doesn't always seem to agree. I wouldn't change it. When you live on the edge of crisis every day, laughter seems one of the few ways to keep perspective. As my grandfather used to say, *'the crisis of today is the boring history of tomorrow.'* There's too much crisis and not enough laughter."

"I don't think your humor will work here!"

"Here's hoping we remain part of the boring history, not the dead history," she countered, not sure her response was even close to funny.

"I don't plan on dying soon," Wang said.

"Nor I, but I bet the money at Monte Carlo isn't on us surviving," replied the President, still trying to keep it light. For a moment there was silence.

"Trust does not come easy, Wang Da," Connie said with flat honesty, in a controlled tone. "When there's no trust, you always assume the worst about your enemy. I remember when President Reagan quoted what President John Kennedy said after meeting the Russian leader, Khrushchev, *'There is something else where the heart is supposed to be.'* Even when a number of Americans wouldn't vote for me, most still trust me and my word. Few, if any in America trust you or China."

"We have hearts, but we also have memories of past wars. We do want peace for our children, good jobs, prosperity like America has. Unfortunately, I fear that Plato was right when he said, *'Only the Dead have seen the end of war!'*"

"I don't want to believe that; I want to work for peace," Freeman replied thoughtfully, "I don't want war. I really don't want war. I've seen a different side of you as we have faced Al-Haram together. I want them to see that side of you, to know more about the Chinese people and their dreams."

"One of my aides has said that U.S. Presidents are like *'Mad Bulls.'* They see red everywhere because their eyes are filled with the blood of madness. Americans think that they alone are good," Wang said calmly. He looked away, staring at a bronze statue in the corner of the room. "We Chinese are people, too. We are your equals, Madam President."

"I am painfully aware of how equal we all are today," Freeman replied. "We both have lost many friends in the last few hours. All of them are dead. This kind of death reminds me of war, not distant statistics. Colleagues and friends we worked with are no longer alive. I don't want war, and I don't want any more to die."

Wang said nothing. Connie confided, "I want our trust to grow. I think one of the most dangerous things that could happen is for any leader to believe in the inevitability of war. Believing that, by itself, can make it happen. Unfortunately, I feel many in my country believe war with your country is inevitable. I came here to fight that."

"Keep struggling, Madam President. I will try to join you," Wang said thoughtfully. "With the death of Min Jian, my biggest believer in winning wars has died with him. Both our countries pay a heavy price for our fears, do we not?"

"I'm afraid we do. We can't afford to blow up the world. We're both on it. We can't let these terrorists do that either. I hope it's not too late for the world to learn another way."

"A man with outward courage dares to die. A man with inward courage dares to live. We must both dare to live, Madam President."

"I have been praying for that, President Wang. May it be so."

CHAPTER THIRTY-THREE

EXPENDABLE HOSTAGES IN THE FACE OF IMPOSSIBLE DEMANDS

**Chinese Embassy
Geneva, Switzerland**

"And the nations shall know that the house of Israel went into captivity for their iniquity, because they dealt so treacherously with me that I hid my face from them and gave them into the hand of their adversaries, and they all fell by the sword."
Ezekiel 39:23 (ESV)

Lin Feng, head of China's Central Security Bureau, had been on a whirlwind schedule all day. Within minutes of the attack, he had met with the Community Party leaders remaining in Beijing and then headed for his waiting plane. His flight from Beijing to Geneva had been entirely too long. His private isolation had unleashed a myriad of memories and potential nightmares. Now, as he walked up the steps from his dark blue limousine into the Chinese Embassy not more than four hundred meters from the Palace of Nations, he saluted the uniformed military guard and turned down the hallway past the illuminated lobby.

The stark gray, windowless walls provided a drab backdrop to the hustle of human activity within the embassy walls. He tried to keep his focus, but his mind moved to the image of destruction he saw from the back seat of his limousine. His friend was in there. *My God, I hope he's alive.*

Lin Feng shifted his briefcase to the other hand as he reached for the conference room door. Behind the oversized conference table sat General Jin Yuan, staring at him from his padded vinyl armchair. Flanking him were General Zhang Ming and Colonel Tang Wei, surrounded by the ever-present ornaments of Chinese leadership, including the obligatory framed portrait of Xi Jinping.

"Comrades," Lin Feng said in a voice that seemed even to him somehow far away.

"Lin Feng. It is good to have you here," General Jin said, raising his head slightly. All three men watched Lin Feng intently for a moment, not making a move. He nodded to Zhang and Tang. Only Tang returned it in kind. Zhang stared back, his narrowed eyes ignoring him with the ferocity of sworn enemies.

General Jin continued, "The head of Swiss security, Guntram Meyer, will be here shortly to brief us on his meeting with the Americans."

"What do you know about the hostages?" Lin Feng asked, trying to remain calm and self-assured.

"It is not good. Of course, you have heard that Foreign Minister Min Jian is dead, as are Shen Kwong and Mun Pai."

"I was told on board the plane. A terrible loss," Lin Feng said softly in a sullen voice. "Do we know anything about President Wang's condition?"

Expendable Hostages in the Face of Impossible Demands

"We have seen both leaders via a taped message. As of fourteen hundred hours, both were alive," General Jin said, leaning forward to emphasize the last few words. "The Americans have informed us that Freeman, using prearranged codes, was able to verify that they were being held together and that they were bound. Since the terrorists have nothing else to bargain with, I assume both are still alive."

"I bring you a consensus opinion from the rest of the Party leaders. In the event of a hostage situation, there is to be no bargaining," he said with emphasis. He could feel his heart beating very fast. His lips tightened, and he was silent for long seconds. He continued with just the right amount of derision, "Understandably, there will be no bombs, no ransom. It was sad how quickly many made it clear that General Secretary Wang was expendable."

General Jin's eyes fixed cooly on Feng, "We have been in contact with Beijing ourselves. This is no surprise. It is not a personal matter. You must be aware that all of us are expendable, comrade. None of us want harm to come to the General Secretary, but negotiation is out of the question and always has been."

"I am aware of that, General, but do not expect me to enjoy it," Lin Feng said, not trying to hide the bitterness in his voice. Ever since the Defense Minister had been demoted to candidate status in Communist Party Leadership, Jin and the rest of the military had waited patiently for Wang's fall from grace. Feng knew they hoped this would provide the fall they desired.

Feng turned to stare directly at General Zhang Ming. Just under six feet tall, he was thin, lanky, almost sinewy. The expression on his bespectacled face was as rigid as his posture in his chair, and his eyes were angry. As an old guard Americanologist and former Communist Party spokesman, he had been promoted to First Deputy Foreign

Minister. Feng spoke directly to General Zhang, "I hope none of us enjoy this."

"We have a duty to uphold the dignity of the Chinese State. No individual, including General Secretary Wang, comes ahead of that," the General warned. An atavistic tension laced the air as he turned to General Shen Gao. "General Gao, do you question my motives?"

Feng's fist hit the conference table with a startling fury. He stuck out his chin belligerently. "We have already lost an entire negotiating team! These terrorists have attacked at the very soul of our country. We had all better be concerned. If individuals are so expendable, it is worth dying for, is it not, General Zhang? I loathe ineptness; I cannot tolerate it. More than ineptness, I am disgusted with bureaucratic cowardice. I have no time for such impediments. Our General Secretary, my friend, is being held hostage. That matters to me!"

"Be more specific! Are you now accusing me of cowardice? Or worse, treason?" Zhang. replied calmly. He crossed his arms over his chest. Although he did not raise his voice, the rebuke was clear. He continued in quiet contempt, "If anyone is guilty of ineptness, it is the men you assigned to—"

"My men died because the foreign ministry did not take our warnings seriously!" Feng said fiercely, "We provided your department with access to a number of dossiers, including one on Ghazi. Why have you not taken advantage of such information? Did you find it convenient to just disregard our intel?"

"This is madness!" Zhang flared, his face red through his neck. "You bury your warnings in piles of reports no one has time to read. If your people were so aware of this threat, why did you not protect your friend yourself if you knew what Ghazi could do!"

Expendable Hostages in the Face of Impossible Demands

"He was one of many terrorists we follow! We had no way of knowing he was the key figure behind this new ... Al-Haram."

"Enough!" General Jin interrupted, his voice raised. "You both stumble where no rocks exist. Guntram Meyer will be here soon; we must be prepared."

Feng said nothing. His heart pounded as his mind struggled with Zhang's words, words he had been saying to himself for hours. With what he knew, he should have been able to stop the attack.

"From your conversations, what has been the reaction in Beijing?" asked General Jin cautiously. Lin Feng grabbed onto the new direction, like a drowning swimmer thrown a life preserver.

"*China Daily* has given minimal details. There has been no public announcement of Min Jian's death or of the terrorists' demands," he said evenly. "But the Western barrage of media news has reached even the streets of Beijing. Many know, and the word is spreading fast. I fear many have gotten used to the loss of many of our leaders over the last few years. The public reaction is not our problem, is it Zhang? This is China. Our people will take care of themselves."

"Our people know too much!" Zhang replied. "Wang's liberal ideas have seen to that. He has attacked the military and crippled the Communist Party old guard."

"He's gotten rid of the dead weight–those who failed to live up to their responsibilities."

"Is it not your team's responsibility to protect Communist Party leaders, comrade? Maybe you should be replaced?"

"There will be no..." Lin Feng broke off in mid-sentence. It was the same scathing indictment he had come to expect from Zhang. It would not change no matter what he said. There was no time for wasted words. Taking a deep breath and turning from Zhang's gaze,

The Summit

Feng asked General Jin Yuan, "Is there any plan established to deal with the terrorists?"

"You, Zhang, and I will be on the Local Negotiating Team with Swiss and American representatives," the General answered. It would again be the usual bureaucracy—the Party, the Army, and the special forces that do the work, thought Feng. Understanding how China was ruled required little more than understanding that fragile balance. He watched as General Jin deliberately paused and then exhaled before continuing, "Kamal Harazi has been chosen as the negotiator."

"The Americans have accepted Harazi?" Feng asked, his eyebrows raised.

"To my knowledge, there has been no problem," General Jin said. "Colonel Tang Wei will be working with the Americans and the Swiss to develop a contingency rescue plan."

"We have already talked with Swiss security," interjected Colonel Tang in a conciliatory tone. Lin Feng. had liked him immediately, a man just under his height, but sturdier built and more graceful. Tang was only forty-one years old, but he possessed a quick mind. He was organized and open, much superior to what Feng had come to expect from the Chinese military. "The parameter at the Palace of Nations is secure. We know the terrorists have a limited force of not more than eight men. But the Swiss are nervous. They want nothing to go wrong. We and the Americans are to be involved in coordinating the rescue."

"I do not think that is wise!" General Zhang warned, leaning forward and pointing a finger at both Tang and Feng. "I have told you. Let it be a Swiss matter! It is their country. It is their failure! Let them fail or succeed on their own!"

Expendable Hostages in the Face of Impossible Demands

"We know your position, but the decision has been made," General Jin interrupted Zhang. "We will work with the Swiss and the Americans to do what we can to secure the release of the hostages."

"You are playing into their hands!" Zhang said testily.

"Who's hands? The Americans or Zhang's supporters?" Lin Feng asked, irked by his continued resistance. He again felt his own anger welling up.

The conference room phone rang. Feng jumped in response. General Jin reached for the phone and listened. Covering the receiver, he confided, "Gentlemen, it is General Williamson. This should be our invitation. Americans love invitations." A forced laughter filled the room.

"Gen. Williamson. It has been years since we talked." General Jin said with an amiable candor that did not match the feeling in the room. Feng watched the others around the table, but there was no change in their expressions.

"Yes, those were under very different circumstances. But we have worked together before. We now need to do so again."

There was another pause. "Yes, that will be fine. We would like you to join us. Until then." General Jin replaced the receiver and stared at the three men. Feng wished he could read the smile that crinkled the lines embedded in the General's face.

"They are on their way here. We shall soon see what it is like to work with an enemy," Jin said.

CHAPTER THIRTY-FOUR

A COMFORTING TIME FOR TEA AND TEARS

> The Domaine de Châteauvieux
> Geneva, Switzerland

> *"Love does not delight in evil but rejoices with the truth. It always protects, always trusts, always hopes, always perseveres."*
> *1 Corinthians 13: 6-7 (NIV)*

The sunlight filtered through the spreading branches of the cedars lining the street as his Secret Service car moved down the country lane. The sky was clear. Martin wished it belonged to another time, another city, a time and place where Connie and he would be together.

His last call had been one of the most difficult ones he had ever made. The hours of news reports had left him utterly exhausted. Although he had tried to close his eyes for a quick nap, he couldn't come close to letting go of reality. Still, he had left instructions not to be disturbed under any circumstances. Martin had wanted to keep people out because there was no one who could really understand.

While watching television coverage, he had heard the news commentator listing the Summit activities that had been planned but would never occur. The sound of her name, Ma Mei, and their canceled tea had pried a wedge into his self-imposed isolation. He usually hated teas. It was a male thing, and he didn't like tea. But almost immediately, the thought had echoed in his mind–*Ma Mei would understand what he was feeling, maybe the only one who could.*

Martin hadn't placed the call immediately; he struggled with his own fears and his perception of the woman he had met for the first time the day before. Attractive, Ma Mei had already won over many Western journalists. Petite with a well-proportioned figure and stylish dark hair, Ma Mei was more than attractive. She was a stylish but intelligent professor of Communist philosophy at Shanghai Jiao Tong University.

The staid, colorless, and submissive image of Chinese wives died slowly. Ma Mei was doing her part to kill that stereotype. The media had missed the opportunity to play up a "Style War" between the first "spouses" of America and China. Unfortunately, the style battle with any male spouse was a war lost before it began. Martin laughed. If it were up to him, he'd have one nice suit and call it his "style statement." Thankfully, Ma Mei had downplayed the attention to appearance as "a little silly."

But it was Ma Mei's smile and warmth that had impressed Martin during their first meeting. She was approachable and pleasant. Any discomfort he felt melted as they shook hands and their eyes met. From that moment on, Martin had actually looked forward to talking with her more. Only the shocking attacks had blunted those feelings and the opportunity.

A tea, yes, a tea. Martin thought back to what she had said about the proposed visit. Ma Mei had said to the press, "We will talk about people, not policy. It's a chance to get acquainted and develop better understanding." When asked what they could hope to do for peace,

The Summit

she had responded with genuine candor in broken English, *"All we can do, we will do."*

The thought again crossed his mind. She would understand. *She would be the only one to understand.* Martin remembered the book *Family of Man*, that Connie and he had on their coffee table at their mountain retreat. His mind raced to the heart-rending picture of two women comforting each other in grief. He had never forgotten the caption, "Women are women's best ally." He had wondered if it extended to men.

Sitting on the bed at the chateau, Martin had lifted the handset in his bedroom to call. An operator's voice answered. Martin gave him the Chinese Embassy number. After what had seemed an interminable time, his call was answered by a switchboard operator who spoke in a gruff voice in French with a Chinese accent. *"Bonjour, L'Ambassade de le Pays de Chine."* Mustering what authority he could find, Martin identified himself in English and asked to be put through to Ma Mei.

Martin had known that he would not get Ma Mei, but he was not prepared for the myriad of buffers that would be thrown in his way to even reach her. He had had a difficult time convincing anyone that it was important to talk to the General Secretary's wife. He had remembered being briefed about the insignificant role wives played in China. As impressive as she was, *China Daily* seldom even mentioned Ma Mei's name.

Finally, he found the right message. The tea was an appointment that must be kept to create some semblance of normalcy. It would also give the press a positive story to focus on. Eventually, Martin's persistence paid off. He had a brief and somewhat awkward conversation with the Chinese first lady. Although Ma Mei seemed a bit confused by his call, she had agreed to meet him for their scheduled tea.

A Comforting Time for Tea and Tears

Martin had had no time to struggle with his own reservations. It had taken all his energy to convince his Secret Service escorts. He decided not to argue, but to inform them of the meeting. He had summoned Agents Oren and McAfferty to his quarters to inform them that he was leaving to go to the Chinese Embassy for the scheduled tea. Their initial resistance faded as they realized he had already committed to being there.

The agents tried to reach Glen Lawson, but he was in a closed planning meeting. When Martin had become indignant and threatened to call his own taxi, they had acquiesced. He had hated acting that way. He respected both men, but he knew that he had to be with Ma Mei.

To protect him, the Secret Service men had taken back roads and had left the limousine in favor of the dark green Ford LTD that would be less of a target for the eager reporters they knew would be near the embassy.

Martin had sat in silence for the entire trip. With only a rare scene to divert his attention, he was lost in his thoughts. He tried to imagine how anyone could have conceived such an attack. Then, as always, his thoughts came back to Connie–her love he treasured and the loss he already felt. He thought again about Mei. *Would she really be able to understand?*

Martin was aware of the car slowing, then stopping. He heard the voices of the surprised press and saw the flash of cameras as they rushed toward the embassy gate. He saw the Chinese flag fluttering in the breeze as the gate opened and the car moved into the embassy compound. The embassy struck him like a Chinese city within walls. *Was it to keep others out or their own in?* Actually, he could understand such feelings. What privacy and freedom they could find was treasured by any spouse married to any superpower leader.

Martin saw Oren roll down the window and show their security clearance papers. He was aware he was undergoing scrutiny by means of a visual monitoring system. They were directed past the main compound to the main residence where they stopped. Agents Oren and McAfferty escorted him to the door. He pressed the buzzer. A raspy voice came through the speaker, requesting his name, citizenship, and business. Martin smiled, but then patiently supplied the information. He was told to wait. The delay bothered him. They knew he was coming. After what seemed like a long minute, the front door swung open.

The Chinese security guard looked alert but nervous. It was apparent that very few were ever allowed to enter this residence. Martin showed his pass and told his men to wait outside. As he went inside through a small foyer, he passed an abbreviated hall that connected the entry room to the main suite. The otherwise dark hallway was illuminated by electric candles. Martin was struck with the silence, was it the deceptive silence in the eye of the storm? He would soon find out.

He was led into a large L-shaped room. It was spacious and airy. A pair of high windows overlooked a beautiful private terrace and garden. The large walnut coffee table at the center of the room was adorned with fresh-cut flowers and a silver tea service. A sudden movement from the far end of the room drew his attention.

Ma Mei entered Martin's eyes locked on her. She was wearing a black suit with a straight skirt and a striking, off-white scarf. Martin had his normal classic suit. He smiled, took a deep breath, exhaled. As soon as he saw Mei smile, he knew he had made the right decision.

"Mr. Freeman. I am so glad you called," Ma Mei said in a pleasing voice, touched with a hint of anxiety.

A Comforting Time for Tea and Tears

"Thank you for letting me come," Martin said gently, his tone soft. An odd kind of calmness washed over him as he reached out to take her hand. "May I call you Mei?"

"Yes, of course!" she said in a hushed voice, squeezing Martin's hand before letting go. "But my English is not too good."

"I understand," Martin said, smiling back at her. "But your English is far better than my Mandarin." Pausing as they moved to the chairs near the coffee table.

"How are you?" Martin asked softly. Tears formed in the corner of Mei's eyes. She looked toward the window, wiping her eyes with her handkerchief. Martin already knew from her face what she was feeling.

"I came, not because I have a lot to say, but because I wanted to be with you," Martin said evenly, watching Mei as she tried to recover her composure. "I wanted to be near where my wife is being held, but they wouldn't let me go, and I understand that." Now, it was Martin's turn to feel moisture form in his eyes. "They said it was too dangerous and too much of a distraction."

"I, too, feel I can do nothing," Mei responded, again looking directly into Martin's empathetic eyes.

"I was tired of watching the television coverage, and I felt so alone. I felt no one else would understand except you, Mei. That is why I called. That is why I am here."

"I am glad you have come. Your wife and my husband are together. We..." Mei said in a choked voice. She bit her lip, shaking her head side to side. Her voice was anguished now, "I'm sorry." Mei burst into tears.

Martin wanted to put his arm around Mei, but it was too familiar to risk. The silence and shared tears brought them closer.

The Summit

"At least, from what we currently know, they're alive." His words were as much to reassure himself as Mei.

"Yes, I saw them," Mei said, wiping the tears from her eyes. "They looked as well as can be expected."

Mei paused, looking directly at him. "Why did this have to happen? They don't deserve this! They won't ever give them the weapons they want. They can't. They're going to kill them!"

The sky was clear—there was no rain and none in the forecast. But the moisture of their tears provided all that was necessary to bring them together.

CHAPTER THIRTY-FIVE

HE IS NOT TO COME OUT OF THIS ALIVE

> The Beau Rivage Hotel
> Geneva, Switzerland

"Those who seek my life lay snares for me, and those who seek to injure me have threatened destruction, and they devise treachery all day long."
Psalm 38:12 (NASB)

Looking impatiently at his watch, Rear Admiral Julian Bishop walked toward his room. He ran his palms up and down his thighs before taking out his key. He waited as a man walked slowly past him toward the elevator. He turned away to avoid the man's stare. He was tired of waiting outside. He opened the door and went to the mini bar for some bourbon.

Thirty minutes ago, Bishop had called the number agreed upon. He wondered why it was taking them so long to get back to him. He tried to calm himself. He was not used to waiting and didn't like the feeling. He took another drink. He still liked Bourbon.

It had been a long day. The terrorist attack had been more destructive than any could have imagined. In an odd way, he respected their effectiveness. While the superpowers lay slumbering, bogged down

The Summit

with bureaucratic red tape and endless committees, men with a mission could still make things happen. But the respect went only so far. Julian hated them, too. If the military had not been encumbered by restraints to the point of practical irrelevance, there would have been no attack. Ghazi and men like him would have been dead! Bishop had continued to support covert CIA operations long after they had ceased to be politically expedient. But constraints and lack of funding had left such operations neutered, trapped in meaningless games while the terrorists and the international crazies continued to run free.

Bishop hated what he saw happening to the military. He hated what he saw happening to his country's will. Julian's eyes burned with a cold, quiet fire born to some men, men who never seem to express their feelings. He moved his 5 foot 10, 190-pound, unathletic, and obviously well-fed body. He knew what others thought of him—he was the resident impatient, combative hawk. The admiral didn't care what they felt. He just feared the West would wake up too late, and China would have its way as the new superpower on the world stage.

Laughing sarcastically to himself, Bishop remembered his earlier doubts about the Summit. He believed the Summit was arranged to pressure a vulnerable American administration to accept Chinese arms control proposals that would be hopelessly self-serving and one-sided. The Summit would end with agreements to increase the cultural and economic cooperation between the superpowers, a cooperation that would open the door for China to beg, steal, and borrow America's high-technology secrets.

He had never seen an arms control treaty he liked, and he hoped never to see one again. The threat of a treaty of Chinese convenience was dashed by the terrorists' bloody assault, but a new threat had been born. With the U.S. and China now having a common enemy, the future was unpredictable and dangerous in new ways.

Julian thought of his brief conversation with his friend General John Westlake. John had been at the crisis planning session. He had been swept up like the rest of them in the spirit of cooperation to save the President and the General Secretary.

Bishop hit his thigh with his fist. He had tried to convince Westlake that John Wayne movies had gone out with the fifties, but like moths drawn too close to the flame, the US Crisis Management Team was moving ahead to cooperate fully with the Chinese and Swiss authorities. Strategic plans and equipment that had taken years to develop were now to be all but given over to the Chinese. The Chinese military wouldn't have to steal or beg. The U.S. would just hand over its technological lead. He doubted whether the Chinese would reciprocate. They would give nothing. The Chinese only knew how to take.

His cell phone rang, and his hand instinctively grabbed it. He said the agreed upon welcome, "The Beau Rivage Hotel."

"The sun is setting, is it not?" a man's voice said carefully in a soft conspiratorial tone.

"Why did you take so long to call?" Bishop demanded with a sharp edge.

"It is not an easy decision to make. It took time," Janik Wocombe said, not flinching. There seemed little apology in his voice. Julian was sure the Vice President of Tyler Defense Industries' International Division was not used to having to apologize to anyone.

"These are not easy times for any of us," Bishop said with heavy mimicry. He did not like the man, but he knew he needed him.

"We cannot afford to let this episode result in a de facto victory for détente and U.S-China cooperation," Janik said gravely. "Our people

The Summit

in Washington have already informed us that the Summit events have put off discussion of our new Strategic Defense appropriations by at least three months if not longer. They report that support for the bill is deteriorating rapidly as a result of the new need to cooperate as a result of the Summit attack and hostage situation. As you can well understand, Tyler Defense Industries cannot afford those kinds of delays."

"Look. You don't have to convince me!" Bishop said bluntly. "I will never trust the Chinese. Their words mean nothing. I believe what George Orwell said about communists, *'Yesterday's weather can be changed by decree.'"*

"You understand that without the appropriation bill funding, your future position with Tyler Defense Industries would be cut," Janik advised.

"You don't need to remind me of that!" Julian snapped, his words blurted in a sudden surge of indignation. "I'm not doing this for money. I'm doing it because it is a mistake to let this new-found cooperation undermine our national preparedness."

"We know that. We just felt it had to be understood," Wocombe said tautly.

"I understand," Bishop said, his fist strangling his cell phone. There was a momentary silence.

"We need insurance. If there is a rescue attempt, President Wang is not to come out alive," Janik said in a controlled monotone.

"Now, you listen to me! I will do nothing that will endanger the President," Julian said flatly, the intensity of his response surprising even himself.

"We want nothing to happen to Freeman, only Wang."

"Any rescue attempt will be the last option, a very difficult one," Bishop warned, not comfortable with the idea of actually killing

Wang. "There is no established rescue plan at this time. The Swiss are trying to get both sides to cooperate. And even if there is a rescue attempt, I have nothing to do with the team."

"We know that," Janik continued as Julian listened intently. "With the information you gave us earlier about the makeup of the American hostage rescue contingent, we have studied the files of all the men involved. Only Major Rip Devins would seem approachable. As the head of the European Delta Force team, he will most likely be in the lead rescue unit. His dad was a POW in Nam; he was tortured under Chinese supervision. He hates China, and he has a reputation as a rebel who is hard to control. He's been passed over for advancement three times. He can't like that. He is black in a white man's army. Two years ago, the major got divorced. It was messy, and he has no savings. He is alone."

"What do you want me to do?" The rear admiral asked earnestly. "I've met him only twice."

"We want you to talk to him. You're on the Joint Chiefs of Staff. He would know your reputation and views on détente with China. You have the military clout to make any offer credible and defensible," Janik said with frank honesty. "We have the money to make it attractive, and the Chinese have provided all the motivation needed to make revenge possible. He's a trained killer. He can get the job done in the fog of attack."

"What if he won't go for it?"

"That's your job. In fact, it may be your only job unless you are effective," Janik warned. "We've placed ten million dollars in a Swiss bank account under his name. There is a matching sum in your name at the same bank. He'll do it, and so will you."

"I'll talk to him," Bishop said. He sat quite still, letting his mission sink in. "With any 'bad luck,' Wang may not come out of this alive. It would be a fitting end to such a tragedy, and a lasting end to détente. Goodnight."

Bishop glanced at his watch. He had much to do. He knew few would understand, but he couldn't sit back and watch any longer. His mind was made up. He would make this happen.

CHAPTER THIRTY-SIX

A CHINESE TEMPEST IS BREWING

**The Chinese Embassy
Geneva, Switzerland**

*"You are my war club, my weapon for battle—with you,
I shatter nations; with you, I destroy kingdoms."*
Jeremiah 51:20 (NIV)

Looking up from the briefing reports, Lin Feng looked at the other three men around the conference table. General Jin Yuan's uniform was ablaze with ribbons. He was proudest of receiving the Order of National Glory, the highest military award of the Republic of China. He wore it proudly.

Like most old men, Jin never seemed to remember the stark terror of combat. It took its toll. Even General Shen Gao, still in his early forties, looked older than his years. Their lined faces and hollow looks as much reflected their tolls in having to navigate years in the upper-echelon of Beijing's military power elite. Their work led to sleepless nights and prolonged periods of tension, made worse by the insulated nature of their existence. None of them had anyone they could risk sharing their stress with. Yet, at some level, these men seemed to thrive on it. Lin Feng wondered if he looked the same way.

Lin Feng went back to the reports. The approach the men used was standard when dealing with such a mass of information. They read everything rapidly, concentrating on the overview rather than the specifics. They had to know the overall landscape before they relentlessly scrutinized the smallest details. Despite the concentration on reading, someone made a comment now and then.

Lin Feng looked up to see General Zhang Ming quickly grab his handkerchief from his pocket and blow his nose. Burdened by a bad cold that had been bordering on pneumonia, Zhang looked flushed and feverish. Lin Feng knew that he had left the hospital against the doctor's advice to be here. With Min Jian dead, Zhang felt he had to be there to support the Old Guard position. Besides, Zhang had never been one to take advice, only orders. He had always been known, less than affectionately as *"Old Fart."* He was a cold fish even for the Communist Party faithful. He never laughed, even when he drank. But he was a survivor. His troops never liked him, but under his leadership, they always fought well in combat situations. Yes, he was a survivor who loved war.

Lin Feng had no idea of the tempest brewing inside Zhang before it erupted. Zhang's face gave nothing away. It never did, unless he wished it to—which was rare. Abruptly grabbing his position papers, Zhang slammed them onto the table.

"There should have been no Summit! This is no time for peace talks. I told Wang that. I told you all. We finally have military superiority over the West, but we won't have it for long! We should not be working with them. We should be using their election-year paralysis to consolidate a stronger foothold in Asia. Our forces are in place. The necessary provocations are available daily. While America remains an impotent giant, we should be making our move on Taiwan. This

Al Haram terrorist attack is deadly distraction. Now, we sit here preparing to give away many of our top-secret military strategies in an attempt to save a man we don't need!"

"You enjoy giving up the lives of others, don't you, Zhang? Or is it that your cold has affected your thinking?" Lin Feng snapped. He felt his anger surging. "Our country cannot expand and survive on military strength alone! Wang's push for increased productivity, more jobs, and improved farm quotas in the last year are beginning to show results. Our people throughout China are starting to talk more about their life in the future than about seeing what new weapons we'll parade for them to see."

"You are a dreamer! Wang is a dreamer. The future of China lies with the realists!" Zhang shouted to little effect of those used to his outbursts. "We committed communists are now in the minority. We have let people have a taste of the decadent West. We cannot afford to keep giving power and hope to the masses. We must control them. You know very well that we cannot even talk about terrorists for fear of creating similar chain reactions of demonstrations and potential violence within our own country!"

"It will take time for any changes to make a difference. I don't suggest that we demilitarize any…"

"Time! We do not have time," Zhang interrupted, his tone offering just the right amount of derision. "Under Freeman, her party is talking about increasing military spending to mobilize a more formidable deterrent to check our influence in the region. Within two years, America will be capable of clawing at our flanks. Taking Taiwan then would be impossible. This is only delaying taking the island that truly belongs to China. This whole…"

The ringing of the conference line brought an end to what Lin Feng knew was another skirmish in a fruitless dialogue. The American and Swiss negotiating team's arrival at the Chinese Embassy had just put an end to the latest skirmish, but there would be more to endure. Lin Feng knew that once joint operations commenced, there would be no turning back. They would be forced to cooperate in spite of their fears. He stared at General Zhang, who had now bowed his head in his hands, his thin fingers massaging his temples. Outdated strategies die hard, and men like Zhang would not let them die gracefully.

The American and Swiss contingent, with the chief negotiator Kamal Harazi walked into the conference room. Lin Feng could see from the look in their eyes that they, too, were finding it hard to accept the need to cooperate. The portraits of Chinese leaders and military immortals stared out at them from the walls. Each man greeted the others curtly. General Zhang gestured impatiently for the newcomers to take their place in the room. Only General Jin Yuan and the aged American General Bud Williamson seemed comfortable. They moved toward each other quickly.

"It has been many years since our last meeting," Jin said warmly, putting a hand on Bud's shoulder and shaking his hand warmly.

"I'm afraid that this time we meet under less than ideal circumstances," Bud said with a concerned cordiality, squeezing Jin's hand before letting it go.

"Yes, we must work together again, like it or not," the general said, looking fleetingly at Zhang, now seated stoically, leaning slightly away from the table. He said nothing, choosing instead to absently gaze at the wall and then back at his notes, notes Lin Feng knew he was not really reading.

A Chinese Tempest Is Brewing

"We'll have to like it, because we can't afford to fail," Bud said seriously. "I suggest we get down to work. Col. Chuck Healey and Major Rip Devins will be joining us shortly. The Colonel is picking up the rest of his men who will be working with Colonel Tang on the rescue team, a team I hope we never have to use."

"Let me remind you, gentlemen, that this remains a Swiss operation," Guntram Meyer pointed out.

"That is right! It was a Swiss failure that got us into this mess. We trust you will not fail us again," General Zhang exclaimed with some venom in his voice.

"Enough!" General Jin Yuan warned, staring directly at his colleague.

"We do not plan to fail, General Zhang. I trust you will do your part to help us succeed," Guntram said with a flat honesty. "We have code-named the operation *'Urgent Eagle.'* In that spirit, I suggest we all have much to do between now and our first direct negotiations with Ghazi."

"We do not have time for this bickering," Kamal Harazi said emphatically. "Your real enemy is in the conference center next to the shattered building less than a mile from here. We are wasting valuable time. We must be together if the negotiations are to be effective. Soon the secure phone lines will be connected for all of us to hear the negotiations. It will then be time to contact Ghazi. I alone will be talking directly to the terrorists during negotiations. I need us to be together and have a basic agreement before that first call. I want to be ready."

"Agreed," Gerald Opfer said, his strong voice filling the room for the first time. "Let's again clarify our position for negotiation, that is, there will be no exchange of hostages for nuclear weapons. I trust that China is in agreement with this?"

"That is our position as well," Lin Feng said quickly, wanting to be the one to speak.

"When each of us entered this room, we understood the limitations of our position," Kamal replied quietly. "The only morality of negotiation with terrorists is pragmatic morality. There is no room for philosophy, only our own brand of utilitarianism. We must accept the greatest advantage for the many over the few. We must not assume that freeing the hostages is beyond hope. But we need time, and that will require giving Ghazi some chance of success. I know him. He will not respond to ultimatums. Routinely, terrorists make death threats. As you have seen, Ghazi and Al-Haram actually deliver on their threats. Ghazi is sane. Misguided and aggressive, but not unbalanced. He will listen as long as we give him something positive to listen to."

"What are you suggesting?" asked General Westlake.

"We will use words and hope to buy us time. We need time to learn more about the number and locations of the terrorists. We need time to find a way for the terrorists to think they are winning even though they are losing. We will try and extend our talks, in hopes that something will occur to our benefit. We will keep them off balance. Ghazi has a strong penchant for media exposure. He wants his ever-expanding manifesto aired. We may be–"

"We cannot unleash the media on this without triggering world panic," Glen Lawson said abruptly.

"The media must be controlled, as all negotiation must be controlled," Kamal said, looking directly at Glen. "Ghazi can be controlled when we help him build an illusion of power, but he is smart. We must control the media. There can be no contradictory messages coming from Washington or Beijing, or your leaders will be dead."

A Chinese Tempest Is Brewing

"Are you suggesting that we let the public believe that negotiating for weapons is a possibility?" Gerald Opfer asked, his eyebrows raised.

"For now, yes," answered Kamal, still very calm despite the storm of emotions visible in the room. "Without actually saying we are considering giving them weapons, we must maintain the illusion that we are not refusing to as long as it is to our advantage. As an Arab, let me assure you that we do not want nuclear weapons leveling the Middle East. Continue with your private assurances but maintain a public position of '*no comment.*'"

There were many questions but little time. Within thirty minutes, it was apparent that Kamal had a wealth of valuable knowledge and the experience to match. Lin Feng had studied him intently. He watched Kamal orchestrate the questions, the attacks, and the ideas into a strategic plan that Lin Feng sensed even Zhang Ming could accept.

Colonel Tang Wei said what many knew to be true, "If this does not work, we will need to be ready with a hostage rescue plan. We still need confirmation on the most current information on the number of terrorists, their location, their habits, their weapons..."

"I understand," Kamal interrupted, nodding. "I know little about special operations, but I do know something about Ghazi and his methods of operation. I will be glad to share any information I have or can secure with your rescue team. If negotiations do not work, we must be ready. As I said, we must work together, and we must work quickly."

CHAPTER THIRTY-SEVEN

THE HERO'S JOURNEY TO GENEVA

> US Military Flight to Geneva

"But you, take courage! Do not let your hands be weak,
for your work shall be rewarded."
2 Chronicles 15:7 (ESV)

The U.S. rescue team's trip from the States had been uneventful, but like the calm before the storm, Rip Devins could feel his body already reacting to what was waiting for him and his men in Geneva. He rubbed his palms against his thighs and hunched his shoulders, trying to relieve the tension. He took a deep breath and exhaled. The preparations were routine; his body no longer even reacted. But this mission would be no practice run, and his body seemed to know that it was more than for real—the world would be depending upon him and the combined rescue team. But no amount of preparation ever really prepared you for the true chaos of combat.

Rip's ears caught the ceaseless tapping of Fast Eddie's thumb on the top of the flimsy, plastic flight desk. Rip turned his face toward the sound, Fast Eddie seemed tightly wound as he busily scribbled a note to his son. Eddie had long since lost the love of his wife, but he didn't want his son to forget him. Rip had written many such final letters. Rip was glad they had never had to send any of them.

Eddie just kept all of his in a brown metal box in his locker. As far as Eddie was concerned, he kept everything worth giving to his son in that box. Rip did not plan on ever having to deliver it. They had always made it through, and Rip was glad the man was along on this mission.

Fast Eddie had specific skills prized in covert operations—demolitions. Hardworking and creative, Eddie had a passion for disintegrating just about everything. He did it with pride and precision, and it helped that he loved loud noises. His expertise in C4 plastic high explosives could prove invaluable. He could knock down a whole section of a wall and still leave a flower standing on the other side. A surgeon of destruction, he also knew how to hold his own in an assault team.

Moisture began to form in the corner of his eyes, forcing Rip to look away for distractions in the fast-moving cloud formations passing by. He tried to center his thoughts, but the pain, as always, was still there. Rip had no one to write a letter to. His wife had given him up for dead when he returned to Afghanistan against her wishes. Deep down, he knew her feelings for him had never even existed. Their relationship had been stillborn from its inception. Getting married was the thing to do, just like going into the military was the thing for young men in his family to do. He had lost his wife when he had been forced to leave for Afghanistan. He felt like he lost that war, too. After all, for all he knew, Al-Haram might be using it as a staging ground outside of Iran. He had not heard of Al-Haram, but knew that many splinter groups were out there. They had one characteristic—they believed that other terrorists were not destructive enough. Al Haram had already proved how destructive they could be. And now, they have the President and the world held hostage!

His feelings were rawer than ever. The last month had been tough. His mother had died—deep feelings buried–even cauterized. He had cried at her grave until he could cry no more. He swore to himself that his last tears were buried with her.

Now, Devins had no one, just the family of men he had forged from Delta Force. They were the only ones who would care when he died. And they would care. He was reminded of what Paul Harvey had once said on the radio, *"The most important factor in determining the number of people at your funeral is the weather that day."* For Rip, he knew that would not be true. Delta Force would be the only ones there, and they would show up no matter what the weather.

The Army had not always been that way for Rip. He had worked his black ass off in a white man's Army—white at the top, black at the bottom. It had taken years for the Army to reluctantly make room for him in a vital spoke in the great white wheel. And now, he wondered if they were calling their black man in to save the great white leader. And if it fails, his black ass would be on the firing line—the sacrificial lamb assigned to what would turn out to be an impossible mission.

Rip could hear the stinging attacks, *"Old Smart was all talk. Coffee-Face blew it! He and his hot-shot crew couldn't cut it when the chips were down. So take that big black spoke out of the big white wheel. He never belonged anyway!"*

He smiled to himself. What did he care anyway? He was getting older now, but he had what he wanted. The rest of his career would be downhill. How many more years could his body put up with the abuse to serve with the men he loved? Even now, his body was rebelling, taking longer to recover from the grueling exercises he demanded from all

The Hero's Journey to Geneva

his men. There could be no exceptions. When he couldn't handle it, he would quit and hand it over to someone who could.

And afterward, what? The best he could hope for would be some desk job in the Pentagon pushing piles of papers. He had seen enough of that world already. It was about as exciting as watching paint dry. He couldn't see himself fitting in to that labyrinth. Rip was a hunter, and he was only happy hunting. He pushed the thought away. His Delta Force team was about to hunt like never before.

The pilot announced their beginning descent into Geneva. Rip focused on the job at hand. This was no exercise. There would be no excuses! All the previous training in the "House of Horrors" simulation room had honed their skills in how to separate the terrorist targets from the captives. The decision was simple but critical—who to kill and who to let live. He visualized the split second it took for the terrorists to shift their attention from the hostages to the explosion. In that second, the Delta Force team would enter the room and neutralize the terrorists before they knew what hit them.

They called it "room clearing." It had to be quick and violent. There was nothing pretty about it. You wanted four men with accurized M-1911A1 .45 Automatic Caliber Pistols to enter a room and go in different directions. The pistol's big 230-grain bullets could slap a man down. Although the bullets traveled slower than the newer 9 mm bullets, they did the job in the hands of a professional, and the bullets stayed in the target. Unfortunately, the newer weapons killed with such velocity that there was always the risk of the bullet going through a terrorist and into the body of a hostage. In this operation, that was a risk they could not afford.

On this team, Rip knew he would be the first man in, and Chuck Healey would be the backup, the last man that enters behind the other four. There was no better man with a 12-gauge shotgun than Chuck. It would be great to work with him again.

There could be no time for error—only a movement to a swift death. All five men would be in constant motion giving the enemy no target. They were ready, and he would bet on them as he always had.

But fear always haunted any rescue operation of this magnitude. Doubts nagged at the corner of Rip's mind. After all, there were the unpredictables—the skill and actions of the terrorists and the hostages. If there were any problems in clearing a room, the wrong people could be shot. You didn't have time to conduct an interview. No time for the subtleties of move and countermove or searching out targets cautiously.

Minds react to images—clothes, skin coloring, weapons. Hostages didn't have guns, but there was no way of knowing how they would really behave. Would they help attack the terrorists and take their weapons? That would put the hostages in peril from the very men sent to rescue them. His Delta Force team was trained to kill anyone carrying a weapon in such a situation. When the shooting started and people began to die, it all came down to the men pulling the triggers. There was no time to train the hostages on how to act. Rip could only pray that they would remain the amateurs they were supposed to be.

Rip knew that he and men like him were unique. They thrived on life and death choices, and they were seldom wrong. But he also knew that perfect soldiers existed only in the movies. Unlike the movies, there are no dress rehearsals or retakes in real combat.

There was an added concern. In this operation, there were the Chinese to contend with. Rip was used to being in charge, or at worst, working with "friendly forces." He knew little about this operation's rescue plans. He had had barely enough time to see the early reports of the attack before he was rushed from the field to the plane. He wanted nothing to do with the Chinese! Shit, you couldn't trust them, but they had to in order to pull this off. He wondered whether they were having the same kind of doubts.

Rip had no time to nurture his private nightmare. The screech of rubber on the runway and the sudden lurch to the right and the plane's correction occupied his attention, bringing him back to focus on the now. It's time to put it on the line.

CHAPTER THIRTY-EIGHT

LORD, DELIVER US FROM EVIL

> **Hostage Quarters**
> **Palace of Nations Conference Center**

"But before all these things, people will arrest you and persecute you. They will hand you over to synagogues and prisons, and you will be brought before kings and governors for my name's sake, in order to give you an opportunity to testify."
Luke 21:12-13 (God's Word Translation)

The President looked at him in the dim light. Wang's eyes were tired, with dark circles under them. Watching the General Secretary's ashen face reminded Connie that she was not the only one who felt racked with exhaustion. How much she just wanted to lie down and let her strength come back to her. Her ropes kept her strapped to her chair.

Although she had tried to nap, the frequent visits by the guards and her restricted movement kept jolting her awake whenever she started to doze. When awake, her head throbbed, and her mind filled with a profound sense of loss, confusion, and anger. She never thought such

Lord, Deliver Us from Evil

an ordeal possible. For once, she hated her own self-complacency–her basic lack of physical fitness and mental preparedness.

Connie thought of Martin, what he must be going through, what resources he would have to marshal to deal with the unbearable uncertainty. *Breathe deep, really deep, and think of Martin.* She told herself. *Think of what you're going to say to him when you see him… what it will feel like to hold him…*

What was she saying? She wasn't getting out of this. She might never hold her family again. *Good God, what was happening?*

The President relived the horrible scene in the hallway, the bodies and blood of lost friends. She tried to find a thread of sense or purpose in this but could find none. She wondered how God could have let this happen. She had tried praying a number of times. She believed and felt His presence, but she couldn't shake her occasional disappointment in God—*Why me!* She screamed at God inside her personal prison. *Lord, deliver us from this evil! Deliver us from this evil!*

In the past, prayer had always anesthetized her pain, settled her mental anguish, lowered her pulse rate, and stiffened her resolve. But now it seemed so many of her prayers seemed to bounce back from the walls that now enclosed them. She had always trusted God, but she couldn't help thinking that God had somehow cut her loose. She wondered why. How could this be His will?

Her eyes caught Wang, staring at her. She wondered what he had seen. She wasn't even sure he cared.

"Do you believe in God?" Connie asked, raising her head, returning Wang's intense look.

"God is for the already vanquished and the children," Wang, answered. "There is an old peasant song that says, *'wishing will make it so.'* God is a convenient lie. No wishing will make it any different."

Connie Freeman did not reply.

"You're a Christian, aren't you?" Wang continued.

"Yes, I am."

Wang stared at her for a time. "But why?"

"If you are wondering where my God is in all this, I can join you in that question. Most of the time, I have a sense of how God's will is working in my life. But I'm struggling right now on that front. At times, I feel his presence, but I am also angry at Him. So many have died here and in the attacks."

"My question remains. Why believe?"

"Because for me, my faith gives me some sense of peace in even the worst times. I can't imagine how this could be any worse, but I'm not afraid. God has earned my trust. He's my anchor, and this hasn't changed that," Connie Freeman said softly. "But at the same time, I'd settle for a miracle right now, if God decided to intervene!"

"I need no crutch," he said, "I am not afraid either."

"I've spent enough time in Washington to understand what you are saying," Connie paused. "Most politicians believe their own speeches. In Washington, they train you to put your trust in men, missiles, tight security, ever-expanding technology, and never-ending position papers, laws, and briefings. If there was safety and wisdom in the sheer volume of paper we put out, we'd be free now. I fear that as superpower leaders, we believed the myth that because of our power and influence, we were invincible. There was always something about Washington that never seemed real. It's all a house of cards that looks good from the outside, but one wrong hit, and things can begin to crumble. Al-Haram has come into our world in a blaze of destruction. Ghazi has us caught up in his plan. I'm afraid he's delivered a blow to the invincibility of both of our countries."

"Yes, we have our share of illusions," Wang confessed.

"Before I was elected President, I'd always found more strength in simple things. A simple faith. Simple and close relationships with people who I knew and loved. Power asks you to let go of too many of those simple things. Sadly, now, I'm not so sure I know how to get them back." Connie paused, turned in her chair, wincing from the rope sores as she did. She continued, "But prayer is something I won't give up. God has always been good. Right now, I'm not so hot, and the situation is even worse."

"I do not pray to any god you know. I have my principles, but if they don't work, I have other principles. I do not need a Holy Church with a biased Almighty to tell me when to switch them," Wang said with an uncomfortable smile. "Now, if your God will help us out of this, I am flexible. But He does not seem to want to help."

"Patience is supposed to be a virtue," she said, trying to convince herself. "There is something that the Disciple Peter said that I hold onto: *Humble yourselves, therefore, under God's mighty hand, that he may lift you up in due time. Cast all your anxiety on him because he cares for you.*" She had to admit that humbling herself and waiting was not something she was currently very good at.

"How long will you wait for your god? In China, they tell the story of an old man, his son, and their donkey. When villagers criticized the old man for riding the donkey, he let his son ride. But when the criticism continued for making the old man walk, both the old man and the son wound up carrying the donkey. God is like the donkey; I have no use for him unless god can pull his own weight. God has been carried by the church and its useless priests for too long. Your god will not save us here."

"The reporters were accurate in describing you," Connie said with a smile. "You have a nice smile but iron teeth." Wang's smile broadened to reveal his teeth below.

"Despite what they say about me, I am a wise man, and I know my limitations. There was a time I wanted to believe, but I have learned to put my hope in other things," replied Wang. Freeman remained silent.

He continued, "My mother died with her faith in God."

Freeman replied, "She was a Christian?"

"Yes. As she grew old, she became more and more disillusioned by the failed promises of communism; she turned back to religion. As leader of the Communist Party, I must profess atheism. I tried to dissuade her of her religious superstitions. I tried to convince her the state could work without a god. Until the day she died, she attended mass in private ceremonies. She never revealed her identity to others in order to protect me. She did not want to embarrass me. Like the leaders before me, I looked the other way while publicly denouncing believers. When people are prepared to die for their beliefs, killing them makes them martyrs. We let them worship and imprisoned the most critical pastors. Most believers are harmless, and their numbers remain few. They will never have power or be officially supported in China."

"Then, in spite of your mother and her early testimony, you do not believe?" Connie asked, thoughtfully.

"I cannot believe," Wang answered. If this bothered him, he was careful not to let it show. "Ghazi has his god. I think his god is winning."

"That man isn't human; he knows no god but himself and his leaders," Connie objected to him comparing her God with that of a terrorist.

"Are you so sure?"

"The God I believe in does not believe in killing innocent people!"

"Have you read your own Bible? Your loving God killed and continues to kill many in the name of His people Israel," Wang said in a monotone. "People with religion see only what they want to see."

"The God I believe in doesn't require killing anyone. In fact, Jesus had but one commandment, to love as he had loved. Jesus chose not to save his own life. He was willing to lose it for those who believe in–"

"I've heard it all before, Madam President," Wang abruptly interrupted. "I heard it on my Mother's knee. If you are so sure of your God, why do you need so many missiles to protect your country from us?"

"That's not the first time I've asked myself that question," she said, trying to sort out her own feelings. "I don't even like my own answers. As we are finding now, our missiles are doing us no good here. That is one of the reasons I was ready for this Summit. You see, I do trust God more than all the missiles. I was hoping to find a way to get both of us to depend less on our weapons."

"I am sorry. I have said too much," he confided. "I still have no words to answer my mother's dying prayer. On her hospital deathbed, she asked me to believe. I couldn't answer her then. I still can't. Communism certainly is no substitute. It has no soul. The party's commitment to the 'Good of the People' is a convenient lie. I have found that they only worry about the good for certain people. As much as I never admitted it, my mother's faith helped provide a moral guide to what was right and wrong."

"So, at some level, God is at least useful."

"People trust my word. It makes me predictable, trustworthy," he confessed. "But they do not know from where my moral anchor comes. So yes, what I learned of faith has been useful. Unfortunately, right now, it is of little use. I find it hard to believe in god or in man this day."

Both sat in silence. Wang stared at the floor, seemingly absorbed in his own thoughts. His head moved slowly from side to side.

At last, Connie Freeman spoke, "Instead of waiting for God or man, I suggest we work again on what we can do here and trust that maybe that is God's way of helping. We have each other."

"You can start by doing nothing further to irritate Ghazi," responded Wang, quite serious now. "You must control your replies. Getting him angry will do no good. Besides, we both will need our strength, and getting beaten for our comments won't help."

"That's good advice," she said with a slight chuckle. "I'm afraid you're getting to know me too well."

"Ah, perhaps that feeling may be mutual," Wang added. "I find you a hard person to hate. But for Ghazi, you are too easy to hate. Do not make it easier for him. They have to keep us alive to parade us before the cameras, Ghazi has captured the attention of the world. You can see it in his eyes when he is in front of the cameras. He is intoxicated with his own power. He will do nothing to endanger that."

"I will control my responses to him. I have been thinking the same thing, but I doubt being friendly to Ghazi will make much difference."

"You are right. Ghazi is smart. He will not be easily fooled. We must work on the others. We must be friendly when they check on us. Debating with them is futile. They will not listen anyway. If we cooperate, they can get on with negotiations. I'm sure we will make no friends, but if we gain three or four seconds of hesitation when our rescue occurs that will save our lives and seal their coffins."

"They can't rescue anyone until they know where we are," the President added.

"True, but we must be ready for whatever comes," Wang said intensely. His eyes narrowed. "We will survive this. We cannot make ourselves more of a target than we already are."

"I like your thinking and your spirit," Connie said. "It's downright American; no insult intended."

"My spirit is Chinese and quite fine," he said, giving Freeman a sudden quick smile. "Maybe no one country has a monopoly on spirit. My father once said, *'That which does not break you makes you stronger.'* I plan on living to be stronger."

"I'm sure we'll both be stronger," Connie Freeman replied. "I'm just not used to being patient. The thing I hate worst about elections is waiting out election night. It's all over. You've finished campaigning, you're finished shaking hands, and you've delivered your last 60-second TV pitch. You know everyone's tired of seeing you and your commercials. And then you wait. All the illusions and trappings of your power fade away in the silence of your room. It's out of your hands. As a leader, you're supposed to be strong for your supporters, but you feel so vulnerable. That's how it feels now, only worse. Our very lives are at stake."

"Yes, we wait. But soon, I'm sure Ghazi will have us deliver another message, and it will have nothing to do with your campaign for November."

Connie Freeman's mind recoiled, momentarily drawing her to the recesses of her mind. She said nothing. She had been thinking about it off and on all day. All the rescue scenarios would require pinpointing their location. Without a location, no rescue would be possible. But in that moment, the solution had become obvious—they didn't have to identify where they were if they could control their location at the time of the rescue.

"That's it!" Connie Freeman said, still staring at the corner of the room, internally checking and rechecking the validity of her thinking.

"What?"

"They need to know where we are before they can even attempt a rescue," she said in a whisper, leaning as far forward as her restraints would allow. "Ghazi craves the media exposure. Up to now, he's settled for recorded messages. They have the equipment for a live feed. If we get Ghazi to broadcast us live, they'll know our location at that moment. They don't have to know where we're being held, if we can control the broadcast long enough for the rescue to occur during that broadcast."

"The negotiating team will not allow a live feed. It is against all negotiation procedures to allow Ghazi that kind of media control," Wang countered. "How will you get the Swiss to allow the direct media access? Ghazi is no fool."

"Neither are we," Freeman said with a calm confidence. "We'll find a way."

The phone on the other side of the room rang; there was a quick contraction in Connie's stomach. They both stared motionless as the phone continued to ring. Never before had Connie so appreciated hearing the sound.

After ten rings, the ringing stopped. Was the phone answered in the other room? Was it ignored? Had the negotiations started? To Connie, it did not matter. It was only a matter of time. A lifeline to their rescue was now at least possible. They would find a way to make it work. They had to. Turning back to Wang, she smiled.

"Do you believe in God now?" Freeman inquired.

"People make calls, not God," Wang said lightly, "When the donkey pulls the wagon, I will be ready to thank God."

CHAPTER THIRTY-NINE

THE DANCE OF THE RELUCTANT WARRIORS

> **Geneva, Switzerland**

"Prepare for war! Rouse the warriors!
Let all the fighting men draw near and attack.
Beat your plowshares into swords."
Joel 3:9-10 (NIV)

The first thing Major Rip Devins saw when he deplaned was Colonel Chuck Healey, his eyes fixed on the door with the cold stare that Rip had come to expect. Chuck always looked serious. But he knew his business. He knew his men, and he took care of both. Chuck clasped Rip's hands warmly as he stepped off the plane. After their brief cordialities, they moved swiftly to the briefing room adjacent to the field. Briefing papers were slammed into their hands, and the all too familiar process was off and running.

"They're dead!" Rip whispered quietly, mostly to himself. He scanned the lines of the briefing notes as if studying the deformed appendages of an obscene, mangled corpse. "I had no idea so many had died—Tom Groden, Jim Naisbitt. It's a who's who of international diplomacy."

"They are the known dead. There are still some missing in the rubble, and many just hanging on by a thread in nearby hospitals. The "whole damn city is in shock." Chuck said flatly, his face drawn, his eyes more hollow than Rip had ever seen them.

Keeping his voice low, Chuck brought the team up to speed on everything that had taken place, from the moment of the first truck assault to the latest recorded demands, to the formation of the Local Negotiating Team and, of course, the backup rescue plans.

Throughout Chuck's recital, Rip's eyes had stayed wide, his clenched fingers wrinkling the edges of the already frayed briefing report. When Chuck had finished, Rip and his men sat motionless, absorbing the full impact of what Chuck had told them—the demands for nuclear weapons, the cold-blooded killing of unarmed hostages, the perilous risk of any attempt to free two superpower leaders that the world could not afford to lose.

"To be clear. If negotiations don't work, it will be up to us." Rip said, staring at Chuck. "And if our rescue effort is not effective and we fail, we got nothing but a shit story left, two dead leaders and a planet on the brink of another world war."

"You got the picture. That's the threat we'll all be working under." Chuck said, leaning forward to emphasize the gravity of the problem with the critical mission. "Unless they're freed safely, we face an almost guaranteed global catastrophe."

"They got the world by the balls on this one, Colonel," Fast Eddie said with a ring of mission and purpose. He looked first at Rip and then quickly back to Colonel Healey before retreating, "Begging your pardon, sir?"

"That describes it well," Chuck said, taking a rare deep breath. An odd kind of calmness washed over the group. Rip could feel the wheels begin to move.

The Dance of the Reluctant Warriors

Like a computer programmed to process and not to feel, Rip's mind took hold of the silence. His task was simple; it was the same in every exercise. All the rescue team had to do was learn precisely where the hostages were being held, develop a tactical plan to rescue them using an economy of deadly force, taking out the terrorists, and freeing the hostages. Executing the rescue would be the easiest part. What they needed was a workable plan to get them the access they needed.

As thorough as Chuck had been, the fact remained that they still needed three things: information, information, and more information. And they needed it fast! These terrorists were not amateurs. They would not settle for long delays. The lives of the hostages would depend upon finding a plan quickly. Rip put little stock in an international negotiation team. There were too many cooks in one kitchen. Rip knew his men would be needed.

"On the positive side, we control the situation outside the walls," Rip said calmly. "We can climb and repel into position to gain entry at the crisis point."

"Yes. We have the full cooperation of the Swiss," Chuck added thoughtfully. "We've got detailed plans of the whole building, and with new technology, we've already narrowed down where they could be holding them."

"We need more than odds on this one," Rip said tautly. "Anything we don't understand in this operation is a risk we can't take. We need the exact location. Until we have it, Eddie, it will be your job to meet with Swiss security to discuss plans. I want you to know everything there is to know about this rathole and how to get in."

"I'll get you in," Fast said effusively. "You just find me the place." Rip knew it was true. Within two hours, Eddie would have memorized the location of all doors, how they worked, which way they opened, how they were constructed, what kind of locks closed them, what locks or controls opened them, which walls and windows could be breached, and how many explosives would be needed.

"You saw the recording," Rip said intently, turning back to Chuck. "What weapons did they use, and how did they handle them?"

"We saw Uzis, and they know how to use them. No amateurs this time."

The questions continued. What about food and provisions? How many men could they possibly encounter? What routines had been observed? Where were the perimeter men posted? What did Freeman and Wang know about how to help as hostages? What position was the negotiating team taking? Where were the media, and could they be kept out of the way? The questions kept coming--questions that needed to be answered to develop any plan. It remained a maddening mosaic with too many pieces missing.

"Who's in charge?" Rip asked. For an instant, his words hung in the air. Silence enfolded the room, thick and choking. Rip's eyes grew wider as a fire burned in his chest. Chuck looked at Rip and then back to the briefing report. Rip saw a tiny quiver beating at the corner of Chuck's eyes that had not been there moments before. Rip knew he was exposing the raw nerves of all the men to the question they had been avoiding.

"The Local Negotiating Team wants nothing to do with the rescue plan; they know they haven't got the expertise," Chuck said cautiously. Rip was not used to his being so careful with his words. "Although I plan to work with you on this, it's your team. You'll be calling the shots for our men. You are to keep the U.S. Crisis Management Team and the Local Swiss Negotiating Team informed, but it will be your game plan we all execute."

"You didn't answer my question. What do you mean that I will be in charge of *our men*?" Rip flared. He could feel the anger leaping through his body.

"You'll work with Colonel Tang Wei, the Chinese Special Forces Officer in charge," Chuck said firmly. "You are to develop a joint tactical plan with Swiss support. Your rescue team will have both American and Chinese special forces. You'll have to work out how many operators you want, the nature of the equipment, and the techniques for entry. You'll work together with Colonel Tang to decide when and if you are ready to go."

"Do you know what you're asking?" Rip said. His hands were clenched, and the corners of his mouth racked with tension.

"You know I know," Chuck said, irked. The air between them seemed heavy. Chuck continued as if deciding to take the fight head-on. "I don't expect you to have a Summit tea party. You don't have to love it. You just have to make it work. We can't afford to go this alone. If anything happened to either leader at the hands of the other, you can put your head between your legs and kiss it goodbye!"

"You'll compromise years of top-secret preparation by Delta Force and the safety of our team, but that's your decision," Rip warned. His mouth momentarily snapped shut with an audible click. The tendons stood out along the sides of his neck. His eyes bored into Chuck with a force neither man had ever risked expressing. "You're putting the lives of my men in the hands of men we have been taught to hate. This exercise in goodwill may just get us all killed."

"I'm not asking you to condone it, Major," Chuck snapped, his face now white with anger. "This isn't a request. I'm ordering you! If you don't do it, I'll put someone else in charge who will. Is that clear?"

The Summit

"Very clear, sir." Rip said bluntly. "Black men are expendable, aren't they, Colonel?"

"I'll forget you said that, Major," Chuck hissed back. Standing up, he ordered in a disgusted tone, "If you and your men are ready, it's time for us to go to the Chinese Embassy. We all have critical work to do."

Cracks of thunder began exploding in Rip's head. His demons danced. He hadn't invited them, and he didn't know how to send them away. Drawn by the undercurrent of anger seething just below the surface, he stood up, walked past the Colonel, and went out the door. He did not hear the sound of the men behind him. He tried desperately to pull the thin veneer of military discipline over the growing tempest exploding within. He wondered if the Chinese officers were feeling the same thing.

CHAPTER FORTY

THE SEARCH FOR A LIGHT TO BREAK THE DARKNESS

**Hostage Quarters
Palace of Nations Conference Center**

*"Those who seek my life lay snares for me, and those
who seek to injure me have threatened destruction,
and they devise treachery all day long."*
Psalm 38:12 (NASB)

Staring at the ringing phone, its stark sounds echoing off the alien walls, Ghazi quelled the emotions churning within. He had not asked for a call, and he did not like surprises. None of his men moved to respond to the phone. It would be his decision alone.

He looked at his watch. The radio broadcast was only seventeen minutes away. But like a magnet, the phone pulled him to its intriguing ring. His body swung into motion as he grasped the phone, covered the receiver with his hand, and drew it to his ear. His fever-bright eyes darted from side to side as he listened.

"If you are listening, Ghazi Saud, this is Kamal Harazi," Kamal said in slow even tones. Ghazi was silent; he was not sure he would

The Summit

even respond to the voice from his past. Images of the rubble in Beirut flashed through Ghazi's mind, reminding him of images he had all but forgotten. Kamal continued, seemingly unperturbed by the lack of any response, "I have agreed to act as an intermediary for the Swiss government in negotiating with—"

"I did not tell them to call! I do not want words; I want weapons!" Ghazi screamed, his voice whiplashed. "Let them crawl to me through the radio with the answer I demand. I need no negotiations!"

"There will be no radio broadcast. There can be no public statement of concessions. if there is to be any discussion of your demands, we will need...."

"You did not hear me!" Ghazi said, his voice again thick with rage. The lines of tension around his mouth were concealed by his heavy beard, but he knew his men could sense it. "You must do as I say, or the monsters will die!"

"As an intermediary, I have no power to agree to that. It is the policy of the Swiss government to disallow media involvement. I will tell them of your concern, but..." Kamal trailed off softly, his words triggering the venom built up in Ghazi's soul.

"We will be heard! I have no time for diplomats! Put away your silver tongue. I have no need for you. Allah has no need for you!" Ghazi spoke the words slowly with contempt.

"You will gain nothing from your attack unless you listen," Kamal replied sternly, but with a certain defensiveness in his voice that was not lost to the keen ear of Ghazi.

"Talking through the media will only paralyze the world and trigger a chain reaction of premature retaliation in the Middle East. The Swiss have convinced the Americans and the Chinese to leave open a window of negotiation as long as the talks remain private."

The Search for a Light to Break the Darkness

Like a jackal waiting silently to pounce on its prey, Ghazi said nothing, not allowing his fast-paced breathing to be heard through the phone. He waited for Kamal to say more.

"They will need continuing proof that the hostages are alive," Kamal continued.

"I will show them no proof, if all it brings me is more talk. I need weapons for our holy war!" Ghazi interrupted. "Do not trick me, Kamal. Tell them they are to prepare three one-kiloton nuclear weapons and deliver them within twenty-four hours at a location I will specify. Our men will verify that they are real and armed. Our own planes, American-made planes, will fly the weapons over the prescribed targets. When all three planes are in position, I will be notified here, and the monsters will be freed. And then we will be ready to die and take the Zionists with us."

It was Kamal's turn to pause. Ghazi listened intently, his hand strangling the life out of the phone as if compelling it to reply.

"I will do my best for you, but you must understand my position. Both the United States and China have absolute no-concession policies. They are bending to political realism. Under the circumstances, their no-concession policy does not mean no-negotiation. I have been authorized to supply you with food and medical assistance. If the hostages are released unharmed, the Swiss are pressuring for your safe transit from Switzerland."

"Just more words!" snapped Ghazi. "They have nothing we need! We have all the food, water, and ammunition we need. We have the hostages. We are prepared to die. We do not want release. You, above all people, must understand our Holy War against the infidels?"

"This will not win the war," Kamal said, his voice now firm. "I am acting as the intermediary with the direct support of many of your

The Summit

brothers: The Islamic Amal, Shia clerics, the senior commander of the Shiite Militia. All agree that the purifying force of violence must be balanced with the cost of retaliation and the deprivation that will result."

"Shut up! You're a liar! A just war knows no limits! That is why Al-Haram will do what they do not have the courage to do!" Ghazi warned, recoiling from Kamal's words. "You have grown soft like the Americans who are not clever enough or brave enough to win any war. Their leaders are clumsy, amateurish, and crude. Their supposed democratic freedom has made their people soft. The Chinese are paper tigers as well. Neither of them can stop us. Like a tree, every time they sever a branch, our warrior tree grows another stronger branch. Allah does not allow such softness. You are a liar, Kamal." He knew he would face many lies, but the way of Allah was clear.

"If you destroy the trunk, no branches will grow," Kamal said, almost pleading. "Israel's policy of the iron fist may sever the tree from its roots. They will not stand by and watch your plane deliver its own destruction. You and I both know Israel has nuclear weapons, and you will force them to use them. Knowing the Israelis, they will not wait for your provocation. They would enjoy unleashing their war machine on the people of Allah. They are as determined to exterminate all Arab terrorists as you are to destroy Israel. Your way will bring no victory, Ghazi. You will only end up destroying your own."

"Are you now joining the voices that believe that the Jews are human?" Ghazi mocked. Ghosts danced in his mind. "Swine are also animals, but extremely disagreeable ones. If the Jews are human, they are like pygmies. They have small minds and are weak. Like wild beasts, they should be severed from the common body of humanity. Our

The Search for a Light to Break the Darkness

captive monsters will help us. They will help us destroy the Zionists, or we will kill them. It is that simple."

"Let me help you keep–"

"I do not want your help! You are a mere puppet crying for peace! While you talk, the Jews move to establish new settlements on Arab land. No more talk! Let your negotiators know that their stubbornness will take them beyond the limits of my patience. They will be responsible for events now. We are blameless. They have twenty-four hours to join us or watch their leaders die!"

Before Kamal could reply, Ghazi cut him off, hanging up the phone. Ghazi stared first at the wall, and then at his brother, Gamal, power throbbing through his veins. The world would listen; it had to listen! *Praise to Allah, for he is with us!*

The phone rang again and again, pleading for an answer. But this time none was to be given. Ghazi did not keep the contempt out of his voice when he turned to his brother.

"All they want is talk. They want to stall, but we will escalate. They cannot control us. We are in control. Soon we will use the very phone lines they have worked so hard to provide. The world is crying to hear our voice. We will now demand to be given the opportunity to speak to the world. They will grant our wishes."

CHAPTER FORTY-ONE

WHEN A KISS COMES CALLING

> **Hotel des Bergues**
> **Geneva, Switzerland**

> *"Then the Lord God said, 'It is not good that the man should be alone; I will make him a helper fit for him.'"*
> *Genesis 2:18 (ESV)*

Brian had all but forgotten the traditional charm and elegance of the Hotel des Bergues. The tragedy with its constant stream of mauled bodies had taken its toll in severing his mind from the beauty of the surroundings. But the hand of Dr. Chen Li. resting lightly on his arm as they walked together through the cool marble foyer did much to bring to life the romantic ambiance of the famous hotel. As they walked past the sweeping central staircase, he was again reminded of the hotel's resemblance to a fine 19th Century private residence. The refined elegance and the special appointments seemed somehow very personal to him tonight. He turned to Li.

"I'm glad you agreed to join me for dinner. I had to get out of that hospital," Brian said gently, enjoying the good feelings being with Chen Li was bringing him. "You don't think your mother would mind your having dinner with a reactionary imperialist?"

"Now, don't start up again!" Dr. Chen said, cocking her head to one side.

"Okay, I just don't want to corrupt you," he said in mock sympathy. She smiled momentarily squeezing his arm and moving slightly closer to him as they walked.

"It's still hard to believe," he said thoughtfully, "This morning we were just two surgeons attending another conference. Eight hours and twenty surgeries later the conference has been canceled, our leaders are being held hostage by terrorists, and I'm going to dinner with a beautiful woman I otherwise wouldn't have met. Not just any woman, but a Chinese woman."

"Why thank you, Dr. Winters," She replied, amused. "But I thought we agreed to the ground rules—no shop talk and no talk of the tragedy."

"You're right! So soon I forget. Not another word; I promise," Brian said, his eyes peering sideways with an exaggerated, slightly lascivious glance. "My buddies wouldn't let me hear the end of it. Alone in Geneva for a romantic evening with a beautiful woman, and I keep talking about a political crisis. I must be forgetting priorities."

"Do you ever stop kidding?" she asked.

"Who says I'm kidding?" Looking now at her eyes as they walked. "I am in Geneva with a beautiful woman."

She smiled and then looked away. Before either had time to say anything else, they had arrived. Brian pulled her up short of the door, bowed formally to Li, and swung out his right arm to point the way into the restaurant.

"Mademoiselle. C'est L'Amphitryon, S'il vous plait," Brian said with as deep a French accent as he could manufacture. With his left arm now firmly placed in the small of her back, he gently pushed her to-

ward the entrance. He whispered in her ear as they walked in, "Is my French getting better?"

"You better let me do the ordering," Dr. Chen whispered, both giving way to more natural laughter as they entered the restaurant. Only the sight of the maître d's serious expression momentarily dampened their levity.

Antoine, the maître d', was so elegant he was almost stuffy. He, along with his backup army of waiters dressed in starched black and whites, provided the only movement to the room. There were no other patrons to be seen. Brian scanned the dining room. The lights from the crystal chandeliers were turned low but were still sufficient to give a subtle yet revealing look at the gold and red velvet walls and the fine crystal and china that graced the room. The lighting revealed a richness that Brian knew he would pay for.

He wisely let Li handle the seating arrangements with Antoine. Brian had long since given up searching through his Berlitz French Guide. He knew that the French waiters loved to watch him suffer. He was equally convinced that his butchered pronunciation provided hours of comic relief for every waiter he encountered. He followed Li and Antoine to a table in an isolated corner. They were handed a menu.

Brian's eyes followed the maître d' as he left. He again became aware that they had the restaurant to themselves.

"It looks like we have the whole place to ourselves. If all those guys are just for us, the tips alone will break me!" Brian leaned towards her.

"Don't worry. We are early."

"Early! It's after eight."

"They eat late in Geneva," she said smiling.

"I'll remember that," Brian said softly as he reached out and touched her arm. Without reacting, she lifted the menu and glanced at it.

"Let me order for you," she said. "Do you like surprises?"

"Every time I order in French, it's a surprise! Besides, with you, I'm getting used to surprises. Why should this be any different?"

The waiter had arrived and listened intently to Li's litany of phrases, responding with well-timed smiles and nods. Brian also listened intently to every word she said. He was aware of how much he enjoyed hearing her talk, even when he didn't understand what she was saying. Her voice had such a musical quality. As she turned to face him, she smiled and stared at him. He saw a certain shyness and the need for his approval. The waiter left as silently as he had arrived.

"That sounded impressive. What did you order?"

"A surprise. Remember?"

"Right! A surprise!" Brian said, his smile broadening. "Well, no shop talk. No current events. No menu. That doesn't leave much for dinner conversation. How about finding out more about Dr. Chen Li, or are you off limits too?"

"Don't laugh too hard when I tell you this," she replied, smiling and raising her eyebrows. "Before Wang, our wise leaders passed a law that forbids us from helping, transporting, or communicating extensively with any foreign persons without expressed permission."

"How much is the fine?"

"For some, as much as a week's wage."

The sommelier bought a bottle of wine and poured the wine in Li's glass. She held the glass up to the light, swirled the wine, and sniffed to check the bouquet.

The Summit

"Tres bon. Merci," she said, turning to the sommelier. Brian watched as he poured the wine and placed the bottle at an angle in a silver bucket next to their table. He left them alone.

"How much French do you know?" asked Li.

"Enough to say *hello, goodbye, I like it,* and *where's the bathroom,"* Brian leaned forward, examining her face again. Then looking around cautiously, said, "In whatever language, with you paying fines for being friendly with an American and me putting fifty dollars on my tab for every bottle of wine that man pours, this night could get downright expensive for both of us!"

"I think for you, yes." They both laughed heartily. She raised her glass in a silent toast, and their glasses met. Each sipped the wine, not taking their eyes off the other.

"Do not be overly flattered. Remember, I am presenting a paper. I have permission to talk to you."

"That's quite a stretch! If they believe that, maybe the IRS will believe this dinner is a legitimate business expense."

"You are right. In China, they probably would not approve," Li said lightly, "but it does not matter. Since Wang, the law has not been enforced. He has, at times, even encouraged us to be friendly. He doesn't support Western ways or our youths' infatuation with their music and clothes, but he does not wish to cut us off from the rest of the world."

"You respect him, don't you?"

"Yes, I do," she said evenly. "He identifies with the average worker. Earlier in his career, he and his wife turned down a much larger apartment that was fitting his position. He has even made private, quiet tours to the small Beijing factories to be available for the common people. He has initiated an attack on waste and corruption within government ministries and the Party organization. Not all in the Party like it, but we can see evidence of real change. Yes, I think he is a good man."

"We did it again! Politics!" Brian interrupted, raising his hand as if to stop any more discussion. He raised his glass again to make a toast. "To our now legal conversation and our own summit."

Their glasses clicked. The smiles returned. The appetizers came and were set down on their plates as gently as if they were made of fine china. Brian stared down at the perfect row of asparagus as the waiter spooned three generous tablespoons of rich creamy hollandaise sauce across the tips. When the waiter had finished serving them and left, Brian picked up the remaining sauce and poured it over the rest of the spears. He took up his fork and raised it to Li.

"The fork is raised," Brian said formally.

"What?"

"Oh, that's what my mother always used to say when we had the fancy silverware and crystal out," he replied seriously, then laughing at himself. "That was her way of saying, *It's time to eat!*"

He took two quick bites from his asparagus and then looked up directly into Li's face.

"A very good choice."

"Thank you. But you might want to wait until you taste the rest of my choices before you thank me."

"Okay. Then we must return to our safe topic," he said evenly, "What about Dr. Chen Li?"

She put down her fork and turned to him.

"My last few years have been the best," she said thoughtfully, pausing. "For the last three years in Beijing, I've worked at the Peking Union Medical College Hospital. I have taught at the university and worked in my spare time to develop our mobile care units. My work has been my life. I guess my career has been something of a refuge from a difficult past."

"Difficult?" he asked. As Li paused, he slipped the tines of his fork through the remaining asparagus tips and dipped it in the remaining sauce twice before placing it in his mouth. His eyes returned to her face.

"My mother Yan Fang-Yi lives on the outskirts of Beijing in a small cottage. She was lucky to marry a good man, we had a privileged life until he died when I was young. I was so young, they wanted us to live with my uncle. He had strong Party connections and was also well off. My mother refused. We made it on our own. I am thankful for my uncle, for he used his contacts to give me the best education China had to offer. I was separated from my mother. It was painful for both of us, but my position has helped her keep her small cottage and the garden she loves. She is a good mother."

"Is she still well?" Brian asked.

"She is well. She is a strong woman, and she is happy living in her small cottage. I went to see her before coming to Geneva. She was afraid I would go to Geneva and not come back. I promised her Brian that I would come back. We are close, and she needs me," Li said evenly. She stopped, staring uneasily at Brian. "I'm sorry! I must be boring you. My past was better than most but not always easy, but my story is not one of your James Bond thrillers."

"No! Go on. It's very interesting. I certainly couldn't top your story," Brian said effusively, his eyes searching hers. He paused before continuing, "Speaking of James Bond, how many James Bond—types have you met?"

"Not enough, I'm afraid," she said, laughing. "I have had no time for them to find me. I only had time to get married."

"Married?" Brian asked, trying to mask the surprise he so strongly felt.

"Yes, but it was like most of my relationships with men, very brief," she said, smiling and taking her last bite of asparagus. Brian watched her as she chewed her final bite.

"When my uncle died, I had no housing in Beijing. It is hard to come by and impossible to continue your studies for those living outside of Beijing. Like many at Shanghai Jiao Tong University, I arranged a marriage of convenience to establish a residence. It was a very short, uneventful marriage. I hardly remember his name. We met only once to register our marriage. It allowed me to finish my studies."

Brian breathed a sigh of relief which he hoped was inaudible to Li.

"As I said, I can't top that," he said. "I'm a New York City boy; grew up in Brooklyn. As far as some are concerned, that was an American Siberia. But it was an alive place. It was a challenge just to survive the day. But I have a legacy from those days--I'm still a survivor."

Brian paused to beckon the sommelier. Li held up her empty glass as the man filled it. He did the same for Brian before leaving. She offered a second toast, "To us all surviving together."

"I have a feeling we will," Brian replied.

The waiter arrived and placed the entrées on the table. Brian took his first bite and chewed slowly. Taking his crumpled linen napkin in one hand, he rubbed it across his face a couple of times.

"Magnifique!" Brian said effusively, "but now that your surprise has passed the test, what is it?"

"Coquilles St-Jacques, scallops in a special cream sauce," said with a comfortable smile.

The Summit

"It's very good. All your surprises have been worth waiting for."

She hesitated and then said, "How did you get out of this American Siberia of yours to become a physician?"

"I played basketball." Brian said pausing. "Do you know basketball?"

"Yes. As an Olympic sport, it is important in our country. One of my fellow students was very tall. They paid for his education and his apartment so he would play in a Chinese basketball league. I saw him play many times. Some of our players compete in your country, your NBA."

"Yes, they do. In Brooklyn, basketball was my life. Since I was nine, I played in the streets every day for hours. I wasn't the biggest and I wasn't the best shot, but I had tenacity. I made All-City my senior year in high school, good old Erasmus Hall High School. It was my ticket to the West Coast. I wanted out of New York. I wanted to go to California. My father said the nation was tilted towards California, and all the nuts rolled down to that end of the country. But my mind was made up. Everybody called me a traitor when I went West. They wanted me to stay home and go to St John's. Instead, I went to UCLA on full scholarship. Just like your friend, they paid for my education. Did your friend ever talk about UCLA?"

"I have heard of UCLA. They were very good, were they not?"

"Yes. They were, but it wasn't because of me. I tore my knee up in a practice scrimmage with the varsity before I ever finished my first season."

"That is too bad," Li said simply.

"It really wasn't," Brian explained. "Oh, at the time, I was destroyed. All my dreams dashed in one sheering second. It took me a long time to bounce back, but I did. UCLA didn't miss me; they went to the finals at the national tournament without me. I would have sat on the bench. I was already getting out of my league. With the coach's support, they kept me on scholarship. I turned my frustration towards my studies, got into pre-med, and lost myself in some new dreams and some new goals. Years later, when many of my buddies were being drafted or forced to sign up for Afghanistan, I was sitting in medical school with a bum knee."

"You almost sound guilty," observed Li.

"Oh, I am, I guess. One of the other All-City players on the Erasmus Hall team, Rich Devens, went to Duke, played damn good ball, but never graduated. He was black, one of the few in our high school at that time. He ended up enlisting. He's still in the service, Special Forces, I think. Your country must have them too, special teams trained to counter terrorist groups. He could be here for all I know; this is his kind of job. He had so much to offer, he never had the chance I did."

"Is he bitter?"

"I don't know. He never said so to me directly. I've only seen him a couple of times since graduation. The last time was at a high school reunion," Brian said almost dreamily. He paused, taking a deep breath. "Basketball was all we really ever had in common. He was black; I was white. He went military; I went establishment. But boy, could we play basketball together!"

Brian was lost momentarily in images and memories.

"Unfortunately, when the basketball died for us, so did our relationship," Brian said, his voice low. As she touched his arm, he sighed again. "I'm sorry. I guess it's my turn to bore you."

Her eyes looked steadily at him. She left her hand on his arm. An all too rare tingle of life stirred inside him.

The Summit

"No, continue," she said, her eyes roaming over his face like a gentle caress. She tilted her head back, and he could feel her study his expression. He looked away.

"What a strange man you are," she said quietly, as if amused by his sudden discomfort.

"Why do you say that?" he turned back abruptly.

"You are so sensitive. I did not expect that from a Western man," she said evenly. Impulsively, she touched his cheek with her fingers.

"Are we Western men supposed to be that different?"

"I don't know. I guess not. Every Western man I have met has been sensitive," she said slowly. Brian took another sip of wine, willing her to continue.

"When you were at UCLA, did you know Dr. Robert Gale?"

"I did not know him when I was there. I left before he arrived, but I know him. He is a special man. Do you know him?"

"In ways, I sometimes wish to forget," she said, turning away. She wiped away a tear with her napkin. "Even with his help, so many died."

"How did you meet him."

"There was an accident—no—an explosion, at one of our nuclear facilities. I was then with the Ministry of Health. I was one of the few physicians that spoke English. I was one of the translators for the Americans."

"This tragedy is not your first. Sounds like you've had more than your share," Brian said, trying to fill a momentary silence.

"We worked twelve to fifteen hours a day. We saved many, but so many were beyond help. One of our doctors that I had gone to school with was a true hero. Knowing the risks, he entered the contaminated building in an attempt to rescue people injured in the initial explosion. He had sacrificed himself to save many. When I first saw him in the hospital, he was still conscious, though delirious at times. He smiled at me as I held his hand. Over the days, we watched his skin literally break down before our eyes. Ulcers spread across his entire body. In a matter of days, he was covered with deep, red skin burns. The morphine did little to ease his misery. He died twelve days later."

"He was a hero."

"So was your Dr. Gale. I cried when the Americans left. I think I will cry again when you leave. If we Chinese are not to trust Americans, I am not doing a very good job," she said with a half-smile, again wiping a tear from the corner of her eye.

"Have you seen Gale again?" Brian asked.

"No, but I will not forget him. After that incident, I could never be the same. I am now a member of the International Physicians for the Prevention of Nuclear War. I have seen what a relatively small amount of radiation can do. War is no longer an option. You are a member, are you not?"

"Yes, but not as active or as committed a member as you, I'm afraid."

"You did not see what I saw," Li said softly, her eyes not wavering from his. "After Geneva, I think you too will not be able to forget."

"I'm sure I won't. That's assuming the world finds a way to get through this without someone pushing the wrong button."

"We will get through this. Remember, we are both survivors." They both smiled.

"We did it again," Brian said. "No more tragedies! This dinner has taken a depressing turn."

"You're right. There are many good memories to share. I remember happier years at Shanghai Jiao Tong University. They say the Chinese are different—harsh, severe, even sullen, but the people are not that way. I suppose there are austere buildings; it certainly is not Geneva. But the people make China special. Many of my fellow students and I would sit for hours sipping coffee and later drinks. It was always a room full of friendly souls. We listened to Western jazz music—Miles Davis and Teddy Wilson. Do you know them?"

"Yes, but not well. I was never that fond of jazz."

"I loved jazz. The music was so free. Tien Chau, the doctor who died of radiation poisoning, would sometimes bring his trumpet. He loved to play in the jazz café. Tien was no hero then, just a good person. I remember the crowd, the noise, the smoke. I am glad he had that good time at the university," she said as if evoking a magic spirit. She seemed inordinately pleased, her smile broadening as she stirred her glass of water with her finger. Withdrawing her finger, the ice in her glass continued to dance as she spoke.

"The government officials never approved, but they understood. They did not stop us. The people were sick of politics and failed promises. They would rather find their joy where they could—whether it was jazz, sports, dance.... We needed an escape."

Brian waited for some additional comment from her, but she made no response. He took his last bite, placing his fork on his plate. As he took another sip of wine, the waiter came and removed their plates.

"You are special," Brian said. He wondered what she was thinking, but her eyes revealed nothing. Carefully monitoring her expression, he moved his empty glass aside so there was nothing between them on the table.

"You are special, too, Brian," she said cheerfully. Then, without preliminary, "I do not want dessert. I would like to go up to your room."

"This isn't the wine speaking, is it?"

"No, Doctor, I'm sober enough to know that I want to be with you now."

Brian's heart pounded so hard it hurt. He thought only teenagers felt this way; that sudden ridiculous panic pulled at his mind. He took another deep breath in an attempt to alleviate it. He looked away and gestured to the waiter who brought the bill. It was not until he rose that his eyes met hers again. They smiled. He was amazed at the flood of feelings that swept over him as she took his arm.

He led her silently to the elevator. The door opened instantly, as if expecting them. He rested his hand firmly on the small of her back, feeling her warmth as he led her in.

As the door closed, she was at his side. He pulled her to him. With his hand, he gently touched her chin, lifting her head back. Their lips were close and their eyes locked. Immediately, his mouth came down over hers, and he pulled her body to him. He felt the heat of her body and the strength of her arms caressing his back. But there was a fluttering terror lurking in the back of his mind. He was losing himself to a woman he knew he could never really have.

He heard her sigh as he kissed her more passionately. His body responded, pulling him deeper into a spiral he did not want to resist. She reached inside his coat, his flesh dancing to her touch. The elevator door opened.

A few minutes later, they reached his room. He unlocked the door and was about to turn on the light when she pulled back his arm.

"No, the lamp will be enough."

Using the light from the hall, Brian crossed the room. He turned on the study lamp near the bed. Li shut the door and locked the chain, banishing the world outside. He watched her from the bed as she turned and faced him. For a moment, they just stared at each other; neither said anything. Without further words, she moved slowly toward him, fueling the desperate hunger he felt for her.

"Li, I..." Brian said with a strange kind of wonderment in his voice. He held out his hand; she took it.

"Be quiet," she said softly as she sat down next to him. "Please. We have said enough."

She stroked the side of his cheek. Now his face was very close to hers. He could see the gleam of sweat on her brow and feel her hand rub over the short stubble of his beard. But most of all, he inhaled her scent. He took her face in his hands, studying it carefully. He could feel the contact building heat between them. In an instant, he put his hands around her shoulders, pulling her body to him.

He remembered her saying, *"In Geneva, the romantic evenings are seldom short."* He was glad.

CHAPTER FORTY-TWO

FOR EARS TO HEAR THE HIDDEN CODE

> **Hostage Quarters**
> **Palace of Nations Conference Center**

"Righteous are you, O Lord, when I complain to you;
yet I would plead my case before you.
Why does the way of the wicked prosper?
Why do all who are treacherous thrive?"
Jeremiah 12:1 (ESV)

"Why are you taking just me?" Freeman asked. Her legs were weak. She stumbled, caught herself, and looked into Gamal Saud's eyes.

"You do not need to know!" Gamal held onto her tightly, leaving the room with sadistic speed, dragging her along.

Now, the President had no allies anywhere. She was on her own. Her chest heaved, and she fought for breath. She felt her own heart beating very fast, as sweat rolled off her forehead.

She tripped again and started to go down. Gamal steadied her before she could fall. Connie staggered but regained her footing, the ropes again biting into her arms. Instinctively, her mind tried to restore order to her growing alarm. *Stay calm. Cooperate. Be hard to hate.*

Keep your head and observe your surroundings. Waste no opportunity. The litany continued as she was dragged into the press room, where the bright lights momentarily caused her to squint.

"Is the proud American Eagle ready to beg?" Ghazi asked. His hand balled into a raised fist. Somewhere, in the back of her mind, she knew how disconnected Ghazi was becoming. She said nothing.

"We are calling a radio station. You will cooperate this time," Ghazi said. Ghazi's eyes squinted, his head thrust out on his muscled neck. He gave the President a wide, wicked smile.

The President nodded her head, but her mind was already running. She was not going to be killed. She was going to be given the opportunity she wanted. She had to be ready; she might not get another. As she watched the men get ready, she concentrated on the problem, surprised by her own calm in the face of pressure. She was even further surprised when, with crystal clarity, the solution came to her easily. *Martin, you've got to listen. You are the only one who can really hear!*

Ghazi moved across the room to the telephone near the President's seat and dialed a number.

"Station manager," the man on the phone said firmly. Ghazi paused, staring at the wall.

"This is Ghazi Saud, leader of Al-Haram," he said fiercely. His voice dropped to a low menacing tone. "We are monitoring your station; we can hear it playing in the background. We want live action, or the American President dies."

Ghazi spoke with controlled fury. The lines of tension grew around his mouth, his eyes glaring. He fired two rounds of ammunition from his Uzi into the wall. The sudden explosions rang unmercifully in Connie's ears. As fast as Ghazi started, he stopped.

"I do not need permission from Swiss authorities. What do I care about your problems? Put us on, or she dies!"

Again, there was a pause, the radio still playing the regularly scheduled music. Ghazi pressed the receiver to the President's ear, her face momentarily losing all color.

"Tell him!" Ghazi demanded.

"I am here. Listen to them," Freeman said carefully.

"Put us on!" Ghazi grabbed the phone and exclaimed into the receiver.

Suddenly, the sound of silence interrupted the music, Ghazi's voice echoing through the room as he talked. Gamal moved to turn the volume down while staying to monitor the radio message.

"We are Al-Haram, and we recognize no other action but destruction," said Ghazi in a voice that was knife sharp. "The urge to destroy is a creative urge. Everything we do is sanctified by the revolution. With Allah's help, we are committed to the sacred cause of rooting out all evil in the world. In Israel, there are no innocents. Their destruction will be a purifying force. The so-called superpowers lay at our feet. Their leaders are not human; they are monsters who will work with us or die. For now, they are alive. Already many have been killed so that you could be warned, so that you could gain some small amount of wisdom." As he placed the receiver against Freeman's ear, he yelled abruptly, "Talk to them, dog!"

Connie began slowly, thoughtfully, "We are fine. They are treating us well. I assure you that the time is short for both myself and General Secretary Wang." *My God, give me the time to get this message in.* She could feel the sweat on her forehead. "I ask you to work with them. Martin, you know how much I love these 15-second spots, but here I can't control the content. I can't wait to see you live. I want to–"

251

"Enough!" Ghazi blurted, his face darkening as he grabbed the receiver. "They have tried to silence our demands. We have now spoken to the world. If you want to see your leaders alive, you must cooperate with us. Deliver the weapons on time, or they will die."

Ghazi replaced the receiver. His face was contorted in a wide, wicked smile. The man was going mad. *Say nothing to antagonize him. Give him no target to look at. Patience... patience...*

A look of loathing and disgust passed across Ghazi's face as he turned to stare at Freeman. He moved toward her.

"Now the mighty are laid low!" Ghazi said without inflection. "It is good for you to crawl. You are learning well."

The President said nothing. She remained silent, her eyes as vacant and unfocused as she could manage.

"Take her back!" Ghazi commanded, dismissing her with a fleeting gesture.

As Freeman was escorted out, a smile formed on her lips. *I got it in, Martin. May you have ears to hear.* Finally, God seemed to hear her prayers. She felt His presence, listening. She remained calm as the familiar words of the Lord's prayer played in her mind. She felt God's comfort. Would Martin listen? Would he get the message to those who would need to act?

CHAPTER FORTY-THREE

WHAT MESSAGE IS THE PRESIDENT TRYING TO SEND?

> The Domaine de Châteauvieux
> Geneva, Switzerland

"Trust in the LORD with all your heart,
and do not lean on your own understanding.
In all your ways acknowledge him,
and he will make straight your paths."
Proverbs 3:5-6 (ESV)

With the nightlights of Geneva reflecting off the lake, Martin's eyes were momentarily riveted to the beauty of the city, a scene that seemed incapable of launching a nightmare. He had been locked in a trance for some time. *You're making something out of nothing. They're experts. Don't get in the way.*

But it didn't feel right. Connie was trying to say something, but what was it? He took a deep breath and uttered another in a string of short prayers that settled his mind. *It will be alright. Neil won't mind. If it's nothing, at least I tried. But what if it's important?*

As soon as Martin heard the broadcast, he started replaying Connie's statement over and over in his mind. He had heard her words repeatedly on the television, but he no longer needed to watch. The words echoed through the synapses of his mind: *"We are fine; they are treating us well. I assure you that time is short. I ask you to work with them. Martin, you know how much I love those 15-second spots, but here I can't control the content. I can't wait to see you live..."*

When Martin first heard the message, he had struggled, another reminder that the woman he loved might never return. *The time was short.* But listening his second and third times had confused and bothered him. Like a series of shocks, one after another, the message had hammered home. She was speaking to him; it was up to him to understand.

With difficulty, he tried to organize his mind and think logically. Something was not right. She never did any fifteen-second spots for any campaign. They had discussed it. She had adamantly refused to be reduced to 15-second commercials—she wanted substance and a chance to connect. She had argued with Neil over that very matter for hours—no short spots! But here she talked positively about them. He knew his wife. She wouldn't say that lightly. It had to be a message. *Connie, what are you trying to say?*

Where was Neil? Martin looked instinctively at his watch. He couldn't understand why Neil had not called. He had left a message with him over half-an-hour ago. Martin knew that they were busy, but it was not like Neil not to make time for him. He paced momentarily in front of the window, determined to distract himself, but it had not worked. His mind refused to let go of Connie's message.

Moving from the window, he went over to the television and turned up the volume. The TV had been droning on hour after hour, a constant companion through much of the ordeal. It was always there, just a steady stream of words and stale images. He had turned it down to help him think, but now, once again, the voice of the reporters filled the room. He was tired, but he knew tonight there would be no sleep. He could not put his mind to rest until he had solved the riddle she had sent him.

Martin focused intently on the new image. A harried reporter was pressing his earphone to his ear while trying to talk over the tumult of a large, milling crowd. His voice had a frightening edge to it. He seemed to hold tightly to his microphone, as if clinging to the last shred of his detachment in an engulfing sea of emotion.

"This is Bill Danson here in Israel. Crowds estimated to be in the tens of thousands have been filling the streets around the US Embassy for hours. The angry demonstrators have been waving banners and holding up signs that sum up the angry mood of the people, *'Swift Death to the Terrorists,' 'Keep Nuclear Weapons Out of the Middle East,' 'No One Is Worth another Holocaust.'*"

But to Martin, however, the faces said much more than the banners and the signs. They were faces of men and women hanging on the edge. Their faces were angry, and they were frightened. The ominous hum of agitated, pleading voices resounded through the reporter's microphone. The reporter tried to brace himself, but he was but one fragile body in a wall of humanity pressing against the US Embassy gates. His body gave ground repeatedly, shifting like a leaf in a stiff wind. The nightmare was spreading. Where and how would it end?

The scene shifted stateside to a special report by Natalie Moreno, one of the few Washington reporters he respected. Moreno's face was flushed, her voice taut. "There are unconfirmed reports from the Naval Air Station in North Island, California, that a C-5A Galaxy transport

The Summit

has taken off, carrying three one-kiloton nuclear weapons in its cargo bay. Unconfirmed, but previously reliable sources have indicated that the weapons are en route to Europe. The White House will neither confirm nor deny this report. This is Natalie Moreno reporting for World Net from North Island, California."

No, it couldn't be. They wouldn't give them the weapons! Martin's mind struggled to make sense of what he could not accept. Waves of apprehension washed over him. Connie would not want this!

The phone's startling reprieve grabbed at his senses. Instinctively, Martin reached for the phone, pulling it to his ear. Neil's greeting brought momentary relief.

"Neil! I'm so glad you called. I just heard Natalie Moreno report that three nuclear weapons are being transported to Europe. Connie wouldn't want this. They aren't really going to exchange weapons for...?"

"Martin. Wait," Neil interrupted. "There will be no exchange. But we want them to believe we may be willing to bend. We leaked the information because we wanted them to broadcast it. Right now, we have nothing but illusions to work with. Ghazi is getting impatient, but he listens to the media. We hope giving him tidbits to hold onto will keep him calm. Right now, we need time."

"They don't seem to know that in Israel," Martin added. "They're all but storming our embassy."

"The Prime Minister has been reassured that there will be no weapons transfer, and he has no reason to doubt us. The bombs themselves have been defused. The Israelis have one of their own men on that transport to make sure there are no problems. They are also monitoring all our strategic aircraft," Neil confided evenly. "Unfortunately, the public doesn't know. We can't let them know. They're a part of the illusion we so desperately need."

"I hope no one gets hurt," Martin said. "Has the negotiator talked to Ghazi?"

"Not since he grabbed the radio airwaves. He isn't answering his phone. Right now, we're just trying to keep the rumors running consistently in our direction until we can get through to him again. I slipped away to call you, but I can't talk long. Your message said it was important. What is it?"

Martin took a deep breath and exhaled. He started slowly, "Connie's message, she's trying to say something to us. I'm just not sure what it is."

"What do you mean?" Neil said sharply. Martin felt there was more to his question than he understood. He quickly continued because he knew Neil was tired and in a hurry.

"Connie has always hated 15-second campaign spots. You remember that. She argued with you about it. But tonight, she said I would remember how much she loved them," Martin said. He paused, but no sound came from the receiver. Martin continued, "When you proposed them, she never wanted to hurt your feelings, but she told me how vehemently she hated short political commercials."

"Come to think of it, you're right," Neil said incredulously. "She nixed them all before we even got to try them."

"Connie wouldn't say that on the radio unless she wanted to communicate something. There is only one thing that I keep thinking after listening over and over. Do you think she might be trying to get you to work with them to let them control the spots, maybe live spots?"

The Summit

His words hung in the air. They were the same words he had said over and over to himself, but now they were exposed. He felt suddenly unsure.

"I'm sorry. It was probably nothing worth bothering you about. I just felt–"

"No, it's not a bother at all!" Neil's crisp words stifled his backtracking. "You're right. She is saying something!"

Neil paused again. Then Martin heard a gasp.

"That's it!" Neil exclaimed. "Let them have their own live feed! Give them all the TV exposure they want!"

"What?"

"Don't you see?" Neil continued excitedly. "Connie knows we can't isolate where they are holding her, but she figured out a way we wouldn't need to. We let Ghazi bring them to us. If we help Ghazi get the television exposure he craves, we have them. We'll control the time and the place! It's beautiful. With at least one of the terrorists busy with the camera and Ghazi strutting in front of the world, we give the special forces team the edge they've been looking for. Martin, you just may have saved the day!"

"Neil," Martin, pausing as a chill ran through his body. "Don't let anything happen to her. I need her; the country needs her."

"We won't," Neil said with the calm, reassuring confidence Martin needed to hear. "For now, stay in the chateau. I'll get back to you when we have everything in place."

"I will for now," Martin said with an edge of reservation. "But before any attempt is made to rescue my wife, I want to be in a place both Ma Mei and I can be together. We belong together for this." He said it in a tone he knew would make it hard for Neil or anyone to refuse.

"I understand. I'll get back to you as soon as I can," Neil said evenly. "Right now, time is the enemy, but you've given us a path to a workable plan."

Martin wasn't sure if Neil even heard him say goodbye. He held onto the receiver after the line went dead. *God, don't let anything happen to her!*

CHAPTER FORTY-FOUR

A DARING RESCUE PLAN TAKES FORM

Rescue Staging Area
Geneva, Switzerland

*"He puts no trust even in His servants, and against
His angels, He charges error."*
Job 4:18 (NAS)

"We've already disclosed more classified information than we should have. It's like giving our operations manual to every terrorist group!" Rip said fiercely, swinging his head suddenly to face Col. Healey.

"Major, enough!" snapped the Colonel, his voice a guttural whisper. They were walking the Chinese Embassy grounds, hearing nothing but the sounds of their footsteps on the pavement. Rip knew it was not in Chuck's nature to be cold. Tough, yes, very tough, but not cold. Chuck continued, "We're not holding back on this one. We can't afford to."

"May I remind you, sir, as important as the President is, we have lost thousands of troops for less," Rip said. "I didn't watch many of

A Daring Rescue Plan Takes Form

my buddies die in Afghanistan to now give our secrets away to the Chinese."

"I picked you because you were the best man for the job. Remember, if you don't want to do the job, I can still find someone to take the lead who does," Chuck countered. "Either you and your patriotism make room for working with us or get out of here now!"

"I'll do the job, sir, but I don't like it."

"Then get in there, Major," Chuck said. "The decision has been made. I just met with Kamal and the rest of the negotiating team. If we can hook Ghazi with the bait of a live feed to the world, you go to work tomorrow. You'll only get one chance, so make it good."

His mind overloaded in a sea of unwanted images, Rip walked back alone to the conference room. General Zhang Ming's cold constant stares had hit him hard evoking images of horrors past. Easier to read was General Jin Yuan, an old warrior no different from those that populated the halls of the Pentagon. Colonel Tang Wei disturbed Rip more. Tang's boundless curiosity and forced cordiality irritated Rip beyond his comprehension. He did not trust him. It would be tough enough to plan the rescue with the Colonel, but it would be even more difficult to carry it out. One misstep and the President would be dead. And Rip and his men could be dead too. He hated depending on men he didn't trust.

Before Rip could finish his thoughts, the briefing was already in progress.

Soon Rip realized he was watching something he had never seen before—men from two enemy camps and two very different cultures trying to find a common ground to work on. Although the words of the planning session had a familiar ring to them, underneath was an undercurrent of betrayal. He wondered momentarily how difficult it was for the Chinese. But the immediacy of the hostage rescue briefing brought him back.

It was clear to all that no detail of the rescue could be left untested—the positioning of the sharpshooters, the timing, placement, and type of the breach explosives, the plan blind spots, the most probable positioning of the terrorists from existing information, the backup operations, the repelling preparations, assault responsibilities, and emergency medical teams. All present at the meeting operated on autopilot, applying expertise and information honed through years of training. The specifics were discussed, dissected, and agreed upon for final approval.

The planning droned on, but no matter how much preparation was done, any rescue attempt always boiled down to a critical six seconds. Once the numbing grenades exploded, the assault team would have six seconds to find and take down the stunned terrorists. Twenty seconds after the initial assault, Guntram's Swiss units would attack the barricaded entrances on the second floor and mop up any additional resistance. But to Rip it always came back to those critical six seconds. If you did not take down the targets or if anything went wrong within that time frame, the leaders' lives would be in jeopardy.

The initial planning phase ended, and the plan was ready to be presented for review to the negotiating team. The plan would work, but could the team work together?

As the other men left the conference room, Rip and Tang were alone. The two special forces leaders stared at each other silently. They could feel the tension both knew was yet unresolved.

"I don't want to work with you," Rip said abruptly. "As far as I'm concerned, your country concerns me more than the terrorists."

A Daring Rescue Plan Takes Form

"You don't really believe that?" responded Tang. "Ghazi and his men are maniacs. I don't have to tell you that. You and I are enemies, and neither of us would pretend otherwise, but we do acknowledge certain rules between us. We are not rabid wolves, we're professional enemies. There is a fundamental respect between us, grounded in fear, but respect nonetheless."

Their eyes were level. Rip broke the momentary silence. "I know you from the dossier in our files, just as you know me from yours. We're enemies, and we'll remain that way."

Tang's eyes danced playfully while he tried to keep a straight face. "Do you want me to be easier for you to hate, Major?" Tang smiled almost tolerantly.

"Don't patronize me!"

"Far be it from me…" Tang said quietly. He smiled again, speaking in a comfortable, warm tone, "Maybe we can have our own summit after this is over. We could meet in California. I have wanted to see California."

"You want to defect? It would be difficult," Rip replied.

"What makes you think I want to defect?"

"No reason," Rip confessed, almost reluctantly. "I just wanted you to know from the start that the Chinese made it clear—no defections."

"I will be no problem," Tang taunted, laughing disarmingly. "Americans seem to think that all Chinese are potential dissidents, simmering with resentment against communist control, and ready to leave at a moment's notice. It may surprise you, Major, but I love my country. Would you like to defect to us?"

"That's ridiculous!" Rip said in a disgusted tone.

"With all your talking about defecting, I thought maybe you were hinting."

The Summit

"Let's drop this!" Rip said bluntly.

"Would it never occur to you that someone might want to leave your beloved America? I have known diplomats who have served in your country. Many have seen enough of your, so-called, freedom. They have brought their families back to China," Tang said triumphantly. "Americans never see themselves as others do. You spend too much time in your Hollywood illusions and your six o'clock news headlines. Some of our agents have lived your way. They looked American; they talked American. They didn't choose to defect. They were more American than you are, Major. They are white. The choices in America are simple: Step outside and get shot on the streets or stay inside and watch others get shot on television. You understand, do you not, major? You are a black man in America. You are more likely to be murdered than to live any American Dream."

"Oh, so the Chinese don't have murders?" Rip said with mimicry. "Many never return from your camps. But I guess that's not considered murder, just educational correction for the misguided!"

"You bore me. You have killed, and so have I. You have been in the field. The first time is so long ago. It is hard for either of us to remember. But you are right. In China, we have murders. We even doctor the statistics to make it less, but we have less murder than your country," Tang said gravely, his honesty taking Rip by surprise.

"Our Chinese murders are secret. We deliberately don't publicize them. Even our accidents and health problems are secret, officially and unofficially. Our killers do not boast, and our witnesses are more afraid of the investigators than the killers. But at least we don't watch it in glorified slow motion every evening on television!"

"We have freedom to report the truth," Rip interrupted.

A Daring Rescue Plan Takes Form

"The truth! You know, of course, this Summit madness is getting top billing in your country. The American press is drooling over it like ants over honey. What products will the killing of our two leaders sell? Do you call that freedom? You will even get to see it in reruns, movies, and documentaries for years to come. Your country has a preoccupation with tragedies. And, oh yes, we will be blamed."

"You think suppression is the answer?" Rip roared defensively. "Silencing people will never work!"

"You don't understand us," replied Tang. "Your experts read our books and you visit, but you still do not understand us. Our system has always been in the process of change. There are phases we have gone through and must continue to go through before the freedoms our people desire are complete. Your country has hollow freedoms, the kind that keep the poor in slavery. You are black. I should not have to tell you this!"

"If you are so free, why do you ban books and program your children," Rip answered sharply. For just a second, he felt the verbal shot hit home. Tang said nothing and turned to face the side wall, smiling.

"Why do you smile?" Rip asked, halfway between fascination and annoyance.

"I have an incurable disease."

"What do you mean?"

"You have it too. We've been trained so long to hate," Tang said evenly. Rip said nothing, choosing only to return his stare. Tang continued with just the right amount of derision, "My father said it could be different."

"Your father?"

"My father is a fisherman. He has worked with Americans for ten years in a joint fishing venture. He has made good money working with the Americans. Politics do not get in the way with my father. He is a fisherman, not a communist. Fishermen are simple, vital people, and they like other fishermen, no matter their politics. My father was the first to teach me some English. He said there could be peace. I am not so sure. I'm afraid we were trained too well for war."

Rip said nothing. Tang was making too much sense to argue.

"I think I'm going to get some rest," Tang said, rising from his seat. "These words tire me. Tomorrow we will be finished with the words; there will only be time for action. I plan on being ready. Maybe we will catch our own fish together in spite of ourselves."

Tang moved silently across the room. As the door closed behind him, Rip stood motionless for nearly a minute, living with the image of Tang's eyes. They held too much truth in them. Over the years, Rip had learned to read men, especially his enemies. Tang was not lying. He had spoken the truth as he believed it to be. They weren't the same eyes he remembered from past enemies. He didn't want to forget, but he didn't want to remember. He closed his eyes, wincing, trying to push away the nightmares from another time.

Suddenly, he felt a jolt of pain in his chest. It was fear, raw fear. He felt trapped remembering memories within memories. Would it be different here?

CHAPTER FORTY-FIVE

NO ONE WINS A WAR IN TODAY'S WORLD

**Palace of Nations Conference Hostage Room
Geneva, Switzerland**

*"Any misjudgement on either side about the intentions
of the other could rain more devastation in several
hours than has been wrought in all the wars
of human history."*
John F. Kennedy

*"Be happy in your hope, stand your ground when you're
in trouble, and devote yourselves to prayer."*
Romans 12:12 (Common English Bible)

"I hate waiting," Connie said in growing exasperation. The minutes were now dragging like hours. She could hardly move her arms, and her legs had all but gone asleep. She once again shifted cautiously before speaking, "I would think we would have heard something by now. I know Martin would understand."

"Understanding and being able to do something are not always synonymous," Wang said softly. He watched Connie's face closely. "The animosity between our peoples has always been a living testimony to that reality."

The Summit

"Right now, it doesn't make much sense, does it?" Connie added thoughtfully. They both hesitated, with Wang breaking the silence.

"Too much living in our own fears," Wang said calmly, cocking his head to one side and raising his eyebrows. "Not enough time trying to understand. We are always reacting. I remember when past presidents responded with economic reprisals against us. Every time they pushed us further into the grasp of Chinese militarism."

"But they felt they had to do something and had so few options," Freeman said quickly, wondering at her own defensiveness so evident in her voice. "What would you have suggested they do?"

"I doubt whether they would have listened to my suggestions," Wang said lightly, both leaders giving way to a shared smile.

"We have predicted for years that communism doesn't work," Connie observed. "Are you admitting it hasn't?"

"You do not understand, do you?" Wang added, trying to check his frustration. The President hesitated. If Wang was upset with what she had said, he was careful not to let it show. "I do not want to change what we call it. I want to make it work better. The more the Chinese dream of economic prosperity for the masses has died, the more pre-occupied we became with militarism. If you cannot cure your own faults, mobilize your people against a distant enemy—the hated impe-rialists from the West. Your actions, your buildups, your presidential provocations gave the ammunition needed to fuel the deep Chinese paranoia about interference and even invasions from the West. We are running from an age of uncertainty by generating fear and revulsion. We have convinced most of our people that the whole outside world is against them."

"We would rather not be against you."

"For now, we cannot afford to make you a friend. China is a multi-ethnic country. Although ninety percent of Chinese citizens come from the Han ethnic group, the other fifty-five different ethnic groups make up a very diverse mix that we refer to as the 'national minorities.' Each has their own demands, but little real power. But with the international media eager to ferment problems, the minorities love to launch a torrent of crusades for 'their people.' They want no communist platitudes or vague promises that somewhere, sometime, they'll have it better. They want changes for the better here, this very minute. With my rise to power and our calls for civic maturity and restraint, there is a fragile peace, but it will not last if needs are not met. We are trying to hide for now beneath the old but familiar cloud and fear of Western imperialism. But many, now connected online or through access to Western programs, refuse to believe that America is our enemy. They want the Summit to work. But if it does, we will be faced with our still unmet promises."

"We do not want war. We want cooperation, but your military buildup sends a message that can't be ignored. You know that."

"What one knows and what one can do may not always mesh," Wang said thoughtfully. "I have always known that America did not want war with us. I have studied the West myself. I believe you even more now, but most of the Party leadership has been unwilling to acknowledge that. We covered our failures with a thin veneer of strength. It was thin, but now our military force is extensive and growing. In their minds, might works. We are still in power, and they remind me that your election to a second term is not guaranteed."

Freeman remained silent, watching as Wang shrugged his shoulders. "We are now an effective and powerful military machine. Do not be lulled into thinking that our military is dull or ineffective. If unleashed, we would most likely win in our sphere of influence. In fact, many of my military men want war. In fact, they feel it is the right time to take back Taiwan."

"What holds them back?"

"I do, Madam President," Wang said evenly, staring at Connie. "I have resisted any offensive military actions of any kind against Taiwan."

Connie stared back. She had been briefed on a China offensive against Taiwan but had doubted its reality. There had been rumors of such a takeover for years. Suddenly, there seemed to be more to Wang than she had ever expected. She wanted to trust him, but she was afraid to under these circumstances. Her judgment may be impaired.

"No one wins with a war in today's world," Connie confessed.

"No one wins in any war. I remember seeing Yevgeny Yevtushenko's Russian film 'The Kindergarten'," Wang said, his voice anguished. "It was war seen through the eyes of children. There were no scenes of patriotic Soviet soldiers beating back the advance of the German soldiers in Leningrad. Just images of Russian faces—the faces of those raped and dying. I remember the eyes, the eyes of men and women suffering. I could feel the fear and panic in the eyes of the children. The Russians lost twenty million in the war with Germany. We have all seen this again in the footage from Ukraine. Yes, we can agree. There should be no room for war anymore."

Wang's steady voice had faltered for a second. She was seeing a new side of him, a side Freeman would have dismissed as unlikely weeks ago.

"With the way I am talking to you, you can understand how many in the Party are not pleased to have me as a leader. For much of the military, I am nothing. Many of those same men, I'm sure, hope to see me die here. I assure you that I do not plan on accommodating them. But we are not in control here. There is no assurance either of us will get out of this."

"If we do get out, what guarantee do I have that you will not use your military against us?" Connie said carefully, her eyes searching his. "My future depends on winning in November. Coming out strong on cooperation with China may not be a winning strategy."

"Guarantee?" Wang said calmly. "You have only my word, which before this ordeal meant nothing. I hope it means more now."

"I think it may," Connie said with a smile. "But what is realistically possible? We both have supporters that would fight such changes. Even if we both want to make it work, I'm not sure there is anything we can do."

"In a Swiss newspaper, I saw a cartoon that showed both of us standing on mountaintops separated by a valley and steep cliffs. The cartoon had you declaring to me, *'You take the first step.'* I know it must be hard for you to accept, but in telling you what I have already said, I'm taking that step," Wang said sagely. "I had not planned on saying any of this to you. It had never occurred to me that you would listen. Being in this room together has changed things."

"I'm really not sure how much our relationship has changed," Connie said evenly. "I've grown to distrust mountaintop experiences and crisis confessions. The hard test of reality is just that, hard! I remember reading President John Kennedy's notes on Khrushchev. When Kennedy tried reason and candor with the Soviet leader, Khrushchev mistakenly took it as a sign of weakness and tried installing nuclear weapons in Cuba. I want to leave you with no such illusion of weakness. If and when we get out of this, there will be time to test both our words and any plans for peace and economic cooperation. But Wang Da, I do want to believe you. I pray that it could be so."

"A farmer once told me, *'It is the wolf you do not see that you must fear.'* I will work with you if you let me. Unfortunately, I'm afraid you believe as much in me as I believe in your God," Wang said, unperturbed. He hesitated for a minute, turning to face the door. They both heard the approaching footsteps.

The President watched silently as Gamal Saud and one of his men entered the room. She looked in their faces for signals that something was different, but there was nothing. Her keen sense of observation scoured their faces for any shades of meaning.

Gamal kept his gun trained on them as his man undid the ropes that bound their hands. The blood rushed through Connie's veins, the tingling sensations awakening her numb body.

Both grabbed at the meager food prepared for them. There were no utensils. Connie used her fingers to scoop the oatmeal-like substance into her mouth. She was hungry, and she knew she would need all her strength. Freeman looked at Gamal's face. He did not have Ghazi's intensity. She had never seen him lose his temper. *Make friends, not enemies,* she reminded herself. It could buy them precious time.

"What are you going to do with us?" Connie asked carefully, looking into Gamal's eyes while she handed his man the empty bowl. Gamal said nothing, choosing rather to divert his attention to Wang as his man took his plate from the general secretary's outstretched hand.

"Do you hate us that much?" she said, again watching his face intently.

"You hate us, do you not?" Gamal said in broken English.

"I don't have it in me to hate you."

"You best find a way. Worry about us, because we are going to kill you."

"You won't kill us. You can't afford to let us die."

"We have wanted to kill you both all year," Gamal snorted derisively. A grim little smile touched his lips. "You are crazy! You forget who is in charge here. We have already killed!"

No One Wins a War in Today's World

"I don't think you are like your brother."

"I will play none of your stupid games!" Gamal said dryly, as he motioned for his man to tie her up. The terrorist grabbed her arms and pulled them behind her. He methodically tied her hands. She continued to watch Gamal.

"You are human, and so are we," she persisted cautiously. "None of this killing will make the world any better."

"You are not human," Gamal said testily. His voice flared as he motioned quickly to tie up Wang. Gamal again stared at the President, "We are more human than you! You are both sick with power. You make the powerless pay. We will now make you pay!"

"We can help your people."

"You have had your chance before, and you did not help. I should kill you for this alone, but for now, you must live," Gamal said, irked.

"Do you have a wife?" Connie asked, her voice softening.

Gamal said nothing, his eyes taking on a faraway look. She studied his expression. If he was ever to find accommodations with any of the terrorists, she must quickly find some way to make a natural connection with this man.

"Do you miss her?"

Suddenly, Ghazi entered. "Enough!" Ghazi's voice echoed through the room. "You do not talk to dogs. You just feed them!"

Freeman could feel Ghazi's eyes fixing her with a sudden intense gaze. The deep black pupils of his eyes were enormously expanded, gleaming, depthless, almost alien. She felt a chill run down her back.

I will not let you win! We will escape! Connie watched as Ghazi, Gamal, and the other terrorist left the room.

CHAPTER FORTY-SIX

WILL JUDAS BE TEMPTED OR TRUSTED?

Rescue Staging Area
Geneva, Switzerland

"Who devise evil things in their hearts;
they continually stir up wars."
Psalm 140:2 (NAS)

Rip's eyes studied the Admiral's face. The dark-haired man stared back. His face was angular, the features sharp, each as definite as if carved by a sculptor more concerned about the details than of the whole. It was a face in quiet conflict with itself, striking yet unsettled. His eyes were engaging and strong, with a deep-set questioning quality about them. At the moment, they seemed like the eyes of a predator, swift to level in any direction, steady, but eager for the hunt.

There was no one left in the bar. All had long since returned to their rooms. That's where Rip knew he ought to be. It had been a grueling day and night of planning, and he had returned to the hotel for some much-needed rest before the final preparations began. But he had learned something in his years in the military: *"Never say no to an Admiral,"* especially a member of the Joint Chiefs of Staff.

When Rear Admiral Bishop had stopped him in the lobby, Rip was willing to talk, but he was surprised by what he heard. Throughout the Admiral's recital, Rip's eyes had stayed wide as he heard him out in absolute amazement. When he had finished, Rip sat dumbfounded, absorbing the full import of what he had told him. The words were still ringing in his ears, *"Take him out! Wang can't come out of this alive!"*

The Admiral's eyes blinked, and he looked away briefly toward the door, his expression troubled. He reached into his brown leather briefcase propped up against his chair. He pulled out a long, thin envelope with curious markings on the backside. He handed it to Rip, fixing him once again with a stare.

"There's more money in this account than you will ever need in your life," the Admiral said in a low conspiratorial tone. "The account is in your name. The director of *La Grande Banque de Geneve* has been instructed to give you access to the account number when the job is done."

"I don't kill people for money," Rip said carefully, his eyes searching the Admiral's. Rip held the envelope in his hand. He had no intention of opening it.

"I don't either," Julian said tautly. Although he didn't raise his voice, the rebuke was clear, "I'm not asking you to do it for money. If they escape, the Chinese will dance for the world, using détente and peace parades to hide their true objective of global military superiority. In a country where yesterday's weather can be changed by a decree, I do not trust their words. I've never met an arms control treaty that was worth the paper it was written on. I, for one, will not let this incident grease our slide into becoming a second-rate power. The Chinese have killed too many for us to ever risk their version of peace. You and I both know firsthand the truth behind the Chinese lies."

There was no sympathy in the admiral's words. To Bishop, it was a loss seared into his memory. Rip had his own memories, a different war, but the similar pain of loss. He wanted to be away from his memories. But now, he was aware of the face of Tang Wei, a man he was to partner with in this rescue. Trust was not there, and there was no time to earn it.

The envelope momentarily twitched in Rip's hand.

"Major, I need you," Bishop said evenly. "You're the only one I can count on."

"If I kill him, I won't be needing this money because I'll be dead!"

"That presumes it was intentional, Major," the Admiral said cautiously with a comfortable smile. "You and I both know more hostages are killed from friendly fire in the rescue attempt than by terrorists. I know your skills. Wang could have a convenient, shall we say, *accident*."

"So, you think you know me well," Rip said, expressionless. Rip respected Bishop's military mind, but he did not admire the man. The former submarine commander was one of those aging men at the Pentagon who justified violence too glibly with self-serving scraps of philosophy while sending young men to their deaths. Rip had learned to loathe such men while in Afghanistan.

"I want him dead, Major," Bishop replied. "Don't you?"

"His death would not bother me."

"I thought so," the Admiral said, smiling, his voice abruptly softening. "The money will be yours, whether you want it now or not. But remember, don't just take him; take him out."

Bishop paused. "And Major, let me make one other thing clear," he said fervently, his eyes narrowing. "This conversation never occurred. If you should mistakenly concoct such a story, I will deny it. The Swiss account cannot be traced to me, and there are no witnesses at this bar. It would be your story against mine, and I would win."

"For a conversation that never took place, you sure make it hard to forget," Rip replied with an edge of disdain.

"Careful," the Admiral warned, his face darkening. "I could find ways to bring you up on charges. Your record isn't clean, you know. I could get you court-martialed."

"Are you offering me a chance to stop the Chinese, or are you threatening me?"

"Both."

Rip could feel the anger shooting through his body, clawing at the base of his throat.

"I won't miss what I'm required to take out," Rip said fiercely. He gave Bishop a withering look. "Since this conversation didn't take place, why don't you go back to the halls of the Pentagon where you belong? Make your pronouncements from a distance and cover your white ass as you leave the dirty work for me. I know your kind lives better that way."

The Admiral leaned forward in his chair, his eyes burning. For a moment, his face went red all the way down through his neck. "You don't have to like me, Major, because I don't like you! But I suggest you get the job done, or your black ass will need more than a Pentagon cover!" Bishop stood erect, grabbed his briefcase, and left the bar.

CHAPTER FORTY-SEVEN

THE BAITED HOOK IS SET

**Rescue Staging Area
Geneva, Switzerland**

"And I will give them one heart and put a new spirit within them. And I will take the heart of stone out of their flesh and give them a heart of flesh."
Ezekiel 11:19 (NAS)

Kamal Harazi's short but eventful career as a terrorist began at age nine. He grew up in one of Beirut's Shia Muslim slums. While visiting relatives in southern Lebanon, his parents had been killed in one of the frequent Israeli raids against the PLO. They had been killed by PLO crossfire. He had grown up Shiite but had been adopted by PLO extremists. He had earned his keep stealing guns and ammunition. He acted as a courier and a lookout, set up targets, and infiltrated military installations as a child that no adult was even allowed near. As a young man, fate intervened to end his short but distinguished career as a terrorist.

He was wounded on a raid into Israel. Two PLO terrorists had been killed. Kamal had resourcefully pulled his small, riddled body into an alcove. He had stopped the bleeding but had lost much blood.

The Baited Hook Is Set

He had prepared himself for death. Kamal had grown used to it. Death had lost its sting.

Unconscious and lying close to death, he had been found by an Israeli woman. She had carried him home, tended his wounds, and nursed him back to life. Kamal could not speak to her. He knew the language, but she was the hated enemy. He said nothing for days, looking into the eyes of this woman who refused to hate. At first, he recoiled to her touch, but soon he craved the moments she washed his wounds and stroked feeling back into his legs. She taught him how to trust. Three months earlier, he would have watched men kill this woman and willingly leave her body to rot.

Then the nightmares came, a fitting retribution for sins seemingly forgotten but now unlocked. They became Kamal's legacy of torment. Forget them? How? He had never learned how to obliterate the memories, but she taught him how to love. He owed his life to this woman who had stepped out of the shadows of a grim past to save him. She, too, died an untimely death before he reached manhood, but her legacy of love had locked his destiny. He had become the foremost negotiator for peace in the Middle East. He had lived in both worlds—he knew the cost of hate. He knew its futility.

He had been a good negotiator. He knew the dialects and the languages, but more than that, he knew the mind of the terrorist. He had learned to be patient because he knew successful negotiations had always followed a predictable pattern. Initially, the kidnappers dominate and attempt to bully the negotiator for a quick settlement. When they realize that is not going to work but that the negotiator is prepared to talk, dialogue begins, punctuated by periods of silence and more waiting.

The Summit

Pressure on the kidnappers increases. They fear that the police will close in on them, and they will get nothing. To kill the hostages was to write off their chance of victory. Soon they were trapped in their own self-imposed web. Kamal would detect that telltale note of urgency and anxiety in their communications, and he was always ready to capitalize on it.

In the final phase, Kamal had always felt in control. He had been successful in arranging for the release of many hostages. Sometimes he had even been able to secure the recovery of the ransom. But it all took time, time he knew he did not have in working with Ghazi. He had always hated the necessity of violence to secure a rescue—men always died. There would be victims on both sides—needless victims to add to the already overflowing graves. But as he looked around the conference table, he knew the truth. If need be, it was time for men to die.

The significance of the meeting was obvious and required no comment. The room somehow matched the mood. There were no windows, no prints on the wall, no extraneous furniture, and no amenities. What Kamal knew of John Calvin, he would probably have approved. Only the quiet whir of ventilating machines gave a unique stamp to the Swiss conference room. The U-shaped table dominated the room, note pads, pencils, and ashtrays in place, and a paper shredder in the far corner. There were three television monitors that silently danced to their own drummer on the far wall, but no one was watching. The real drama was about to unfold in the room.

Kamal had already greeted each man curtly, and each understood. It was not in his nature to give in to a rescue attempt this early in the negotiation process, but he was frightened by the implications of Ghazi's actions. Guntram Meyer sat on his right, Gerald Opfer on his left, and General Bud Williamson one chair removed so he could

The Baited Hook Is Set

lead the review of the rescue plans presented by the young Major Rip Devins and his Chinese counterpart, Tang Wei, both seated across the table. The rest of the Local Negotiating Team was also there. The room was packed. The seating order was a pecking order rooted in logic. Most of the questions would be directed at Devins and Tang. They had swivel chairs that allowed them to face all members and the large digital screen which would help provide the visual detail of their plan. It was time for Kamal to provide direction for the meeting.

"It has been a difficult day, but I'm glad we can speak again with a single voice," Kamal said evenly, thoughtfully pausing as the eyes of all present were drawn to him. "It is the consensus of the entire Local Negotiating Team that a rescue attempt be initiated as soon as the live television coverage can be arranged. Unfortunately, Ghazi has refused to answer his phone, and although we have successfully controlled his media access to avoid a repeat of yesterday's media circus, we still are awaiting the opportunity to plant the bait. I'm sure it is no surprise to any of you that long periods of silence are the norm in negotiations of this kind. Let me assure you that Ghazi will answer on his own time-table, and when he does, we are ready. If we had time, I believe the negotiations would be successful. As you know, it is the opinion of all on the committee that we do not have the time to wait. The hostage rescue plans have been agreed to by all involved. We are here for the final review."

While talking, Kamal watched intently as Col. Chuck Healey turned to Major Devens and discreetly slapped his knee in support for what all knew would be a grueling review. Col. Healey was smiling; Rip Devens was not. *Was it anxiety, or was it more?* Kamal had immediately sensed the reluctance of the intense black warrior. He had hoped the hours of planning would have mellowed Rip's distrust of his new Chinese counterparts. If it had, it was not showing.

"Gentlemen. I do not need to tell you the importance of this plan. We are here to support each other, but we are also here to be critical of any possible flaw. Do not hold any reservations back," Kamal said slowly, letting his comments break into the group's collective consciousness. He turned his gaze to Major Devens, watching him intently for a moment before speaking. "It is my understanding, Major, that you are responsible for presenting the plan for review."

"Yes, that is correct, sir," Rip said calmly, returning his gaze with a fixed stare of his own.

"You look tired, Major."

"Nothing that will limit the team, sir," agreed Devens, "We have had few breaks, but we have all been trained to work under the worst conditions. I'd say our being tired is the least of our worries, sir."

"I'm sure you're right," Kamal added with a comfortable smile. "Are you ready then to proceed?"

"Yes."

Kamal and the others watched intently as Rip Devens turned his attention to the critical screen and the information it provided.

Lowering his voice, Rip Devens, with an occasional aside by Chuck Healey and Tang Wei, proceeded to tell the group everything that was to take place, from the moment of beginning team preparation to the final assault and rescue scenarios.

Throughout Rip's recital, Kamal's eyes had stayed widened, his fingers clenching his pencil against his notepad while hardly making a mark. His early years of terrorism were truly child's play when compared to the science of destruction it had spawned. Kamal was impressed and absorbed in the detail, simplicity, and finality of the plan.

The Baited Hook Is Set

There had been the obligatory questions from all in the room, but every one of them had been handled without a flaw—the weapons, the breach explosion, the positioning of the teams, and the medical and troop support backups. The men were ready, but Kamal had come to appreciate that the only place that perfect plans existed was in the artificial light of bureaucratic conference rooms. Kamal knew who would know the plan's true weaknesses: Devens himself. Devens had listened to all the concerns with an odd acute intensity, and he had fielded them well.

"Tell me something, Major," Kamal asked thoughtfully, leaning forward in his chair, his eyes leveling on Major Devens. "You have all but toyed with our questions. You are prepared. I compliment you."

"Thank you, Sir," Rip said evenly. "It has been a joint effort. Colonel Tang and his men have contributed as well."

"Oh yes, I am sure," Kamal replied. He paused, searching for the right words. "There is nothing like one's own mirror to reveal our cruelest faults. You have lived with your own plan all day. Where do you see the problems? Ghazi is a professional. He will not go easily."

"Ghazi does not bother me," Rip said evenly, his voice full of suppressed excitement. Kamal watched as Rip turned momentarily to face Tang and then return his eyes to him. "Ghazi is like a crazed animal. He is a professional, but he is human. If he had time, he would use every trick in the book. But he will not have the time. The breach explosion will stun all in the room. We will have six seconds to clear the room. If we act quickly and as planned, once he is in our sights, he will die quickly like all men."

"Then you see no problems?"

"I did not say that. I said Ghazi will not be our problem." Rip again looked at Tang.

"Where is the problem, Major?"

"The General Secretary himself, sir."

"Just what do you mean?"

"Freeman has no military experience. She doesn't even know how to use a gun. Most likely, she will freeze," He concluded, cocking his head to one side as he continued. "The General Secretary is familiar with the use of weapons."

"Not true!" General Zhang Ming flared. Kamal and others gave him a withering look that immediately silenced him.

"Continue," Kamal said.

"Colonel Tang has confirmed that the General Secretary is no stranger to weapons. If he gets access to a weapon, he knows how to use it," Rip said carefully.

"Are you suggesting that he might use it against the rescue team?" Lin Feng interjected, defending his long-time friend.

"No sir. I am not," Rip suggested, shaking his head. "If he has a gun in his hands during that initial assault, he may very well be shot by our men."

"What are you saying, Major?" General Williamson snapped.

"Our men have been trained to make split-second decisions that mean life or death to the people in that room. With milliseconds to respond, anyone with a gun becomes a target," Rip continued calmly. "It isn't a choice. It will be a reaction honed by years of training."

"What does that mean?" Gerald Opfer interjected, his eyes widening as he spoke. "Would you shoot him in the shoulder or what?"

"No, sir. We're shooting each target twice, right between the eyes."

"You mean you can really do that? Running?"

The Baited Hook Is Set

"Yes, sir. We've all trained to do that," Rip said in a deadpan that seemed to impact all but Kamal. He had seen men trained to kill before. He knew it was so.

"Well, we can't control what he does," Gerald countered.

"You may want to start praying. If he picks up a weapon or tries to be a hero, he could be killed," Rip continued with a matter-of-fact tone.

"Is that true?" General Jin Yuan turned and asked Col. Tang.

"Yes, sir. What he says is a very real risk."

The silence weighed in the room like a heavy fog. Before any could respond, the frantic message of an intruding aide put all doubts prematurely into the grave.

"He's answered the phone!" he said anxiously, staring at Kamal. "He wants to talk to you!"

Kamal immediately moved his chair towards the phone, remembering his planned opening. But it was something in Rip's eyes that still nagged at the corner of his mind. He knew the look. He could not decipher it or was it because he didn't want to? He wasn't sure. He let it go, concentrating as he lifted the receiver on what he was going to say next. He knew the others were well aware of the plan, and he also knew he was ready.

"We did not tell you to call us!" Ghazi said, his voice rich with emotion but controlled and coldly angry. "What do you want?"

"Reluctantly, Washington and Beijing have agreed to ship the weapons to Iran as you requested," Kamal said slowly. He hesitated a moment for his words to sink in and then continued, "But certain conditions must be met."

The Summit

"We have your leaders!" Ghazi said fiercely, but with an ever-decreasing intensity that left him halfway between fascination and annoyance. "There will be no conditions unless we establish them!"

"You will have your weapons, Ghazi, but only when the assurances we specify are met."

"What assurances?" he demanded, his tone sharp but shrewd. "I have no time for your petty delays. You must deliver the bombs tonight!"

"There will be no delays. In fact, we require a speedup in your timetable," Kamal said, his reply sucking the air from Ghazi's sail, leaving him still in the water. Ghazi said nothing. Kamal took the initiative.

"The weapons must be delivered tonight to avoid press coverage and panic. Is that clear?"

"What else do you demand?" Ghazi said cautiously, but still with an unmistakable menacing air.

"The planes will not leave for Iran until we have direct proof of the condition of Presidents Freeman and Wang. The planes will be ready for flight at 19:00. They will take off for the destination of your choice in Iran as soon as we see both leaders on the TV screen from a direct line broadcast you must provide from the Palace Press Room."

Kamal felt the hook sink in. Like the silent pause before the great marlin runs with the bait, Ghazi gave no reply. Kamal jerked on the line one last time to set the hook.

"We have already notified the media of your request for a live telecast. Everything is in readiness from their side. As far as they're concerned, you have demanded it to address the world audience. They know nothing of our plan to use the direct telecast as proof of the condition of the hostages."

The Baited Hook Is Set

Kamal could feel the tightening of his stomach muscles. *Had he miscalculated? Would he break the tenuous line?*

"You will give us permission to say what we want?"

The hook had set. The smile from the others in the room reaffirmed what he already knew. There would be no further need for planning. Soon it would be the real thing. It was time to taunt the beast to move him closer to his death.

"What you say is up to you but have the hostages visible to us, or the planes do not move," Kamal said evenly, his voice taking on a patronizing tone. "I suggest you make your case to the world with the time you have. Because the horror you plan will never be accepted..."

"It does not need to be accepted! We hold the monsters. And they will have helped us obliterate the Jewish scar that discolors the Middle East!" Ghazi raged. Kamal could almost see his eyes afire through the phone. "You will see your leaders lick the soles of my boots, but you will see them. We will leave you the location for delivery dropped from the east window at 18:00 hours. Is that clear?"

"That is clear? We will notify the press to be ready for the direct line feed," Kamal said, continuing to taunt him. "Do you need any assistance to set it up?"

"We need no assistance. We have never needed your help!"

"We want the leaders released before the weapons are given over," Kamal demanded what he knew would be refused. *What a fool. You are so drunk with your own power you are blind to the realities you face!*

"No! You will have the dogs released when the planes deliver the weapons, and no sooner. You will not be allowed to shoot down our planes before they get off the ground," Ghazi blazed. He ordered in a disquieted tone, "You have waited this long; you will have to wait longer."

The Summit

"If anything happens to…."

"Be watching at nineteen hundred!" Ghazi interrupted, hanging up before Kamal could respond. The line was dead. The marlin was now off and running. The line was reeling out, but soon it would be time for Ghazi to die. Kamal spoke the words no one in the room doubted.

"He bought it! It is now up to us to execute. Nineteen-hundred it is!"

CHAPTER FORTY-EIGHT

PRAYERS FIT FOR THE WAITING GAME

> The Domaine de Châteauvieux
> Geneva, Switzerland

*"A friend loves at all times, and a brother is born
for a time of adversity."*
Proverbs 17:17 (NIV)

Martin Freeman reached out a hand. As if the contact caused Mei to speak, she said impulsively, "After last night, I was embarrassed. I haven't cried like that with anyone in years. I'm glad you were there with me."

"I, too, am glad. I cried a few tears of my own."

Martin gave Mei a heartfelt hug, moisture again forming in the corner of Mei's eyes. Pulling back, Martin held her shoulders, looking at her smiling. Mei brought one of her forefingers up to wipe away her own tears, beginning an uncomfortable laugh as she did.

"Look at us. We're starting all over again," Martin said warmly with a smile. He tried desperately to keep it light. "We really are quite the pair."

"What?" Mei asked, a confused look in her eyes.

"I mean, we are so alike," Martin said sincerely.

"Yes. I understand," Mei said quickly, nodding her head. Martin could sense relief spread over her face.

"Thank you again for seeing me," Martin said, his voice soft and hopefully reassuring. "Once it was decided to attempt a rescue, I knew I had to be with you again."

Awkwardly, Martin asked her to please have a seat. Mei confided unhappily how she was still confused as to what was to be done. Martin sat down on the corner of the nearest oversized armchair and began to explain, as best he could with what he knew of the plan. He went over and over the rescue plan, explaining what he knew in the simplest English he could find.

"Thank you for being so patient with me," Mei said gratefully.

"It is no problem," Martin replied kindly.

"To the people in embassy, I am a problem. They will not tell me anything. They never do," Mei said. Her voice had suddenly gone metallic. For just an instant, Martin wondered whether she had been serious. "When the General Secretary goes to the West, they order me to join him. That does not mean they need to tell me what is happening."

"Being the spouse of a great leader is not easy in any country," Martin responded, trying to relieve Mei's emotional wound. He wanted her to know she was not alone.

"You knew there would be a rescue," Mei said with a harsh tone. "If you had not come, I would not have known."

There was a peculiar, tense silence. Neither looked at the other, as if trying to hide from the bitterness in Mei's response. Martin watched as Mei returned his stare, and again he had the sensation that she was seeing him for the first time.

"You know," Mei said softly with a smile. "You are not at all what I thought you would be like."

"Not spoiled rotten?"

Mei smiled, and they both laughed, "Yes. Not rotten at all."

"We have gone through much together, but I still know so little about you, Mei. Your children?" Martin asked, seeking a safe topic to help her regain emotional balance.

"We have one son. His name is Wang Yiyun. He is now in Sweden. He is in, how do you say...? The foreign service there," Mei said with pride.

"Our sons live in California. Neither wanted anything to do with Washington," Martin said evenly. His mind traveling the distances he wished were never there. "One is a lawyer. The other owns a number of auto dealerships on the West coast." Martin could again sense his English had outstripped Mei's comprehension. He moved quickly to explain.

"He sells cars, autos."

"Yes. I understand," Mei replied, smiling broadly as she nodded. "Have you talked with them?"

"Yes, we have talked often. They are very concerned, as you would expect. I have tried to keep them informed and reassured that everything that can be done is being done. As you must be aware, there is little we can share about the rescue plan. The less any of them know the better."

"I understand. My son is unaware as well," Mei shared.

"At a time like this, I know Connie and I would be joining together to pray. Would you mind if I did that right now with you?"

Her eyes showed concern as she confessed. "I do not have a faith in God. Zhou's mother did, and I talked to her often about her beliefs,

The Summit

but I do not share her faith. I do not know how to pray. God would know."

"Let me do the praying for us. Would you hold my hands?" Mei grabbed his hands and joined him in bowing her head as he did. *"Lord, we humbly pray for your presence with us. We ask you to be with the rescue team. Protect and empower them to be a mighty force in rescuing Wang Da and Connie. And Lord, protect them both from any harm and bring them safely back to us. You promise to hear us and be with us in this our time of need. We praise you and rest in your will. We ask this in the name of your son, Jesus Christ. Amen, Lord."*

"How did you do that? How do you know what to say?" Mei asked.

"I just talk to God. I believe that he listens. I also trust that he has no need for fancy words. He knows our hearts when we pray. I've always found God to be faithful," Martin confessed. "I don't always get answers in the way I want, but I've always found my faith helps me handle whatever comes. It gives me peace to pray. God is the rock I hold on to in tough times."

"Thank you," Mei said. "Strangely, it helps me as well. Thank you for praying for Wang Da."

"You may be surprised to know that we have been praying for him for a long time. Jesus called on us to pray for our enemies," Martin said with a smile. "That is not always easy, but it certainly is now."

Martin could feel her grow more comfortable as he talked. He was not sure whether he was trying to help Mei, or just trying to maintain his own sanity in the face of the fear that kept creeping in. Suddenly, the reality of their plight was brought back to him again.

"It will be dangerous. Will it not?" Mei asked, in a voice suddenly fraught with apprehension.

"What?" Martin asked, his stomach betraying his own concern.

"The rescue attempt," she said, refusing to retreat from her worries. Martin could see her take a deep breath before continuing, "Many men have died in such rescues. Is that not true?"

"Yes," Martin said anxiously. "Any rescue attempt is always dangerous, but we have the best team you could have."

Before the words had had a chance to sink in, a resounding knock at the door riveted their attention. An aide moved quickly into the room. His face said more than his words to confirm their own growing fears.

"Pardon me," he greeted them. He seemed as tightly wound as a spring. "They want both of you at the Summit staging area. The rescue plans are now in motion. They want you there. You will be safe. Please come with me."

CHAPTER FORTY-NINE

TRAITORS ARE ENTITLED TO A FIRING SQUAD

> U.S. Embassy
> Geneva, Switzerland

"As no one has power over the wind to contain it, so no one has power over the time of their death. As no one is discharged in time of war."
Ecclesiastes 8:8 (NIV)

Rear Admiral Julian Bishop walked into the US Embassy conference room escorted by two Marine MP's. His angular face was set, his eyes darting around the room fixing on no one. He tried to look strong, but he was obviously anxious. His broad-shouldered frame and well-tailored blue uniform was kept crisp from a compulsion of vanity. Today, like a man trapped, his body was rigid, with no easy fluidity of movement.

His face was a hard-baked mask that was about to be cracked. Once confronted, Chuck Healey knew it would shatter under the weight of the charges. He could see the admiral's increased breathing through his uniform jacket. A thick trickle of sweat crawled down the line of his sideburn. He had seen it many times before. The Admiral's years in the military aside, Chuck knew the man was petrified. Try as he might, Bishop's eyes could not conceal his inner fear.

General Bud Williamson, sitting next to Chuck, spoke first, addressing the MP detail. "Thanks very much, gentlemen. You will not be needed for now. Would you please wait outside?"

"Yes, sir," said the man on Bishop's left, saluting and then nodding to his companion, as they both turned and started for the door.

"You've interrupted my dinner, and I expect…"

"Shut up, Admiral," interrupted Williamson, quietly but forcefully. His tone was cold, the General's lips tightly pressed, hostility and disapproval radiating from his every move.

The door closed, and Bishop took several angry steps toward the conference table, but to Chuck the anger was too contrived, too forced. It had been summoned to mask the fear running through him. "I have a meeting with Guntram this evening, and I…"

"He has been notified. Your meeting has been canceled," Bud said evenly in a lifeless tone. Chuck could feel the noose tightening around the Admiral's neck. His own heart beating faster by the minute. Chuck knew instinctively that the trap door was about to fall.

"This is outrageous! I demand an explanation!" The Admiral's eyes were intense. He licked his lips, his mouth dry.

"You're entitled to a firing squad," Bud said softly, fiercely, leaning forward as Bishop gasped. "And I think you know why Admiral?"

"What are you talking about!" The officer's eyes grew wide. He swallowed as the color left his face. He turned to his long-time friend General John Westlake sitting quietly on Bud's right. "John. Tell me this is some sort of joke!"

"This is no joke," John murmured in a voice of such contempt even Bishop's feigned insolence appeared shattered for an instant. The Admiral looked crestfallen as his friend continued, "I told you that you were going too far, but I had no idea you would go this far."

Bishop became rigid again, brows arched, eyes clouded, a military man resigning himself to name, rank, and serial number. "I have nothing to say to you. I have no idea what you're talking about."

"You've got a great deal to say, and you're going to say it. And you are going to say it quickly," Bud said in controlled, forceful tones. "And if you don't, I'll personally send you to the deepest cell in Leavenworth that I can find, and you'll never get out. To put you on trial would be far too dangerous to the security of our country—and too damaging to our reputation."

"No! You can't! I did nothing wrong! I am right. We are right!" the Admiral said, obviously agitated. He had begun to tremble, his hand reaching out to use the table as support. "Those who understand will agree. We had to do something. Our national security cannot be compromised by the weak-minded."

He paused, trying to regain control, but the mask was already cracked. Fear turned to desperation as Bishop whispered, "What are you saying I've done?"

"In violation of your oath as an officer, you have conspired to kill the General Secretary of China," Bud stated with firm conviction. Chuck watched the General. In the Pentagon he had been nicknamed the "Pit Bull." He was well known for his indomitable spirit and his fierce determination. His teeth were sinking in, and he wasn't about to let go of his prey.

"And to whom did I conspire with? Answer me that?" the Admiral interrupted, his eyes flaring.

"It doesn't matter."

"It does! It's everything! They are lying!"

"Admiral, you had no authority to...."

"You can't trust that black bastard!" Bishop screamed, his voice touched with hysteria. His words echoed through the room, momentarily silencing the General. Chuck could see how disconnected he was becoming. The Admiral's eyes were glaring with the fear of a trapped predator.

"It's Devens word against mine! He's a troublemaker and a liar! You ought to be court-martialing him!"

In the last few words, a degree of uncertainty crept into his voice. Chuck could feel the hairs rise on his arm. He looked at General Williamson and then back to the Admiral, Bishop's eyes dancing frantically from face to face, seemingly aware that the inquisition's verdict had already been sealed.

"I never mentioned Major Devens' name, Admiral," General Williamson pointed out simply, giving Bishop no time to recover.

"It must have been Devens," Bishop said fearfully, his voice now grasping for threads of logic that weren't there. "That's why Colonel Healey is here. That's how I knew."

In the ensuing silence, nothing was said. Bishop took a halting step, then another, desperation showing in his wide eyes. He began barely above a whisper, the words growing louder with a zealot's dying conviction.

"For God's sake, can't you see? If we didn't do something, it would all be lost. I couldn't stand by and let our military retreat again behind the skirts of détente. We have been weak before. You men know we can't let it happen again. One man's life is not worth a whole nation being crippled!"

The Summit

"Enough!" said Bud, leveling his eyes and waving his hand as if dismissing his every word.

"You can't silence me!" Bishop straightened his broad-shouldered body, a condemned man knowing that the ultimate justice of his convictions would bring him a pardon. "The people of our country will recognize a giant. They won't turn their backs on me because short-sighted politicians and weak-kneed military men fall short of their calling. I will speak to them! They won't stand for it!"

"Damn it!" Bud raged, pounding the table and immediately silencing Bishop. In a democracy, Admiral, it isn't your right to determine what is best for our country," Bud said with just the right amount of derision. "It isn't your right, and it isn't ours! Now, Admiral, you're going to start talking. We don't have time to listen to your bullshit!"

Bishop wiped beads of sweat forming on his brow, denying the unsaid emotions screaming at him in the silence. A flush came to his cheeks. Quickly, control returned, and he tried to feign detachment.

"I'm listening, Bishop."

The trigger words spoken by General Williamson opened locked drawers in the Admiral's mind, drawers he had never planned on opening. The Admiral sat down in the chair next to him. He was trembling. For what seemed like a very long time he did not look up or acknowledge their gaze or respond in any way. He remained motionless, face somber, staring down at the conference table as if trying to find a way to salvage his perilous situation.

Bishop talked slowly in a voice that showed the considerable strain. His mind released in a stream of consciousness. The words flowed without prompting. As he spoke, Chuck listened in amazement, a thoughtful frown creasing his brow. An outpouring of names, dates, events: Afghanistan… the China Connection… South Africa… and then Rip Devens.

Tyler Defense Systems and other defense contractors had contributed millions to perpetuate their own interests—money for lives. Chuck could feel the rage welling up inside him. His feelings were kept in control by the urgency of the situation. The mandatory questions were asked, the extent of Rip's involvement scrutinized over and over again. The skeleton took on flesh, and Bishop's testimony confirmed what Devens had already said. *He's clean! Thank God, he's clean!*

"Sir," Chuck interrupted the questioning, pulling Bud's eyes to him.

"What is it, Colonel?"

"In light of the Admiral's testimony, Devens' statements have been corroborated," Chuck said evenly, looking first at his watch and then back to the officers. Seeing no response in the face of either General that would contradict him, he continued, "This inquiry has already taken valuable time from our rescue preparations. I would like your permission to take leave to join my men. We still have much to do."

"I loathe ineptness and arrogance," Bud said, looking briefly at Admiral Bishop. "I cannot tolerate it, but more than that, I hate impediments. You are right, Colonel. I see no reason to delay Major Devens' involvement. In fact, I commend him. What is Colonel Tang's reaction to Devens remaining with the rescue team?"

"He has left it up to us, but he privately made it clear that he is willing to work with Devens, if his story was corroborated?" Chuck said, trying to keep his own bias out of his report.

"Then take your leave, Colonel," Bud said, smiling. "You have much to do."

"Thank you, sir," Chuck said, rising from his chair. He saluted both officers, ignoring Bishop. He started to leave and then turned to both men, his enthusiasm prompting him to add, "Devens may be running around with his own demons chasing after him, but he's a professional. He's survived in the field for ten years and has made Delta Force what it is today. I'm glad his name has been cleared." Chuck did not wait for a response. He continued with conviction, "And now it's time to get the job done."

CHAPTER FIFTY

THE WORLD WAITS
AND WONDERS

> Hotel des Bergues
> eneva, Switzerland

*"Love is patient and kind; love does not envy or boast;
it is not arrogant or rude. It does not insist on its own
way; it is not irritable or resentful."*
1 Corinthians 13:4-5 (ESV)

Turning after the call ended, Brian faced Li sitting next to him on the bed. "I had a feeling this was going to happen. Terry said the whole country is in a state of shock. Classes have been canceled at the University. And, let me tell you, they don't cancel classes for just anything. Last time I remember, it was after 9/11 and the terrorist strikes." Pausing momentarily, with furrowed brow, he continued, "I hope that's not a bad omen."

"What do you think is going to happen?"

"Your guess is as good as mine," Brian said. He rubbed the side of his nose. His shoulders lifted and fell. He continued almost reluctantly. "You saw what they did to those people we operated on. They're capable of doing anything. They can't give them weapons. I don't know. It's just so frustrating!"

The Summit

"I understand. I feel the same way," Li said carefully. She reached out her hand, placing it on Brian's arm.

"You feel so helpless just sitting, waiting, and watching television, but I guess that's the sign of the times. The worst in this world seem to have the passionate desire to inflict their hateful violence wherever they can, while the rest of us lack the conviction or the power to do anything about it," Brian said, his voice shadowing the exasperation all felt. "We settle for watching it unfold on television, helpless..."

"Don't be so hard on yourself," Li said softly, in soothing tones. "I think everyone, no matter how passionate about making a difference, is feeling powerless right now."

While looking at her and smiling, Brian reached out to push back her hair from her face. He kept his hand touching her cheek. Li leaned into it, momentarily closing her eyes. At that moment, his frustration was gone, lifted again by this woman he swore he couldn't love.

"Speaking of good men with passion..." Brian said in mock pride, his eyes lighting up.

"Oh, stop it!" Li said, laughing and pushing his arm away.

"What? You don't remember?" Brian pleaded.

"You are impossible!"

They both laughed. He faced her seriously with a boyish grin.

"What were you saying about men with passion?"

"Nothing that involved you, Dr. Winters," Li said calmly, but he could feel her breathing slow. He felt her direct, challenging sexuality, his face only inches from hers.

"What am I going to do with you?" Brain asked, more to himself than to Li. She smiled, looking back into his eyes as if looking for an answer to the same question. "After this ordeal is over, I won't want this to end."

The World Waits and Wonders

"Brian, I'm going back to China," Li said abruptly, as if having to let the words go for fear her growing feelings for him might bury the truth forever. She looked away in the uncomfortable silence.

"I know that," Brian added softly. Her eyes returned. He could see moisture in the corner of her eyes, pulling tears of his own. "I will be going back to the States, but I don't want to let this die. I want to work with you. We could do some research together. We could present at...."

"I don't know if we should. It will hurt enough to leave you once."

"Now wait a minute!" Brian interrupted, bringing his raised finger up to his face and cocking his head. "We're survivors, remember? I'm from Brooklyn, and you're from China. Don't run from a little hurt. We're used to it."

She said nothing. He tried to study her face carefully, but she pulled him to her, holding him tightly. He inhaled her scent. He tried to shift on his side to be more comfortable. She was clinging to him. He felt the tranquility of her slow breathing, but his mind searched for her answer that wasn't there. He didn't want this to be the end. *Tell me you'll see me again...*

For several seconds, he hardly heard the rumbling cell phone next to his bed. It was her reaction that drew him to the sound. She tried to break his hold. Brian quickly recovered, picking up his cell and placing it beside his ear.

"Yes?"

"Is this Dr. Winters?" The voice greeted him, serious but with an air of urgency.

"Yes, who is this?"

"It's Dr. Junliang."

"Yes, what is it?"

"We need you here at the Hospital. I cannot explain over the phone, but you are to tell no one and come immediately."

"Is it an emergency?"

"That's all I can say. Please come, doctor. By the way, I've been unable to reach Dr. Chen Li. If you see her or can reach her, please notify her that she has also been requested to report here immediately."

"If I see her, I will tell her," Brian said evenly, unable to stop the smile forming on his lips. He replaced the phone in one motion, now again staring into the eyes of Li.

There were many questions still left unanswered, but now there was no time. He remembered the comments of one of his mentors, *"Doctors can hide in the urgency of the life and death struggle of their jobs, never having to face their own fear of intimacy."*

But right now, he wanted to hide from the final answer he feared she would say. Without saying a word, they got to their feet and moved to find their clothes. There was no longer even a hint of warmth, just the smooth, efficient professionalism of doctors preparing to do their jobs.

CHAPTER FIFTY-ONE

DELTA FORCE ADVANCES AT THE POINT OF THE SPEAR

> The Conference Area Roof
> Geneva, Switzerland

"See, I lay in Zion a stone that causes people to stumble and a rock that makes them fall, and the one who believes in him will never be put to shame."
Romans 9:33 (NIV)

Like a picture postcard, the lights of Geneva cast their own special reflections across Lake Geneva. It proved only a momentary distraction for Major Rip Devens and his men as they glided effortlessly along the roof of the Palace of Nations. Dressed for the mission, they wore black field pants and jackets, unpolished GI boots, and dark blue Navy watch caps. Their faces were covered with ebony face paint, making it all but impossible to tell where the caps ended and the jackets began.

Each wore large bright red circles stitched on the front and back of their jackets. To avoid reflection, the circles had been covered with black tape. Once ready for the assault, the tape would be removed to help identify the rescue team in the confusion of the assault that would surely follow. No one wore any visible insignias.

Besides Rip, there were eight men on the team—Chuck Healey, Tang Wei, Su Cai, and Fast Eddie joined Rip to make up the primary assault team. Three additional men, two Chinese and one American, were picked as roof operators. Two of the men on the roof would coordinate and secure the repelling operation, the third would provide backup weapons support if needed. All eight men moved silently, each moving as if one unit with their weapons and equipment attached.

So far, all had gone according to plan. Rip saw the polished movement of Tang Wei as he moved the final ten yards to the target position. Tang thrived on plans. Like Rip, they both knew that without well-thought-out plans, things could go wrong, and men could die. Tang and Rip were right on time. Rip respected the man. He hoped Tang felt the same about him.

With silent stealth, Rip moved his body past the final open area to his position next to Tang. He stood motionless and then crouched as he watched the other men to follow his lead. They made no sound as they moved into position.

Looking at his watch, Rip glanced at Tang and smiled. The elapsed time was no more than eight minutes. They were right on schedule. Tang gave the familiar thumbs up gesture.

It had been a hectic afternoon for Rip, and he was glad to see things running smoothly again. There had been hours of hectic planning, his disclosure of Bishop's involvement, the grueling cross-examination, and the final flurry of activity as they moved into action. There had been no time to think, no time to feel.

Rip unbuttoned his field jacket, checked his tight body armor underneath, and then gripped the handle of his .45. He made one final check of his weapons, his ammunition and the affixed new precision laser light system designed to help the team zero in on his targets. He adjusted his goggles and positioned his weapons to the ready. They had the best state-of-the-art equipment, but Rip still knew it would be the men and their years of specialized training that would make the difference.

It was always the men that made the difference. It had always been that way. He thought back to the final minutes before the men had climbed onto the roof. Everyone had been high-strung. Fast Eddie had asked to read something from his Bible, and since Tang had not protested, Rip had agreed.

Fast Eddie had read from 1 Samuel about the Philistine champion Goliath and David's prayer. The words still echoed through his mind, *The Lord who delivered me from the paw of the bear will deliver me from the hand of the Philistine.*" He had given David the tools and the strength. Eddie had led them in a brief prayer for their own strength and guidance. *You didn't bring me out of Afghanistan to fail. Give me your strength, God. Let us do our job.*

Rip looked out at his men at work. They were readying the repelling ropes while Capt. Radman kept his 40XB Remington heavy-barreled sniper rifle in the ready position, scanning the terrorist windows for any activity. The rifle was especially designed for Delta and would deviate less than a minute of an angle at 100 yards. Radman could put a bullet on top of a bullet. Rip had seen him do it many times.

Radman was the right man for the backup all hoped they wouldn't need. All involved had years of experience to hone their skills and timing. Tang and Su worked well together. Rip smiled, thinking that he hoped he would never have to meet them as enemies. They would be formidable adversaries. It wasn't safe to know your enemies if your job was to kill them.

There was almost no movement now. The ropes were in position, all were waiting for the scheduled window check by the terrorists. As soon as they passed, it would be time for the final positioning.

Like the rest, Rip remained inside himself. He thought about the years he had spent in Delta Force, all the names and the faces. Like a collage of colors and texture, the moments raced before him. He felt the sweat streaking down his face. He touched the roof under him to steady himself.

What would they actually find when the breach explosive was detonated? Would they all be in the press room as planned? Would both leaders be there? Could Ghazi and his men have been trained to overcome the startle-freeze reaction? Would the explosion give them adequate entry? Would the backup Swiss units overcome the other terrorists?

But his main concern was if the hostages would have the sense to hit the floor, leaving the terrorist targets easily identifiable. He hoped they would. He knew that fifty percent of your chance of success in saving hostages depended on timing and the other fifty percent on luck. It was time for luck to be with them. He prayed it would be.

He sensed the movement before he felt the hand on his shoulder. Fast Eddie motioned him to move to his repelling position. The guard had made his rounds early in preparation for the soon-to-occur video transmission. It was now time to move down the wall. There was no more time for doubts. It was time to act.

Moving effortlessly to the roof's edge, Rip was in his harness and ready for the descent. Like spiders bounding to their trapped prey, all five of the assault team stepped out over the roof together and repelled the three floors within seconds. Only the dark strands of the ropes were left as visible evidence of their presence. There remained an illusion of calm.

The descent had taken them to the row of false windows which had long since been sealed off with concrete, the result of remodeling in the press room. The security arrangements were designed to keep men out, but they had made it easier for experts to breach. A well-placed explosive would make a gaping hole with more than enough room for all to get through. And now it could be done with the surprise necessary.

The sealed windows made detection all but impossible. The five men clung to the wall as if they were a part of it. They watched intently, as Fast Eddie pulled out a small package of lead sheath explosives from a canvas pouch attached to his stomach. They all knew that explosives could take out the wall, but, depending upon the technician's skill, they could also blow out your eardrums. Rip wanted into the room, but he wanted in without drawing blood from his ears.

Eddie used a diamond glass cutter to get inside the glass pane of the false window; he then attached the soft rolls of plastic explosives to the concrete wall with the detonator wires extending from it. For Eddie, explosives were not to be feared. They were part of his family. Each one was a new baby that he took pride in bringing to life.

There in the darkness, Rip could feel the enemy. Ghazi was close now, and he could sense it, feel it with every breath he took. They were two animals now, two predators stalking each other in the darkness. But one had the advantage—Rip knew when the time would come. The darkness would be good to Rip. It had always been his friend and sanctuary. He knew it instinctively. He now felt it again strongly.

The Summit

Soon, he would provide living proof that Ghazi would be no match for him. Rip did not come out of the early days, the terrible days of horror, to lose. He knew there would be death on both sides, but as with any cancer, some good tissue is excised with the bad. There would be a cost, but in the end, the cancer would be gone. As each moment passed, he felt nearer to what he felt would be his destiny.

And they waited, each member of the team was fighting their own private battle with their fears and their god.

CHAPTER FIFTY-TWO

SEARCHING FOR HOPE BEYOND THE HELPLESSNESS

> **Palace of Nations Press Room**
> **Geneva, Switzerland**

"For behold, the day is coming, burning like an oven,
when all the arrogant and all evildoers will be stubble.
The day that is coming shall set them ablaze,
says the Lord of hosts, so that it will leave
them neither root nor branch."
Malachi 4:1 (ESV)

Wang tried to open his eyes, but only slits formed. He smelled only the sickening stench of his own vomit. His shirt and trousers had been drenched and stuck to his skin. In front of him were gradations of black, intermittent shadows of gray, and flecks of light that bobbed and weaved in his blurred consciousness. Like a man struggling out of a deep, dark tunnel into the daylight, he closed his eyes, still unable to take the intensity of the blaring light. Wang Da felt a dull pain everywhere, centered in his stomach, rising through his neck and throat to his face and head, which felt swollen and numb.

He had been beaten severely; he had never known such pain. In that twilight zone somewhere between consciousness and unconsciousness, frantic images danced through his head.

He had thought he would die. They had beaten him, but they had wanted more. Holding his head in a viselike grip, Ghazi's huge hands had twisted the side of his jaw, forcing his mouth to open. Wang involuntarily trembled as he remembered Gamal forcing the bronze nozzle of the hose down his throat. He had cringed at Ghazi's words, "You will feel what it is like to drown." Ghazi had pinched his nostrils as the water surged down his throat. He had gagged, masking his hysterical, muted pleas as he struggled for his life. He straightened in his chair, fighting the bonds that held him and trying vainly to push back against the alien force violating his body. He had felt the convulsions in his throat and fought to maintain consciousness from what he feared would be his watery death.

It was at that moment that he heard the last thing he remembered, *"Do you enjoy being helpless? What a poor creature you are, but so typical of pampered leaders. You are all weak!"* Wang felt as though his whole body was blowing up, and, indeed, it was. And suddenly, he lost consciousness.

Awakening, he had not been killed; that told him something. His mind was still reeling, like a thousand devils with pitchforks were jabbing pitchforks into his brain. He struggled to rediscover his senses, his mind searching for allies he feared he had all but lost. He felt his stomach lurch menacingly, and he coughed, the acidic sourness again making him gag. Terror was creeping in at every corner as he felt as if some part of his vital life force had been ripped from him.

Again, Wang strained to bring his senses in focus. There was that urgency of survival like the drowning man struggling with his last gasp of air for the ever-evasive surface. Gradually he was able to open one of his eyes, the other was caked shut with blood, his eyelid swollen. His eye burned, but the images steadied. Freeman was still there, her eyes searching him, seemingly willing him back to life. As the image focused, the swollen features and the half-closed left eye gave evidence of the President's own personal struggle.

"You are alive," Wang mumbled through a swollen mouth.

"I told you," Connie said unevenly. She paused, grimacing from her own pain. "God's not done with me yet." Her abuse at the hands of the terrorists had been no less severe, but she had more time to recover from her torture.

Wang tried waiting for the dizziness to pass. He still felt on the verge of blacking out. He tried mustering a forced smile, "If this is just the preliminary, I do not want to be around for the main event," he continued to gaze speculatively at Freeman. "Your God has a funny way of showing his support."

"For now, I'll settle for both of us still being alive," she said slowly.

Wang moved his wracked body carefully, but the final hurdle back to consciousness sent spikes of pain jolting through his body. He sat back, slumping in pain. "I think I'm glad." He took a deep breath, the air stinging the raw flesh of his raped throat.

"They have kept us alive. They still have use for us," Connie said. Wang felt it was as much to assure her own doubts as his.

"What time is it?" Wang asked.

"I don't know. I was unconscious. We just have to stay alert," Connie said through pained lips. "They won't let us sleep. They beat us. They take us to the edge and expect us to break. They want to shame us. We've got to hold on until they come to rescue us."

For a moment, there was silence between them. She had said the words neither of them fully believed, but both now knew it was their only hope.

"I want to believe–"

Wang was cut short by the muffled sound of fast-approaching footsteps that echoed from down the hall. He stopped, looking first at Freeman, and then they both turned to face the door.

The sight of Gamal's scowl and his menacing face caused Connie's body to tense. Her hands bound behind her now balled into fists, straining against the ropes, all but oblivious to the pain. Her mind was blind with rage at the man who had tortured them. Her one good eye narrowed to a slit.

"So, it's back to more torture?" Wang said contemptuously. His grotesquely marred face going hard, his rage driving color to his cheeks and neck. He had survived the first round, but his brashness communicated more his anger than any new-found confidence.

"We are through playing games," Gamal said, spitting at his feet. He had a determined, cold look. Gamal and the second guard Ibn, roughly untied their wrists, jerking them to their feet.

"Courage. God is with us," Connie said, her eyes communicating the President's support he knew was real. Ibn jerked Connie through the door.

"Just words!" Gamal said, his voice like a whiplash. His hands pinched the life from Wang's arms, thrusting him forward. He grunted, "Move, or we will fill you with water again."

Wang stumbled forward as he was pushed out into the hallway.

It was as if there were no people in the room. All eyes were riveted on the screen. Martin did not want to watch, but he could not look away. A prolonged and lasting damper had descended over their nervous conversations as soon as the smooth voice of the anchormen had taken over the coverage.

She had described the day's events, the throng of protesters, the riots in Israel and the United States, and the telecast that the world was waiting for that now was only moments away.

They had wanted Mei and Martin to be at the Summit staging area but had not realized how much of an impact their presence would have. Martin could sense it the moment they had come into the Rescue control room, the whispers, the side glances, the awkward silence. He could understand. *Don't they realize I understand?* How do you talk candidly about the operation with a spouse in the room? *They could all die. But God, don't let it happen.*

Martin was relieved when the rescue assault team left. It had given everyone something to focus on as they made progress on the roof. But now that they were in place, the moments seemed like hours. Waves of apprehension washed over the room. Martin rubbed his palms on his thighs and took a deep breath. He looked at Mei. She looked glassy-eyed. There was a tiny quiver beating at the corner of her eye. It had not been there before.

The words of the commentator echoed through the room. Martin concentrated on every word, "There is every indication that the Vice President has given in to the terrorists' demands. Although he refused to officially comment, reliable sources have confirmed that the weapons are in transit."

Her words hung in the air like icicles from a winter ice storm. Martin knew they were having the same shocking effect all over the world.

The Summit

"Near riots have erupted in New York, spurred on by blistering editorials in the *New York Times*, and I quote, 'We cannot condemn too severely the transparent way in which Vice President Wallace has turned tail and run in the face of the biggest challenge to human decency and world peace in decades.' And so agreed the *Washington Post*, the *Los Angeles Times*, and the *Boston Globe*. Demonstrations by pro-Israeli groups have been unleashed across the states in most major cities."

Like everyone in the room, Martin knew it was all a grand charade, but would it work? He looked at his watch.

It would soon be the beginning of the end. Whatever the outcome, the pain of waiting would be over. He felt Mei's hand slip into his. Martin was comforted at the flood of warmth and relief that swept over him with her touch. She squeezed his hand, turning to Mei, Martin tried to share a reassuring smile.

God, let it be over. But let it be over and everyone survive.

"What's the matter? There are no smiles this evening?" Ghazi said, giving Freeman and Wang a wide, wicked smile.

"We do have something to celebrate!" Ghazi continued, walking towards them. He felt inordinately pleased. His skin wrinkled as he smiled, as if the lines that scored his rough face were direct evidence of the price his victory had extracted from his body. But the price had been worth it.

Seeing the fear in their eyes was payment enough. Even the mighty would listen to him now. But Ghazi did not care about these leaders. They were vermin upon the Earth. He had enjoyed torturing them. He would enjoy even more strangling the life force from their bodies. Death was his companion. He carried it with him everywhere he went. After all, he had killed already, and he was in the mood now for more. Their time would come. It would be easy. A smile, arrogant, contemptuous, and, as always, superior smile formed on his lips.

"They will never give you what you want," the President said, her ripped lip slurring her words as she spoke. New blood trickled from a cut that refused to scab.

"You know nothing!" Ghazi blurted. His voice dropped to a low menacing tone, each word landing like a sledgehammer. "Your puppets miss their masters. They have agreed to our demands."

Ghazi watched the words sink in, twisting their already fragile brains, sinking the hook in deeper, tearing at their core. THESE ARE NO LEADERS! LIKE BALLOONS THEY CAST A BIG SHADOW, BUT THEY EASILY BURST.

"You doubt it!" Ghazi continued, sticking his chin out belligerently, using his words as a cutting sword. "You underestimate the power of the American bleeding hearts. They cannot let you die. Betraying the Zionists is a small price to pay. You hate the Jew, too. This gives many the excuse they wanted. Our war is holy, our cause just. Allah is with us."

"Ghazi," Gamal said evenly, adjusting his headset and turning to face his leader. "We are ready for the broadcast."

Ghazi turned around. He could feel the light of triumph emanating from his face. His moment was here.

"I knew you dogs had no guts. Where is your courage now? It seems we know your kind better than you know yourselves," Ghazi exclaimed. He laughed and jerked his head back towards Gamal. But something was amiss, his trained eye, automatically aware. His face darkened.

"Where is your weapon?" Ghazi said fiercely.

The Summit

"It is over there!" Gamal objected, recoiling from his scalding words.

Like lightning Ghazi moved to his side, swinging his arm in an arc and knocking his headphones off his head.

"Never leave your weapon!" Ghazi said sharply, not flinching. Carelessness was death. Ibn brought the weapon placing it next to Gamal. Gamal stared back but said nothing. He replaced the earphones and turned away.

"We are now ready!" Ghazi said, a forced smile again returning to his lips. He turned to face both leaders, seated hunched in their seats. For a moment, Ghazi watched them, drawing energy from their helplessness. But there was another look there, he did not understand. It nagged at the corner of his mind. They were not broken, but soon they would be. The red light on the camera clicked on, resounding through the room. Ghazi turned to face the camera. He would now have his opportunity to praise Allah before the world. *Praise be to Allah.*

"We are destined by Allah to be the enforcers of the final solution. We do not fear death. We welcome it as the supreme reward," Ghazi said bluntly, feeling a genuine surge of power flow through his body. "For you in Israel that sit secure in your homes resting on land stolen from our Arab brothers, you will pay for your arrogance. Your allies are now betraying you for these leaders. At this very minute, a plane with nuclear weapons..."

Out of the corner of his eye, Rip could see Eddie's thumb trigger the near-instantaneous timing device. Eight seconds to detonation. He ticked off the seconds in his head. For an instant, he was immobilized and numbed; there was no explosion.

Don't move. It will go. It has to go!

These were men used to finding amusement in the sudden exposure of another's weakness. They were never comfortable with their own. They had only their strength; there was nothing else they really believed in. The seconds challenged the shadows of their own deepest fears.

Instinctively, Rip wanted to look, but curiosity could kill. The contour of the building was his only protection. He fought his own impulses.

Damn it all! Don't fail us now! BLOW!

He wanted to scream, but he didn't dare. His insides churned with the force of trapped eagle wings. His face moved a fraction of an inch, enough to see Eddie move toward the bomb.

The roar of the explosion tore into the silence of the night. He watched in horrifying slow motion as Eddie's arms and face were blown away by shards of glass and cement. The baby had taken his mother with him. No time for memories–one more friend had been ripped from him.

Rip's body was frozen, figures in the night swinging past him into the fog, but he couldn't move. The operator's litany played in his mind: *Surprise, Speed, Success. MOVE! MOVE YOUR BLACK ASS! IT'S KILLING TIME!*

His legs propelled him back and through the hole, his body moving and his gun in hand as soon as he hit the floor. Like a cold, lifeless calculator, he manipulated the odds. *And now, there are three.* His senses were alive, bringing life and death to the room. There would be no time to think; *it was kill or be killed.*

CHAPTER FIFTY-THREE

SURVIVAL OR DEATH IN THE FOG OF WAR

**Palace of Nations Press Room
Geneva, Switzerland**

*"And the Lord sent you on a mission and said,
'Go, devote to destruction the sinners, the Amalekites,
and fight against them until they are consumed.'"*
1 Samuel 15:18 (ESV)

eath hung in the air. The President could feel it descending with sadistic slowness, intent on suffocating her. Her sore body heaved and fought for air. She saw faint shadows and heard noises. Even though hoping for a rescue, the President was locked in the grip of her own shock and disorientation. Her body refused to move. The ringing, *wouldn't it stop?* The seconds seemed like minutes. Connie's mind was blurred. She fought the crosscurrents of her own fears. But she wanted to live. She wanted to move but didn't know where to go.

She heard the sounds of Ghazi through the explosive cloud of smoke and dust, "Liar! Liar! You all will die!" She heard screams, other shouts, commands, and counter-commands filled the room. There seemed no beginning or end, just a furious frenzy. She crouched down as best she could. Men were all around her.

Then she saw him through the smoke. Ghazi was in a low crouch twisting his body towards her. His face was grotesque, the mouth stretched like a rabid dog's. As if in slow motion, the muzzle of his Uzi swung in an arc until she was now directly in his line of fire, Ghazi's widening eyes now staring at her. Time seemed to stand still. She wanted to move, to pull back, but like a frightened mouse mesmerized by the hypnotic swaying of the adder's head, she froze.

Ghazi's smile turned into a savage grin. He lifted his weapon higher as he moved closer. "There is nothing left now but this! It is time to die, dog!"

He heard the gunshots sputter and the bullets tear through the wall, but Freeman saw nothing but a blur. Her body shoved and then propelled forward by an unseen force onto the floor. She wanted to scream, her body wracked with the pain of recent abuse and now rebelling against the weight of the body now over her.

"Stay down!" Wang said quietly but with urgency. Before she could even reply, the General Secretary was off her and moving in the other direction.

Instinctively, Connie clung to the floor. She had no choice now but to try to make herself a small target. Her heart pounded as the sounds assaulted her, but she was alive. She heard the pounding of boots and the clatter of guns fired. She hoped that the right men were dying.

Wang had saved her, and he didn't have to. *This was it. Take a deep breath and pray. You wanted the rescue, and now you've got it.* God be with them all.

Smelling the harsh stink of cordite and the heavy scent of fear, Wang moved quickly in a crouched position. He did not intend to wait for death. He had been in death games before, and he had always won. Memories flashed through his mind as he moved. He hated weapons, even feared them. For that reason, he had learned to master them. In the early years he thought he might have to use them, but when he rose to power, he had thought he had put them to rest. But now he wanted one. He needed a weapon. Inside, he knew that in the death games terrorists played, doing nothing was not an option. He had to do what he could.

He felt an adrenaline surge. He knew his target was near. *Ghazi will die. I will kill him myself!*

In the fog of the attack, Wang reached for the gun propped next to Gamal. He had heard screams from that area just moments before. He would find a gun, or he would find his own death. He moved quickly. *Death waits for no man!*

Flares were now providing some light. Shadows were still on the move. A booming shot whined away just to his left. He gasped and dove beyond the camera equipment. He landed on a body. It was Gamal–two bullets in his forehead–his eyes glaring into the heavens. There was no time. *Find the gun!*

He extended his body, reached out, and using his hand, brought the weapon to his body. He flipped the safety off. The noises grew louder. If Ghazi was still alive, it was his time to die!

The tremendous explosion had completely shattered the wall. The force of the detonation had knocked Abdul Gosaibi flat on his back. The blood on his right cheek and neck had come from the flying cement that struck him. Now groggy, he tried to recover his senses and understand what had just happened. It was at that moment that he saw the last thing he would ever see. A black-clothed phantom attacked him. He felt as though his head was blowing up, and indeed it was. His body was blown backward, and he knew no more.

The first thing Rip saw was Gosaibi's face blasted by the steady fire coming from Colonel Tang's M-191A1 Automatic Pistol. Su Cai had already left for the hallway, ready to neutralize any reinforcements. The killing had started. Tang would handle Gamal.

With Eddie gone, Ghazi was Rip's alone. Rip landed in motion, traversing the room. There was enough light, but it did not help. Ghazi was not where he was supposed to be. He was already dead, or he had moved to cover. Searching for answers in the slowly settling dust and smoke from the explosion, Rip heard shots. *KEEP MOVING!*

Momentarily tripping over debris, he quickly righted himself and moved on. Before getting sight of Ghazi, Rip heard his voice and the blaze of Ghazi's weapon strewing lead into the distant wall. He took a few more steps, his heart pounding. Ghazi was still alive, and he would kill if he wasn't stopped. He heard the sudden scream and the stream of shots behind him. Gamal was dead. *Soon, Ghazi will join you!*

There he was. Ten feet away, crouched in the ready position and moving cautiously toward the conference table, his Uzi leveled and ready for the kill. Loud spits of automatic fire from the hallway caused Ghazi to spin toward him. The eyes of two professionals met. Ghazi's eyes were fever-bright.

The men were so close neither needed to aim—too many years of training, too many triggers pulled in combat. The muzzles leveled quickly. Someone would die, and someone would live. An instant before the bullets left his pistol, Rip saw the understanding come into Ghazi's face—his own death mirrored in his cruel frozen eyes.

Rip felt a tiny muscle twitch in his forefinger as he began to squeeze the trigger. He saw in a blur the other weapon moving upward with appalling swiftness, and he knew with each passing second, he was losing his advantage. He squeezed twice with even control. He watched the bullets stream from his pistol bringing death at 850 feet per second.

Both shots connected. Ghazi was lifted off the floor and twisted halfway around from the impact. His Uzi dropped from his hands as he fell limp against the floor. Images flooded through Rip's mind, blotting momentarily the identity of the man lying dead before him. Like all dead men, there was no expression. Rip was shaking. The pistol, tight in his hand, was still aimed at his victim's body. He was breathing hard, and his heart was racing.

Behind the table, Rip saw movement. It was the President. She was alive. She was rising slowly, carefully, her eyes glazed with shock. *THANK GOD!*

Out of the corner of his eye, he caught movement coming toward the President. Like a computer limited to the information it receives and given only milliseconds to spare, his instincts read the intruder: *No black. No insignia. Moving with a gun.*

Without a moment's hesitation, the pistol leveled on the moving target. It was a matter of survival. His finger squeezed, too late to stop. *The shouts, what were they saying? ABORT!*

In his last willful action, he tried to jerk his weapon away and watched transfixed as the bullet sped toward its target.

Rip did not see the bullet strike home. He felt an awful pain in his back, emanating through his chest. The pain took over his being as he slumped to the floor. And then he felt nothing more.

Her mind tried to function. Freeman saw the soldier whirl around and bring his .45 to bear on Wang.

"Don't shoot! It's Wang!" Her pleas ricocheted off the walls. Her vocal cords were strained, her muscles taut.

"No!" the President yelled. The cry that was wrenched from her throat came also from the center of her soul. *"YOU CAN'T LET HIM DIE!"*

Her screaming plea came a moment too late. The gun roared. The muzzle came up in recoil. She saw a strange expression on the soldier's face, somehow disconnected and bewildered. It lasted but a second. His body exploded, splattering blood before her as a second volley of shots sounded. Through the haze, she saw the soldier stumble and fall. He clutched at his chest, blood coming through his clenched fingers. His eyes were wide and staring. A look of disbelief suffused his face. His sightless eyes stared ahead motionless.

She did not even look to see where the shots had come from, she was already turning. Where was Wang? Panic-stricken, her eyes picked out a motionless body. *My God, it can't be!* She moved as fast as she could, but her legs were wobbly from the ordeal. She stumbled, fell to her knees, and crawled to Wang's body.

"Wang's been shot! Get a doctor!" Connie yelled. Her mind was racing, but she was momentarily frozen by the sight of blood flowing from an open wound in Wang's chest.

Before she could say another word, a soldier was at Wang's side applying a compress and testing for a pulse. The President stared in stunned, bewildered silence. She moved closer, her furtive eyes searching frantically for a shred of hope. She could hear men shouting and boots approaching. She was moved to the side, but she watched the men huddle over the General Secretary's wracked body.

"He's alive! Keep him alive!" Sweat was running down Connie's face, her own hands and face still bleeding from the ordeal. She thought for a moment that she would vomit. She had passed over the edge of hysteria. She had to pull herself back. She was safe now. She had to get ahold of herself. *God, don't let him die. Please God, answer my prayer!*

"Medic! Get a medic in here. We need blood here! Stat! We're going to lose him!"

Tears dripping from his chin, Col. Chuck Healey stood motionless. He watched Rip's prone body, studying it for any sign of movement. There was none. There was blood strewn all over the floor, blood he had brought with one shot from his weapon. There was no need to check for a pulse; he had seen death too many times to miss its reality.

As if controlled by a hypnotic trance, Chuck dropped his gun, now somehow defiled. He forced himself to turn away. He had to keep functioning. He wanted to get away from the nightmare he knew he would relive forever. *You deserved better. My God, Rip, I'm sorry... I'm sorry.*

CHAPTER FIFTY-FOUR

WORLD PEACE IN THE BALANCE

Geneva, Switzerland

*"A time to love and a time to hate,
a time for war and a time for peace."*
Ecclesiastes 3:8 (NIV)

All over the world, viewers in this real-life drama stared in stunned silence, bewildered by the events enfolding in front of their eyes. They were mesmerized by the images of death that danced before them. The unattended camera had continued to record history as never before seen. The lighting was marginal, the smoke from the explosion had made detail foggy, and the unattended camera left most of the action off-camera. But it was live. This was no movie, no simulation. This was death on prime-time television. And thankfully, the good guys were winning.

Some had screamed in horror as they watched Ghazi turn his weapon on President Freeman. It had happened so fast no one could tell whether Wang's attempts to save her had come too late. There was no instant replay or commentator to spare them the agony of waiting. Most cheered when Ghazi had been shot and cheered again when

Freeman had peered from behind the conference table. Millions had huddled close to the screen riding the roller coaster of emotions while they tried to make sense of the rapidly moving figures.

Some would report later that they didn't even see or hear the gunshots that leveled the General Secretary and Rip Devens. Their own emotional filters trying to screen out the reality they did not want to see. But Brian Winters could not escape the scene unfolding. The images played over and over in his mind as he stood transfixed. He sat along with the medical team assembled, ready if needed.

"They shot him!" Li exclaimed. Her eyes moistened. She bit her lip, shaking her head in disbelief. "What is happening? Why are they doing this? I thought they were safe."

"My God, he shot him," Brian said incredulously. His voice did not sound like his own. He had already felt as tightly wound as a spring. *He shot him! My God, is he dead?*

"What?" Li asked. She turned to face him, her eyes fixed on him, leaving the screen for the first time since the attack had started. He did not see or hear her. His eyes were sad and far away. She grabbed his arm and asked in a voice harsh with strain, "What did you say?"

"He shot him. It was Rip Devens," Brian said solemnly. Momentarily, they were both speechless. He wondered if she could read the pain, the sadness welling up within him. He stared into her eyes. He tried to think, without success, of words of comfort and understanding that refused to come because, perhaps, they did not exist. He shook his head sadly and sighed, speaking but hardly recognizing his own voice, "I don't understand. It must have been a tragic mistake."

For a very long moment, there in the hushed ready room, Li stared at him without expression. She started to say something but seemed to decide against it. He wasn't sure, but she seemed to move imperceptibly away from him.

In an attempt to keep his world on an even keel, Brian turned toward the other anxious faces on the assembled medical team from the US and China. He wanted reassurance, but he found something else. His own tone had been too obviously alarmed not to bring distress to the team.

"Are you saying that man was an American?" One said what all felt.

"Yes, he was an American."

"What the hell was he doing?"

"I don't know. Wang had a gun. I think he mistakenly thought he was a terrorist."

Brian turned his back to them. He had nothing more to say. For a long time, he, no more than they, could speak.

The night air was fresh and cool, yet for President Freeman, everything was still oppressive. She was still confused, both by the chaos of the rescue and by her own helplessness.

Suddenly, as she was led from the area, through the milling crowd, she caught sight of him. The face seen sporadically through the weaving, colliding military and medical staff was no illusion. It was Martin.

Their eyes locked. They both seemed to hesitate, frozen still by the moment. Then yielding to impulse, something she had seldom done publicly since becoming President, Connie Freeman began running as best she could toward Martin. Her wracked body responded, oblivious to the residue of pain, still her constant companion. The surprised Secret Service Agents moved quickly in pursuit, unsure of what to do but unwilling to let anything else happen to their leader.

Martin had been told to wait and had not moved. He waited, moving only as she approached. Connie's blood-smeared face was radiant, softened by the stream of tears flowing from her eyes.

"Thank God!" Martin cried out, clutching her and pulling her to him, tears streaming down his face. "You're safe! I was going out of my mind!"

Connie said nothing. She was overwhelmed by the flood of relief and emotion that swept over her as he held her close. Connie pulled back. Martin took her chin in his hands, staring at her marred face and then at her eyes.

"I never thought this moment would come!" he said in a whisper, kissing her softly on her wounded lips. "God, I love you! I am so glad you're safe." "Martin said, kissing her again, holding back some ready tears.

"Don't start. I've been crying enough for both of us," she said in a hushed but relieved voice. Momentarily distracted by the frantic activity of the medical team rushing Wang from the room to the waiting ambulance, she turned again to face Martin.

"I don't know how often we will be able to rest after tonight," she said, her voice anguished now.

"How is the General Secretary?" Martin asked.

"What I heard does not sound good, but he is alive. I heard them say that he had a weak pulse and had lost a lot of blood," Connie sighed. "But he's got to live, Martin. It was one of our men who shot him."

"I know. I saw it on the television," Martin said evenly. "The whole world saw it."

She said nothing at first, her mind again reeling to yet another jolt, "You mean the camera was still on?"

"Yes. We saw the whole thing. They were starting to play it back when I left the staging room."

"My God. I can't believe it!"

Behind them, they heard the ambulance doors being opened, a white minibus with red cross emblems and a flashing light on the roof. Without saying another word, both hurried toward the ambulance. Martin immediately moved to the side of Mei standing near the ambulance. The President went with him, pushing their way between two startled Chinese agents guarding the Chinese First Lady.

"Mei," Martin said, touching her arm. He stared into her eyes that seemed somehow dead. Mei said nothing.

"Mei, I'm sorry," Connie said, searching for words she had a hard time finding. "It should be me there. Your husband saved my life. I will do everything I can to…."

"No! No, no, no. Nothing can help!" Mei cried in anguish, her self-control slipping.

"You have my word. I can help you, and I will. As President…"

"Help!" She screamed, vulnerable to the core. "It was one of your men who shot him!"

"Mei, I'm sure It was a tragic mistake!" Martin pleaded.

Connie said softly, "Your husband has become my friend. We both suffered together. I…"

"You both suffered, but you are alive!" Mei said, her composure totally shattered and giving way to sobs.

Martin put his arm around her shoulder as they watched Wang put into the ambulance and the doors closed. Connie watched as if hypnotized. She could not take her eyes off Mei and Martin. She could see and even understand the bond both had found in each other. She knew the bond she felt for Wang. *Oh God, please! You can't let him die!*

The Summit

The Chinese guards carefully separated them, guiding Mei to the awaiting car. The limousine left in hot pursuit of the ambulance.

Martin again hugged Connie. The President turned to the nearest Secret Service agent, "Get us a car. We're going to the hospital."

"Madam President, the Swiss are suggesting you not go to the hospital. Security is...."

"I don't give a damn what security wants!" she shouted. "If that man doesn't live, all the security in the world may not help. Now, get us a car!"

The Presidential limousine screeched past the ruble surrounding the Pregny Gate of the Palace of Nations onto the Avenue de la Paix. At the same time, a waiting staff of surgeons and nurses with a mobile gurney, navigated General Secretary Wang into surgery. The attending surgeons, Dr. Chen and Dr. Winters, one Chinese and one American, examined the massive bleeding from his chest wound, exchanged dubious glances, and began to work.

Within minutes of the rescue assault, the world press feasted on a compelling lifeline to the emerging drama. The world watched. Like vessels surging blood to the muscles of a weary marathoner, the news service satellites and networks literally throbbed with activity. The world, eager to devour whatever news it was fed, had come to a standstill. Streets emptied, and office buildings suddenly became silent. People were awoken from their slumber. Televisions, streaming coverage, and radios around the globe had but one focus—the rescue and the life now in the balance!

At the Hotel Bergues, Joan Bashnel, a reporter from the *Los Angeles Times*, began writing her story, instantly transporting it halfway across the world: *"Miracles do happen, but fairy tales do not always have a happy ending. Surrounded by hundreds of special forces agents involved in the unprecedented attempt to rescue President Freeman and General Secretary Wang, there is no rejoicing. There is an invisible pall of tragedy, created by the awesome reality that the head of the Peoples Republic of China has been critically wounded by an American Delta Force officer involved in the rescue operation. Major Rip Devens, the man responsible for the Chinese leader's wound, was shot seconds after shooting General Secretary Wang at close range shot by his own commanding officer, Col. Chuck Healey. Wang is now in surgery being operated on at this moment by a team of American and Chinese surgeons. Before leaving for the hospital, President Freeman spoke to the press, calling for 'prayers for the Chinese leader.' The President's husband accompanied her to the hospital as they awaited the outcome of the surgery. There are unconfirmed reports that..."*

An NBC commentator expressed a more pointed summation: "The world watched in horror as viewers were taken from heaven to hell in five agonizing seconds...."

Within hours, the mobs of protestors in Israel and around the world had turned from brandishing upraised fists and placards to solemn reflection, offering prayers of supplication. Many wept openly. For now, the Al-Haram threat had been neutralized. The Middle East had been spared a nuclear holocaust, but the world now braced itself for the potential confrontation between the superpowers that Wang's death could bring.

In the limousine, Generals Zhang Ming and Jin Yuan had commanded the driver to take them immediately to the hospital. It had been a silent journey, both men left to their own thoughts.

"They've killed him, Jin!" Zhang snapped, adding just the right amount of derision. "I told you that they were not to be trusted. Wang can be buried in his blessed détente. There is no place for peace with the West!"

"Wang is not dead!" General Jin warned, recoiling from his comrade's intensity. "Do you wish him dead?"

"That's absurd! I do not wish him dead, but it's not important that he live. Mother China will go on whether he lives or dies. If he does not recover, the myth of peace will die with him. That will be good. We have peace only in our strength and the silence of imperialist guns!"

The limousine screeched to a stop in front of the hospital, leaving both men no time to continue their argument. Jin knew that arguing was of no use. After what he had seen, he was a reluctant defender of the Americans.

As they moved through the entrance, the strong figure of Gen. Bud Williamson was waiting for them.

"General Jin, we must talk," Bud said with respectful but adamant firmness, moving towards the two Chinese leaders.

"Have not your guns done the talking General?" Zhang taunted. Both generals came up short, refusing to shake the General's outstretched hand.

Bud said evenly, in controlled tones. "I understand your reaction. If the situation were reversed, I might feel the same way. Yes, it was our man who shot him, but one of our own took him down. I am sorry to say, we have every indication that it was an unfortunate tragic accident."

"There is no proof that it was an accident!" Zhang shouted, suddenly threatening, swinging around Jin and confronting the General. "The whole world saw it! He shot him for all to see! Do you deny that he was involved in the initial plot?"

"That's enough!" General Jin cautioned.

General Bud Williamson looked around frantically trying to control his voice to avoid making a scene. He said directly to General Jin, "It was Rip Devens who killed Ghazi! It was Rip Devens who turned in Bishop! Yes, he shot Wang, but Wang was moving towards Freeman, and he had a gun. Special forces are trained to neutralize a visible weapon."

"Are you saying that Wang was going to in any way harm...?" Zhang countered.

"Of course not! But in that moment of decision, Devens had no way of knowing that! If he had been trying to kill Wang, he would have been dead with two bullet holes in his forehead." Bud asserted, now looking for some hint of understanding in the face General Jin. "You know yourself, general. There are no dress rehearsals in war. In that moment, it's kill or be killed. There will always be mistakes! Devens paid for his mistake with his life!"

"Do not think that is enough, General!" Zhang said, not flinching. "If Wang dies, the cost will be high!"

General Jin and General Williamson were left with a silent stare, their eyes searching for some hint of shared hope and understanding.

CHAPTER FIFTY-FIVE

IT'S HEALING TIME ON THE OPERATING TABLE

**Hôpitaux Universitaires de Genève (HUG)
Geneva, Switzerland**

"Yea, though I walk through the valley of the shadow of death, I will fear no evil: for thou art with me; thy rod and thy staff they comfort me."
Psalm 23:4 (KJV)

The wound in his chest was deep and severe, quite possibly immediately fatal had not the .45 bullet been partially deflected by the rib cage, lodging itself just millimeters from the heart and next to the spine. Had the bullet entered millimeters on either side, the vital functions would have ceased. There was bleeding, but nowhere near the damage that there could have been.

Dr. Winters and Dr. Chen had already been working over an hour, their surgical greens already showing signs of the pressure they were both under. He had performed more complex surgery, but never more important. Their hands were in constant motion performing the delicate work that had exposed millimeter after agonizing millimeter of traumatized tissue. There could be no room for error. Everyone in the room knew that, even though it was never expressed.

The only part of the General Secretary not covered by drape was the exposed wound area and an unruly clump of hair not hidden by the mask covering his face. It was as if no one wanted to admit that this was anything other than a typical patient.

Brian had never had to defend his professional integrity before, but he had also never operated on a world leader that one of his friends had shot. He had understood why the Swiss and Chinese authorities had been reluctant to allow him to operate. After watching the General Secretary being shot by an American, they didn't want to let an American physician finish the job.

He had tried to reassure them. He remembered his words: "Gentlemen, let me assure you that I will give the General Secretary the very best care I can. I won't be holding anything back. I can't make any promises, but if there is any way of giving him back to the world alive, we'll find it."

They had known his credentials and heard his words, but it was Dr. Chen's support that had swayed them. "Brian did not pull the trigger. He is the best surgeon available. He knows the operating room because he helped design it. Most importantly, I trust him, and as the chief Chinese surgeon, I will be assisting him."

She had put her career on the line. In China, they would not tolerate mistakes in judgment, particularly not fatal judgments involving the General Secretary.

Concentrate! Don't let her down! Brian kept pulling his mind back to the operating challenge facing the team. Before he began, he thought of his mother. She would say a prayer, a powerful prayer for him right now. *God, I don't know any powerful prayers, but there are many people out there praying. Listen to them, and help this man survive!*

The Summit

With a nod, Dr. Winters indicated the nurse could suction some of the blood clots out from the exposed chest cavity. Wang's blood pressure had stabilized at 90/60. His pulse was steady but weak.

Again, using the light scalpel, Dr. Winters directed the laser as he instantaneously cauterized and welded the ends of damaged vessels severed by the bullet. The rest of the surgical team watched, the new technology doing work that previously would have taken far more time.

Finishing what he could, he stopped, giving way to Li's steady hand. He watched Dr. Chen as she wielded the meniscus knife, trying to sort out yet unexplored layers of tissue in the wound. And then there it was, the operating room lights revealing the bullet lodged where the x-rays had indicated.

The nurse slapped fine-toothed surgical forceps into her gloved hand. There was no conversation as Dr. Chen delicately removed the bullet from its resting place. Brian's eyes locked on hers, a smile visible through her mask matched his own.

"God is with us today!" Brian said. "Let's put this man back together!"

As she turned to place the bullet on the tray, she took a loaded needle holder and sutures from the attending Swiss physician. Brian dropped his head momentarily to make a notation on his medical chart.

Dr. Chen reacted first, her sudden movement pulling Brain back from his notes. The concern in her eyes said more than any words could. Brian looked with her at the slight change in the blip trace as it moved across the oscilloscope screen. His blood pressure had suddenly dropped; it had fallen for no apparent reason. Then there were two more abnormal ectopic heartbeats. The change in the audible rhythm caught the attention of the rest of the surgical team. Fear returned to Brian in a moment's rush, his own heart now racing.

He knew all too well that such runs of irregular contractions followed by compensatory pauses were often the immediate harbinger of cardiac arrest. Something was wrong… something could be very wrong. *God, don't let this happen now!*

His mind raced ahead for answers he hoped he wouldn't need. Perspiration coalesced on his forehead and dripped off the bridge of his nose onto his notes as he stared first at the monitor and then at the open wound. His own clammy skin reminded him again of just how important this case was.

Brian spoke first in agitated tones, "Do you know what the hell's going on?"

"I hope nothing," Dr. Chen said, the pattern momentarily returning to normal as they watched. They had done nothing. Maybe God was listening!

"Has he had any history of cardiac problems?"

"None to my knowledge."

"Well, I'm afraid we may not have him out of the woods yet," Brian said. "Let's get him back together before we have a cardiac arrest on our hands!"

"Look, I'm fine!" Connie said, reassuring the doctor.

"I understand," Dr. Horrowitz said, noticeably reacting to the President's impatient tone. "After I treat this, I'll just check your heart. It will only…."

"My God, Arnie! If it made it through that ordeal, I think my heart is good for a few more years!" Connie pleaded, still knowing that she would have to put up with their worries, more to reassure them than herself. She knew she was okay. There were cuts and bruises, but nothing critical.

Dr. Horrowitz said nothing, choosing to finish dressing her wounds rather than to add any commentary.

"Hey!" Connie exclaimed, jumping in response. "That hurt!"

"And it will continue to unless you stop complaining so much!" Dr. Horrowitz said softly with a smile. Connie smiled, knowing full well it was a game both of them always played over every physical. But Dr. Horrowitz was good, and he was thorough—something she knew that she needed, something the world needed. They needed to know that she was OK. Now, we just needed to know that Wang was OK.

As her fine doctor attached the electrodes, Connie's mind went to Martin waiting with the others nearby. She was almost glad that she had been called out. The room had been stifling. One by one, they had gathered in the small waiting room, holding out for some word that would put an end to their worries. Martin had felt more restless than usual; he had walked back and forth ceaselessly. There were long moments of silence, broken only by his attempts to comfort Mei on the couch across the room.

Connie could still remember staring at Martin taking time to hold Mei's hands. They were close, and Connie understood. She was glad to see that connection.

Lin Feng was seated near them, chain-smoking steadily. Martin hated the smoke, and he knew it wasn't allowed. But he had decided to forgo the international incident his complaining might initiate. Lin Feng was Wang's best friend. Martin knew Connie had enough to worry about without irritating one of the few positive Chinese voices left.

It's Healing Time on the Operating Table

It had not all been bad since they had arrived at the hospital. The first half hour at the hospital had been a blur. There was a conversation with her Vice President in Washington and questions from Swiss authorities. She had given them all what little emotional reserves she had left. She had thought the hostage ordeal had been draining. She had forgotten how taxing just being President could be. But then again, she was alive. She felt blessed, as blessed as a terrorist captive could feel.

But it was the last hour in the waiting room that had been the most difficult. Like most, she had not felt like eating. She had filled her system with the high-octane Swiss coffee. She knew she had been in captivity too long; she had even liked the muddy brew. She smiled to herself. She decided to blame any heart irregularities on the coffee.

Connie heard the knock at the door, but Neil was in the room before she or the doctor even had the opportunity to respond. Neil was smiling like the child who had just pulled the plum out of the pudding.

"Sorry Doc," Neil observed, cracking a smile. "You look good, Madam President. No makeup available, but the natural look works!"

"Oh, shut up!" Connie said, smiling back, cracking again the cut on her lip. She touched her lip, showing the blood to Neil. "Big help you are! Look what you made me do!"

"Will you two stop it!" Doctor Horrowitz said, but even he was clearly smiling. "I'm trying to get a reading on this."

"Sorry Doc," Neil said in hushed tones, bringing a bigger smile to his face.

"It's good to see you, Neil. Check that, it is good to be seen, period!"

"Agreed!" Neil said affectionately. "Seriously, you look great!"

The Summit

"Watch it. You're going to make me self-conscious."

"I don't think I could if I tried," Neil said in mocking tones. "The world's waiting for your face, and they will take it any way they can get it. Do you want to make a statement?"

"Not until we know more about Wang. Let's step outside," Connie said. She took a deep breath and walked out of the waiting room. She exhaled before continuing, "I don't want to answer questions I hope I won't have to. God, we all hope he pulls through this. Is there any word?"

"Nothing new. They are still waiting. I just finished talking with Colonel Chuck Healey. He's really having a tough time of it."

"I was briefed on what happened, I was there. I saw it, but it's still hard to believe."

"As far as Chuck is concerned, he feels responsible," Neal said, trying to sort out his own thoughts. "He feels like Rip did his job and paid a price he did not deserve."

"I'm sorry. There is cost all around," Connie said. "His wife is distraught. That's why I wanted to step out."

"That is understandable, but, with Chuck, I don't know how you recover from killing a friend who was just doing his job," Neal continued. "In Chuck's eyes, Rip wasn't going after Wang. The General Secretary just happened to be holding that gun. Rip was in the killing business, and he died doing his job."

Connie reflected before responding, "Men primed to kill, sacrificed to the altar of man's futility. I am so sorry we need such deadly talents. But after experiencing Ghazi and his hatred, it is necessary."

"I'm sorry," Neil said, apologizing. "This is not the kind of conversation to welcome you back with."

It's Healing Time on the Operating Table

"No, it fits," Connie confided. "I learned something in there. The work of civilization is to try to keep one's own country a little less insane than the rest of them. There will be other Rip Devens and other Ghazi Sauds. I just hope Wang lives to help us make them a little less necessary."

"You respect him?"

"Yes. He saved my life, but it goes beyond that. I trust the man. We've got a bridge. God only knows if Major Devens has mistakenly burned the only good one we've had in years. God, I hope not!"

CHAPTER FIFTY-SIX

A HEARTFELT CALL FOR WORLD PEACE IS PLANTED

> **Hôpitaux Universitaires de Genève (HUG)**
> **Geneva, Switzerland**

"Behold, I will bring to it health and healing, and I will heal them and reveal to them the abundance of prosperity and security."
Jeremiah 33:6 (ESV)

The minutes turned to hours. Mei had not left the waiting room except to go to the bathroom. She did not eat; she had no stomach for it. When someone brought her coffee, she drank it. There were words that floated in and out of her awareness, but she did not take the time to even understand them. She wanted her silence. She sat still, clasping her hands. Martin and Connie provided what support they could provide. She was no longer angry, just afraid she would lose her husband.

She was desperate to have Wang live. There was a seemingly never-ending stream of memories, and then she would think of him lying on the operating table. Connie and Martin had asked to pray with her.

A Heartfelt Call for World Peace Is Planted

She allowed it. She tried to convince herself in those hours of waiting that if only the prayers would make a difference. *God, he had to be alright.* That was all that she could pray to a God she was not sure even existed.

She knew she loved Wang. He was her only friend. She did not know how she felt about anything else. She did not care about the international ramifications of his living or dying. Without him, world peace would just have to take care of itself.

All Mei knew was that there was a darkness that pulled her into the blackness of the night. It was a darkness that clawed at what light she had left.

Martin and Connie had gone to what the hospital called its "chapel" to take time to pray for Wang. But soon, they returned to the waiting room. As the minutes slowly moved on, Martin tried rifling through the pages of a magazine left in the room, finding momentary distractions in the pictures. That was all he had; he couldn't decipher the text. Connie was alone in her thoughts, looking with sadness at Mei's struggle. At times Connie would close her eyes. Martin knew she was praying.

Neil had long since left, returning to give what information he could to the waiting press. He knew the beasts would be hungry for their next meal by now, but he had little to share.

General Bud Williamson entered the room, providing a fresh distraction. "I just talked to intelligence," Bud said with relief. "They had just picked up unconfirmed reports out of Iran. A combined counter-terrorist attack by moderate Arab forces has overrun the Al-Haram stronghold not too far outside of Tehran. Maybe Allah has a way of taking care of his own."

"That is good news," Connie said evenly.

"I just left General Zhang Ming and General Jin Yuan," Bud said, now turning to Lin Feng seated next to Martin. "It went as well as could be expected, but they refused to join us here."

"I'm sure comrade Zhang was not too understanding," Lin confided, shaking his head.

"No. He wasn't. I'm sorry to report."

"Any word on Wang?" Bud asked, his face taut.

"No." the President said softly. "But the doctors did say that the longer the time the better the chances. It's nice to know they are still working, but it doesn't make the waiting any easier for any of us. From what I know about Wang, he's strong and a fighter. I pray to God that he's got more fight left in him."

"The Chinese aren't the only ones that want to put a stop to détente," Bud said, looking first at Lin and then at Connie. "The Admiral has been spilling his guts. He's admitted that the conspiracy has implicated two executives from Tyler Defense Systems. The whole stack of cards is crumbling."

"Has the press got wind of it yet?" Connie inquired.

"No," Bud replied, raising his eyebrows. "But when they do, they're going to have a field day of implications. You thought dealing with terrorists was tough. You may wish you were back in that room."

"Not a chance!" Connie said, looking at Martin as their eyes locked, then smiling before turning back to face the general. "It isn't important. We can stop their influence as of now. With full disclosure, we can put it behind us."

"I agree. But remember, we didn't stop it. Major Devens did."

A Heartfelt Call for World Peace Is Planted

"I know." The President said, turning to face Lin Feng and then back to Bud. "I've explained to Mei what we know and what we did. Full transparency."

Lin Feng said with feeling. "We've looked at the recordings, and Colonel Tang has confirmed the initial assessment. Devens was no traitor; he was a hero. We knew such an accident could happen. We are only sorry he had to die for his error."

"I hope the rest of your comrades will be half as understanding," Connie said with a sigh.

Without fanfare or warning, Dr. Winters and Dr. Chen entered the room, their white masks unfastened and hanging from their necks, possible signs of surrender or victory. There was no waiting or clarification needed. Their professional demeanors were already compromised by the smiles radiating from their faces.

"He'll recover," Brian said, his smile broadening and his eyes lighting up. He continued feeding on the electricity suddenly surging through the room. "He won't be entertaining any new Summits for a while, but he'll live to see his share."

"Thank God!" President Freeman exclaimed, rising to take the hands of the two surgeons. "Congratulations! You have both done an immeasurable service to your countries! Thank you! The world thanks you!"

Brian and Li accepted the outstretched hands from the throng of sudden admirers. The cheers, the released laughter, and the words of gratitude just added to the explosive release of pent-up anxiety and unleashed joy.

Mei stood motionless, a ray of sunlight coming through a hideously destructive storm. Tears trickled down her cheeks. She smiled widely, beginning to sob desperately. She felt the arms of Martin and

The Summit

Connie hug her, encouraging her to believe, "He's going to be alright! Mei, He's going to be fine!

"When will he be out of recovery?" The President asked. "I know Mei will want to see him, and I would also like to speak to him."

"Now wait," Brian cautioned, his voice still light and neutral, but his left palm pushed forward and his eyebrows raised. "I understand your desire to talk with him, but he's very weak and will be for some time. It's my job to make sure he stays a good patient."

"Of course. I understand. I just..." Connie agreed fervently.

"Dr. Chen, when can I see my husband?" Mei asked, carefully touching the doctor's sleeve. Her face was sunny with relief, like the earth alive after a sudden Spring shower.

"As soon as possible, you will be with him. He will need you there," Dr. Chen said with feeling, stroking her hand.

CHAPTER FIFTY-SEVEN

TRUST EARNED...FAITH SHARED

> **Hôpitaux Universitaires de Genève (HUG)**
> **Geneva, Switzerland**

"Blessed are the peacemakers, for they shall
be called the children of God."
Matthew 5:9 (NIV)

"Mei said you were feeling better," Connie said, peering out from behind the door to Wang's hospital room. "She said you would make time for a fellow captive."

The smile on Wang's face said it all. Connie had not planned on crying. She had felt no tears were left. But as she moved into the room, tears flowed down her cheeks. She tried in vain to check the emotions that welled up within her.

"Didn't think I would die on you. Did you?" Wang asked, reaching his hand out to his friend.

"You did have me worried."

"Surely you know that we Chinese do not die easily," Wang said. His voice was light, his touch warm. "I told you that."

The Summit

"Okay. I believe you, but you didn't have to prove it so dramatically," the President said with a chuckle. She continued in a more serious tone, "You know we have taken care of…"

"I know. Mia told me," Wang stopped her, patting her arm and looking into her eyes. "She also told me about how you and Martin…" He paused, tears coming to his eyes. He did nothing to stop the tears. "How you held her… and prayed with her."

"Don't make me cry again," Connie said, half laughing but wiping the moisture from the corner of her eyes. "I've done enough of that already today."

They stared at each other, Connie pressing her hand against his.

"Mia is a wonderful woman. You are very lucky."

"We are both lucky. You and I can never be enemies again. Our partners will not allow it." They both smiled.

"You could have let Ghazi kill me, but you didn't."

"I told you before," Wang said, pausing but for a moment. "You are a hard person to hate. I know you tried to stop the Major. Captivity has served us well, though it leaves me a bit sore." Wang grimaced from pain, pausing to move his body. The President helped adjust the pillows.

"That's better," Wang said with a sigh, settling into his new position.

"In the end, it may have been worth the price, but it should not have had to occur," Connie said with a soft but serious tone. "We must stop the proliferation of weapons that makes this madness even possible. Our own countries do not always act sane, but at least we know that we are not crazy. We must help our countries stop acting that way."

Trust Earned...Faith Shared

"Do I hear a hint of trust?" Wang said in a hushed voice, his eyebrows raised. "Look out, Madam President. Don't you know that they train us Chinese to be nice? Nice, long enough to stab you in the back."

"Believe me. I have been warned," Freeman countered, smiling. "But something tells me neither of us will believe all our own prior propaganda after this ordeal."

"Do you really think it will make a difference?"

"As I say in my campaign, 'Quick fixes don't fix big problems.' This is no different," Connie continued, leaning forward in her chair. "But I see it in the eyes of the men out there that worked together to get us out. Now, they make unusual enemies."

"But there are still men like Bishop and Zhang. They seem to thrive on distrust and hating enemies. They have even shown that they can kill to maintain their fears."

"Don't get me wrong," Freeman said, a smile returning to her face. "I don't think I could win in November with you on my election committee."

"Nor could I control the Communist Party with you in Beijing," Wang replied, trying to laugh but grimacing again from the pain in his stitches. "You are right. It is a journey we are only beginning, but a journey we both want to take."

"Yes, it's one worth taking," The President said, inordinately pleased. "Besides, I'm not one for having to be popular. Never been good at keeping my finger to the winds of Washington."

"In Beijing, you put your neck to the winds. I'm afraid that it will still be so."

The Summit

"Not now. I bet you'll be on a honeymoon for months. Patriotic people always love a wounded, fearless leader. I'm sure the Chinese will be no different."

"You may be right," Wang said, smiling.

"I have thought about what you said last night," Connie said in a tone that she knew would bring Wang back to the gravity of the challenge. "We must keep our countries strong, no quick disarmaments. Our people and the diehards who love to hate will put up even greater roadblocks if we move too quickly. We must become enemies that are hard to hate. I will take you up on your offer to speak to your people yearly. You must do the same when you visit Washington. I want you and your people to know our country. I want my people to know the China you love. It is easy for strangers that peer through binoculars to push red buttons that start wars. Maybe the next generation will not have to be such distrustful strangers."

"We have much to learn about each other," Wang said. Connie wondered whether he was as optimistic as she felt.

"Remember something about Americans," Connie said, tone softening. "We love to forgive and adopt our enemies. It's a longstanding joke. The smartest thing Japan ever did was lose their war with America."

"May I remind you that we did not lose any war. We won this war together! We do not need to be adopted, but we will need your help."

"I understand."

"You can help us build critical sectors of our economy."

"Weakening you does not strengthen us," Connie asserted. "I will work with Congress to open up more trade possibilities and cultural exchanges. It should be people to people—sports, culture, media, education, the arts, any way that we can find a way to cooperate together. I'll try and authorize more funds for the Institute of Peace so they can coordinate the exchange programs from our side. We'll always have the next Olympics to enjoy."

"Of course, but don't expect to win."

"If we don't win, it's just because you were the one wounded, and China deserves a little break."

"Americans. Always excuses."

"You are better!" Connie said with a grin and a wink. "The banter returns."

"Yes," Wang said, shaking his head while sighing. "There must still be room for some back-and-forth rhetoric. Gradual changes last. Understand Madam President. If you hear of statements that I make that do not sound conciliatory, I make them to keep some in line. I fear I will recover from one wound only to invite another if I move too quickly."

"I understand the need to please," the President replied, for the moment serious. "You don't need to be elected, but it would be nice to stay alive."

"After all of this, I would hope so."

"But with each other, we must be clear and direct," Connie said evenly with emphasis. "We must pay each other the tribute of candor. When we talk, we both need transparency, at least as much as possible."

"You are a good leader, Madam President."

"Thank you," Connie said, staring into Wang's eyes and feeling reassured. "One thing is certain, however. Martin has already informed me that the hotline will be used for another purpose. Mei and Martin are already cooking up plans for when they meet again."

"I'm sure." Both smiled.

The Summit

"Wang. The world is waiting for a statement from us," Connie said cheerfully, again pressing her hand on his. "I wanted to do it together before distance makes the words more easily distorted by the media. I don't want to promise anything specific. But the world deserves some hope after the ordeal we've put them through. Can I get Neil to bring in the designated press people? They promised to have only one camera and to keep it short."

"Certainly," Wang said enthusiastically. "Am I right to assume this news footage is going into your campaign propaganda chest?"

"You better believe it!" Connie agreed, laughing as she spoke. "I have to get something out of this. With a beaten-up face like this, I'm going to need all the help I can get."

"You don't need that much help. Our God will come through."

"Our God?"

"When we were sitting in the press room with Ghazi waiting for the cameras to roll, I was praying. It was a selfish prayer, but it was real," Wang said, then paused, looking at Connie intently and grasping her hand. "I told you. I saw what faith did for my mother...and you."

"You must tell me more."

With a sudden knock, the press had arrived in Wang's room. They set up their equipment efficiently. The designated Chinese and American reporters were trying to build their own seeds of cooperation, but they're finding little support from the Swiss. They were back in control, and they liked it.

The lights were positioned and turned on, shining in their faces. There was the familiar aura, the emanations, the electricity of rapid movement that only the media could provide. It was time for their feeding, and the world was ready.

The image of the superpower leaders projected on the screen from his hospital room touched off a crescendo of cheers around the world. Both leaders smiled, and Connie raised Wang's good arm in celebration of the support they had both received. Then the world slowed down to listen. It was Connie Freeman's words that they heard first. They were words they would not soon forget:

"We are in this world together, holding on to a promise of doing the hard work of peace. May God be with us both in making that happen."

Not all that they said would be remembered, for what was said at that time was not really that important. The world, for a moment, stopped for a glimpse at a potential paradise. There was a fleeting glimpse of peace, a whisper of hope. Horns sounded. Voices were raised. The beer and wine flowed.

At a table in a Geneva bar, Dr. Winters and Dr. Chen raised their glasses one last time, for now. It was Brian's turn, his voice raised in cheer, "To the survivors, to our leaders, and to peace worth having!" Li added her own, "And let it begin with us." Both smiled.

"You remember what I said about my mother?" Wang asked, pausing to remember himself.

"Yes, she was a believer. I remember," Connie answered.

"I told you that there was no room for me to believe and stay with the Party. But what I did not tell you is what she said to me before she died," Wang said, pausing to look at Connie. "She said that she prayed for me... that I would come to know God. She said that he would not let me go. His Spirit would pursue me."

"I think He did," Connie said with a smile.

"He found me," Wang confessed. "Every time you prayed with me, I felt God tugging at my soul. In that final day, as they tortured my body, I too prayed. I felt His presence. God helped me through it all."

"Now, God is in our story," Connie shared.

"I think he has been all along," Wang confessed.

"I have a feeling your mom is smiling right now," Connie said, putting her hand on his shoulder. "You know, now we both belong to the same kingdom. The kingdom that counts the most. I guess, in the long run, that makes us brother and sister."

"I think so. I trust God will continue to be with us," Wang said.

"Amen, Wang Da. Do you want to pray with me?"

"That would mean a lot."

Connie smiled, "You start. I'll finish!"

"People want peace so much that one of these days, governments had better get out of their way and let them have it."
Dwight David Eisenhower

THE END

ABOUT THE AUTHOR

Dr. Paulson has a PhD in clinical psychology and a MA in lay theology from Fuller Theological Seminary. In addition to being a contributing author to *Epoch Times*, he's an op-ed columnist for Townhall.com. He's author of *The Optimism Advantage, They Shoot Managers Don't They,* and *Leadership Truths One Story at a Time*. As a professional speaker and trainer, he helps leaders and teams leverage optimism to make change work. He's past president of both the National Speakers Association and the Global Speakers Federation and is a member of NSA's Speaker Hall of Fame. Dr. Paulson has conducted over 4,000 practical and engaging programs for organizations such as IBM, 3M, Merck, SONY, and Starbucks. You can contact him at AuthorTerryPaulson.com

Printed in the USA
CPSIA information can be obtained
at www.ICGtesting.com
LVHW021622280924
792309LV00012B/369